Nicholas Rinaldi is the author of two previous novels, *The Jukebox Queen of Malta* and *Bridge Fall Down*, and three collections of poetry. His stories and poems have appeared widely in literary journals around the world. He teaches literature and creative writing at Fairfield University, and lives in Connecticut with his wife, Jackie.

www.**booksattransworld**.co.uk

ALSO BY NICHOLAS RINALDI

The Jukebox Queen of Malta
Bridge Fall Down

BETWEEN
TWO RIVERS

Nicholas Rinaldi

BLACK SWAN

BETWEEN TWO RIVERS
A BLACK SWAN BOOK : 0 552 77181 3

Originally published in Great Britain by Bantam Press,
a division of Transworld Publishers

PRINTING HISTORY
Bantam Press edition published 2004
Black Swan edition published 2005

1 3 5 7 9 10 8 6 4 2

Set in 10.5/12pt Melior by
Falcon Oast Graphic Art Ltd.

Black Swan Books are published by Transworld Publishers,
61–63 Uxbridge Road, London W5 5SA,
a division of The Random House Group Ltd,
in Australia by Random House Australia (Pty) Ltd,
20 Alfred Street, Milsons Point, Sydney, NSW 2061, Australia,
in New Zealand by Random House New Zealand Ltd,
18 Poland Road, Glenfield, Auckland 10, New Zealand
and in South Africa by Random House (Pty) Ltd,
Endulini, 5a Jubilee Road, Parktown 2193, South Africa.

Printed and bound in Great Britain by
Cox & Wyman Ltd, Reading, Berkshire

Penguin Random House is committed to a sustainable future for
our business, our readers and our planet. This book is made from
Forest Stewardship Council® certified paper.

Printed and bound in Great Britain by Clays Ltd, Elcograf S.p.A.

For Jackie

With special thanks to Dan Conaway for his enthusiasm, insight, and inspired suggestions, and to Bill Scott-Kerr for his keen eye and richly probing comments. And with particular appreciation for Nat Sobel and Judith Weber—for their patience and their caring attention, their belief in this book, and their always helpful guidance. And to Isabelle, my sister, lasting gratitude for the phone calls, the affection, the wisdom, and the abiding good cheer.

Contents

PART THREE

Prologue

Farro Fescu's
End-of-the-World
Friday Fantasy

At Echo Terrace, the ground-floor lobby is a large open space with marble walls and a marble floor, and a vaulted ceiling high enough to accommodate the Jamaican thatch palm growing in a brass urn by a black leather couch. The desk area—Farro Fescu's domain—is light oak, off to the left as you come through the front door. The couch and the palm tree are to the right, and the two elevators, east and west, are straight ahead but spaced far apart, a gracious expanse of blue marble between them.

It's a few minutes past ten, Friday morning. In the mail room, around the corner from the desk, Farro Fescu, the concierge, is sorting the mail. He's fifty-eight and of medium height, wearing thick-soled shoes that add ever so slightly to his stature. He takes his time with the mail, noting the return addresses as he puts the envelopes into the appropriate boxes. A letter for Mrs. Abernooth, the widow, from her niece in California, and a stack of bills for the Rumfarms, recently back from a week in Copenhagen. For Dr. Tattafruge, the cosmetic surgeon, some junk mail and a magazine. For Aki Sato, a letter from Tokyo, and for Harry Falcon, dying of cancer in the penthouse, a large brown envelope from his third wife's attorney.

The building is changing. Farro Fescu senses it. It started to go wrong when a twelfth-floor unit was bought by the clothes designer, Ira Klempp, an anorexic young man with spiked yellow hair and green eyebrows, his bony body clad in outfits of his own creation, tight-fitting

13

black shirts open at the throat, and loose, baggy pants made of brightly colored patches sewn together at odd angles. He glides through the lobby with his eyelids half closed and a marijuana joint hanging from his lips, as if deliberately bent on ruffling Farro Fescu's old-world sense of propriety.

Only a few months after Ira Klempp's arrival, a sixth-floor unit became available and was purchased by Juanita Blaize, a singer from the Bahamas and a hot number on the charts, with pink hair, two dalmatians, and a band of unsavory friends who visit all hours of the day and night—young men with unshaven faces, and braless women in Benetton sweatshirts and acid-bleached jeans, sporting metallic shades of makeup on eyelids and lips. For Farro Fescu, it's no trouble at all to imagine what's happening up there on the sixth floor—the sticks of incense, darkened rooms lit by candles, pillows scented with cologne, torsos draped languidly across the neo-mod, foam-bloated furniture, blue-mooded music from the sound system stirring drug-laden dreams and torpid hormonal urges. It's as obvious as the clock on the lobby wall: the building is going to the dogs.

All day long the lobby is busy, service people coming and going, the phone buzzing, heels clicking on the marble floor. But there are moments when the movement stops and Farro Fescu sits alone, quietly expectant in a slow and ripening silence. He feels the pulse, the heartbeat, as if the building were a living, breathing thing—as if there are wires running from his fingertips to every room on every floor, a web of wires connecting him to the doors, the balconies, the closets, the breakfast nooks, the sofas and soft chairs grouped around the fireplaces, the pool in the rooftop solarium. Delicate, tremulous, invisible wires linking him to the beds in the bedrooms, and the Ferraris and BMWs in the basement-level parking den. He owns it, possesses it—imagining, for the moment, that with his own hands he made this building, I-beams, cement, and the fancy interiors, right here in Battery Park City, lower Manhattan, the crisscrossing wires weaving an intricate, lacelike pattern, and there he sits, at the center, in a quiet, brooding rapture, gray eyes gazing intently, all the wires leading to him and from him.

What he knows, with a knowledge rooted in his bones, is that a building—any building, and especially this one, Echo Terrace—is a great deal more than steel and glass and hardwood floors. It's an organism, feeding and growing, a life-form that moves and breathes, continually changing and evolving. So care has to be taken. If care isn't taken, instead of growth there is decline. Entropy sets in, quality deteriorates, pride vanishes, reputation goes downhill, and before you know it the good times flatten out and it's time to move on.

He's thinking not only of Ira Klempp and Juanita Blaize but of Mrs. Abernooth on the ninth floor, whose apartment is crowded with a chaotic assortment of birds, turtles, monkeys, lizards, and snakes. He's seen it. The place is a mess. When her husband, the entomologist, was alive, there were only a few birds and animals, and the apartment was orderly and neat. But since his death, Nora Abernooth has been adrift in a kind of oblivion, passing dreamily through the lobby, with a raincoat over her housedress and blue slippers on her feet—and she has stocked the apartment with so many animals that it's now a boisterous, smelly menagerie, and, no doubt, a hazard to health. Something, obviously, will have to be done, but what, exactly, is not at all clear. Farro Fescu has raised the matter with the governing board, in reference to Clause 9, which limits the number of house pets, but the board members—Rumfarm, Knatchbull, and Neal Noelli—have shown little inclination to involve themselves in an action against a widow. In certain fanciful moments, Farro Fescu imagines he might take it upon himself—barge in and send the birds out the window, dump the reptiles down the toilet, and toss the monkeys and turtles out on the street, let them fend for themselves in the downtown traffic.

When he's done with the mail, he goes to the men's room and steps up to the urinal. There's a small red

15

pimple on his penis, on the thick cowl of flesh where the foreskin had been cut away—a pimple or some sort of wart, something he noticed only a week ago. He stands a long time there before his water flows. When it does, it's a thin, interrupted stream, and he thinks of his prostate, how age takes its toll. He rinses his hands and runs a comb through his hair, but it's a superfluous piece of grooming, his hair still firmly flattened by the generous amount of gel he applied at home. It's surprising, even to him, that his hair, at his age, is still black and full, with no hint of gray. He adjusts his tie—dark red stripes on a field of Prussian blue—and brushes some flakes of dandruff from his maroon blazer. The blazer is a light-weight polyester, for the summer, something he picked up at an off-season sale. Even on the warmest days he never takes it off. It's molded to his body, shaped to the contours of his stooped shoulders.

Behind the desk, he puts on his reading glasses and turns on the computer, a new machine with acres of memory, replacing the old 286. Everything is logged there, all the jobs that need doing: who needs a limo, who needs a plumber, who needs the housekeeping service. Who needs a basket of flowers, and when. They're all there, all of the residents, in the files he's kept ever since the condominium first opened its glass doors, nine years ago. Even the ones who are no longer there are still present, locked in electronic memory: the ones who sold and bought elsewhere, the ones who vacationed in Palm Beach or Rio and never returned, the ones who went broke and were forced into more modest digs, finding other doors, other elevators, other windows to look through. And the ones who died, those too, still there in the limbo of the hard drive: the stockbroker done in by a bad pancreas, the disk jockey killed by AIDS, and the Maltese soprano, Renata Negri, who collapsed with a cerebral hemorrhage while warming up for a perform-ance as Leonora in Verdi's *La Forza del Destino.* Passing through the lobby, she would give Farro Fescu coy, furtive glances and sometimes a wink, leading him to

16

suppose that in a different circumstance something worthwhile might have developed between them. One Christmas, for a tip, she gave him a pair of cufflinks. Another Christmas she gave him gloves lined with lamb's wool. Then, amazingly, she was dead, and her absence lingered like a missing word in a newspaper story—your eye runs down the column and suddenly an important word is not there, a necessary word, a word on which the sense of the entire article hinges, and its absence renders all of the other words simply meaningless. For Farro Fescu, Renata Negri's sudden passing left just such a confusion, and for the longest time, whenever the door of the west elevator opened, he expected to see her stepping into the lobby. But it would be Rabbi Ravijohn with his cane, or Luther Rumfarm with yet another of his pompous suggestions.

When the eighth-floor apartment occupied by the Blorgs became available, it stood empty for a time, and it was eventually sold to Karl Vogel, a German air ace who had come to America soon after the war in Europe came to an end. In the 1960s, he wrote a book about his combat experiences, which was highly regarded, and for a while he was the darling of the talk shows. Though short of stature, he had an appealing presence, and with his angular jaw, blue eyes, and crisp, assertive manner, he cut a striking figure. Now, though, white-haired and a bit shrunken, he finds himself less in demand and feels neglected.

Farro Fescu likes him, though this is, perhaps, too strong a way of putting it. They exchange small talk—the weather, the pain in Vogel's back, the latest on cholesterol. It isn't a fondness, nor is it friendship, merely an amiability born of an unexplained sense of connection. At the very least, Farro Fescu doesn't feel toward him the outright antipathy that he feels, say, toward Rumfarm, who gets under his skin even more than Ira Klempp does.

When Farro Fescu was seven, living in a mountain village in the Balkans, he lost a grandfather and an uncle in a German bombing raid, and he remembers the harshly bright, sunlit day in April when they put the bodies in the ground. He can still recall his mother's angry, wrenching sobs, and the smell of the flowers they put on top of the hastily constructed wooden coffins. But none of this is anything that he ever mentions to Vogel. Small talk is what they share, not the baring of souls. And besides, the past is long gone, and the war, by now, is a fossilized piece of ancient history.

Vogel, pausing at the desk, complains about an aching molar. Farro Fescu complains about the pains in his feet. They compare notes on chiropractors. Farro Fescu passes along a tip on a horse. He recommends a jeweler to repair Vogel's broken watch. Coming into the lobby one day with a bag of oranges from the market on South End, Vogel takes one out and puts it on the desk. "Good for the heart," he says with an unmistakable accent, even though he's lived in America almost twice as long as in Germany. "Fresh, juicy oranges. I eat three a day, they cure everything." Juicy is choocy. Oranges is owanges. Three is twee.

Vogel is short, approaching seventy, but Rumfarm, in his late forties, is tall and portly, with pale eyes, small ears, pudgy hands. He's with an investment group in the Trade Center and has a practiced affability that is unctuous and, at times, overbearing. When not in his business suit, he wears splashy casuals and a Mets baseball cap that seems quaintly incongruous above his big nose and beefy face. His voice is smooth and softly urgent, a tone that Farro Fescu associates, in its mellowness, with a television commercial for toilet paper. Ever since he wormed his way onto the governing board, he's managed to make a nuisance of himself, coming up with one obtrusive idea after another. This month, it's the waterfall. He wants to install an electronically controlled cascade, twenty feet high, in the lobby, on the wide marble wall between the two elevators. It would flow down into a granite catch basin, with hidden pumps cycling the water in a continuous, rushing flow. His plan includes colored lights playing on the water, and artificial shrubs at the rim of the basin, with a stuffed egret or two.

The thought of a waterfall in the lobby—the sheer noise of the thing—pushes Farro Fescu to the edge. When he hears Rumfarm talking it up among the residents, he manages, through a sheer act of will, to remain outwardly calm, but a slow anger builds inside him and his blood boils.

Only two days ago—Wednesday—Rumfarm was in the lobby, on the leather couch, smoking his pipe. Smoking is taboo in the lobby, but Rumfarm, now a board member, takes his liberties, and for that too Farro Fescu dislikes him. He was pretending to read his mail, but was in fact lying in wait for anyone who happened along. The first to turn up was Karl Vogel, perspiring, back from one of his long walks, in khaki pants and a blue pullover.

"Right over there," Rumfarm said pridefully, pointing with his pipe toward the wall between the elevators. "That's where we'll put it." He was wreathed in smoke from his meerschaum. In yellow slacks and a bright, flowered sport shirt, he seemed a tropical tree that a bird might nest in.

Vogel, frayed from his long exertion and ready for a nap, was slow to respond. "A waterfall?" he said, with delayed surprise, appearing to hear of it for the first time, though he already knew of it from Tattafruge, who had it from Mrs. Sowle, who had learned of it from Louisa Wax. "Here? In the lobby?" He touched a handkerchief to his brow, blotting up the beads of perspiration.

"It will freshen the place no end," Rumfarm said, warmly encouraging. With his pipe in hand, he made a large, sweeping gesture that took in the whole of the lobby—the high marble walls, the palm tree and the couch, and, across the way, the desk area where Farro Fescu sat behind a long oak counter that was covered by a slab of polished granite. He was in his high-backed leather chair, busying himself over a clipboard.

"The place needs some livening up," Rumfarm said.

"No doubt, no doubt," Vogel nodded, seeming to agree.

"But tell me—tell me about the water." His accent thickened ever so slightly, the word water coming across not as *water* but as *vasser*. "Will it be chlorinated?"

Rumfarm, unbalanced by the question and uncertain where it might lead, hung back cautiously.

"I ask," Vogel pursued, "because if it's chlorinated, there could be, you realize, an unpleasant odor. Is that what we want? A lobby smelling like a swimming pool?"

"No, no," Rumfarm answered. "Of course not. That's not what I had in mind. Not at all."

"On the other hand," Vogel added, "if the water is untreated, imagine the unpleasantness."

"What unpleasantness?"

"Bacteria," Vogel said. "Mold spores."

Rumfarm stared coldly. "Are you suggesting a health problem?"

"Of course a health problem. The ones with allergies, ask them. You think Mrs. Klongdorf wants this? You think Sandbar and Rosen, and Mrs. Marriocci?"

Rumfarm had already spoken to Sandbar and Rosen and Mrs. Marriocci, and they hadn't mentioned anything of their allergies.

Vogel put his hand on the marble wall. It was cool and silky smooth. Faint veins of yellow and gold branched through the dark blue slabs, the blue transforming itself, in places, to milky white, or to charcoal and pale gray.

"Could they make it soundproof?" he wondered.

Rumfarm arched his eyebrows.

"Yes, yes," Vogel went on, "you know—a waterfall with a minimum of sound, with a device to hold down the noise. Technology, these days, can do everything."

"Frankly," Rumfarm said, with barely concealed annoyance, and a clear sense that Vogel was putting him on, "with a waterfall, the sound of the thing is more than half the charm. Don't you think?" He puffed on his pipe, shrouding himself in a cloud of smoke.

Vogel touched the silver button on the marble wall, summoning the elevator, and let out what seemed to be a sigh, though it may only have been a partially restrained yawn. "Oh," he said, "I'm only thinking of poor Mr. Farro Fescu over there, who will have to listen to it all day long."

Farro Fescu did not glance up at the mention of his name. He turned to his calendar and, rather deliberately, put large black Xs through the days of the month that had already passed. The elevator arrived, and Vogel stepped aboard.

"We could pipe in music," Rumfarm said, with a special urgency. He knew he had lost Vogel, yet he kept on with it, refusing to give up. "It could be very soothing—music mingling with the sound of the waterfall. I want you to think about this, Mr. Vogel. I want you to give it some thought. Will you think about it? Will you?"

"What kind of music," Vogel asked, in a tone that didn't expect a reply.

The elevator door whispered shut, and Rumfarm was left standing there, by the marble wall, near a small lacquered table with a vase of freshly cut flowers. Far above the table and the flowers, some twenty feet up, was the clock, elegantly simple, just two bronze hands on the wall, with brass markers for the hours, the hands sweeping across the delicately veined marble like knives slicing relentlessly through time itself. Above the clock was a small, narrow ledge, an accent piece, pink jasper, and on a few rare occasions, birds had found their way into the lobby and perched there. A sparrow, a pigeon, a gull.

At the desk, Farro Fescu drew more Xs on top of the Xs he'd already made, then phoned for a limo for Juanita Blaize.

That, the exchange between Rumfarm and Karl Vogel, had occurred two days ago. Today, Friday, it's ten in the morning, and the day, which began with bright sun, has turned cloudy. There are predictions for rain.

Through the glass doors, Farro Fescu sees a delivery car pulling up in a rush. It's Poppo Pizza, with a sign on top that proclaims: 24-HOUR-SERVICE.

21

Farro Fescu shows the delivery boy where to sign on the log. The pizza is for Ira Klempp, on the twelfth floor, pepperoni and mushrooms. The delivery boy, a light-skinned Hispanic, is young enough to be still in high school, wearing, by sheer coincidence, a pair of Krazy-Kolor pants cut from an Ira Klempp design, each leg made of irregularly shaped patches of brightly colored denim. Pimples on his face, and on his upper lip a line of scraggly black hairs that he's trying to cultivate into a moustache.

"Twenty-four hours?" Farro Fescu says doubtfully, unwilling to believe that a pizza shop, any pizza shop, Poppo's, was really open around the clock.

"Well, it's a little slow in the wee hours," the kid says, a streetwise slant on his lips, "but it picks up around seven." Farro Fescu figures if he weren't delivering pizza, he'd be pushing drugs.

"Nifty pants," he says. And to stir some mischief, he tells him about Ira Klempp, who invented Krazy Kolor and uses it not just for pants but for shirts and underwear too. "He'll give you his autograph," he says, pleased at the thought that Klempp, who eats pizza at this ungodly hour, is going to be imposed upon.

The kid winces, thinking Farro Fescu is pulling his leg.

"Why would I do that," Farro Fescu asks.

"I don't know. You look like you're up to something."

"That's what you think?"

The kid tilts his head, skeptical.

"Just last week," Farro Fescu says, "he put his signature on somebody's back pocket. Don't you want his John Hancock on your ass?"

"Bullshit," the kid says, smiling now, wanting to believe it's true.

"You old enough to drive?" Farro Fescu says.

"I drive, I drive," the kid answers, and it's plain he's driving with a phony license.

Farro Fescu raises an eyebrow. He rings Ira Klempp, letting him know the pizza is on the way.

"Ask for his picture," he tells the kid. "He passes out eight-by-tens. In color."

"Now I know you're just pissing," the kid says, vanishing up the east elevator.

Farro Fescu puts a sucking candy in his mouth. The flavor is ambiguous, hard to identify. It reminds him, for some reason, of the color lavender, if the color lavender could be said to have a flavor. The lobby, this moment, seems a mausoleum. It's as if time has thickened, as if it has solidified and been bent and twisted out of shape. He feels it, the bending and the twisting, and knows that he's part of it—and perhaps, in some crazy way, he is the source of it, this warp in time, creating it, a lavender deformation from which there is no way out.

More than ever, the building seems alive to him, and more than ever, now, he hates it. It owns him, feeds him, puts blood in his veins. It holds him in a strange belonging, a bond so intimate that he no longer knows if he is part of the building—a fixture, an extension—or if the building is part of him, his dream, his creation. Him and not-him. The sounds, the smells, the hum of the elevators, shoes on the marble, the comings and goings—and the dim silences. It's a form of hate-love, a love so fierce that it twists into hate, and a hate so pure it can only be understood as a sign of desire—the hate and the love vibrating on the same wavelength. The other name for it—he knows—is hell, and once you've become used to it, why would you want to be anywhere else?

He pushes up from his chair, steps around the desk, and goes through the heavy glass door, leaving it open, the stopper in place. Far up the block, to his right, beyond South End, the traffic hurries along on West Street. But here, by the condo, no traffic at all, the street empty except for a few pigeons, and weirdly quiet, as if, for the moment, it's been sealed off from the rest of the world.

He crosses to the other side, giving himself some distance, going toward the river, and then, turning and looking back, simply stands there, hands in his pockets, scanning the building, Echo Terrace, from top to bottom, the stolid, fifteen-story structure clad in a maudlin skin of gray-green granite, the rows of balconies forming a monotonous grid that reveals nothing of the luxury inside. His eyes rove, window to window, and he sees, at the top, a slanting angle of the rooftop solarium, glass panes blazing in the morning sun.

Many times, in the news, he's seen how buildings are demolished, the charges set with scientific precision and detonated with perfect timing—the outer walls fold in on themselves, and the building drops straight down, a neat gravitational plunge. Implosion. It enters his mind that he can do this. By simply wanting it, focusing his attention, he will make it happen. Implode the building and bring it down, the entire bad-luck heap of glass, steel, granite, and wallboard. Make it crumble. Now.

He wills it.

Intends it.

Wants it to happen.

Touches a button in his mind, and with a surly, snappish roar, the charges detonate. The solarium shatters, and the building's outer walls shiver, the granite skin straining and tearing open. Windows burst. The whole outline of the building trembles and disarranges itself. There is the barest hint of a pause—the building hovering in slow motion, as if trying to pull itself together, resisting collapse, clinging desperately to its own memory of itself. Then, with a kind of shrug, it lets go and collapses thunderously, dumb tonnage, the low, slow rumble amplifying in an ear-splitting crescendo as the floors plunge and shatter in a ground-thumping, bone-shaking crash. It's gone, all of it, nothing there but a tongueless heap of wreckage. Mrs. Abernooth's zoo, Ira Klempp's closets full of Krazy-Kolor pants, Muhta Saad's cigars, Juanita Blaize's couches and pillows, all smashed, crushed, compacted. Nothing but sticks and crumbled mortar, twisted steel, torn wires. Rumfarm's blueprints for the waterfall—gone.

Farro Fescu is still out there on the street, basking in the thought that he made this happen—he, and nobody else. He's still good for something, still capable, able to do, able to perform.

He looks down and sees a pigeon, inches away from his left shoe. He gives it a swift kick, lofting it like a football, and the bird, stunned, but with no serious damage, unfurls its wings and flies, mounting the air in a flutter of bright feathers. A tugboat on the river hoots a mournful sound. A blue car, a Saab, comes down the street and turns into the underground garage.

In the lobby, back at the desk, he fills his white mug with coffee from a thermos. It's still Friday morning. Summer, hot July. 1992. The vase of flowers is still on the lacquered table between the two elevators, daisies and roses. Blue lights are blinking on the phone. Mrs. Rumfarm needs a taxi at noon. Muhta Saad has a leaking faucet. Mrs. Marriocci has lost her rosary beads and would he kindly keep an eye out for them? Mrs. Wax has no hot water for her bath.

The east elevator is on its way down. The door slides open and the pizza kid steps out, moving briskly, and there is no joy in his face. His eyes are two dark holes. When he passes the desk, he says to Farro Fescu, without looking at him, "Up yours, motherfucker."

"Yeah, kid," Farro Fescu answers blandly. "Same to you. Have a fun day."

The kid is out the door and into the car, burning rubber as he speeds off. And Farro Fescu, sitting there, watching the kid disappear, is hauled back, through some magical mind-bend, to his own youth, fifty years past, in another place, a part of the world that he doesn't think about often, but now it comes rushing back, with a bittersweet pungency that twists him around and fills him with loneliness.

His people were from Craiova, in Rumania, but soon after he was born, they moved across the border into Serbia so that the men could work the copper mines at Bor. The labor was hard, yet his father and his uncles did well and there was always enough food, and a movie once a week in

25

the village hall. The village was on the flank of a long hill, looking across at a higher hill. Not many were living there, in that village, mostly Rumanians who had come across for the mines, which were owned by a French company. There were dances and gatherings where the men drank too much, and the women too, and a great deal of laughter, and more than enough weeping. And pies, cakes, and the nougat candy that he liked so much. Then the Germans came, and everything changed. April 6, he remembers, was when it started, the big guns firing shells, planes strafing and bombing, and the heavy armor moving in, big tanks pushing along on the roads and the fields. A ten-day war, that's all it was. The army collapsed, and the Germans had Yugoslavia. They already had Rumania, Hungary, and Bulgaria, which had simply let them walk in. But in Yugoslavia, the Serbs and others had opposed a pact with Hitler, and after the army's defeat, many of the soldiers fled into the mountains and waged a guerrilla campaign.

Farro Fescu remembers that he stopped believing in God when he was seven years old. That was the year the Germans attacked, 1941, and his grandfather and one of his uncles were killed. The uncle—Grigor—was his favorite uncle, the one who taught him card tricks and chess. They used to play for hours. Then came the bombardment and the blitzkrieg, and his uncle was nineteen years old when the bomb killed him. Sometimes Farro Fescu wonders if up there, among the attacking planes, Karl Vogel may have been strafing and bombing. He should hate Vogel—yes. And yet, oddly, he does not. It's as if somehow, through the death of his uncle, in that awful time, they've been brought together, without reason or logic, and now they meet in the lobby and talk about their arthritis. He's never asked Vogel where he flew in the war, and he doesn't want to know.

Two years after he stopped believing in God, he stopped believing in love. There was a girl he was obsessed with, a light-haired girl who was too old for him, but still he had a crush on her. He was nine, and she was sixteen. During a dance at the village hall, he found her in a back room that was full of coats. Her lavender dress was pushed down off her shoulders, down to her waist, and with her was his oldest brother, Barbu, fondling her breasts. They were on the floor, and the smell in the room was the smell of the coats, of wool that was wet from the snow that had been falling all through that day.

He thinks often of that room and that moment, wondering what if it had been him lying there with the girl, instead of his brother? How different, perhaps, his whole life would have been. And many other things he wonders about and remembers. That village of old shacks on the side of a hill, and the sound of the whistles at the mines, far off. How different if the Germans had never come!

He had fooled around with a harmonica when he was a child, but that was long ago, and now he can't even hum a tune. He never collected stamps, or coins, or pictures of movie stars, and sports he's never been keen about. And he dislikes oranges, they irritate his stomach. When Vogel gives him one, he drops it in the basket as soon as Vogel has walked off. He wonders if they still dig in the copper mines at Bor—it's something he should find out. He would like to go back and visit, to see what, if anything, is left of that small village.

And then, with a buoyancy, almost a light-headedness, he's thinking again of Renata Negri. What if, at this moment, she were to come through the door, with her wanton glances and her bold wink? She who sang the Verdi operas so wonderfully before her premature death—and how many times he stood outside her apartment, in the foyer, listening as she practiced her arias. What if she should appear now, in the lobby, and invite him to dance?

"But you're dead," he would say, and she would give him one of her long, slanting looks.

"Yes, yes," she would answer, "it's true, I'm dead. But does it matter?"

And what if he were to take her in his arms and dance with her across the marble floor, past the elevators, the palm tree, past the desk and the mail room filled with everyone's mail? This would be better, he thinks, than bitterness and despair. So why should he blame anyone? Why blame his uncle Grigor for dying? Or his brother Barbu for taking the girl of his dreams? Why blame Rumfarm, or Ira Klempp, or Mrs. Abernooth with her messy animals? Or Harry Falcon in the penthouse, dying of cancer. One thing he is sure of, because he's given it hard thought and has made up his mind. If the waterfall is installed in the lobby, he will resign and go elsewhere.

He leaves the desk, boards the elevator, rides down to the subbasement, and walks snappily along on the painted cement floor, past the boiler room and long ranks of insulated piping, past valves and intakes and shutoff cocks, past the emergency electric plant and the telephone interchange. Fire hoses, and water pumps if there should ever be flooding. And far down, in the southwest corner, he comes to a locked room that has stood empty and unused since the condo's opening. It's broad and spacious, and early on there had been arguments about how to use it—as an entertainment parlor with pool tables and video games, or as a smoking room, with roulette and baccarat, or simply as a reading room. But the residents had never been able to agree, and the large, wide room remains empty. Farro Fescu unlocks the door, throws on the fluorescents, and there before him, on the far wall and across the cement floor, is the zigzagging crack he discovered only a month ago. At first it had been a mere thread, but now, in places, it's half an inch wide. It runs down the cement wall and onto the floor, where it divides into two long branches that seem bent on mischief.

Time is good, he thinks, and time is bad. And he suspects, on balance, there is more bad than good. There are gray days, slow days, quick days, and blue days— smart days and days that are utterly foolish. Perhaps the

28

building will fall on its own, from its own internal weakness, with no help from him, simply crack open and split apart, sooner than anyone knows. It's the Rumanian blood in him that thinks this, the Balkan darkness, always waiting for the next shoe to drop.

Part One

Venus, favorite of men and gods, through you all living things are conceived . . . For you, O goddess, the earth puts forth flowers, for you the sea laughs, and heaven glows with a radiant light . . . You put the passion of love into the hearts of all creatures, and they beget their kind, generation to generation . . . Without you, nothing comes forth into the world of light, nothing joyous, nothing lovely . . .

—LUCRETIUS, *DE RERUM NATURA*

. . . we are now in a hot little sidewheel steamer jammed with men, dogs, bags and belongings, partially cured and rather bad-smelling skins, and the like . . . In ten days we shall be at the last post office, San Luis de Cáceres; and then we shall go into the real wilderness.

—THEODORE ROOSEVELT, LETTER TO HIS WIFE, EDITH

A Green Dream
of the Jungle

1

In Nora Abernooth's ninth-floor apartment, there are finches, canaries, three marmosets, a defanged cobra, a tortoise, and a macaw with blue and gold feathers. There is also a rhesus monkey that answers to the name of Joe, and a glass-enclosed formicarium loaded with ants.

She lets the finches out of their cages and they flit about from room to room, perching on the chairs and lamps, and on the lemon tree in the living room. In the kitchen, which is hung with white cabinets, they flutter among the morning glories by the window, and in their busy way they poke at the grapes and the apricots in the fruit bowl. Her husband, Louis, who had had a burgeoning career as an entomologist, has been dead now for six years, yet there are times when it seems he's still alive, moving among the animals. She hears him in the library, browsing through his books, or in the kitchen, fumbling with the coffeepot. There are moments when she seems to glimpse him from the corner of her eye—but when she looks up, there's nothing, merely a finch gliding by, or one of the snakes readjusting itself on the sofa. She lives with echoes, shadows, dim rustlings, as if every wall in the apartment were a foggy mirror tossing up tarnished images and vague, elusive glimmers.

In the winter months, when the heat is on, robbing the air of moisture, she keeps a humidifier going day and night. The animals suffer when the air is dry. She turns on the showers in both bathrooms, letting the steam flow warm and wet into the other rooms. The air thickens and grows heavy, like the air of the rain forest in Ecuador, where she spent several months with Louis soon after they were married. Their jungle honeymoon, she called it, their lush, decadent romp in the tangled wilderness.

For the finches, there is a mix of millet and canary seed, with cuttlebone and grit. The macaw is spoiled on peanuts. For the tortoise, a mash of fresh fruit and vegetables, with bonemeal. Because of the moisture in the air, there's a problem with mold. Dampness clings to the white walls, forming patches of varying shapes and sizes—in the living room, above the mantel, a magenta smear that shades off to pale yellow, and in the dining room, above the buffet, a gray smudge tinged with red. In the master bedroom, small green spots have appeared on the white louvred doors that open onto the walk-in closet. She used to be diligent about wiping the mold away as soon as it formed, but now it's simply there, growing at will, allowed to make its way in whatever shapes and colors it chooses.

After her bath, as she towels herself dry, she wanders from room to room, wet feet leaving a meandering trail on the beige wall-to-wall that carpets the apartment. Her trail winds through the bedroom, the dining room, Louis's library, through the long foyer, and ends in the large but sparsely furnished living room, where she picks up a Bible from the coffee table and stretches out on the floor, on the bearskin in front of the fireplace.

She is pink and warm from the bath, and pleasantly drowsy. The Bible is a Gideon that she took, years ago, from a motel in Ithaca. It's the only Bible she's ever owned. That time in Ithaca, it was her first night with Louis, before they were married. "I want this," she said, taking the Bible, tenderly, as a reminiscence. It disappeared for a while, buried in a box of books, but after Louis died, when she was cleaning out and rearranging, she found it again, and now it's a comfort for her, a source of solace and consolation. Scarcely a day goes by that she doesn't linger over a few verses, deriving a haunting satisfaction from the old words and rhythms.

The bearskin is from a giant grizzly, *Ursus horribilis*—this one was cinnamon-colored, the fur thick and reddish brown. It was given to her long ago by her grandfather, when he was very old and she was very young. She runs her fingers through the fur and leans down into it, into the bear's warmth, into the hard-soft clumps of hair, and the Bible falls open to a page she's looked at many times before. *The Lord is my shepherd, I shall not want. He maketh me to lie down in green pastures: he leadeth me beside the still waters.* She lies down into the bear's fur, into its silence, and thinks of Louis, gone forever, yet at this moment, in his vague way, he is here in the room with her, breathing as she is breathing, and waiting to be touched.

Her face is deep into the pelt, into its rugged smoothness, and this, she thinks, is death, the beginning of it, the slowness of it, the valley of the shadow, shaped in darkness. And yes, she thinks, yes, I will fear no evil. Her fingers clutch lightly at the bear's wool and she breathes heavily, tugging at the humid air. The rhesus watches her. The cobra glides across her ankles. A finch flies from the mantel to the lemon tree, and she lies there, on the bearskin, in a green dream of the jungle, thinking of Louis.

In the rain forest there were monkeys in the trees, high in the canopy, and birds with warm, burning wings, toucans and tanagers, and always the insects, the glorious, swarming insects, incessant among the flowers and rotting logs. It was because of the insects that they were there, she and Louis, those slow three months in the first year of their marriage.

They were gathering specimens. Louis was on leave from the university, on a government grant, studying the insects and finding some that no one had ever seen before. He searched and collected, and she used the camera, her father's old Leica, capturing on film the rare

35

and unknown species that Louis plucked from the soil and from the decaying wood of fallen trees. They searched and photographed—and, as if there were no other reason for their being there, they touched each other, a finger on an arm, his hand on her thigh, and, with a wild passion, they made love, coming at each other all hours of the day and night, insatiably, in ways she had never imagined, with a panting restlessness that seemed to grow out of the heat and murmur of the jungle itself, out of its ripeness, its sensuality, the sullen throb of emotion in the calls of the animals and the birds. Those three slow months in Ecuador, it was a fever, a level of desire she'd never felt before. Time was so wonderful, she thought. It spreads out, weaving and wandering. It turns and folds over on itself, full of surprises.

In the forest, Louis taught her about the ants, though she wasn't sure she wanted to know anything more than the little she already knew. He showed her a swarm that moved glisteningly on the carcass of a bird. Ants were what he knew best, he'd written about them in his doctoral dissertation, dense pages packed with research and field observation.

"Aren't they incredible," he said. "They have such tiny brains, and yet they know exactly what they're doing."

He picked one up and showed it to her through a glass: the gaster, the mandibles, the thorax, the intricate eyes. Magnified, the ant had a weird, otherworldly beauty, but still she wasn't won over.

"In their small way," he said, "they're so much like us. In fact, there's probably nothing out there that's more like us than they are." He bent down and scooped up a whole handful, letting them roam across his hands and arms. "They hunt, they farm, and they kill. Some ants keep flocks and herds—they round up aphids like cattle and milk them for the fluid they excrete. There are ants that loaf, and ants that get drunk. And some, the Amazons, keep slaves—did you know that? Isn't it astonishing? And there are slave ants that help their masters make slaves of still other ants. What could be more human than that?"

"I hate ants," Nora said.

"The weaver ants weave, and the leaf-cutters cut. There are murders and kidnappings. And all sorts of fun!"

His favorites were the warrior ants, whole armies that go on the warpath. A colony some twenty million strong, eating anything in its way. When he did his fieldwork in Africa, on a single day, in Kenya, warrior ants invaded the village he was in, near Nairobi, and devoured eleven chickens, five rabbits, and an entire sheep, right down to the bone.

"Do any ants sing?" Nora asked.

"Not that I know of."

"Do they dance? Do they read novels and go to the opera?"

His eyes narrowed. "Some people eat them, you know."

She had the camera and was photographing the ants as they crawled across his arms. "If you want," she said, "I'll bake some in a pie for you."

"I had some in Uganda," he remembered. "They were fried. Very crunchy."

"Ants don't really get drunk," she said doubtfully.

"Sure they do. The red ants. They drink the secretions of the *Lomechusa* and they walk away tipsy."

An entire chapter of his doctoral dissertation had been devoted to the red ants. The males of the species had only one purpose in life—to fertilize the queens—and that, in the strange way of things, could be risky and less than lucky. In Siberia, the red ants in the Tien Shan mountains had developed a mating ritual in which the female climaxes the sex act with a quick snap of her jaws, severing the male's thorax from his abdomen.

While Louis rambled on about the plight of the Tien Shan males, Nora photographed his left ear, his nose, and his right ankle. She took a picture of the back of his head, where already the hair was beginning to thin. She removed his shirt and photographed his left nipple. Then she removed his pants and photographed his penis, first in repose and then in tumescence.

"I can't wait to be back in New York," he said.

"Really?" she said. "I rather like it here. I think I could stay forever."

"You didn't take a picture of my tongue," he said.

"I'll do that later," she said.

"If we were ants," he said, "would you cut me in half with your razor-sharp jaws?"

She spent some time thinking about that. "I don't know," she said, unwilling to commit herself. "I really don't know."

All of that—the ants, the forest, the Leica, and the many new species that Louis was discovering—was nine long years ago, when Nora was thirty-two, and Louis was about to turn forty. When they returned to New York and he was back at the university, he published his findings and had, for a time, a wonderful success. But then, in his foolishness, he was suddenly dead, and what Nora was left with was not him but an echo of him, a fading video-tape playing over and over again in her mind. He was gone, living only in memory, and what she had now was the apartment, the lemon tree, and the albums filled with photographs, and the books he had pored over, the articles he had written, and the lazy, languishing animals—the python curling across the sofa, the tortoise hiding in his shell, and the macaw talking in his garbled way, saying the unpleasant words that Louis had taught him: *Merde* . . . Murder . . . *Sacre bleu* . . . Take off your pants, chum . . . Up yours!

The macaw is thirty-seven years old. They had purchased him from a dealer in New Jersey, with papers testifying to his age and country of origin. At thirty-seven he is only a few years younger than Nora, and she wonders if he will live to be fifty, as some macaws do. He shows signs of aging, a crankiness, he's picky about his food, restless, stiff in the joints. He complains, making a low croaking noise that is less than pleasant. He is hopelessly in love with the cockatiel, a bird of lavish pink and blue feathers. The cockatiel struts by, paying no attention, and when the macaw sees her he blushes, the whites of his eyes turning deeply, vividly red. Any number of times Nora has seen him trying to mount the cockatiel, but with no success, the cockatiel nipping at him ferociously, then spreading her wings and darting away.

There is a time of day when the macaw, listless, uncertain where to turn, comes up to Nora and, in an evident state of malaise, utters yet another of the choice phrases that Louis had taught him: "What's for lunch, baby?"

2

On a wall in the living room, above the couch, hangs a photograph of Theodore Roosevelt on the verandah of his big home on Sagamore Hill, dated 1907. There is mold here too, on the edges of the walnut frame and under the glass, on the photograph itself. It's Teddy, the indomitable bull moose, with his big moustache and bluff, impervious gaze, and beside him stands a much younger and smaller man, Nora's grandfather, with rimless glasses and a stick-pin in his tie, and a wan smile on his thin, enigmatic lips. He became part of the team in the final years of Teddy's presidency, helping to write some of the speeches, smoking cigars in back rooms, hobnobbing with the politicos, and it saddens Nora to think this picture on the wall and the bearskin on the floor are the last things in the world that she has left of him.

When she was five, he was eighty-two. When she was fifteen, he was already several years in his grave. Now she's beyond forty, and she sees how time has a way of closing in on itself. She's been to Oyster Bay, on Long Island, and has stood on the verandah, on the spot where her grandfather stood when that picture was taken, and has seen the same distant view across the tops of the trees.

Time is too painful, it twists and turns, it teases and torments. It tips you upside down and leaves you dangling. She remembers the smell of tobacco on her grandfather's breath, his white moustache and yellow, ground-down teeth, cavernous wrinkles in his cheeks and forehead. He talked to her about how much he had loved to hunt, days and weeks in the wild, on horseback. He'd been on many of the trips out west, when Teddy was shooting buffalo and bear, and whitetail. The bearskin in her living room is from that time, though she never had it clear whether the bear had been done in by her grandfather or by Teddy. Even her grandfather, when he gave it to her, seemed uncertain. He was, by then, confused about so many things, but always talking, talking, bits and pieces, and she suspects, now, he may have been making much of it up.

He gave it to her when she was eleven, on her birthday, because he saw how much she wanted it, the thick fur, and the head with the pointed ears and thick snout, the fur shaggy with the feel of the wilderness, and a pathos too, a loneliness she thought she understood. She wondered why the bear had to be dead, why it couldn't be alive and running in the woods, and one day she had asked him just that. Why, if it was so strong and big and beautiful, had it been necessary to kill it?

"I don't know," the old man said, hoarse and throaty, struggling with the question as if it were a problem in calculus. "You kill what you love, I suppose. That seems to be the way it is. What do you think, Nora? Tell me how it seems to you."

The bear had been a big one, a thousand-pound grizzly, nine feet long, gutted and made into a rug, and she cherished it like nothing else she owned. When she returned from Ecuador, with Louis, and they set up in the new apartment, which they bought with money inherited from her grandfather, she took the bearskin out of the box where it had been stored and spread it out on the living room floor, and they made love on it, the touch of it on her naked skin igniting a special excitement, a sexual keenness and elasticity, as if, as Louis bore down on her, past and present were commingled in the fur of that dead bear, and the bear itself seemed alive, brought to life by the oily sweat of her body, her limbs tensing and flowing in the dreamy ache of her pleasure. It had been her idea to make love on that rug, on that particular day. It was she who suggested it. And when she thinks of Louis now, sometimes, oddly, his face is a blur, a tangle of gray shadow—and sometimes, even more strangely, Louis's blurred face becomes her grandfather's face, the face in the picture, when he was young and had all of the world in front of him.

That one time when she went to Sagamore Hill, she climbed the stairs to the top floor, where, in an earlier time, the servants had lived. It was a house of more than twenty rooms, with one cook, two maids, a waitress, and someone to do the laundry. The maids dusted and swept, made the beds, and filled the vases with flowers. Their wages were twenty dollars a month, and meals. She wonders what it must have been like, living in that big squat hilltop house with all those rooms, with the gables and dormers and mustard-colored shingles, and the chimneys for the eight fireplaces, and all the famous people passing though. The foundations were twenty inches thick. In the basement, two furnaces warmed the house with hot air. A brochure that she picked up at the door explained it all, telling her more than she really wanted to know. On the ground floor, the Great Room was stuffed with trophies of the hunt, buffalo heads and antlered elk and deer, and elephant tusks from the safari in Africa, the year after his presidency was over.

Nora's grandfather was with him on that trip to Africa. They killed bull elephants and rhinos, and zebras, lions, klipspringers, oryx, bohor, and kob. They gave the bones and tusks and most of the hides to the Smithsonian, some thirteen thousand specimens and three thousand skins. While they were camped at Mount Kenya, in Meru country, runners brought a cable

41

from Commander Peary, who had reached the North Pole. "The Pole is ours," the message said, and Nora's grandfather told her of the excitement in Teddy's face, the sheer boyish delight, when he read it. Later, on the White Nile, on their way to Khartoum, they needed four hundred and fifty carriers to help them along as they passed the rapids.

She wonders if Teddy, the hunter of big game, would have enjoyed searching for insects in the rain forest in Ecuador. The small ones with silver wings, and the smaller ones with no wings at all. Would they have been too infinitesimal to hold his interest? He had been always so eager to bag the big things, elephants, bears, bison, as if size, magnitude, were the all-important thing. Would he, on the insect hunt in Ecuador, have been simply bored?

When he was fifty-five, after he lost in his run to regain the presidency, he went off to Brazil, deep into the jungle, not for insects and not for game, but to explore a river, tracking its course through a dangerous succession of rapids and waterfalls. It was the River of Doubt, Rio da Dúvida, and it nearly killed him. Nora's grandfather was with him on that trip too. There were piranhas, mosquitoes, poisonous snakes, and jungle fever. They ran out of food and ate monkeys and whatever fish they could catch. The river was nine hundred and fifty miles long. Three men died. One drowned when a boat capsized, and another, crazed by a fever, shot a companion and ran off into the jungle to die. The Brazilian colonel, Rondon, lost part of a foot to the piranhas. Teddy himself, with an abscess on his leg, feverish and close to death, urged the others to go on without him. They carried him on a litter, through dense foliage, and at the end of April, after two months of struggling with the river, they came out of the jungle at San João and caught a steamer to Manaus, and on to Belém. He had lost over fifty pounds. Five years later, at sixty, he died in his sleep of an embolism.

Nora never knew him. He was dead long before she

was born. She toys, at times, with the notion of an after-life, and imagines how pleasant it would be, some Saturday afternoon, in the green pastures, by the still waters, if her grandfather and Teddy should come strolling along, and her grandfather calls her over and introduces her to the great man. What, if anything, would they say to each other? Would they talk about the River of Doubt, and the one who drowned, and the one who went mad, and the dysentery and the terrible piranhas, or would he want to forget about all of that? They would listen to the robins and the meadowlarks and watch great flocks of geese passing overhead, black against the sky, their big wings beating the air. Would he offer her, possibly, a cigar? And if he did, would she accept?

Time, she thinks, is so confused, so lacking in definition. It turns back on itself, and you are never where you thought you were. She begins to think of time as something she could hate, as something she could cut into tiny pieces with a pair of scissors, letting the pieces blow away in the wind.

3

It's Tuesday afternoon, but it could be any day at all, Monday, Saturday, Wednesday. She takes out the camera and spends some time photographing the cobra. He seems to know he's being photographed. His body lies neatly coiled, the head rising nobly, self-consciously, staring at the camera, showing his magnificent cowl. He turns to the left, briefly, offering his profile, then to the right, and she clicks away, shot after shot, catching him in all his moods. He rears back, tongue flickering with a show of meanness, eyes gleaming with a special intensity. But then, suddenly, the intensity is gone, and in a kind of exhaustion, as if weary with it all—as if, in his defanged state, he is disappointed with himself—he withdraws and settles down, twisting himself into a tight, slumber-some ball.

She turns on the music. The only tape she plays, these days, is Ravel's *Bolero*, booming it loud, the slow, pounding rhythms laboring and lumbering with lush monotony, building hypnotically. It's the same tape she had with her in Ecuador, in the rain forest, where she played it again and again, and the mood, the rhythm, became synchronous with the mood of the forest. And she feels it again now, the heat of it, steam rising from the jungle floor, the seductive tempo of the flute, the sensual clarinet and sheer lust of the bassoon.

The animals love it. The macaw, with a feathery flutter, hops onto the coffee table and moves with an awkward grace, as if trying to keep time with the music. The marmosets swing rhythmically on the ropes in their cage. The canaries sing, and the finches dart wildly. The tortoise hides in its shell, and the python, draped across the sofa, sleeps.

She takes the rhesus by his hands and moves with him in a slow dance, as if drifting underwater, in slow motion, turning and weaving in some dark, primal dream. The drapes are drawn, and the only light comes from the dim lamps. They move and turn in the flow of the music, the rhesus making a low, churring sound. He's barely half as tall as she. They're at arm's length, only their hands touching, the music wandering, flowing over and through them. In the jungle she had danced with Louis like this, bodies far apart, only their hands touching, in a clearing by the tents, the music bleeding from the speaker, swelling and rising in the damp air and filtering through the leaves. Birds with scarlet wings hovering in the shadows.

4

During the past month or so, she's become friendly with Theo Tattafruge, a slight, fragile-looking man who lives on the fifth floor. He's a surgeon, specializing in cosmetic adjustments. He does face-lifts, breast implants, and liposuctions. They had passed each other often, in the lobby, but didn't actually meet until, one day, they were on the elevator together, coming down. He studied her face intently, frontally and in profile.

"A few tucks here and there," he said, "and the years will disappear. It's a simple procedure, I do it in my office. You won't recognize yourself."

"But I like to recognize myself," she said, in her calm, pleasant way.

"That's a good attitude," he said, not meaning to be patronizing. "Yes, always be yourself. I encourage my patients to have a good attitude about themselves. It will surprise you, after the procedure, how young you will seem."

"How old do I appear to you to be?"

"Forty-six, forty-seven," he said, too quickly, giving her, carelessly, more years than she had.

She said nothing.

He was remorseful. "Forgive me," he shrugged, "I'm a terrible fool when it comes to guessing ages."

Tattafruge himself, she learned later, was approaching fifty, though he seemed younger.

They didn't see each other again until two weeks afterward, when he was stepping off the elevator and she was coming through the front door, into the lobby, laden with packages.

"Let me help you," he said, insisting. He was slightly taller than she, but thin to the point of appearing frail, and it seemed incongruous to her that he should offer to help with her burden. His skin, she noticed, was dark, a rich bronze tone, and this, she learned later, was from a Nubian woman somewhere in his bloodline, from a time when his Belgian ancestors were sojourning in Egypt.

At Nora's door, he saw, from the plaque above the lintel, that the apartment was named for Edward Hicks, someone that he'd never heard of.

"Oh, just some old American artist," she said.

Hicks was remembered, mainly, for his many "Peaceable Kingdom" paintings, in which lions and lambs lived at ease with each other in an earthly paradise. And Nora, with her own love for trees and animals, had always considered it fortuitous to be living in an apartment named for someone who had such a visionary attachment to nature.

When Tattafruge stepped inside, carrying the packages, he had his first glimpse of Nora's pets. The cobra was wrapped around the telephone on the marble table by the door, and the macaw was on the umbrella stand. The rhesus was stretched out on the Persian throw rug, on his back, one leg crossed over the other, gazing at the finches perched on the hat rack.

"It's a mess, I know," Nora said apologetically.

He was amazed. "You have these wonderful friends," he said.

"They're not so wonderful. Sometimes they're cranky pests."

"But they're marvelous. What a splendid idea!"

"It's my rain forest," she said.

He was particularly taken with the macaw, which approached him in a bold manner and uttered a wicked mouthful.

"Did you teach him all those dirty words?"

"He teaches himself. He's a very nasty fellow."

"You must tell me their names. Do they all have names?"

Even the finches—so many, more than twenty of them—had names, though she admitted to sometimes mixing them up. The marmosets were Larry, Moe, and Curly. The macaw was Franz, for Kafka, and the cobra was Charlie, for Chaplin. The cockatiel was Sappho, for Sappho.

The python slid off the sofa and approached Tattafruge in a friendly manner, gliding across his shoes, but the cockatiel avoided him. One of the finches squirted on his shoulder.

What she understands about Theo Tattafruge—what she understood from the start—is that he doesn't want sex from her. They simply share each other's company. They have tea a few times a week, in her apartment, and he watches the marmosets as they play in their cage. He handles the snakes and talks to the macaw, teaching him new words, as unsavory as the ones he already knows. Sometimes, on the couch, sipping tea, he and Nora don't even talk, they simply sit, munching on the cakes he brings, relaxing, subsisting with the animals. And this, his being there, the few times a week that he comes, is the extent of their relationship. They don't go out together, nor has he ever offered to show her his apartment. They are, in their deliberate way, a quaint pair, wanting only what they have, this little time that they spend together among the animals, fearful that anything else, any change in the routine, might upset the balance. On a few occasions, tired after performing surgery, he has stretched himself out on the couch and gone to sleep.

He's fussy about his tea, using a blend he buys from an Indonesian dealer on Canal Street. He's left a supply in Nora's kitchen, in a black and gold tin, and when he visits, he insists on making the tea himself. The water must be boiled to exactly the right temperature, and the tea itself must sit in the water for just the right length of time before the leaves are removed with a strainer. Nora senses that he learned his tea ritual long ago, when he was growing up in Cairo. And she agrees, it does make a difference, very special tea indeed.

But the man himself, so thin and slight—chest and rib cage so pancake-flat that he seems like a character in a cartoon, just run over by a steamroller. His jackets hang loose from his scrawny shoulders, and even his face is skinny, as if his head had been turned and pressed flat when the steamroller came along—eyes set close together, the nose long and thin as a wafer, and the skull, from temple to temple, so incredibly narrow. Not a persuasive advertisement for someone practicing cosmetic surgery—so spindly, so angular and odd-looking, he seems entirely right among the birds and animals, one more exotic species in the bunch. Sexually, she thinks of him as neuter, neither masculine nor feminine, without appetite or any hint of desire. There had been a wife, some years ago, whom he's mentioned, but it ended in divorce and he never remarried.

"I'll make the tea," he says, after sitting for a while on the floor and examining closely, with a magnifying glass, the markings on the tortoise's back.

"Yes, yes, let's do tea," she says, not looking up from the newspaper she's reading. She's in the easy chair to the left of the sofa, by the fireplace.

In the kitchen he notices a jar of ginseng on the counter, and steps back into the living room with it, studying the label.

"Have you been using this? The ginseng?"

"Oh, no," she says, glancing up from the paper. "That's very old, I only took it out to throw it away."

"I've never tried ginseng."

"Well, you don't want any of that," she says. "I really wouldn't trust it."

"People put it in their tea. I have a patient who swears by it."

"Louis used to put it in his coffee. That's how old it is."

"I'll add a pinch to the tea."

"God, no, it's rancid. I think it might kill us."

He unscrews the lid and sniffs the jar, catching from it a scent that seems familiar, but he can't quite place it. "It doesn't seem rancid, but it does have an odor." He hovers uncertainly. "I know this smell. Where do I know it from?"

But Nora is up now, briskly, out of her easy chair. She takes the jar from him and screws the lid on firmly.

"It would spoil the tea," she says, carrying the jar back to the kitchen and putting it in a cabinet. "You of all people, so fussy about flavor. I'll buy a fresh jar, if you really want to try it."

"The theory is that it bolsters the immune system."

"Yes, yes, I know. Louis used to say it was good for his warts."

"Really?"

"He had warts on his feet."

"It's a root. They dry it and grind it up. I really don't think it could have done anything for his warts."

"Tell me about the Nubian," she says.

"Which Nubian?"

"The one who gave you your dark skin."

"Ah, her," he says, putting water in the tea kettle. "She belonged to my grandfather. His name was Anhelm, from Brussels. He was on a dig at Luxor, working on one of the temples, and they took a fancy to each other. He brought her to Cairo and they lived together for fifteen years, till he died."

"So—your grandmother?"

"I suppose so, yes. But they never married, you understand. The relatives referred to her as Anhelm's woman."

"You grew up on the Nile," she says wistfully.

"Oh, we were on the outskirts, at the edge of the desert. I hardly ever saw the Nile. I was only there till I was seven. My father died, and my mother brought me here and we had an apartment in Chelsea. I went back to Cairo after I interned, but I found it boring."

He talks about the crowding, the noise, the traffic, the poverty, on and on, as if some gate had opened, and as she listens, there in the kitchen, while they wait for the water to boil, she realizes how little she knows him. The times when they sat quietly together, sharing the tea and the animals, or browsing through the newspapers, everything had felt right for her, as if she knew him thoroughly. But now, when he talks like this, about his past, she suspects that if she knew him better, he might turn out to be a person she doesn't like, someone she has nothing in common with and doesn't want to know. She wants him to stop talking. She's tired, more tired than she'd imagined. He's pouring the water from the kettle into the blue teapot, and all she can think is that she can't wait for him to leave.

"Are you really sure about that ginseng?" he says. "If the cover's on tight, you know, stuff like that can last a long time."

5

In the rain forest they had had three tents: one that they
slept in, one with the cooking utensils and supplies, and
the other with the field equipment and the microscope
and the small vials for the specimens. There was a table
with mounts, lights, and reflectors, where Nora
photographed the specimens. When they returned to
New York, Louis had seven new species with him, and
through the rest of the year he wrote tirelessly, at a
furious pace, preparing his articles for the entomology
journals.

Among the new species he had found was a yellow fly
that hovered like a hummingbird, and a spider that wove
bright blue webs, always in the shape of a triangle. And
a wasplike creature with a green head and azure body,
with a buzz like an angry bumblebee.

But by far the most exciting find, for Louis, was a
damselfly that from a distance looked like any ordinary
damselfly, *Odonata*, but upon closer inspection it
showed some remarkable variations. Nora still remembers the moment, on a Sunday morning, when she heard
him calling to her from a distance, urgent and excited.
"Nora—look! For God's sake, come take a look at this!
Bring the camera!"

She rushed from the tent and found him in the tall
grass, by a small pond, holding the damselfly by two of
its wings. It had a dark red body and purple wings, and
on each of its wings a brilliant yellow dot. They discovered later that the yellow dots glowed in the dark.
And, instead of the usual four wings, this species had six.
He named it after Nora, calling it *Odonata noraensis,* and
brought several of them back to New York. He had one of
them sealed in a cube of clear vinyl, with the wings
spread, as if in flight, and set it on the mantelpiece, under
a recessed lamp in the ceiling, where it still is, the overhead beam igniting the damselfly so that it seems more a
jewel made by an ingenious artisan than an insect
plucked from the wild.

The day that he found the damselfly, there was something in the air, a shimmer, a kind of electricity. They both felt it. First there was only that one damselfly, but then, amazingly, there were dozens, and they were mating, coupling in the air, flying about in tandem, male connected to female, in swirling loops above the pond and the tall grass. The thing in the air, the shimmer, was not just in the damselflies. Nora felt it in herself, keenly, a rush of hormones, feverish, and she saw it in Louis too, a simmering eagerness that lifted them out of themselves, transforming them, in the dense blue air by the pond. She gave him a hungry, sidelong look, and then, abandoning the camera, she began to run, across the grass and into the trees, weaving and glancing back, and as she ran she was pulling off her clothes.

He went after her, following her up a low rise and then down the far slope, into a flat area thick with mahoganies, across gnarled roots and ant-laden soil, among chameleons, geckos, pulsing salamanders, through dense undergrowth. He chased her, and, catching up, he grabbed hold, lightly, but let her escape and run again, and when he caught up to her the second time, he pulled her down into a mess of ferns and magnolia leaves, and when she remembered it later, all she could think was that they were like fire in each other's arms. She wrapped her legs around him, and they leaned into each other with a hard, wild desperation, as if the world and everything in it would in a moment come to an end. And when they had exhausted themselves, limp and breathless, all spent, they lay side by side, and he was saying the words, dredging them up from memory, intoning them, the words that he liked so much, and she remembered thinking how incongruous it was, if not actually blasphemous, because the way he said them, he made them sound as if they'd been written for no other reason than for this wild, lustful moment in the ferns.

The Lord is my shepherd; I shall not want.
He maketh me to lie down in green pastures: he
leadeth me beside the still waters.
He restoreth my soul: he leadeth me in the paths of
righteousness for his name's sake.
Yea, though I walk through the valley of the shadow
of death, I will fear no evil: for thou art with me; thy
rod and thy staff they comfort me.

It was the only part of the Bible he knew by heart, the only verses that seemed to hold any meaning for him. He didn't believe in God. God, he thought, was merely nature itself, spreading out, evolving, generating itself in an endless dance of sex and death, a wilderness of begetting and dying and new birth, unfolding forever. And the best of it, on the very finest of days, was the green pastures and the still waters, and the wild ferns and magnolia leaves. He was still saying the words, drawing them up like water from a well—*thou anointest my head with oil, my cup runneth over, goodness and mercy shall follow me all the days*—and as he was saying them, he was warm again, ready for more, and she was up already, on her feet, taunting him, prodding him with her toe, and she was off again running, and this time he let her run a very long way before he caught up with her.

In January, they left the warmth of the rain forest, and he went back to the university in triumph, with the seven new species that had never been seen before. He was teaching again, but he also spent a great deal of time writing, and before the year was out he had a whole rash of articles accepted for publication, in *Tetrahedron, Insectes Sociaux, Oecologia, Journal of Insect Physiology,* and *Studia Entomologica.* Within a very short time, he'd made a considerable name for himself.

But at home, Nora was aware of subtle changes. He was grumpy, and there was an unwonted gruffness, which she attributed to overwork. He complained about the money they'd spent for the apartment, going over their heads to buy into a river view. It had, in fact, been expensive. The money came from an account that Nora had inherited from her grandfather, and Louis felt now that they should have used it more wisely. When Nora offered to sell the apartment and go into something more reasonable, he became even grumpier, muttering it was a bad time to sell. He was right, it would have been a mistake to sell in a depressed market, yet Nora sensed in all of this that it wasn't the apartment or the money that was bothering him, but something else.

The spring semester came to an end, and they made it through the summer. But then, as the fall semester started up, it became clear that something was very wrong. Often he wasn't home for supper, and there were times when he didn't return until very late at night. Sex seemed more and more perfunctory, and there were long periods when there was no sex at all.

In November he sat down with her and told her he'd been involved with one of his graduate students. She was a girl Nora had never seen, from Montana. It had started with coffee and donuts in a shop on Bleecker, then there were afternoon movie dates and strolls through the Square, and visits to the two-room unit she rented on East Thirteenth. Then, for reasons he said he still didn't understand, the girl quit the program and went home to Montana. "Anyway," he said, "it's over. Finished. Done and over with." His hair was tousled. He hadn't shaved for several days.

Perhaps it wouldn't have been so painful, she thought, if he hadn't insisted on giving her all of the details. They were in the kitchen, he was brewing a pot of coffee. He used a strong Turkish blend that she bought for him on Mercer Street. He told her everything, or most of it, minimizing the amount of time they'd spent in bed but accepting full blame for his waywardness. He'd been working too hard, he said, trying to accomplish too much in too short a time, and had made himself vulnerable. He'd lost his bearings. But it was over, he said, it was all behind him—done and finished. And he was sorry. Really sorry.

"When did it start," she asked.

"Last spring."

"And the summer?"

"She was in Montana. She sent some letters."

"And now?"

"Still in Montana."

He was remorseful, saying he'd been a damn fool, and for a few moments, while the coffee perked, it was she who was consoling him.

"All of this, all of what's happened, it's temporary," she said, feeling the bond between them was too strong to be threatened by a mothy schoolgirl. "It will pass," she said. "It's going to be all right."

"It *has* passed," he said. "I promise you."

He took the girl's picture out of his wallet and handed it to her, but she didn't put a hand out to accept it, so he put it down on the hickory table, where she could look at it without touching it. The girl didn't strike her as particularly pretty. There was a roundness in the chin, and a blandness, a kind of apathy, in the eyes. The eyebrows too thick and close together, and her hair short, brushed back behind her ears, and she wore drop earrings that did nothing for her. Yet there must have been something about her, physically, that had appealed, though she couldn't see exactly what.

"It's over," Louis said.

"Is it?" she asked.

The picture lay on the table, and there was an awkwardness, because it wasn't just a picture, not just a thing, but a third presence in the room. There was a strained silence, a sense, plainly, that something had to be done. Slowly, Louis picked the picture up off the table and tore it into four pieces, and, just as deliberately, he put the pieces down, as if expecting she would complete the ritual by picking up the pieces and throwing them into the garbage.

But Nora was already up and on her way out of the room, leaving him with the torn photograph, to toss it into the compacter under the sink, or, if he so chose, to keep it and do with it as he wished.

54

It was around that time that they started buying the animals. Nora wanted finches, many finches, and she kept them in a large cage. It wasn't until after Louis died that she let them out, to fly around at will. Louis selected the macaw, which they purchased from the same dealer in New Jersey from whom they had bought the tortoise. He spent a great deal of time teaching the macaw to talk. They got through their days and nights that way, busy with the birds. Nora saw some marmosets in a midtown pet shop and positively wanted them, so small and furry, so full of fun, but Louis just as definitely said no.

"They're cute, true, but being so small they frighten easily and they bite. My roommate at Colgate had one and it was impossible. You know what their favorite food is? Baby chicks. Turn a marmoset loose in here and he'll eat all your finches."

Still, she was captivated: their eyes, their hands, their funny little faces, the soft, dense fur, the tufted ears, the way they moved and swung about, and the name itself, marmoset, so wonderfully haunting. What a name for a species! Marmoset, marmoset, it rang with mystery, she walked around whole days with the name singing in her head.

Instead of a marmoset, she bought the Burmese python, and more finches. The cobra came later, after Louis's death, as also the rhesus. The cockatiel was a very late addition, and somehow there was something never quite right about it—it seemed not to belong, it had a difficult time fitting in.

Another summer came and went, and they managed reasonably well. But then, in the fall semester, he was behaving oddly again, and she was aware it was all going wrong.

"She's back, isn't she," she said, over supper.

He didn't respond. For several days he was uncommunicative, and then, when they did talk, he acknowledged that the girl had in fact returned, though she wasn't in the program. She was working at a flower shop in Tribeca.

"So where does that leave us?" Nora asked.

"I don't know," he answered coldly. "I just don't know."

When they spoke again, the following evening, he was sympathetic, accepting blame, yet he was also talking about a need for realism, saying he thought it might be time for them to rethink their relationship. Without spelling it out in just so many words, he seemed to be suggesting that it was time for them to go their separate ways.

They did not split up, yet a form of separation did set in. He was often not home, and when he was, there were long silences and petty meannesses. The nasty words he taught the macaw, she was sure, were directed against her: gripsack, scuzz, saucebox, *poule*, *füchsin*, pain in the ass. Times when she expected him home, he would be late, and there were other times, whole weekends, when he didn't come home at all. She bought more finches. She set up a terrarium for newts and chameleons. She thought more and more about the marmosets.

And then, quite suddenly, he was dead. It was their third summer at home, after the honeymoon in the rain forest, and he was complaining of cramps. He'd been working hard, sending more articles out, spending a great deal of time working in the lab and researching in the library. He attributed his malaise to overwork. He took antacids, and for a while the cramps diminished, but then they worsened. She encouraged him to visit a doctor and offered to call for an appointment, but the pains subsided, and he put it off.

Then, on a Wednesday afternoon, she received word that he had died. It happened in the least seemly of circumstances, in a midtown massage parlor, a place with a reputation for offering more than massage. An ambulance was called, and the police became involved, and when a woman police officer came to bring her the news, she wanted all of the details. He had apparently been on his feet, about to put himself on the massage table, when it happened. The young woman who was there, the masseuse, had described what seemed an obvious heart attack, the way he clutched at his chest, gasping, and fell to the floor. When the ambulance arrived, he was already dead. The officer asked if she had been aware of a problem with his heart, and Nora mentioned the pains, saying yes, there had been pains in his chest, and she had been urging him to have himself checked.

She declined to have an autopsy performed, and after a brief service in a funeral home, attended by a small handful of his colleagues from the university, she had him cremated. When she was given the urn, several days later, she carried it to the riverside promenade and sprinkled the ashes into the Hudson. The same day, late in the afternoon, she went to a nearby pet store on Beaver Street, and she bought the marmosets. She also bought the cobra, and a pair of lovebirds.

Love, she thought, was a sordid, abominable thing. It takes you and tangles you up, twists you, bends you, and pushes you around. It drowns you, and brings you back only to drown you again. What she felt, going home in a taxi with the marmosets, was that she never wanted to bother herself with love again.

6

After Louis's death, she was afflicted with nightmares, and one in particular kept returning. Even now, after six years have passed, it still bothers her. In this dream she sees Louis dead, in the room where he died. She had never actually seen the room, but in the dream she knows this is the place and this is the way it was. He lies naked on a bed, on his back, on crumpled sheets, blue eyes glassy and staring. Ants crawl all over his body, on his torso, on his arms and legs, on his face. They are on his dead eyes, and on his genitals. She has a can of insecticide but doesn't use it, simply watches as the ants explore his body, in and out of the various orifices.

Someone is singing in this dream, a faraway voice chanting indecipherable words. The music seems to be *Bolero*, but she knows there are no words to that. Who is singing? She goes to the window, wanting to hear the words, but outside there is nothing but traffic and a great commotion of cars and trucks.

There is a variation on this dream, and this too comes back to her, more often than she cares to remember. It isn't Louis lying there naked but her, and she's not on a bed but in the jungle, on the damp soil among putrefying leaves, and the ants are everywhere, in her ears and on her breasts, and into her nostrils. She makes no effort to shake them off. They're on her arms and legs and down among her pubic hairs. This is the way life is, she thinks. This is the definition of her existence. She lies there, covered by ants and knowing it's a dream, and she blames Louis, because if it hadn't been for him, she would never have been to the rain forest in Ecuador, and none of this would ever have happened.

He was right, though, about the marmosets. Cute and small they were, weighing only a pound or two, with fluffy fur and tiny hands and toes—but impossible. One bit the python, inflicting a nasty wound, and another ate one of the canaries. One night all three of them took it into their heads to demolish the finches, killing seven before she managed to round them up and bring them under control. There was no way, no solution but to put them in a cage, under lock and key. It was a stabbing disappointment.

7

It wasn't until Theo saw the photograph on the wall for the third or fourth time that he realized the stout man on the left, with the moustache and the spectacles, was Teddy Roosevelt.

"And who is the young one next to him," he asked.

"My grandfather."

"They were friends?"

"He helped with some of the speech-writing. They went hunting together." She showed him the bearskin in front of the fireplace, the pelt with its lush cinnamon fur spreading hugely. The rhesus was on it, dozing, his body twisted in an obscene posture, his rump high in the air.

"When I was a girl, I had this darling little teddy bear. Oh, how I loved that plump, stuffed thing! They called them teddy bears, you know, because of Teddy, he was always off hunting for bears, and he looked so much like a bear himself. He hunted everything, elk, deer, wildebeests."

"You had fantasies about him?"

"Oh God, yes. My grandfather talked so much about him and showed me so many pictures. I used to dream about him. When I was nine, I wanted him to be alive again, so I could marry him. Isn't it shameful? I wanted to make love to a dead president!"

"He hunted?" Theo says, pondering the image. "He rode horses?"

"He rode until the horses went down under him. Do you ride?"

"In a car."

"Do you hunt?"

"I wouldn't know how to load the rifle."

Her eyes narrowed, teasingly aggressive. "Ah yes, yes, I know about you, Theo Tattafruge, you are only happy when you're working on breasts and buttocks. And noses."

In fact, he hated the nose jobs. His patients were rarely happy with the outcome, they fretted, uneasy with the new face in the mirror. The reality was never equal to the expectation.

"What's a wildebeest," he asked. "I don't believe I ever saw one."

Nora had never seen one either. "It's some sort of an antelope. A subspecies."

"I know moose," he said, "but not antelope. Is an antelope a moose?"

"I don't think so."

"Look at the macaw, he's leaning against the wall."

"He's lonely. He's getting old."

"We're all getting old."

She heard in his voice an invitation, a shy hope that, together, they might explore some deeper emotional level, but she chose not to pick up on it. "You know," she said, "when Teddy Roosevelt decided to run again, that last time, on a third-party ticket, they called it the Bull Moose Party. That's because one day a reporter asked him how he felt, and he said he was as fit as a bull moose. My grandfather fed him that line, expecting that it would go somewhere. That was my grandfather's big contribution to history, he was responsible for the Bull Moose label on the Progressive Party. When they lost the election, they went down to South America, into the wilderness, and explored the River of Doubt. That's how they handled their disappointment. But it was a horrible time, fever and dysentery. Teddy very nearly died."

"And your grandfather?"

"Oh, he made it through without a scratch."

As she reflects on it, she thinks there was something symbolic about Teddy's going to the River of Doubt. As if, having had so little hesitation in his life, always so buoyant and self-confident, he was now discovering diffidence, uncertainty, existential confusion, after his defeat at the polls. It was 1914, he was fifty-five years old. What was left for him? There was nothing big out there waiting on the horizon, nothing but the horizon itself.

"Life is too strange," she says.

"Stranger than strange," Theo agrees.

They're standing, at this moment, by the French doors, gazing idly at the boats on the river. The doors open onto a balcony, but she keeps them closed because of the animals.

"What do you think?" he says. "If we let the birds out, will they find their way back?" He means the finches, dozens of them, all about.

"Them?" she says. "Find their way home? No IQ at all. If we let them out, it would be the end of them."

8

In Nora Abernooth's apartment, on the ninth floor, it's snowing. Outside, on the street, it's July, but here, inside, snow falls in the living room and the bedrooms, and in the kitchen. Even in the two bathrooms it's snowing. The animals like it, except for the tortoise, which keeps its head tucked in.

Snow covers the couch, the piano, the bearskin rug. The finches fly excitedly through the falling flakes. The canaries sing. The marmosets, in their cage, don't know what to make of it. The monkey, standing, turns in a slow circle, a look of wonder in his eyes.

It's dry snow, so dry that when she touches it, gathering it in her hands, it feels like the artificial snow that was used at Christmastime when she was a child.

She pushes a pile of it off the bearskin, clearing a space for herself. What a predicament! Who would have thought? She sits there, on the bearskin, hugging her knees, watching the macaw, the cockatiel, the rhesus, their quiet amazement, and the finches diving and fluttering.

The flakes fall so thickly now, they block the light, creating a shimmering dimness. She stares intently into the darkening snow, searching patiently, and it's with no surprise at all, after a long time of waiting, that she sees him. He's leaning against the piano, slouching, in casual abandon.

"It's you," she says, though she doesn't physically say the words, her lips and tongue not moving.

"Yes, me," he answers, speaking, like her, without words, his mouth a blur, his eyes dark and empty.

"I don't want you," she says.

"But you have me," he answers.

"I guess I do," she says.

For a long time neither of them says a thing. They look at each other through the falling snow, with accusing eyes.

Then he comes closer and says, "You had no right, you know."

"Didn't I?" she says. "What recourse did I have?"

The snow thickens, and for a moment he seems to be gone. Then, dimly, she sees him again, and he appears to be floating.

"You have no softness in you," he says. "No forgiveness at all."

"Is that what you think?"

"You had no right," he says again, still floating, hovering.

"Nor did you," she answers.

"Maybe not," he says, and the snow falls so thickly now she can hardly see him, only his face and shoulders. His legs and the lower part of his body are gone. Then the shoulders go, and then she doesn't see him at all.

After a while, the snow stops and there is only a thick white mist. It's as if time has turned itself inside out. The animals are perfectly still. The finches perch on the branches of the lemon tree, like sculpted ornaments.

In the bathroom, she soaks a washcloth with cold water and presses it to her face. Life is too short, she thinks. The cobra seems not what it was, slowing down, too old, perhaps. Something's wrong. The monkey, Joe, seems melancholy. The macaw hasn't said a word for days. Love is a drowning, a tormented dream. She isn't sure if it's better or worse that Louis is dead. Dead, she still has him, owns him, possessing him as she never possessed him in life, because death is, after all, a kind of seal, a lock on the door. But what she knows, as well, too late, is that she too is in bondage, held in place by the same foolish lock on the same stubborn door.

"I'm so tired," she says to the rhesus. "Are you tired? Why aren't you tired?"

She wanders over to the bearskin and lies down into it, pressing against it, the whole weary length of her body, and the fur of the bear is her fur, because she knows better now than ever before that she and the bear are one and the same, the same self, same animal, running among the trees and dead leaves, its bone, its cartilage, its fevered brain, hunted, pursued across rushing streams, where light falls in flickering pinpoints, and there is no escape, pushing herself deeper and darker into the bear's fur, and wherever she goes, the fear and the flight are her fear and her flight, *Ursus horribilis,* her hunger and her craving, her emptiness. And what she senses, in the gathering darkness, is that there is only one bleak and maddening way in which any of this can ever end.

9

For some time now, Theo has been reading about Teddy Roosevelt. He's browsed through several of the biographies—Thayer, Putnam, Edmund Morris—and has even dug into the Roosevelt monographs and some of the diaries and letters. Had he never seen the photograph in Nora Abernooth's apartment, Teddy Roosevelt would have remained, for him, a nebulous unknown, but now he's a fascinating immensity, a rich reservoir for the anecdotes he rolls out in the operating room, entertaining his assistants while performing the liposuctions and breast augmentations.

"His appetite was gargantuan," he says, poised to put a breast implant in place. The incision has been made, and he's prepared the pocket where the implant will go. He favors silicone, but with the ban that just went into effect, he now uses a pouch containing a saline solution. "What do you suppose supper was like, on the ranch? Can you guess what Teddy ate after riding the range all day?"

It's Marie, the short perky one with black hair, who picks up the challenge. "Three Big Macs," she says, "and a chocolate malt spiked with gin." She's the comic on the team, he likes to banter with her. Jennifer, the other one, is taller and prettier, but dreamy, not very quick.

"No, Marie, not even close. Supper on the ranch was—" He purses his lips, unhappy with the way the implant fits into the incision he's made. "You know, this one is—not the way I want it. Something seems—not right in there." He's all concentration, maneuvering the breast, manipulating the saline pouch. There's a cloudy moment when it all seems hopeless and impossible. But then, in the next instant, it's solved and he's ready to apply the stitches. "For supper on the ranch," he says, "for supper—get this—it's broiled antelope steaks, smoked elk meat, fried prairie chickens, and saddles of venison, with baked potatoes, and don't forget the buffalo-berry jam. And apple pie. How's that for a menu?"

"He ate all that?" Jennifer, the slow one, says.

"Not always. Sometimes it was only a dozen eggs, and then the pie."

There is a photograph of Teddy when he was twenty-five, in a cowboy outfit, buckskin, with a big gun sticking out of his holster, looking for all the world like Billy the Kid. He weighed only a hundred and twenty-five pounds when that picture was taken. Later he would soar to two hundred. Theo found the picture in one of the biographies. He brought it to a photo lab and had it copied and blown up into a poster, and now it hangs in his waiting room.

The story behind the picture is that it was taken a short while after the death of his first wife, Alice Lee. Devastated, he went west and ranched in the Dakotas, as a way of coping with his grief. He broke horses and branded steers, and hunted, big game and small. And when he wasn't hunting or riding the range, he was on the verandah, reading poetry and listening to the birds, and writing, constantly writing. He was tuned to the song of the meadowlark, haunted by it—"a cadence of wild sadness," he wrote, "inexpressibly touching." Theo underlined those words, and marked others too, descriptions of dim hills reddening in the dawn, morning wind blowing across the plain, the scent of flowers on the sunlit prairie.

Despite the hard-bitten, gun-toting facade, the roughrider from Manhattan was a restless romantic.

10

The animals are dying. They are dropping off, and rather quickly.

The finches are the first to go. Theo, stopping by after a game of squash at the health club, is immediately aware of their absence.

"They're gone," Nora says.

"What happened?"

"I don't know. I felt something was wrong yesterday. They were lethargic, not flying around very much. Then, overnight, they all went."

She has them in a box on the dining room table, a gray carton in which she had received some mail-order clothes from L. L. Bean.

He lifts the lid. The finches are lined up in rows, seven rows with seven birds in each, stiffly dead, feet sticking up like silly little twigs, but their feathers still alive with color, flaming orange and metallic blue, lavender and yellow, all neatly arranged like Christmas tree ornaments waiting to be hung.

"The macaw?"

"Franz? Oh, he's around, somewhere. Brooding, talking to himself."

"This is terrible," Theo says, picking up one of the finches and examining it, studying it, trying to discern what killed it.

"They must have caught a cold," Nora says, not wanting to make too big a thing of it. She knows what he's thinking: if there is something in the apartment that killed the birds, it could spread and infect the others.

"I'll get a postmortem," he says, putting the finch back in the box. "We have to find out what did this."

She hovers, as if thinking it over and inclined to agree. But then, firmly, she says: "No."

"It's important," he insists. "I know someone, a vet. He's very good."

"I'll take care of them myself," she says, making him feel, for the moment, that he was intruding.

Her intransigence surprises him. "Don't you understand?" he says, trying to reason with her.

But there is no changing her mind. She looks at him calmly and again she says no, saying it without urgency, in a quiet, deliberate manner. "I don't want to go into this," she says, and it's plain that she feels, simply, that he has no rights in this matter.

He glances about, frustrated, searching for a way out of the unpleasantness. The cobra is on the couch, the cockatiel is on the bearskin. He steps over to the rhesus monkey, which is curled up on the Morris chair, and examines his eyes, noting they are more bloodshot than usual.

"Is he eating?"

"Oh yes, he eats."

"Have you changed the food? The diet?"

"It's nothing, nothing, we'll get through all of this, we'll manage. It was just the finches, they're very fragile. I've seen it before. Something runs through them, and poof, the whole flock dies."

He gives her a long, complicated look, as he does when a patient describes symptoms he can't diagnose.

"I think this is wrong," he says, turning to leave, so annoyed with her that he won't stay for tea. "Very wrong. And really, you know, very foolish."

That night, after dark, she carries the box with the dead finches down to the river. There is a long promenade, bordered by grass and shrubs, with an iron railing running along the river's edge. She walks some distance, to a place where there is an opening in the fence and access to the water. There are boats, yachts, far off, moving slowly.

One by one, she takes the finches out of the box and puts them in the water. They float, bobbing among the ripples. They don't sink. Across the river, the big Colgate clock is lit, and lights in the high-rises define patterns in the night. The moon is up and the finches drift, carried off from shore, bobbing gently in the moon's reflection, which lies shattered, like millions of sequins cast across the black water.

The next day, Tuesday, is her shopping day. She picks up a few items at the supermarket, then stops at the pet store. She spends a great deal of time looking at the iguanas. Once, in college, she saw a play about an iguana, but can't recall if it was Arthur Miller or Tennessee Williams. The iguanas in the display tanks are small and young. They will grow to be six feet long. Already the python is seven feet, and she wonders if, instead of an iguana, she would be better off with a swan.

She buys seed for the finches, white and yellow millet, and canary seed, and cuttlebone and grit, as if they were still alive. And mice for the snakes, and a pound of sun-flower seed for the macaw, but it's a waste, he's too picky, preferring peanuts and bits of toast. It isn't until she is back in the apartment that she remembers the finches are dead, and here she is with all this fresh seed that she's bought for them.

When Theo visits again, a few days later, he quickly grasps that there has been a disaster. The cockatiel, the tortoise, the macaw, the cobra, and the python are all gone. Only the rhesus is still alive, but he isn't well at all, and it's clear that he will not last very long.

"You should have called me," he says.

"I thought you were busy."

"I was."

"Well, I managed."

"Where are they? What did you do with them?"

As with the finches, she has brought them all down to the river.

He's upset about the macaw. He had grown fond of him, the blue and gold feathers, and the arrogant manner as he barked his nasty words, running through his scurrilous repertoire. So deliciously ribald. Several times he rewarded him with caviar, and one night he got him wonderfully tipsy on blackberry brandy.

He walks through the apartment, as if expecting, at any turn, that the macaw will appear. The rooms vibrate with a powerful emptiness. The rhesus is on the bearskin, but all the other life is completely gone.

Not until now does he realize how sparsely furnished the apartment is. In the living room, only the couch and the Morris chair, and the bearskin in front of the fireplace, and the upright piano. No paintings on the walls, only the one framed photograph of Teddy Roosevelt and Nora's grandfather, and, on the mantel, the vinyl cube containing the damselfly. Without the birds flitting about, without the macaw and the snakes and the cockatiel and the tortoise, the apartment feels barren.

He goes to the kitchen, to prepare the tea, and she stays in the living room, on the floor, comforting the rhesus. While the water boils, he searches the cabinets, and in a place where she keeps sugar and salt and small jars of spices, most of which have never been opened, he finds the jar of ginseng and opens it. And again there is that queer, distinctive odor, which he couldn't identify before, but which he now remembers, from his lab work in medical school.

He doesn't confront her with the ginseng, which he knows, now, is more than just ginseng. It would be, he feels, simply pointless.

When he pours the tea, she's standing by the mantel, gazing at the damselfly in its cube of vinyl.

"Why?" he asks, trying to understand the reason for what's happened.

"Why what?"

"Why are they all dead?"

"How would I know a thing like that," she says wearily. "They're dead because they're dead."

"Was it necessary?"

She seems in a daze, apathetic. "Everything is necessary," she says. "That's how it is. Nobody has the power to change what happens."

Looking at him now, with his teacup in hand, she

understands again that she knows so little about him, and has no inclination to know more. He does breast enhancements, face-lifts. He changes people so that they can lie to themselves about who they are. And what she feels now, looking at him, is that she hates him and doesn't want to be near him. She wants to tell him how much she loathes him, but instead she says, "You've been a good friend. I want to thank you for that, Theo. You're a good, kind, generous person." There's a flatness in her tone, as if she were saying good-bye.

She steps over to the French doors and looks across the river, toward New Jersey, where the windows in the high-rises are already lit. There's a long, wispy cloud, like a red scarf, where the sun has gone down.

"Why do you think of me only as a friend?" he says, putting down his teacup and joining her by the door, where he sees the same red cloud, shading toward lavender and gray.

She turns and looks at him, and they are, for a moment, very close—closer, she's aware, than they've ever been. She can feel the heat coming off his body, and she hears his breathing.

"How should I think of you?" she says, resisting, putting him off. It's the first time she's ever felt anything sexual about him, and she hates him for it, for reminding her of her own lurking needs. She doesn't step away from him, but neither does she offer any encouragement—projecting instead, despite their nearness, a sense of distance, as if at this moment his mere presence, his simply being alive, was a form of transgression she will not abide.

11

The next evening he's late at his office, and when he comes to her apartment, after nine, the rhesus is dead. She's put him on the bearskin, carefully laid out, his hands clasped across his chest.

"I'm to blame," she says. "I'm responsible for his death." She's speaking now not about the rhesus but about Louis, and through some mysterious leap of understanding, Theo knows exactly what she means. He expresses no surprise, because, in a vague, half-conscious way, this is what he's suspected now for quite some time. It's as if she were two different people, the one who sips tea with him, enjoying the animals and the fluttering finches, and this other person, dark-souled and distant, dispensing poison from a jar she keeps in her kitchen. But she isn't two people, she's only herself, the different sides of her personality layered and folded together, woven into a strangeness, and it's this strangeness, more than anything else, that draws him to her.

He sees exactly how it must have happened, the way she slipped the poison into the birdseed and into the fruits and vegetables that she mixed in the blender, doing it almost unconsciously, barely aware, as if doing it in sleep. Yet there was, he thinks, a genuine intention, a deliberateness, because the dark thing inside her wanted them all dead—the birds, the snakes, the macaw—needing them dead because in the logic of it, with Louis gone, the animals too had to go, their death canceling out his and somehow restoring a balance.

"He had no right," she says, speaking of Louis without naming him, "no right doing what he did. He thinks I'm the one who had no right, but doesn't he see? Can't he understand? He was the one who set it all in motion. It was so wrong of him, turning away from me the way he did."

There's a mirror in the foyer, above the phone. Theo takes her by the hand and leads her there, and he shows her, with great concern, what he'll do for her.

"I'll make you beautiful again," he says, standing behind her and reaching around, touching her face, drawing back the thickened, wrinkled skin. "There. You see? If I stitch this back, over here—look, you're young again. Your entire body, all of you. You'll be young and beautiful."

"But it wouldn't be me," she says. "I'm not that person."

"You can be whoever you want to be."

"I don't want to be someone else," she says. "To be beautiful, you have to be beautiful inside. I'm not beautiful inside. They're all dead. Don't you see? Whatever I love, I make it die."

She thinks of death, her own death, and she hates it, yet she doesn't want to go on living. She hasn't figured out yet how she'll survive tomorrow and the next day, waking up every morning and wandering through the rooms, every one of them empty.

She looks at the rhesus, dead on the bearskin, and goes down close to him, studying the hair on his face, the closed eyelids, the lips, the ears, the rigid body emptied of breath and filled with a silence that she finds unbearable.

A light summer rain is falling. Theo wraps the monkey in a blanket, and they go down on the elevator and into the night. They don't take an umbrella. He carries the rhesus in his arms, heavy, hidden in the blanket, and feels secretive, as if carrying a dead child, a grown boy, disposing of the body. Nora hurries along beside him.

They turn left, toward the river, then left again, onto the promenade, toward a stretch of low junipers where there is a gap in the fence, and they pass through, down onto the big rocks, to the water. The river is murky and dark. Theo puts his burden down and Nora pulls the blanket away, and together they move the rhesus off the rock and slip him into the water. Theo gives him a gentle shove, pushing him off. He seems to float for a moment, then the water closes over him, and he's quickly gone, carried off by the current.

They stare at the black spot, and in the weirdness of the wet summer night, it's as if none of this ever happened, as if the animals and the birds had never existed, and therefore they never died.

The rain, now, has subsided into a heavy mist. On their way back, returning to the high rise, there is a slight distance between them, and neither of them says a thing.

The next morning, Theo, in his fifth-floor apartment, takes his breakfast on the balcony. The humidity has lifted, and though it's still midsummer, the temperature is down and it promises to be a pleasant day. As he sips his coffee, he gazes at the street below, people coming and going, in and out of the condos. And the cabs, the cars.

He thinks of Nora, and, not wanting to return to her apartment, he wonders about a day out together, any-where. The park, or a museum. It would be a change, certainly, something they've never done together. With the birds and animals gone, she may be ready for some-thing different.

He goes inside and phones up to her. "I thought we might go walking, take some fresh air," he says. "We could have lunch somewhere. How do you feel about that?"

"I don't think so," she says sluggishly. "Actually, I already have plans. I'm leaving right now, in fact."

"Well, fine, then," he says, feeling rebuffed. "That's good—good you're going out. We'll try another time."

"Yes," she says. "Another time."

She sounds not herself, as if it's not her talking but someone else who has moved into her body.

"You're sure you're all right?"

"Yes, yes," still with the same flatness.

He puts down the phone and sits for a while, wonder-ing what he might do with his day. Then, knowing she's about to leave, he returns to the balcony and looks down into the street, waiting for her to appear. He feels a per-plexing desire to see her, even from such a distance, a need to look down from the fifth floor and watch, he doesn't know why. It's a whim, a fancy. He leans over the railing, waiting, and a cab pulls up, he thinks for her—but it's for the lawyer, Goldfarb, who steps in, lugging a briefcase and a carry-on. He sees Mrs. Marriocci walking her schnauzer, and Knatchbull sliding into a limo. Old

Karl Vogel, white-haired and trim, in shorts and a sport shirt, coming from the lobby and hurrying along at a quick pace, off on his daily walk. For a long time no one comes out the front door, and he suspects Nora may have changed her mind. She had sounded tired, sleepy. He was about to give up on her, ready to go inside, but suddenly, there she was, out on the sidewalk and moving toward the curb, wearing a gray blouse, and a dark skirt hanging far below her knees. Her feet are in white tennis sneakers. Her oversized sunglasses cover much of her face.

She's looking around, turning this way and that, uncertainly, as if deciding which way to go, toward the river or away, in the opposite direction. Theo feels voyeuristic, watching her, looking on without her knowing that he's there. A few cars go by, two cabs and a Mercedes. She steps off the curb, but instead of crossing to the other side, she walks along in the middle of the street, heading away from the river, toward West Street. The traffic isn't heavy, but it's sudden, and Theo watches with alarm as a cab, coming from South End, turning the corner, veers left, barely missing her, and runs up onto the sidewalk.

She walks on, heedless, past South End and on toward West, and he knows he should do something, rush down, run to her and drag her off the street. But he's frozen, caught in a paralysis of looking. And how could he reach her anyway, she's already so far off? And what would be the point? Because this, he sees, is her solution, her answer to everything, this willful recklessness, walking into the traffic.

He wants to call to her—but from this far away, how would she hear? And even if she could, would she bother to look back? So he simply watches, and knows it for what it is. She is ridding herself of the past, ridding herself of Louis, who is dead, and the macaw, who is dead, ridding herself of the snakes, the tortoise, the rhesus, and all the flying things that flew not just in the apartment but in her mind, tormenting her with the fierce, bright beauty of their wings. She strides deliberately into the traffic, with abandon, ridding herself not only of the finches and the canaries but her grandfather too, whom she knew only in his old age, with yellowed teeth, and his boss, Teddy Roosevelt, whom she never met but he was always with her, looming and mythic, with his guns and horses, and his obsession with the wilderness. Ridding herself of the folds and layers, the blankets of confusion, the hate and the love and the dreams, those too, unloading all of it, solving her bitterness and guilt in the only way she knew. So why should he try to stop her, when she was already too far off and so deep into it?

The last he saw of her, she was far up the street, plunging ahead, aiming for the intersection with West, into the brisk traffic moving to and from the nearby financial district. And only then, when he lost sight of her and heard the horns honking and brakes screeching, did he call to her, the cry bursting from him involuntarily. He called her name, shouting it, again and again, long after she was out of sight, and felt, in the calling, a kind of bafflement, because not since he was a boy had he opened his mouth to shout in such a way, with such force, such power and anxiety. And, in spite of what he knew, with such hope.

From Trance to
Venial Sin

It is one of the features of Echo Terrace that each of the units bears the name of a famous person from the past—the Whittier, the Gershwin, the Eleanor Roosevelt, the Scott Joplin. There is a unit named for George Washington Carver, and one for Edna St. Vincent Millay. Maggie Sowle's apartment is the Helen Keller. Mrs. Snow is in the Robert Frost. Knatchbull, a descendant—on his mother's side—of General Stonewall Jackson, is in the Abraham Lincoln, and he doesn't feel happy about that at all. The penthouse, where Harry Falcon lives, had been named for Audubon, on the theory that more birds would be visible from that far up than from any of the other apartments—but even the architect who came up with that idea didn't really believe it was true.

In the original design, each floor was to hold three units of differing size—the A units being the largest, with three or four bedrooms, the B with two, and the C with one. The A units were accessed by the west elevator, the B and the C by the east. But it quickly developed that on some floors the B and the C were merged to form large, expensive units, while some of the large A units were broken into smaller apartments, with the result that the geography of the building has become a shifting, amorphous thing, changing year by year.

Even the names of the units, protected by the building's bylaws, are not immune to change. When the owner of the four-bedroom Jefferson split it into two units and offered them for sale, the Jefferson had obviously ceased to exist and the new units, with board approval, supported by a vote of the resident-owners, became the Amelia Earhart and the Dolley Madison.

As more and more restructuring occurred, the board members maintained a cautious attitude when reviewing the names submitted to them—though it appeared, to some, that there was, at times, something arbitrary in their decisions. The same board that had allowed Stonewall Jackson, Mae West, Warren Harding, and Sitting Bull, shied away, for reasons never fully explained, from Marilyn Monroe, Geronimo, W. C. Fields, and Crazy Horse. Jack Kerouac didn't make the cut, nor did H. L. Mencken, or Nikola Tesla, the Croatian-American who had become famous for his work on alternating current.

It was part of Farro Fescu's job, as concierge, to keep a record of the board's approvals and disapprovals, and he did so with great diligence, saving the results in computer memory as well as on hard copy. With respect to Kerouac and Mencken, he couldn't care less, not knowing much about either of them. And Marilyn, she of the adorable body and the tempting smile, he felt she belonged where she was, in the movies, not on the door of a luxury condo unit. And as to Tesla, he couldn't have been happier about his being dumped, because even though he had become an American and was probably a good person, still he had Croatian blood in him, and the Croatians, in the war, had gone to bed with the Nazis, and they did some terrible things. And in such matters Farro Fescu thinks it is better to have a long memory than to shrug and forget.

Many years ago, in an effort to impose some order on his life and to increase the range of his knowledge, Farro Fescu decided to acquire an encyclopedia and read as much of it as he could. This would broaden him, he thought, and increase his ability to function in a world where so many of the people he served had college degrees. A concierge should have a nimble mind. He should know things, should have many points of reference, should exude an air of knowing life beyond the immediate details of summoning cabs and helping with packages. At a second-hand bookstore on Fourth Avenue he picked up a complete set of the *Encyclopedia Americana*, a 1958 edition, in thirty volumes, and he started with the first volume, intending to read every day. But he quickly understood that, long before he ever finished the thirty volumes, he would be in his grave, so to hurry things along, he decided to read only the articles that were accompanied by pictures. If he lived long enough, he could return to the items without pictures, but by then would he really want to?

The pictures were wonderful. Right off, in the first volume, color plates of Africa and Alaska, and the handsome black-and-white photos of Afghanistan, Albania, the Alps. And airplanes, so many pictures of the old planes and newer jets, and American paintings too, and famous American writers. And the amusing old Jell-O ads under Advertising. So much to learn, and too much to absorb. A great deal of what he read he quickly forgot, and some of what he remembered he wishedhe could forget. Did he really need that article on acids and the acid industry? Or on anatomy? It made him queasy, looking at pictures of ribs and arteries and internal organs, laid out in grotesque tones of purple and red. If this is what he looked like inside, he didn't want to know.

Over the years he kept on with it, pushing along from volume to volume, and now, to his own amazement, he is all the way to Volume 27, which opens with an item on Trance, and ends with Venial Sin. There are no pictures accompanying the article on Trance, so he skips that, and glancing ahead at Venial Sin, he notes that it too is pictureless and he will leave it unread. But then he already knows about sin, both venial and mortal, not just the petty transgressions in his own life but the big-time stuff all around him, sin boldly rampant, gone wild, uncontrollable—the violence, the recklessness, the killing, the trading in vice and drugs, the pride in wrongdoing. Daily slaughter on the highways. And you, a simple private person yourself, trying to lead a good life, but you cheat on your income tax, or try to, and what kind of sin is that, mortal or venial? You eat too much pastry, you drink too much brandy. You don't vote and you don't contribute when the blind person calls on the phone. You blame God for everything, and you are so angry with life you put your fist through a window. In such a world, is there hope? Where lies the future? Where is peace?

So much, so much to read and know. In Volume 27. Trees, Tropical Birds, Tunnels, Turtles, Turbine Navigation. On and on—United Nations, USSR, pages and pages on the United States, and then Uruguay. And Utah with the pictures of Zion National Park. Should he go to Utah? Should he see with his own eyes the Rainbow Bridge, a natural bridge of salmon-pink sandstone carved by wind and water, above what is now a dry creek bed? It rises 309 feet and has a span of 278 feet. But to get there, the last sixteen miles are along a packsaddle trail through canyons and gorges. Well, he must think about that. He must consider. Maybe they had a road by now.

For the moment, right now, it's the lobby, with the palm tree and the marble walls, and in these brief minutes of quiet, he has been reading along, skipping Utica and Utilitarianism but pausing over Utopia, even though it is unaccompanied by pictures, because he has always considered utopia to be an interesting idea, even if unattainable.

And then, when he glances up, there before him, at the desk, is Dr. Tattafruge, who needs a cab today because his car is in the shop. So enigmatic, this skinny man, a doctor, a plastic surgeon. Changing the way people look. This too Farro Fescu finds unsettling, because if you change how you look, then who are you? Are you no longer who you were but somebody else? And as he dials for the cab, he is thinking again about Zion, for which a packhorse is not necessary, you can get there by car, and perhaps he will do that, go to Zion, see the cliffs, the tall rocks, the monoliths. Perhaps, yes, next year, though it's far more comfortable, and cheaper too, to stay at home.

Mist on the Sepik River, Drums Beating

On the rare occasions when the building's front door is locked, a plastic card lets you in. The card is gold at one end, silver at the other, the name Echo Terrace printed in gothic letters. You slip the gold end into a slot, and the massive glass door clicks open. The same card opens your apartment door, but now you use the silver end, into the slot, and you're home.

Theo Tattafruge has his door rigged so that when he enters, the sound system comes up, playing Vivaldi. The selections are randomly arranged—cantatas, motets, a concerto for oboe, several pieces for the transverse flute. After a long day of surgery at the hospital, or of seeing patients at the office, he stretches out on the white leather sofa and the rhythms of Vivaldi sweep over him, flowing under and around him, and for a while there is nothing inside him, only the music.

His preference for Vivaldi goes back to his early youth, when his mother purchased a recording of the *Le Quattro Stagioni* and played it over and over on the phonograph. This was after his father had died, and they had left Cairo and had taken an apartment in New York. His mother loved that recording, and he, listening with her, learned to love it too. Even when she wasn't home, he would throw the switch on the phonograph and he would lie on the floor, on the rug, losing himself in the rise and fall of the violins, the ebb and flow of mood and emotion.

Before he was born, his mother had been busy with long lists of possible names, and the one she fastened on was Theophilus. But it was wrong for him. Growing up, he not only didn't feel like a Theophilus but had no idea what or who a Theophilus might be. Nor was he happy with the shortened form that his mother used, Theo, because Theo meant god, and, though he had a high estimate of his own abilities, he never quite thought of himself as being in any way divine, and in any case he wouldn't have wanted the responsibility.

Early on, while he was still in grade school, he began to think of himself simply as Tattafruge. He liked the crispness of the *t*'s, balanced against the smoothness of the *f* and the *r*, and the soft *g*. There was a firmness to it, Tattafruge, a solidity and a sureness, the sound evoking, for him, an array of good feelings about himself. Later, at the prep school on East Eighty-fourth, where jackets and ties were the rule, his teachers used only their surnames, never Tom or Bill or Jack, but Kelly and Rizzo and Bonabeau, and his own habit of thinking of himself as Tattafruge was reinforced. Even now, so many years later, on the not infrequent occasions when he talks to himself, scolding himself, complaining, or patting himself on the back and urging himself on, he speaks not to Theophilus or Theo but to Tattafruge. On the squash court at the club: Come on, Tattafruge, move it, put some zip into it. And in the locker room, in front of a mirror, seeing again how thin and bony he is: Put some weight on, build some muscle. More red meat, Tattafruge, more pasta, more chocolate bars. But to no avail, because eat what he will, his weight doesn't rise. And it's hopeless too about his name. Theo is the name his mother gave him, and still, that's what they call him, the people who know him well enough not to address him as "Doctor."

He had moved to Battery Park City only three years ago, not long after his divorce from Estelle. His apartment at Echo Terrace is the Harry Houdini, and when he first saw it, the name struck him as perhaps whimsical. Houdini? He ranks with Jefferson, with Winslow Homer? With Eleanor Roosevelt? With Jack London, whose name appears on the neighboring unit on the same floor? But

Farro Fescu, who knew everything about the building, explained to him that soon after Jack London's death, his widow, Charmian, had a brief but torrid affair with Houdini, and someone on the architectural staff had deemed it appropriate that London and Houdini should have this opportunity to coexist, side by side, on the fifth floor of Echo Terrace. In her diary, Charmian spoke of Houdini as her "Magic Man," her "Magic Lover."

The Houdini is one of the smaller units, yet the living room is ample enough to hold the canoe that Theo brought back from a trip to Papua New Guinea. It's a funeral canoe, a handsomely carved dugout that had been used to ferry the dead to a burial ground a mile downriver from a village that he visited. He found it, and bought it, during a three-week trip that he treated himself to after the stormy time that he'd had during the divorce. Estelle had made it hard for both of them—the bickering, the demands, the back and forth with the lawyers—and in the end, spitefully, she moved to Seattle, taking their boy with her, barely five years old, imposing this huge obstacle of distance, a whole country, some three thousand miles, between him and his son. She took the BMW, the silverware, the paintings (a Benton and an early O'Keefe among them), and the antique rocking chair that they'd bought at auction. And there were, of course, the monthly payments—he felt he was choking every time he wrote the check. What had ever possessed him to marry her? He hardly knew, and now that it was all behind him, he thought it better that she was far away. And he would have been delighted if she went farther still, across the ocean, disappearing into the thickets of the Malay Peninsula.

When he made the move to Echo Terrace, he enjoyed the good feeling of starting over, everything new, white sofa, white easy chairs, white rugs, white shelving for the books, the whiteness erasing the scribbled mess of his last few years with Estelle. It was a welcoming white-ness, like the white of a fresh sheet of paper on which the remaining years of his life could be written.

And the best part of it, he thinks, is that if Estelle had never left, going off to Seattle, he might never have gone to Papua and found his funeral boat, and wouldn't be sitting here right now, this instant, gazing at it, the stained cedar, reddish brown, glowing with an inner fire, and the bird on the prow so neatly carved, the beak, the eyes, a slash of chiseled wood suggesting feathers. The bird of death or bird of life, however you might want to think of it. He'd been on a road following the Sepik River, in a rented jeep, north of the Highlands, and came upon a village where a funeral was in progress, the coffin being taken from the village in a canoe. It impressed him powerfully, morning mist on the water, the plain wooden coffin in the canoe and other canoes following, oars dipping in the brown river, and the natives solemn, wearing necklaces of pearl shells. In two of the canoes, shirtless men were beating on drums and chanting, and even after they disappeared around a bend, the sound of the drums carried through the distance.

Several natives stood on the riverbank, but they spoke no English. Moving about, he found a woman who spoke a form of pidgin, and, with some awkwardness, they were able to converse. She explained that most of the islanders were Lutherans and Catholics, but here, in this village, they had their own religion. They believed that everything was God. The river was God, and the tiny tree kangaroos were God, and the parrots and the cockatoos. She showed him her fingernails, broken and gritty from digging for taro roots, and said, with obvious pleasure, that her fingernails were God. And it seemed to him, that morning, with the mist hanging over the river, a fine idea. He hadn't been a believer for quite some time, yet at that moment, the air echoing with the sound of the drums, it pleased him to think that if God did exist, perhaps a piece of God was in everything—in the lizards and crocodiles, the butterflies, the anteaters and the scarab beetles, and in the killer snakes, the adders and the taipans. When the canoes returned, the drums were silent and there was no more chanting. The canoe that had carried the coffin was the first to touch shore, and he saw how much finer it was than the others, with the carved bird on its prow. It was sturdy and simple, solid, cut from a large cedar—hard to imagine anything better for ferrying the dead across the water. And, looking at it, he wanted it, needing it so he could remember this rare morning of the mist and the drums.

He asked the woman to speak to the man who paddled it, and she did. The man's face wrinkled in a frown.

"He say if he sell you the boat, there be no way no more he bury the dead."

"Tell him I pay, I pay. He can make a new boat."

"It no good," she said, "it takee him a month do that."

Theo glanced about at the crowd that had gathered.

"Tell him I'm a doctor and everyone here is perfectly healthy. No one is about to die. Tell him I am not just a doctor, but I am God too—as the pigeons and the crocodiles are God. For a whole month I will not let anyone die."

When she told this to the man, he laughed, not scornfully but with childish delight. He was small, with narrow shoulders, naked to the waist and hollow-chested, in a pair of cutoff jeans. His hair, cut close to his scalp, was turning gray.

Theo opened his wallet and took out a large amount of kinas.

"What does he say?"

"He want more."

Theo took out more.

"What does he say now?"

"He thinkee you crazy."

"Tell him he's right," Theo said. "I thinkee me crazy too."

The man took the money and with the help of his friends he put the canoe on his pickup truck and drove it to Wewak, where Theo paid someone to package it, and he made arrangements to have it flown home. And now, three years later, relaxing on the white couch and gazing at the boat, he still remembers the excitement of that morning in the village on the Sepik River. The canoe brings it all back to him, the mud and the mossy forests of Papua, the delta plains and mangrove swamps, the stilt houses on the riverbanks and the crocodiles and the flower-clogged lakes.

And, looking at the boat and remembering, he thinks not just of Papua but of Nora Abernooth, his dear friend Nora, lying close to death, in a coma, in the Cabrini Medical Center, after being hit by a cab on West Street almost a month ago. He'd known her for a year, he on the fifth floor, she on the ninth, and though there was nothing sexual in their relationship, there was a closeness, an intimacy, and it was a torment for him to think he was losing her.

On the day of the accident, he rushed to the emergency room and consulted with the doctor who had worked on her, a dour man with heavy black eyebrows and a tortured expression on his face, as if suffering from a severe case of indigestion.

"She's your patient?"

"Just a good friend," Theo said.

"Then I think you should notify her next of kin. She's in rough shape."

The X rays were a map of fractures. An arm, a leg, a wrist, an ankle. They could work with that. But there were internal things, something with the spleen, and an injury to the brain. She had been conscious when they brought her in, but now she was in a coma, and it wasn't at all clear that she would pull out of it soon.

The first week, even though a neurosurgeon was handling her case, Theo visited every day, studying her chart, checking her pulse and heart rate. The room was filled with flowers—from Vogel, Muhta Saad, Harry Falcon, and the Japanese businessman, Aki Sato. A small bouquet from Farro Fescu. And from the cleaning service too, carnations, with a card signed by all of them, Oscar, Yesenia, and Muddy Dinks, and the others. That was in July. But by mid-August, the only flowers were from the lady on the fourth floor, Mrs. Sowle, who had a reputation for the quilt blankets that she made. Every week she sent a rose in a basket of baby's breath. Theo himself never sent flowers, considering it pointless, because Nora was, after all, in a coma.

If she could make it past the injuries, he thinks, past the broken bones and internal damage, and if she could find her way back to consciousness, then he would take her the rest of the way. He could repair her face and reduce the scarring on her legs and arms, make her presentable again. But something inside her seemed to be saying no, refusing to heal, and as the weeks passed, he began to think of it as a choice she was making, a rejection, a willful turning away from everything she'd known.

He touches her face. Takes her wrist and feels her pulse. Puts the stethoscope to her chest and listens to the heartbeat. He thinks of the times when he visited in her apartment and they sat quietly among the finches. Just sitting there together, on the sofa, the small talk and the long silences. The lemon tree. So peaceful, a calmness that his own days didn't give him. And then that terrible moment in July, when some inner darkness took over and she stepped into the traffic, and everything went horribly wrong.

The only living relative was a niece in Los Angeles. He remembered that Nora had mentioned her—she was trying to break into acting, just starting out, taking small parts at a downtown theater. When he went through Nora's things, he found the address and a phone number, and after several tries, when he reached her, he told her what had happened. Her name was Angela, Angela Crespi, and, hearing about Nora, she was distraught. He could hear, feel, how troubled she was. She said she would fly in right away to see Nora, and to help, do anything, handle her affairs if necessary. There was the play, yes, but her role was a small one and she would work something out, fly back and forth, and when she couldn't be there, they would use someone else.

"I don't think she's going to last," Theo said.

"It's that bad?"

"I think so, yes. I'm sorry."

Sorry was an empty word, it didn't say half of what he felt. He was, he knew, not terribly good about expressing his feelings, and worse, he had a knack for saying the wrong thing at the wrong time. Should he have said that over the phone, about the likelihood that Nora wouldn't make it? Couldn't it have waited? And anyway, how did he really know about that? What made him so sure? There were, he knew, cases of deep coma in which the patient held on for years, and recovered. So why, now, so soon after the accident, was he taking a dark view and preparing for the worst?

At forty-nine, about to turn fifty, he has hints of gray in his hair and is less than thrilled about passing through the midcentury mark. Like crashing through the sound barrier, in a way, but this isn't sound, it's time, a time barrier, age barrier, life barrier, death barrier, and what is it like on the other side, on that downward slope?

He was born in Cairo during the war, in the year when the Germans, under Rommel, threatened to overrun Egypt but were turned back at El Alamein, with heavy losses. 1942. His mother, born in Germany, had become an American citizen, living for a while in New Haven, and it was there that she met the man who would become his father. He was the son of a Belgian archaeologist who had worked many years at Luxor and had lived with a Nubian woman, who went with him to Alexandria, and then to Cairo, where they were together until he died. So the bloodline, for Theo Tattafruge, was a complicated thing, a mix of Belgian, German, and Nubian, and in the color of his skin it was the darkness of the Nubian that was dominant.

Twice a week, on Tuesday and Thursday, his thirty-second commercial airs on the radio, on WQXR. While a selection from Vivaldi plays in the background, a woman's voice says: "The Aesthetic Cosmetic Surgery

Salon of Dr. Tattafruge is here to serve you. Enhancement and reconfiguring. Stop in for a consultation. We perform total body surgical transformation."

In recent years he's moved heavily into sex-change operations, male to female and female to male. Before he operates, he requires that his patients spend a full year in the new way of life they're choosing, the men dressing and living as women, and the women as men. He puts them on a regimen of hormones and has them work with a therapist, to confirm, before surgery, that they'll be psychologically capable of living with the changes. And the changes, he stresses, are merely anatomical. The newly created penis will deliver no sperm, and the vagina of a former male will have no womb attached, no fallopian tubes, no ovaries.

More than once he's wondered about Nora, if there might have been some deep sexual confusion that she'd been wrestling with. There seemed a lingering unhappiness in her life, a disorientation, at peace only with her animals. He wondered if a sex change might have been of any help to her. Would he have liked her more, or less, as a man? If she had been a man, the marriage to Louis would not have occurred, and the whole long tissue of her life would never have unraveled in the way it did. She wouldn't be, at the moment, in the hospital, in a coma, lingering between life and death.

He keeps a notebook in which, periodically, he jots down his thoughts. There had been a time when he wrote about everything in his day—where he ate, the people he met, the women he slept with—but now he only sets down occasional reflections that catch his attention, random thoughts that hold a special meaning for him, focusing a mood, a feeling, an attitude. When he glances back, turning the pages, he's often amused by his own seriousness, and sometimes terrified. Yet he scribbles on, groping for meanings that seem, somehow, beyond his reach.

—Summer almost gone, and soon the chill of autumn. When I saw my father dead, I thought it was the end of the world. When I saw my mother dead, I knew that death was not just terrible, but that it had to be opposed. I thought of death as asymmetrical and blue. And I understood, also, that it is better to kick death in the teeth than to go quietly.

—Again and again, the body betrays us, it tells the wrong stories. It lies, it cheats, it deceives. In the operating room, I shape and reshape until the story comes out right—or as nearly right as I can make it.

—Esse est percipi. Berkeley, I think. Or Hume? No, Berkeley. And still so right. Surface is everything, to be is to be perceived. And in being perceived, we find the hard edge of our existence. Image, image—the glint of an eye, slant of the jaw, the angle of a lip at the moment before the face breaks into tears.

Despite his many years at surgery, he is still enthusiastic about his work, driven by a fascination with form—a sense of comeliness, a desire for balance and harmony in the way the parts of the body relate to each other. He works with forceps, scissors, the ribbon retractor, the French suction tube, the Kantrowitz clamp. The spoon, the grasper, the side biter, hook knife and chisels, nippers and splitters. And there are moments when he feels a sense of mission, caught up in something larger than himself, a struggle against nature and time, a desire to create beauty, or at least some sort of gracefulness, out of the mess of sagging flesh and misshapen bones everywhere around him. Line and form, shape and contour, these obsess him. The texture of the skin, the shape of an ear.

His own appearance, he knows, has little to recommend it. "Thin as cardboard," he overheard Mrs. Wax saying, as he passed one day through the lobby. Thin is what he is, a shade above average height, but scrawny, with a sunken chest and light bones, his head elongated and narrow, his eyes set too close together. Surgery could repair the drooping eyelids and the wrinkles, but what could it do for the shape of his skull? Does it matter? Does it? What matters, he thinks, is that he can work, cutting and shaping, his hands steady, and that's what he lives for, human tissue, sculpting, giving new life.

He's done especially well with the sex operations. He has a reputation, and people, talented people, come to him now from all over the country. One, after the operation, became a volleyball star in Hawaii, and another became a CEO with a firm in Cincinnati. There are so many—a dancer, a dentist, a college professor, a chief of police, and the mayor of an upstate town on the Hudson. They are all his secrets, and one of the greatest secrets he keeps is that the rock singer Tony Indigo, now living at the San Remo, overlooking the park, is a changeover. Before the operation, he was Martina Martinez, a singer with a guitar, playing the theater-district bistros for a meal and a meager stipend, hoping to be noticed but going nowhere fast. But now, after the change, as a man he is amazing, the throaty voice seething with sexuality, shoulders and hips weaving and gliding with a ferocious energy that galvanizes audiences clear across the country. His promoters bill him as a superstar from Mazatlán. He does in fact have relatives in Mexico, but the plain truth is that he was born in Brooklyn.

One night, clicking through the channels, Theo spotted him in performance at a stadium in Wisconsin. He watched, riveted, as Tony Indigo swept across the stage, sheer dynamite, the close-ups showing powerful emotion in the face, the eyes, the movement of hands and body. I did this, Theo thought. I made him. Created him. He felt a surge of pride, a feeling of accomplishment, knowing that had it not been for the surgery, Tony Indigo would not exist, he would have remained a very mediocre Martina Martinez.

Yet he knows—suspects—there are problems. Tony Indigo doesn't come in for his checkups. He's out there rocketing across the country, and Theo wonders if he's using his hormones properly. He's seen it before in other transsexuals, a tendency to play with the dosages, brewing hormonal cocktails that lift them into expansive moods, at the risk of sudden letdown and depression. One of his patients abandoned a job at a bank and ran off to an uncertain future in Alaska. Another, a young woman, jumped from a bridge. He wonders where it will end for Tony Indigo, if he will be one of the lucky ones, going on and on, or if, one of these days, he will fold and vanish from the scene. A high-speed crash on the highway, or an overdose in a hotel room.

He's on the white couch, relaxing, enjoying a flute concerto, the flute feisty, quick and slow, ranging from mood to mood, and as he lies there, head on a pillow, he's thinking of his son in Seattle, only five years old when Estelle took him, and already he's turning eight. They exchange letters, phone calls. "How's your spelling? Not so good? Working at it? Are you? Still playing checkers? Have a girlfriend yet? Next time I'll bring a chess set, you'll like it, I know you will." Twice a year he flies out, they go to the park, the zoo, the movies. What to do with a son you haven't seen for six months? He buys a gigantic stuffed zebra. An Erector set. A remote-controlled fire engine. Physical distance, the space between New York and Seattle, is a wedge between them. They hardly know each other, and he sees, dismally, how it will be: they will know each other less and less, and eventually they will be strangers. Send a birthday card. Maybe a CD, a flute concerto, *La Tempesta di Mare*—but will Estelle let him listen to it?

When he shops, he uses the market on Cedar Street, at the corner of Washington. Cold cuts, frozen dinners, fresh fruit. A good store, with a wonderful array of breads. He takes the pumpernickel, but occasionally the Hungarian rye. Flowers too they have, he often buys a bunch and puts them in the prow of the canoe, by the carved bird. Daisies, snapdragons. A few times a week he eats out, at the Au Bon Pain or the *ristorante* next to the tailor, and sometimes he has a meal delivered in, from Wan Lu's or Alfredo's. He likes mustard, puts it on everything, and often makes mustard sandwiches that contain nothing else, just the mustard.

It's Wednesday, his day off. In an hour or so, the girl from the building's cleaning service will arrive to vacuum and dust. He could arrange to have her another day, when he's not home, but there is something about her that fascinates him, so he makes a point of always being there when she arrives. He offers coffee, which she always declines, and he keeps on hand a box of chocolates, from which she will take a piece—one, never more—and glad if it's a caramel. She goes quickly to work, plugging in the vacuum, and before he steps out to do his shopping, he lingers briefly, watching as she moves about, siphoning up the dust.

He remembers the first time he saw her, almost a year ago, when she first joined the cleaning crew. He was gripped by her beauty, the way her eyes, lips, nose, and chin blended so perfectly, and the warm texture of her skin, the light brown tone—with her vacuum cleaner and the feather duster, in her gray working uniform, the boxy pants and loose-fitting top, ready to work on his apartment. No artifice, no makeup, nothing but straightforward simplicity.

When he asked where she was from, she said she'd been born in El Paso, but her parents had brought her to New York when she was a few months old. Her mother was mestiza, from Ciudad Juarez, and her father was black, from Carlsbad.

"Do you like Vivaldi?"

She smiled, confused.

"The music," he said, pointing to the speakers.

"Oh. Yes, yes," she said vaguely.

She listened to the melodic rush of the violins, but her eyes were on the canoe, and he saw that it was of greater interest to her than the music. And why shouldn't it be? A canoe, twelve feet long, in a living room, right there with the couch and the easy chair and the bookshelf and the fireplace. He saw her looking, but he held back. How to tell her about it, how to explain that a canoe, made from a tall cedar on a far-off island, could become an antidote, a source of comfort, a balm in a time of crisis?

"I want to take your picture," he said, fetching his Polaroid from a cabinet in the wall unit.

"No," she said.

"Why not?"

"Not like this," she said, touching her hair, her working clothes.

"You're perfect," he said. "Perfect."

But her face, her whole posture, expressed resistance, and he knew it wasn't her hair or her clothes that worried her, but him—her being there in his apartment, alone with him, the camera creating an intimacy that frightened her, as if he might suddenly ask her to take off her clothes.

He snapped a picture of her face, front on, the flash catching her by surprise, and the photo came through the slot and they watched as it developed.

"See?" he said. "What's so terrible about that?"

Then he brought her to the canoe and insisted that she sit in it, and he took more pictures, quite a few, left profile and right profile. He didn't ask her to take off her clothes, because mentally he could see right through them, through the baggy pants and the button-down, all of her, shoulders and breasts and waist and thighs, seeing them as if touching them with his hands, because if he knew anything, it was the human body, the curves and crevices, the hollows, the slopes and rises, the hidden hair. And there she was, a kind of miracle, in that drab janitorial uniform. He needed the pictures as a way of confirming for himself that she wasn't a mirage. And he could use them, too, with his patients, showing them what was possible, what to do with the nose, the cheeks, the jaw. He took more, many more, then let her select a few that she liked, and the rest he put in a drawer, and as she started her vacuuming, he went out for a walk, to the Amish Market, to buy bread.

Yesenia, that's what her name was, in white print on the small black nameplate she wore on her blouse, and though he was caught by her beauty, he felt no hormonal pull. That's how it was with him, and still is, how it's been with him for a long time—a general flatness sexually. And why, he thinks, should it be otherwise? He spends his days handling women, measuring, touching, cutting into their flesh, redesigning their bodies. Each woman, naked on the table, was a job, a problem to solve, meat and bone, cartilage and fat. As he worked with the forceps, with the angled clamps and scissors, sexual desire was dormant. For weeks and weeks there was no appetite, and he was comfortable with that. But then, every month or so, the urge would be upon him, libido surging irrepressibly, and when that happened, he would shut down, cancel appointments, and he would visit a woman on the Upper East Side, in the Eighties. She was expensive but good, better than good, rare, uncommon. Her name had been given to him by Ned Knatchbull, who had learned of her from Charlie Rohr, who knew of her from a stockbroker with whom he sometimes played tennis.

She was María Gracia Moño, handsome, appealing, with dark hair and luscious brown eyes, and when he visited her the first time, they spoke very little. He didn't want to talk, didn't want thought or feeling to interfere with the plain earthiness of the moment. They were quickly into bed, and he thrashed about with the vigor of a man half his age, coming at her again and again, as if the semen had been storing itself up inside him, and now the dam had cracked and an entire reservoir was emptying out. He became a different person, not a doctor, not a surgeon, not an admirer of the music of Vivaldi, but someone else altogether, driven by animal appetite. He thought of it then, and thinks of it now, whenever it happens, as a kind of rage, a devil that possesses him, and after a day or two of round-the-clock sex, the rage wears itself out, and he's free of the need for weeks, or even a month or more.

He's been seeing her for more than a year, and, with her

long experience, she is more than a match for his needs. But she likes to talk, he sees that, conversation is part of her style, and he resists. He puts his hand to her lips, stopping her, and he bends her to the task, keeping his time with her single-mindedly physical. Knatchbull was right, she is special, more than good, with the charm and comfort of a woman in her early forties, which she in fact is, but with the vigor and zest of someone who has yet to see thirty.

They do it on the bed, and off the bed too, on the Egyptian carpet in the bedroom and on the Persian in the living room. They've done it in a closet, with the light on, and with it off. He's put her on the butcher block in the kitchen, on her back, her legs hoisted high over his shoulders. They've done it standing in the shower, lathered with Palmolive, warm water rinsing over them, always Palmolive, he brings it with him, the scent of the soap doing something special for him, hauling him back to some childhood memory of arousal in the bathtub. She leads him barefoot to the living room window, and she leans there, on the sill, inviting him to come at her from behind, and he does, taking in the full view, all that she has to offer and the window too, glimmer of the East River, and the hospital and the brick co-ops of Roosevelt Island, slow traffic on the FDR below, barges on the river and gulls wheeling, and a helicopter angling across like a clumsy bumblebee.

Forty-nine, he thinks, and still going strong. Still at it, still capable. Is this him? The rage, the craziness. Or is it not-him, some alternate self from deep inside that takes over and turns him into a ravenous beast. He remembers how Knatchbull had spoken of her, that she was sympathetic, wonderful to talk to, but it isn't sympathy or talk that he wants, nothing but the language of the body, the vocabulary of thrust and counterthrust, cling and hold, playing the rhythms of the body until the body becomes a kind of music, a desperate song. Talk was something else. He talked with his patients, with his nurses, his attorney, his tax accountant.

He likes the throaty sounds she makes—the moans, the whimpers. They sleep, and when they're awake, he's at her again, thinking oasis, acres of date palms, thinking jasmine and pomegranate. She gnaws, she nibbles. She bites. He likes her mean.

"Shall I sing?"

He doesn't want singing.

"Shall I hum?"

No humming either.

He spreads apricot jam over her breasts, and as he licks, her nipples come up hard to his tongue.

"This is silly," she says. "Isn't it silly? Life is silly. Death is silly. It's so wonderful—don't you love it?"

Love it, yes, until they punch hard and break your bones. One of his patients lost half of her face when a mugger hit her with brass knuckles. And another, a college boy, a compulsive gambler, when he failed to pay up they cut off his nose. The boy was the son of a television anchor whose sagging neck skin Theo had fixed.

And she too, María—she too, he knows, is not immune from hurt. She works only with clients on her list, approved and recommended, men of consequence, well positioned and of good reputation. But in her apartment one night, a congressman, in a sexual frenzy, beat her so hard he broke two of her ribs. And a rabbi, in a hotel room, enjoyed her so fiercely he gave her a black eye. It did not happen often, yet it was always there, a possibility, something in the wind.

This time, when they make love, it's arduous, he's out of breath, heart racing. It's a Friday, overcast and dreary, the streets wet with small rain. He rolls over onto his back, exhausted, and for a while, as he lies there, he's a boy again, in Chelsea, his mother putting the record on the phonograph, *Le Quattro Stagioni*, and he wonders what happened to him, that boy who was born in Cairo and was brought to New York—what ever became of him?

They go to the kitchen for coffee, sitting at the same butcher-block table on which they'd had sex a few months ago. He's tired, a loneliness inside him. And now, oddly, he does want to talk, wants to tell her things, wants to tell her about Nora Abernooth, whose body he never touched, never entered, Nora and her animals, the macaw, the cobra—but the moment passes and he says nothing. And another moment when he wants to tell her about his son, taken from him, gone, in far-off Seattle, but he lets that pass too, and between them now, on the table, there is just the coffee.

And then, when he does talk, it isn't about his mother, his father, or the Nubian grandmother, or the son Estelle took from him, but about Antonio Vivaldi, the priest who taught music at the girls' orphanage in Venice, the Ospedale della Pietà—he of the red hair, how brilliant he was, playing the violin, and how he wrote and wrote, prolific. He didn't say mass or do the priestly things but gave himself to the music, composing restlessly. And with him, living with him, his companion, his favorite contralto, Anna Giraud, and her half-sister, Paolina. They lived with him in Venice and traveled with him across Europe, to Rome and Amsterdam and Bohemia. What was he doing with this saucy prima donna and her sister? Giving them voice lessons? Improving their vocalization and expanding their range? Anna was seventeen when she first performed in one of his operas, and he an energetic forty-eight, famous in Venice, famous in Mantua, with his brisk, buoyant rhythms, and the red hair fading to gray. At the end, he dies poor in Vienna and is quickly forgotten, the music gone, lost, and who cared or remembered?

But then, amazingly, sheer luck, a hundred years later, some of the scores are found in Dresden—and more, many more, in Piedmont and elsewhere, the concertos and cantatas emerging here and there like glowing secrets that had been hidden so long they grew wings, and now they were out of their cocoons and flying in the sun.

"Did he fuck them?"

"Who?"

"Anna and Paolina."

"What do you think?"

She slouched down in the kitchen chair, languid, running her fingers through her hair. "I think they must have eaten a lot of pastry, those two girls, while he was writing his operas."

Pastry yes, and pasta. And when Anna sang, what did Paolina do? Did she knit? Did she dream of black swans sleeping in the grass?

It rains, then the rain stops. It's September, the air crisp, the sun going down over New Jersey and igniting the clouds, turning everything crimson. The sky, the trees, the glass towers, the sidewalks, the river. He goes to her now more often than in the past, no longer the great gulps of time between visits. Not monthly now but weekly, and sometimes more.

She puts on her wigs for him, the blond that hangs to her waist, the red that drops only to her shoulders, the aquamarine that plunges garishly to her breasts. And the mature gray with a schoolmarmish bun, reminding him of one of his grade-school teachers.

He wants to shave her hair.

"Are you out of your mind?"

"Yes," he says. "Mad. Why else would I be here?"

"No," she says.

He pleads with her.

"But I can't. I have other clients."

He goes to his checkbook and writes a draft for a very large amount.

"Don't do this to me," she says.

He tears up the check and writes another, even more extravagant.

"Why?" she wants to know.

"It will be wonderful," he says. "More wonderful than you imagine. I want to make love to your naked scalp."

"Go away," she says, rejecting the check.

He leaves, and a week later, when he returns, he comes with a barber's kit, all the paraphernalia, scissors, electric shears, razor. And another check, bigger yet, and this time, cursing herself for being hopelessly corrupt, she submits.

He shears away her hair, the lush ebony locks tumbling away, and she is close to weeping to see them fall. He finishes with the razor, applying foam and drawing the straight edge across her scalp with great care. He applies oil, and her scalp glistens. In her baldness, she is exotic, strange, alien, a brown-eyed archangel from another part of the universe. He holds up a mirror. "See? See?"

There is nothing in her eyes. Emptiness. Loss. Distractedly, she grabs a handful of her shorn hair, holding it, fingering the silky smoothness. Gone.

In bed, there is a new wildness in him, his hands and lips and tongue on her skull, the shape of it, a living death's head, feeling the heat there, the touch igniting for him a special excitement beyond anything he's known before. He grows inside her, lengthening and thickening, and the music now, simmering in his brain, is an untempered, unrestrained oboe, and for a hot, tense instant he is transformed, becoming Vivaldi, the red priest, *il prete rosso,* in bed with his favorite contralto, Anna Giraud, and the women merge and blend, María is Anna, Anna is Paolina, and all three of them are his ex-wife, Estelle, whom he can't abide, and he is into all of them, riding them, thinking of the mist and the drums on the Sepik River, in Papua, and the canoe on the water, the funeral canoe with a bird carved on the prow, and the sound of the oboe, deep and dark, but soaring, floating.

And then, in the heavy breathing of the aftermath, it's as if he has slipped into a dream, seeing a hush of blue light on the river. The light is his mother, alone, just her, she's the corpse in the canoe, and she wakens, comes alive, sits up and gazes at him across the water. But as they draw close, it isn't his mother that he sees, it's María, her sweaty body, amid the crumpled sheets, her pouty mouth, black eyebrows, her shaven head—why, why did he do that to her?—and a faint bruise on her chin.

And still she wants to talk, because that is her way. Wanting to know more about him, about where he grew up, about his mother and father, but he doesn't want to remember any of that. And she wants to tell him about herself, he can see that, how important it is for her to say everything out in words, but he doesn't want that, has no need for it.

She's been faking her orgasms, he knows that, it's the art of her trade. And she does it so well, to perfection. Fakery is truth, he thinks, lies are better than reality. He jots that down in his journal. Life is never enough, deception makes it better.

He returns to her a few days later, and that's unusual, too soon. It breaks the pattern. There is a heaviness in his manner, a quiet seriousness. They're by the ficus in her living room, by the window, she's in gray pants, a half-eaten apple in her hand. She's covered her baldness with a new wig that she's bought, delicate, soft, the hair seems alive, it seems her own.

"Give me a son," he says.

He catches the look in her eye—the stabbing glance that says he's gone too far and needs therapy.

"You can do this for me," he says.

"No," she answers. "I can't. You know I can't."

"You must."

"I won't."

He wants a son from her to blot out the son he's had from Estelle. Estelle he's blotted out with María Gracia, and now, to complete the process, he needs a son from her to cancel the son that Estelle has stolen from him, taking him clear across to the opposite side of the country and making a mockery of the visitation rights. That was her style, vindictive and punishing, always punishing. And she's ruining the boy, pushing him into the wrong things, into ballet, into sissy stuff like shuttlecock and croquet.

"Don't say no," he says, not wanting her to cut him off. "Tell me you'll think about it."

"But you know how impossible it is."

He pleads with her, telling her how important it is for him. How he needs something to live for.

"What you need is a wife," she says.

"I've already had one."

"If not a wife, then a surrogate mother. You're a doctor, you can find one."

"But that's not what I want," he says. "I want someone I know. Someone who means something to me. Why won't you do this?"

He isn't asking her to marry him, and she understands that. He wants her to carry a fetus, his seed and her egg. He wants to borrow her womb for nine months.

"I have a profession," she says. "Don't you see? I can't just say to my clients that I won't be available for a while because I'm pregnant. That wouldn't do. It wouldn't do at all."

"Haven't I been good to you?"

"You've been very good. Yes, you have."

"But?"

And he saw then, painfully, that though she cared for him, it was only in the way that he cared for his patients. The caring was genuine, but it was a professional caring. In bed, she was performing a service, as he was performing a service when he did a face-lift, and beyond that they were in separate orbits. Why should he have expected more?

"Don't you see?" she says. "Don't you understand? It simply can't be."

He does see. But he doesn't want to.

"I could set you up," he says, "you'll have nothing to worry about. You won't need to have clients anymore, you'll be on your own. To do what you want."

"I think you really don't hear what I'm saying," she said. "I like living the way I do. It's my life. How would you feel if suddenly you couldn't have patients to work with anymore?"

He stares long at her, studying her eyes, as if reaching into them, straining to touch her inmost feelings. "Think about it," he says. "Give it time."

101

He leaves, but he's back again the next afternoon, early, with dozens of red carnations. He carries them up on the elevator and dumps them on the bed, and they make love there, on the carnations, in the spicy red smell, on the long green stems and cushion-soft petals. There are carnations in her mouth, and carnations on her breasts and down between her legs, and as they turn and move, the intoxicating scent becomes a long lake they are swimming in, holding and letting go and holding again, losing breath, and breathing again. And when they're done, lying side by side, relaxing in the slow rhythm of the afternoon, sunlight spilling through the window, he wants to ask again, wants to put the question, but the mood is too good and he doesn't want to ruin it, doesn't want to risk that she will again say no.

A day later, in his apartment, early Sunday evening, he's in jeans and a yellow shirt, at the kitchen table, taking a light meal of scrambled eggs and toast. The morning *Times*, which he is just getting to, is spread out across the table, and the window at his elbow opens on a bold slash of vermilion where the sun is going down. He glances through the headlines, then spends some time scanning the book section and the magazine.

The phone rings, it's Farro Fescu at the desk downstairs. There's a visitor in the lobby, wanting to come up, and Theo hears, with surprise, that the visitor is Tony Indigo.

He hangs silent, hesitating, and then, against his better judgment, says, "Yes, yes, send him up." And knows it's wrong, because you never see a patient in your home, you don't do that. And why is he here anyway? With a problem, certainly, of one sort or another, and who needs that, yet another problem. On a Sunday no less, when the sun is going down.

When he opens the door, he's startled to see how terrible Tony Indigo looks, nothing like what he was, none of the dash and glitter of two months ago, when he was on television. His eyes bloodshot, something shadowy at the mouth. Slouching and breathing heavily, in a white shirt open at the throat and a black jacket, pink pants. He is shorter than Theo and young, just over thirty, but with the burnt-out look of somebody long ago over the hill.

They stand facing each other in the wide vestibule that opens onto the living room. The vertical blinds are open, the big window in the living room showing a tired dusk settling over the river. Looking at Tony Indigo, the face, the trembling hands, Theo is sorting it out—thinking blood tests, a physical, maybe a rest cure. Check the androgen levels, and back to the psychotherapist. What's he into—crack cocaine? Standing there, on the red-tiled floor of the vestibule, he wants to say all that, jump right into it, but what he says is, "How about some coffee?"

Tony Indigo hovers, seeming about to say yes, but then, with some firmness, says no and lifts his face boldly. "You ruined my life," he says.

Theo draws back, surprised. Says nothing.

"Look what you've done to me," Tony Indigo says, hands gesturing toward his body.

"But you're a success," Theo says. "A huge success."

"Am I?"

"Aren't you?"

"Look at me—what you did."

Theo gazes at him, the pink pants, black jacket, and understands, knows what he means. He's taken away the breasts, the womb, the sexual organs. "You want a child," he says. "Is that the problem?" And as he says it, he thinks fleetingly of his own son in Seattle, growing up without him, and how he hates Estelle for taking him away.

"Doesn't everybody want one?" Tony Indigo says. "Isn't it the normal thing?"

"You can adopt. That's what they do, the others."

"It wouldn't be the same."

"But you wanted this," Theo answers. "You were desperate for it, pleading with the therapist."

"Her? That one? What does she know?"

"You're in depression," Theo says. "It will pass."

"No, it won't."

"It's temporary."

"Life is temporary."

In the changing light from the window, he becomes aware of a faint thickening in Tony Indigo's face, almost a plumpness, the skin glistening with a puffy smoothness. A denseness in the neck too, and in the hands.

"You're on estrone," he says.

"It's none of your damn business what I'm on."

"Isn't it?"

"No."

"It can't change you back, you know."

"Don't you think I know that?"

"It will make you feel cold and it will sap your energy. And it will make you fat."

"Go to hell," Tony Indigo says.

"That's what you came here to tell me?"

"No," he says, "not for that." He looks away, and then, with some fumbling, he takes from his pocket a small black pistol, so small it seems a toy.

Theo feels a tightening in his chest, around his heart. "Put it away," he says in a sinking tone.

"It was wrong, so wrong," Tony Indigo says, waving the gun uncertainly. "You made me over, but inside I'm still the person that I was."

Theo looks intensely into his eyes. "You're anyone you want to be," he says. "You have to understand that. You're what you think you are."

"Not so," Tony Indigo says. "Maybe for the others, but not for me. I'm still who I was."

"But you were so eager—what happened? A whole year we made you think about it, before I operated."

"And now it's the rest of my life."

He straightens, lifting the gun, and takes a deep breath, aiming unsteadily. And Theo, seeing the barrel only a few feet away, pointed at his head, feels a strange fatalism. He doesn't move, thinking maybe this is right, if it has to be. It is nothing he'd ever imagined or expected, not this, but if it has to be, then, in the whole scheme of things, let it happen.

Tony Indigo pulls the trigger and the gun jerks, the noise a sharp, dry sound, like a firecracker. Theo doesn't flinch. He sees the flash, hears the report, smells the burnt powder, and doesn't move, not even when he realizes the shot missed and he is still alive. Simply stands there, looking at Tony Indigo, still with the gun and with his head angled, tilted like the head of a mannequin in an awkward pose, readying himself to shoot again. But then, with a great shudder, he lowers the gun and folds in on himself, a rush of tears springing from his eyes, and as the gun falls away, clattering on the vestibule tiles, he puts both of his hands to his face, sobbing fiercely.

"See? See what you've done to me?"

Theo puts a hand on his arm, and with that, Tony Indigo leans into him, weeping, his head on Theo's shoulder. Theo catches the smell of perfume in his hair, attar of roses. And then, reluctantly but with feeling, he puts his long arms around him, holding him as he weeps.

And standing there, in that odd embrace, he looks beyond, through the window and across the river, the lights coming on in the high-rises on the other side. He thinks of Nora in her coma, and the finches that flew in her apartment, all gone. He thinks of María Gracia and Estelle, and his son far away in Seattle, and here now, in his arms, this sorry piece of life, this body that he transformed, this mistake. He never should have taken him on. He'd had an inkling, a suspicion it might go wrong, and feels now an anger about life, how upside down it is, how it twists away, turning right into wrong, good into bad. He thinks of his mother dead, and his father dead, and the mist on the Sepik River in Papua, and the drums beating, and the mist and the drums seem the only reliable things to hold on to.

The small black gun is on the floor, like a dead mouse by the potted fern. There is a box of chocolates on the coffee table, and an unlit log in the fireplace. The canoe is at the far end of the room, the carved bird on the prow seeming somehow alive, as if at any moment it might rise and fly off.

The Jamaica Avenue El

She's nineteen and pretty, Yesenia, one of the house-maids on Oscar's janitorial crew. Wears her hair long, drawn back behind her ears, and uses a faint hint of blush on her cheeks. Her mother works for the telephone company, making enough for the rent, the food, and now and then some new clothes for the two of them. Her father, a bartender, left a long time ago and they never hear from him—and Yesenia feels bad about that. She lives in Queens, with her mother, on Jamaica Avenue, where the trains on the el run past her window and she can see the people riding by.

The year Yesenia turned seven, she tripped and fell while jumping rope and broke her leg. That was in the month of May, when Mount St. Helens blew up and she saw it on television, a lunatic mountain exploding, throwing trees about like toothpicks, and it stuck in her mind. Her leg was in a cast, and she spent most of her recovery time sitting by her window, watching the trains as they came by, so close to her, slowing as they prepared to stop at the station up ahead. And through the windows of the trains she saw the passengers, so many of them, standing and sitting. Some, seeing her, smiled with surprise. Most stared blankly. She saw the beaded neck-laces, earrings, wristwatches. Women with hair cut short, and others with long hair busy with ribbons and barrettes. That springtime of the broken leg, she sat by the window, memorizing the faces and waiting for them to come by again—the gray-haired lady in blue, the man

107

who wore sunglasses even when it rained, and the handsome white boy in a jacket and tie. She had a crush on him, wishing she could meet him, wondering if he noticed her as she noticed him. The faces, so many. And now, at nineteen, she is one of them, traveling the same line, the J train, wondering if someone at a window will see her and wait for her to pass by again.

On her way to work, she boards at 111th, into the rush hour crowd, and as the train grinds along, she daydreams, barely noticing the stops—Woodhaven Boulevard, then Eighty-fifth, and the big slowdown as the train groans through the long S-curve between Cypress and Crescent, and on to Alabama and beyond, all the way to Marcy, past the dome of the old Williamsburg bank and the massive Domino sugar plant. Then over the bridge, with the big view of Manhattan, and quickly down, underground to Essex, then Bowery and Canal and the stop near City Hall, and on to Fulton, where she gets off. And that's where she is right now, in the morning crush, quickly out of the train and stepping along on the platform, up the stairs and on her way to Echo Terrace, where she will dust and vacuum all day, room to room, apartment to apartment.

As she comes up out of the subway, she's thinking about her name, saying it over and over to herself. Yesenia, Yesenia. I had my name a long time, she thinks. Should I change my name? Is there a better name would be more me? She waits for the traffic light, then crosses, past the throbbing hoods of cars and taxis ready to lunge as soon as the light turns. She's in a pleated skirt and sleeveless blouse, with a faded pink backpack that holds her work outfit and her lunch, ham on rye and a juicy pear, and she looks forward to the noon break when she'll sit on a bench by the river and look at the boats and think of all the good things lying ahead for her. Good things? What good things? Delirious. Maybe another lifetime. But she can imagine, and what's wrong with that? A bike swishes past, and another. A tall girl blazes by on rollerblades. A cab, a bus, a Mercedes. A stretch limo.

She's in the morning sun and it's Tuesday, wonderful Tuesday. It could be Monday, but it's not, or Wednesday, but not that either. This morning, when she dressed, instead of her usual jeans she put on the skirt, not knowing why. It was a whim, a fancy. Her red skirt and the sleeveless lavender blouse, her arms and legs free, open to the weather, Indian summer in mid-October, the air crisply warm, touching her skin. She has a sweater along, just in case.

Today she'll do Vogel, Tattafruge, Nora Abernooth's place, and Mrs. Sowle. Mrs. Sowle is her favorite, she always puts out apple juice and a plate of cookies. She makes quilts, beautiful crazy quilts, full of wonderful shapes and colors, and it's always exciting to see the new pieces that she's working on, each of them so different. Vogel too she likes. He has a fancy collection of toy trains, and when she's done with the vacuuming, he always wants her to run the trains before she leaves. She turns the control switch, speeding them up and slowing them down, across the bridges, through the tunnels, past the little Alpine village and up the hill covered with tiny trees. It's pretty, she thinks. Quaint. One day, as she sent the train uphill, he put his hand on her behind, and she let him do that, because what harm could there be in it? He was just an old, white-haired man, enjoying his memories.

Dr. Tattafruge she doesn't care for at all. He's thin as smoke, with a long nose and a head so narrow it looks as if the doctor that delivered him must have squeezed too hard with the clamps. One day he took her picture with a Polaroid. She didn't want him to, but he insisted, a whole bunch of pictures. He gave her some and kept the rest for himself, and she wondered what in the world was going on. But it ended there, he didn't put his hands on her. When she was in school, at Richmond Hill High, the boys were always grabbing at her, catching a quick feel, touching her breasts, her buttocks. But with Tattafruge, it was nothing like that, just his peculiar way of looking at her, studying her, and she wondered why on earth would he want those pictures?

After the long walk from Fulton, she crosses West Street and on the next corner turns down South End, going past the pharmacy, the food market, the Chinese restaurant, then she swings toward the river, and in a moment she's there, at Echo Terrace, going through the big glass doors. She waves a hand at Farro Fescu, sitting cloudlike at the desk, and down she goes on the elevator, to the basement level, the gray-painted room where they gather to check in before starting the day.

Verna and Luke aren't in yet. Nor is Hollis, or Smoke, or Oscar, the supervisor. But Chase and Blue are there, and Muddy Dinks, who is squatting down, doing his shell game on the cement floor. He used to do it with walnut shells and a pea, but now he does it with three plastic cups and a dime. He puts a dime under the yellow, lifts the green and the red to show nothing is under them, and shuffles the cups around. Lifts the yellow to show the dime is still there, then shuffles some more.

"Come on, Yesenia, where's the dime?"

She's been through this before.

"Ain't nowhere," she says, with no enthusiasm for the game.

"Nowhere?" He lifts the green and there it is.

He shuffles again, and again he looks to her, and this time she guesses red.

But it's not there, nor under the other cups either. Muddy Dinks holds up his bare hands. He's in a sleeveless shirt, so it can't be up his sleeve. He steps over to Blue and tells him to open his mouth. Blue opens wide and Muddy reaches in with thumb and forefinger and pulls out the dime.

"Was there all the time," Yesenia says.

"Was it?"

He looks to Blue, and Blue looks to Yesenia, shaking his head and holding up both hands. "I swear," he says, "I swear."

"Don't swear," she says. "You'll maybe go to hell. Both of you."

"On the street they pays a clam to play," Muddy says, boasting. "If they find the dime, they win a cock and hen. But they damn never find it, I make sure of that." Weekends, he hustles his game by the Metropolitan Museum, where there is good crowd flow. He uses a small folding table with a surface slightly over a foot square. If a cop comes along, he collapses the table quick and hikes over to Broadway and sets up there. Always on the move, ahead of the cops.

He has a high bony forehead and his face is light brown, but the hollows of his cheeks are dark, almost black, and his neck, under his wedge-shaped jaw, is also dark. He's shuffling the cups again, smiling at Yesenia, lips peeled back in a devilish grin. "Come on," he says, his eyes darting.

But she turns away and heads for the bathroom, where she changes out of her skirt and blouse and puts on the gray Dacron pants and the button-down with her name on it, the name on a piece of black plastic pinned high near the collar. The Dacron is light, easy to work in, not thin enough to see through, though when she bends and turns, the lines of her bra and panties show. Somebody's smart idea of what a maid with the cleaning service ought to look like.

Verna and Luke do the toilets. Blue polishes the brass and mops the white marble floor in the lobby. The marble has streaks of gold and crimson in it, and Blue likes that, can look at it forever. Muddy Dinks does the risky things, like climbing the tall ladder to change the lightbulbs high up in the lobby ceiling. He has eyes for Yesenia, and she knows it. And hands too, grabbing her arm, touching her nose, patting her ass. Once, in the lobby, she was bending over, making an adjustment on the vac, and he came up behind her and put both hands on her rump, grabbing hard.

She jumped. "Don't *do* that," she said, with a flash of anger.

"Why not?"

"It ain't decent is why. Don't you know?"

111

"Decent? You want decent? How 'bout a burger and a movie, they got a new Dracula over at the Hoyt."

"I don't think so," she said.

"You turnin' me down? I'm not meat enough for you?"

"Go away, Muddy."

"How come?"

"My mother told me not to mess with black boys. My father was black and he run away when I was six, all the way to Atlanta."

"That makes you half black," he said, putting a hand on her again. "All I want is half of you anyway, the sugar half. Half a loaf is better than none."

"Damn," she said, pushing him away and shoving the vacuum nozzle into his face. "*Damn!*"

Her senior year in high school, she had taken up with a boy who looked like Muddy but not as tall, with a mellow tan skin and tight, kinky hair. They were hot for each other, having sex in an abandoned tenement and in a car he stole off the street. They were into each other for maybe three months, then he was picked up for dealing drugs, and they put him away. "Didn't I tell you?" her mother said. "Didn't I warn you?" She hated her mother for being right, and hated herself for being so dumb. And now, if she wants, she can have Muddy, but it's a big if. He works hard and doesn't do drugs, doesn't seem to, and that much is good. But he spends weekends hustling his shell game, and was she really ready for that?

And she thinks too of her mother and father and how it went wrong for them, how her mother still hates him for running off, hate feeding hate. When he left, her mother went back to using her own name again, Rivera, and that became Yesenia's name too, Yesenia Rivera. But it left her, so young, a little confused, thinking maybe she should change her first name too.

Muddy Dinks comes in from Harlem on the A train. So does Blue. Verna comes in from Brooklyn on the M. Chase comes on the 6 from Mott Haven, in the Bronx, and switches at Fourteenth, grabbing the N or the R. Oscar drives an old Chevrolet from Richmond Hill, in Queens, and parks in the underground garage, but when he expects gridlock, he leaves the car home and takes the E to the World Trade Center and foots it from there.

Today, Tuesday, before she starts with the dusting and vacuuming, Yesenia changes the flowers. They're in two big boxes from the shop on South End, one waiting for her at the east elevator, and the other at the west. On each floor, the elevators open onto a foyer, and in every foyer there's a small table and a vase. Oscar, the supervisor— Oscar Acciuga—has told her about the vases, how precious they are, from Venice, Holland, Vienna, Barcelona. And the pretty colors, ruby and apricot, coral and aquamarine. And because they're so precious, it worries her when she handles them. What if she were to drop one? What if a vase were to slip from her hands and break?

She's told Oscar how it worries her, and he's done his best to reassure her. He's a good man, she can talk to him, his face round and honest, with dark, serious eyes, and he works hard, doesn't just stand around telling you what to do. He climbs ladders, lugs heavy buckets. Not a tall man but not short either, with thick shoulders and a heavy middle, his dark hair with a few splashes of gray. Pushing fifty. Some days he brings bagels for the crew and passes them around, and sometimes he brings bubble gum.

"Don't worry about it," he told her, "don't let it bother you. It's in God's hands, we just do what we can." And the way he said it, it sounded as if there were days when even God could drop a vase. Then, seeing how troubled she was, he reached out and put a hand on her elbow. "Look—you're careful, right? Then don't give it a thought. If you worry and you're nervous, you'll drop one for sure. But even if that happens, no problem," he said, with a jerk of his head, "the rugs are so thick, the vase will just bounce."

This week it's red roses, fresh and tight-fisted, just opening—a few roses into each vase, with sprigs of baby's breath and some ferns. It takes her all morning, but she enjoys the aroma, the heady scent, and doesn't care about the time, how long it takes, though she knows Oscar would really like it if she moved faster. She doesn't begin the vacuuming till after lunch. She does Tattafruge first, then Mrs. Sowle. Then Vogel. Nora Abernooth's apartment she does last, feeling eerie about it, because Nora Abernooth has been in the hospital for more than two months, in a coma, and nobody expects she'll ever come back. It was Candy who used to do Mrs. Abernooth, but Candy has left for another job, and this, now, is Yesenia's first time there.

She unlocks the door and goes in, dragging the vacuum, a low steel cylinder on wheels, with a hose attached, and stands in the living room, looking around, seeing the room as Mrs. Abernooth left it. The lemon tree, the couch, the old brown photograph on the wall show-ing two men with cigars. The walls moldy, in need of a painting, and the furniture marred and stained from the animals that she'd kept. Yesenia has never seen them—the birds, the snakes, the tortoise—but she's heard plenty about them from Candy, who hated them because of the mess. They're gone now, all of them, and Oscar has told her just to vacuum and dust, not to worry about the stains and the dying plants.

And now, as she stands there, in the living room, her eyes rove across the room and come to rest on the bearskin by the fireplace. She's never seen a bearskin before. She bends down to it, touching it with her hands, running her fingers through the thick, bristly fur. She studies the head, the ears, the snout, and again she runs her fingers through the fur, aware of a flow of energy there, as if, somehow, she was touching the dead animal's life. She wonders what kind of an existence it had been, out in the open, in deep grass, and a forest to hide in. She kneels there, on the fur, feeling the bear's life underneath her, warm and strong, and senses a primal loneliness, the loneliness of trees and grass, and she's drawn in, pulled as if by some powerful, invisible force. And then, fearful of the mood that threatens to swallow her, she tears herself away, breaking loose and jumping to her feet.

She doesn't stay to do the cleaning. It can wait till next week, and maybe she won't come back at all. She'll ask Oscar to send someone else, because it's too unsettling, the animals dead and Mrs. Abernooth so long in a coma, and this strangeness that she feels, that she has to escape from. She gathers her stuff, the feather duster and the vacuum with its hoses and nozzles, and locks the door behind her. It's late anyway, close to quitting time, the whole morning with the flowers and then too much time with Mrs. Sowle, so she heads down to her locker in the basement, fetches her things, and changes out of her work clothes.

Everyone is on the move, Oscar seeing them off, good-bye Blue, good-bye Muddy, go Luke, see you Smoke, all of them heading home, Chase and Hollis, Verna with the orange ribbon in her hair.

And Yesenia too, out of the building, but instead of heading for the subway and home, she walks down to the bottom of South End, under the arcade, past Gristede's and the shoe repair and the Japanese restaurant, and where the street ends she goes on the long path through the park, heavily treed with evergreens, and beyond that onto the open grass, passing the war memorial with the big bronze eagle and the names of the dead, making her way to the ferry.

At an outdoor phone she calls her mother, knowing she won't be in from work yet, and leaves a message, telling her she'll be home late. Better that way, leaving a message, because her mother was always giving her an argument about getting home late, and who needs that? She buys a hot dog from a stand, mustard and sauerkraut, and, entering the terminal, she rides the long escalator that takes her up to the waiting room, thinking why not, why not? It's her gift to herself, the half hour trip on the water, to Staten Island, and a half hour back. The waiting room is big and round, crowded, wooden benches full of people waiting, many standing, and big windows all around. She can see the Brooklyn Bridge. So good, so good, sitting on a bench and finishing the hot dog, waiting for the ferry, and when it comes she's up with the crowd, lining up and waiting to board.

As the ferry pulls out, she stands in the rear, by the gate, looking back at the big green terminal, how it shrinks as the ferry moves away. And the huge glass buildings of lower Manhattan, slick and smart, reflecting the sky, seeming to change shape as they fall away in the distance, and, looming above them all, the Twin Towers of the Trade Center, so tall there are days when the top floors are hidden in clouds. It's better than anything she knows, being out there on the water, feeling the breeze as the ferry picks up speed. The foam of the wake, and the gulls, and the other boats, sometimes a freighter. She likes the motion, the water, the beat of the engine. And then, passing close to the Statue of Liberty, off to the right, how big it is, high on the pedestal, green folds of the robe and thickness of the upraised arm, the bright gold of the torch turning red in the slanting sun. They pass a tug hauling two barges loaded with coal, and a white speedboat goes zipping about, circling the barges.

She leaves the back and, passing through the long cabin, makes her way to the front and takes the last half of the trip from there, facing the breeze. Dead ahead lies Staten Island. The ferry pushes on, steadily, and she looks down, watching as the green-brown water washes against the prow and splashes into white foam. They pass a ferry coming in the opposite direction, painted orange, same as this, the pilothouse on the top deck, nobody up there except the crew—and down below, at the front, people at the gate, just like her, hair blowing in the wind.

To the left, now, she sees the Verrazano Bridge leaping high over the Narrows, from Brooklyn, and off to the right the clutter of sky-high derricks and the white oil domes of Bayonne. They pass a garbage scow pushed by a tug, and a freighter at anchor, three tall cargo booms sticking up from its deck like red fingers. To the right, close by, a white lighthouse rises from the water on a pile of black rocks. And then they arrive, a slow glide between bundles of tarred poles jutting up out of the water. On one of the poles a small white gull stands motionless, so near. Yesenia reaches out to touch it, but not close enough. The boat thumps against the pier, and they're in.

Two large gangplanks swing down, locking onto the ferry, and the gate opens, and Yesenia moves off with the crowd, into the terminal. In the past, she's stayed for coffee and a sandwich, then boarded the next ferry back—but tonight she heads out, taking the long uphill walk through the bus depot and out to the street, Richmond Terrace, which runs along the shore.

It's a long trek from the terminal to the street, and her eye is caught by a large building up ahead, with wide steps and six massive columns on the portico. She crosses over for it and climbs the stairs, twenty-nine steps she counts, lifting her high above the street and bringing her up to the columns, and when she's there, touching them and looking up, seeing how lofty they are, she feels completely dwarfed. A sign by the door says COUNTY COURTHOUSE—a small sign, she thinks, for such a big place. With both hands she pushes back her hair, and turning, she looks out across the water and sees the sky-scrapers of Manhattan lit by the late sun, and she's stirred by it, so glad to be there, the red sun putting streaks of fire in everything.

Beneath her, on the street, the traffic is light, some cars, some cabs. Across the street there's a parking lot, and beyond the lot, tall on the water, is the orange ferry she came in on, on its way back. Off to the right are the long lanes for the buses, and beyond it all, across the water, the many gleaming towers, glass and steel, rising with cozy arrogance, a sun-splashed manic fantasy leaping up out of the waters of the bay. So glad, so glad! She sits on the top step, elbows on her knees and chin in her hands, watching as the sun sinks and the whole scene dips and turns, clouds in the sky all crimson and even the sky-scrapers burning, all of it alive and fierce. And, knowing dark will be coming on soon, she thinks she better move along, back to the terminal, but lingers, captivated, watching as the clouds simmer to purple and gray.

On the trip back, the sun is gone, but there's still light in the sky, and now, instead of standing up front or in back, she sits inside, on one of the blue vinyl seats, relaxing, dreaming away the end of what has been a very good day. Closing her eyes, resting, then awake again, gazing. The ceiling gray, the floor covered by a dark linoleum speckled with white. Overhead fluorescents light the heads and faces of the ones crossing over. Not many at this hour, after seven. A few young couples, a few old, two girls in leather pants, a black man with a red bandanna around his forehead and a gold ring in his left nostril. A woman with a baby. And others, some sleeping, some gazing. A girl arguing with her boyfriend. And everywhere the signs—

LIFE PRESERVERS UNDER SEATS
LIFE PRESERVERS UNDER SEATS
LIFE PRESERVERS UNDER SEATS

And other signs too, in black lettering on the walls, NO LITTERING, NO RADIO PLAYING, MEDICAL EMERGENCY KIT IN PILOT HOUSE. The name of the boat is *Andrew Barberi*, and she likes that, the sound of it, wondering who Andrew Barberi might have been, and how lucky, having a whole ferry named after him. A few seats across from her, a girl with red hair opens a can of Coke—she looks sad, there are lines in her face, an unhappiness, her eyebrows tense and her forehead wrinkled. Two teenagers, boys, playing cards. A baby crying. An old Jewish man, bearded, in black, with a black hat and a black cane. Through the window, she sees a fat October moon rising over the water.

Coming off the ferry, she feels a surge of energy and wants to walk. She could catch a subway right there, by the ferry, and change later to the J, but instead she sets out along Whitehall, stretching her legs, feeling jaunty, free. It's dark now, but light spills from the streetlamps, and the skyscrapers are lit, and the beams of passing cars sweep across her body. Past Bowling Green she goes and up Broadway, hoofing it, a quick, easy stride. She could cut over and pick up the J at Wall and Broad but keeps on, enjoying the crisp night air. Taxis on the street, a police car cruising. Five or six blocks farther, there's another station, but she passes that up too and keeps going. A car slows and the driver calls to her, asking if she's available. She keeps walking and the car pulls away, snorting as it accelerates through a red light.

Crazy, crazy, she thinks, beginning to tire, thinking of tomorrow, up early and back to work. Why am I doing this? From Broadway she angles over on Park Row, passing City Hall and the park, all lit up, the trees, the grass, the cupola, her thoughts drifting. Thinking of her mother, her father, and Muddy, who wants her but she doesn't want him, and Jinx, the boy she had sex with in school. And high to her left the tall Woolworth Building swaddled in light, the top looking like a green pyramid, luscious green, pistachio, and she remembers a five-and-dime her mother used to take her to, not many of those around anymore. Wondering if she'll grow fat and cranky like her mom and doesn't want that, no, keep fat and cranky far away. And her pa skipping out when she was just a kid—but still she likes him, remembering. Used to tickle her under the arms and lick her forehead, the rich tan smell of whiskey and cigarettes on his breath, and eyes like brown neon. That other woman that took him away, kick her hard, real hard, dump her in the trash. And the trees she just saw where the ferry took her, some already turning, glorious red, strange to see that on a day that was so warm—autumn leaves in Indian summer. And only two weeks to Halloween. God, where is the time going? That's what her mother used to say. Still does. Time's movin', girl. Do the shoppin', clean the stove. Time movin' and you not even begun yet.

And then the big intersection and the traffic coming down off the bridge, and in a few moments she's at Chambers Street, and there she quits, gives up on her long trek. She enters the vaulted arcade of the Municipal

Building, passing under the high tiled arches, and goes down a steep flight of stairs into the subway, through the turnstile and down another flight, to the track where the J comes in. On the way down, she passes a transit cop going the opposite direction, on his way up, leaving the station. He's middle-aged and he eyes her, giving her the once-over, and she eyes him right back.

It's one of the bigger stations, wide and cavernous, with several platforms and four sets of tracks. Square columns rise from the platforms, each column covered by white tiles. From where she stands, she looks across to another platform, and another beyond that. She sees no one, nobody there, nothing but the underground stillness and the white glare of the fluorescents and the stale subway smell, and a vague uneasiness. She's used to the rush-hour crowds, the push and shuffle, shoes clicking, twist of the turnstiles, roar of the trains. When the motorman applies the brakes, the ear-splitting screech of metal wheels on metal rails. But now nothing, no sound. An eerie hollowness. She goes to the edge and leans over and looks down the tunnel, the tracks disappearing into a lonesome blackness. She thinks the train will never come.

On the neighboring platform, across the tracks, someone is suddenly there, in jeans and a maroon T-shirt, a woolen watch cap on his head. She thinks maybe he was there all the time, she just hadn't noticed. He's at the foot of the stairs, in dirty white sneakers, hands tucked into his pockets, looking across at her, and it bothers her, makes her uncomfortable, and she's glad he's over there, the other side of the tracks, rather than here. But the way he's looking at her, she thinks he might jump down onto the tracks and come right across.

She walks down the platform, trying to escape his gaze, but feels his eyes still on her, drilling into her. She never should have stayed so long, watching the sun go down. Should have caught an earlier ferry and would be already home by now. She takes a few more steps, approaching the end of the station, then turns and sees with surprise that he's no longer there. She breathes easier, relieved, thinking maybe he wasn't real, just a figment, something she imagined, a subway ghost haunting the trains. And why had she been worrying anyway? Silly, silly. Just tired and tense after a long day, and her own foolishness getting the better of her.

She's in motion, drifting slowly from the far end of the station back toward the middle—and then, with a start, she sees him coming down the stairs, right there ahead of her, onto the platform, and now he hangs there, looking at her through the distance, as if owning her. She stands rooted, more than nervous now, and nowhere to go. He moves toward her, coming slowly, taking his time, with a kind of arrogance, the long jaw and half-shut eyes, maroon T-shirt snug around his spare frame, his long, thin legs hugged by tight-fitting jeans that are faded, worn, grease-stained. Long arms and big hands, and it's hard to know just what he is, his skin an odd color, like tea with too much milk in it, some kind of mixed breed like herself, black and Latino, but he has a heavy dose of white and other things, from deep in Europe, or the Middle East, or God knows where. And the half-closed eyes, fierce hazel, yellowish, intense and piercing. Where did he get those hideous eyes?

She just stands there, watching, and when he's covered half the distance toward her, he pauses, pulls out a pack of cigarettes, taps one loose, and lights up, long jets of smoke steaming from his nostrils. He grins, unpleasantly, and she sees his teeth and wishes she'd taken that earlier ferry, so dumb, so dumb. Maybe part Navajo, she thinks. She met a Navajo once, had skin like a baked potato, just out of the oven. What's happenin', she wonders, what's happenin' to me? Why am I thinkin' crazy?

And then, from the dark of the tunnel, she hears the squeak and groan of an approaching train—and there it is, sudden and shining, all lit up, coming into the station, the J, and it's over, she'll be all right now.

She steps aboard, and the blue watch cap slips on too, into the same car but at the other end. The seats are in two long rows, facing each other, blue vinyl. She glances his way, and there he is, on the opposite side, at the far end. The cigarette is gone, and his arms are folded, long legs stretched out, the half-closed eyes still on her, staring. She looks away, thinking the eyes are maybe just make-believe. Colored contacts, like they use in the movies.

There are others in the car, a middle-aged couple, a woman in white, a man in a gray jacket, a black woman in a pink sweat suit, a teenager with earphones. She wonders if the blue watch cap will get off, or if he'll stick with her the whole way. What to do, she wonders. Maybe jump off at the next stop, just before the doors close. But what if he's quick and gets off too? What then?

She tries to distract herself, reading the ads that run the length of the car, above the windows. THE BAHAMAS—FOUR DAYS—FLY AMERICAN. MADAME GARDENIA, PSYCHIC. HOME MORTGAGES, QUICK APPROVAL. JESUS CARES ABOUT YOU! There are three sets of doors on each side of the car, polished steel, and at each end, a door leading to the next car. The floor is linoleum, musty brown. The woman in a pink sweat suit is sleeping.

At Canal, the man in gray steps off, and a girl wearing shorts and leotards gets on. The blue watch cap is still at the other end of the car, and Yesenia wonders about the cap, why a woolen thing like that? Doesn't he know it's Indian summer?

Above him, there's a poster warning the passengers not to stand close to the edge of the platform. AGUDICE SU SENTIDO DE SEGURIDAD EN LA PLATAFORMA—the picture shows footprints crossing the yellow line, and a big red don't-do-it sign. *Seguridad*, she thinks. She knows some Spanish, her mother taught her. But what good is Spanish if there's a dumb dude on a train staring hard at you and he won't let go? And again she's wondering about him, who is he and where from, thinking maybe some Arab blood in him—or a pale Pakistani? That odd color to his skin, too light to be dark, too dark to be light. Not Jewish, she thinks, or Lithuanian. But what does she know about who people are and where they're from? She used to think Oscar Acciuga was Spanish, from Spain, but it turns out he's Italian, from Richmond Hill.

As the train pulls into Bowery, the middle-aged couple are up, ready to exit, and the woman in white too, and the girl in shorts and the teenager with earphones. In a panic, she thinks she should go, stay with the crowd, hope to find a transit cop—but something holds her back, a weird paralysis, fear of finding herself suddenly alone out there, with him. And again she's thinking what then, what then?

A man with a violin case comes aboard, though he doesn't sit, just leans against a pole. It's him and the black woman in a sweat suit, and at the far end, the one with the watch cap, still looking her way.

The doors close, and as the train grinds up, picking up speed, the lights blink off, then on again. And then, only a minute or so out from the station, it slows and stops, and for a few minutes they're just sitting there, in the tunnel. From the corner of her eye, she sees he's still locked on to her, as if telling her something, sending a message, and whatever it is, she doesn't want to know.

The train starts up again, and when it pulls into Essex, the man with the violin gets off, and the black woman in a sweat suit, suddenly awake, leaps for the door, just in time. And Yesenia, heart pounding wildly, sees now that it's too late for her. She's stuck with him, alone. And as the train begins to move, she looks down the length of the empty car and watches as he pulls out his pack and lights up again, exhaling a long stream of smoke.

Quickly, then, she's up, electrified, going for the door at her end of the car, to skip through to the car ahead. But the handle sticks. She struggles with it, pushing hard, and when the door finally slides open, the roar of the train wraps around her in a foul gust of wind. Signals and tunnel lamps flash by, and in the car ahead she sees a bald man sleeping, a woman with orange hair, a priest, and a bearded man with a newspaper. But the blue watch cap is suddenly there, behind her, and before she can open the door to the next car and pass through, his hand grips her wrist and draws her back.

He slides the door closed, shutting out the wind and the noise, and drags her toward the middle of the empty car. He's a foot taller than she is. His switchblade is out, open, and with the long blade he stabs upward into the fluorescents, through the vinyl shield, breaking the tubes, putting them out, a flurry of wild thrusts, and hits a nerve, something vital that throws a spark, and all of the lights in the car go out. The only illumination is from the dim emergency lamps, and from the light filtering in from the cars ahead and behind.

"Don't hurt me," she says.

He grins. "Hurt you? Not you, darlin'. You my sweet-meat, my sugar juice. My butter cream pie. I ain't gonna hurt you, I gonna eat you up and shit you out my itchy ass. Then, if you want, I gonna kill you good."

He draws the point of the knife slowly across her cheek. She feels the sting, and when she puts her free hand up to her face and touches the wet, she knows it's blood. God, God, she thinks. He cut me, cut my face. Thinking now she was dead for sure, he won't stop till he's killed the life out of her. The noise of the train is inside her, the rumble, the growl, the rocking and swaying, and the thought of death, her death, puts her in a panic, and she goes dizzy, refusing, not wanting to believe any of this is real. She shuts her eyes, closing out what little light there is—and then the dizziness again, swimming up inside her, and she folds over, collapsing onto the floor.

When she comes to, she's where she fell, on her back, her backpack pressing into her spine. Her knees are up and her skirt is pushed back and he's between her legs, driving hard into her dryness and cursing her, *fuckin' pig, fuckin' pig.* And when he's done with her, sweaty, out of breath, he pulls away and stands up, over her, and only then does she realize the train is motionless, stopped, and from the floor, looking up through a window, she sees they're out of the tunnel and in the open, into the night. Outside, there are lights, glimmers.

He adjusts his jeans, then bends and pulls her up by her hair, and shoves her against the door. He's behind her, leaning hard. Through the door's window she sees where they are—on the bridge, above the East River. Stalled there, God knows why, and she's hoping maybe the conductor will come through. She sees the lights on the other bridges, and a plane passing low, lights blinking. And lights in the buildings, in the windows. Windows everywhere, lit up. All those lights, she thinks, and nobody knows. She tries to pray, *Hail Mary, full of grace,* but the words swim away from her. It's her mother who prays. I should pray more, she thinks. Maybe if she had prayed, this wouldn't be happening.

Then, with a wrenching groan, the train is moving again. Off the bridge and onto the el, and as it pulls into Marcy Avenue, he has his hand high on her left arm, above the elbow, gripping hard, and when the doors snap open he steers her onto the narrow platform and hurries her to the stairs—moving her down fast, onto the street and propelling her along, past a deli, a newsstand, a bridal shop, a kosher market. They pass a Chinese restaurant and Colossus Drugs, and a discount house called 99¢ Dream. Most of them closed but all of them well lit. Hustling her along, under the el, past the parking meters, past a gray-haired Latino in a torn sweater sitting in a doorway, smoking a cigar. A bearded man walking his dog, a clot of girls by a camera shop, giggling. Two Hassidim walking rapidly, each with a newspaper under his arm. A cabbie, parked at the curb, eating a sandwich. Then away from the el, around a corner, and into an area of old brick warehouses, broken sidewalks, smells of raw sewage, urine, dog shit. A few homeless sleeping in doorways. Sheets of newspaper scattered on the street, and in her mind she's trying to pray again, but the prayer is fragmented, in pieces.

The building he takes her to is a five-story brick, the windows on the lower level boarded with plywood. The front door is steel and padlocked, dark red, the paint peeling. Some kind of old factory, she thinks. Warehouse, maybe. The plywood over the windows weatherworn, blackened by rain.

He unlocks the door and gets her in, throws on the lights, and, his hand still tight on her arm, hurries her into the elevator, a wide, clunky thing, little more than a cage. It grumbles its way to the top floor. He puts on the lights up there and it's a big empty space with a tin ceiling, the white paint dingy, yellowish, patches of rust where water has seeped from the roof. The floor wooden and old, with holes in it where machines had once been screwed down. Could have been women here working on sewing machines, or men stamping out metal buttons, and all she can think is they're gone, gone, nobody here, and she feels so helpless and alone.

He pulls off her backpack, yanking roughly, and empties it onto the floor. Picks up her uniform, the pants and blouse, and tosses them aside, then grabs the wallet and takes the bills and change. Nine singles, counting, and stuffs them into his jeans. And then, grabbing her, he throws her to the floor and he's on her again, and the only sound now is the sound of his thick breathing, the grunting and heaving as he forces his way in, yet in her mind there is still the sound of the train, the grinding of the wheels, metal on metal. She is sore and hurting where he pumps against her, and she hates it, doesn't want it, but despite her anger, the pain slides over into pleasure, and, still resisting, thinking never, never, she is plunged into a turmoil of fear and hate and sensual appetite all mixed together, an erotic surge flaming inside her at the same time that she curses him aloud, shouting *no*.

The knife is in his left hand, the blade pressed flat against the side of her neck. "You liked that," he says. "Say you liked it."

But she says nothing. The knife still there, against her neck, and still she doesn't answer, thinking nothing, emptiness, death, thinking loss and abandonment, not wanting the thing she's just felt and hating herself for having felt it, thinking now, more than ever, this

126

is the time. If he wants to use the knife, let him.

He rolls off, away from her, and lies flat on his back, on the floor, the knife still in his left hand. And they're that way a long time, she on her back and he on his, and she hears distant sirens, a fire somewhere, and wishes the fire would come right upstairs and burn them both, and there would be nothing to think about anymore.

Then, out of the long silence, he's talking. "The first one," he says, "was a skinny old woman in an apartment in Rego Park. She was seventy-one, and couldn't get enough of it. Every day I stuck it to her, and she wants more. Paid me money to do it to her any way I liked. Sometimes she hid in the closet, waitin' for me to find her. She hid under the bed. She liked those little games. After I killed her, I carried her up to the roof, six flights up, and dropped her down into the street. Garbage, that's what she was. Garbage."

He lights another cigarette, the smoke rising in slow billows toward the rusted ceiling. He seems to be meditating. Remembering.

"There was another used to make chocolate puddin' for me. Can't recall if she was the third or the fourth. Can't remember her name. She had red hair, fat legs, and considered herself an expert in the makin' of puddin'. Took the powder from a package and poured it into boilin' water and stirred it, gettin' it real thick and addin' some milk, and set it out to cool, then put it in the fridge to give it a chill. Put whipped cream on it, and a cherry. A whole month I was with her. She wore silly lace underpants she thought were a turn-on. But it wasn't the lace turned me on, it was the thought all along that I was going to twist the knife in her guts, and she knew nothing about that, never even imagined. Just kept shovin' that chocolate puddin' at me. Then, when the right day come, I spread puddin' all over her. She thought it was kinky, it turned her on. It was the best sex we ever had. But when I stuck the knife in her, was she surprised."

His cigarette burns down and he rubs it out on the floor. He's still on his back, gazing at the tin ceiling.

"The best one," he says, "the best was the one that hated me. She had curly yellow hair, but it was dyed. When she was young, before she went gray, the hair was black. She been married to a trucker, he been killed when his rig went off the highway. I tied her to the bed, spread-eagle, arms to the posts at the headboard, ankles to the posts at the footboard, and she didn't like that at all. I had to punch her in the jaw before I got her all tied down. I greased her with olive oil from the kitchen and give it to her good. She hated me, spat in my face. But before I was done, she was hummin' and moanin'. I didn't like the moanin', it got on my nerves."

He lights up again. Exhales, and flicks a shred of tobacco from off his tongue. "You know who that one was? The one I tied down? That was my Aunt Veronica. She took care of me after my mother died. She was thick and dark and not pretty and always resented my mother being dead. She hated raising me. So after I was grown and gone, I went back that once and fixed her good. It was my way of thankin' her."

He's silent for a while, and then, still looking at the ceiling, says, "What about you? You got any stories to tell?"

She doesn't answer.

"You gotta have somethin'," he says.

She just lies there for a while, silent, thinking she should pray, but the words aren't there for her.

Without looking at him, she says, "Where you from?"

"Louisiana," he says.

"You don't sound like Louisiana."

"That's 'cause I lie. It's a habit I have. Louisiana seem a fun place to be from. Truth is, I'm from Brooklyn. Sheepshead Bay."

"You always lie?"

"Most of the time."

"Don't you get tired making things up?"

"I get tired livin'." And then, leaning toward her, he takes off his woolen watch cap. His head is shaved, and there's a knobby scar running from high on his forehead to the back of his head. "Happened in the army," he says. "Sonofabitch sergeant cracked my head open. Like it? Do you?" He leans close. "Lick it," he says. "Go ahead and lick it with your tongue."

She doesn't.

"What's the matter? It makes you shy? You don't like my scar?"

"I want to go home," she says.

"They all do," he answers. "Me too. But where is home? Have a cancer stick," he says, extending the pack of Marlboros.

"I don't smoke," she says.

"You should, it calms the nerves."

There's another long silence, and then she says, "How much longer?"

"Before what?"

"Before anything," she says, unable to say the words for what she's thinking.

"Before I kill you, you mean? That's what you thinkin'? Don't worry, sugar. We have a lot more yet, before it comes to that. Don't rush things, it don't pay. That's what my Aunt Veronica used to say, though it didn't help her none."

He's up, buckling his pants, and pulls her to her feet, pushing her toward a narrow door with a padlock. He unlocks it, yanks the door open, and shoves her inside. It's a closet-sized john, the toilet to one side of the door and the sink to the other, barely enough space for her to stand. A string hangs from a naked bulb above, and he reaches in, jerks it, and the light comes on.

"Be right back," he says, closing the door, and she hears the padlock snap shut.

The sink is old, stained with rust. The wood-framed mirror is spotted and dull, but still she can see herself, dried blood on her face, the cut running from the corner of her eye down to her chin. Her face is ruined, but it means nothing to her. She's numb, anesthetized. As if in some way she has already died, and the physical death yet to come would merely be a confirmation of the inner

129

death that has already occurred. She turns on the hot water, but nothing. Then the cold, a slow trickle, and she rinses her hands, no soap, just the water, rubbing her hands together, wanting to wash them clean, but she knows she can't.

The toilet is filthy, the bowl blackened, swirls of dark slime in the water. She flushes, wishing the slime away, but as the water fills the bowl, it rises dangerously, and, fearing an overflow, she moves quickly, lifting the cover from the tank and reaching in, pushing the shut-off valve. Just like home, she thinks, toilet never works. As she replaces the cover, she's aware how heavy it is, a thick slab of old white porcelain, chipped at one corner. She'd like to crack him over the head with it, good and hard. Real hard.

She turns down the wooden lid on the toilet and sits there, holding her head in her hands. How long will he be, she wonders. Maybe he'll never come back. He doesn't live here, that much is clear. No bed, no kitchen, nothing. Just the toilet. Maybe he lives on one of the lower floors, or somewhere else, another building. Maybe he's left for Louisiana, skipped town and will never come back. But it's too much to hope for.

She closes her eyes, thinking she'll sleep, but can't. She wonders what it will be like when he returns—will he want sex again, or will he just look at her, staring, the way he stared on the train. Something inside her is still hoping, not wanting to believe the trouble she's in, not wanting to believe the meanness, the ugliness, the foul words whispered in her ear, and his thing deep up in her body, and the knife, that he would actually use it. And the stories he told, too insane, she thinks, too impossible to be true. There was no old lady playing hide-and-seek in the closet. No fat redhead making chocolate pudding, and no Aunt Veronica. He was making it all up, to scare her.

And now, for a moment, she doesn't altogether hate him, and thinks maybe she can help him. She can change his lies, bend them and soften them, and make him feel better about himself. She could do that. But even as she thinks it, she knows it's crackbrained, over the edge. And yet, over the edge is the best hope she has, because if he really did kill those women, then what chance does she have? She's hungry, starved, a gaping hole in her stomach, and imagines him coming back to her with food, with chocolate bars, and pizza, and strawberry ice cream. She roves from one to another, tasting them in imagination, and it's the chocolate she wants most. She tastes it, chews it, smells it, swallowing and wanting more, so good, so good. And she thinks, now, Muddy is right, so right, been right all along, life is nothing but a shell game. Now you see it, now you don't. Pay your dollar and take your chance.

Her stomach hurts with hunger and she feels a headache coming on, a low whining thing, like a wire humming in her brain. The window is too small for her to pass through, and even if she could, what good would it be, five stories up? The moon is high and she sees other buildings like this one, some taller, some shorter. She tries to open the window but can't. She could break the glass and shout for help, but who would hear?

She's tired, so tired, and sinks onto the floor, resting an arm on the closed lid of the toilet, and leans her head against her arm. Shuts her eyes and sits that way, almost sleeping but not quite. She's awake but dreaming—on a boat, sailing, and then awake again, looking up through the window at the moon. Nothing to eat since that hot dog at the ferry. Dumb, she thinks. Never should have looked so long at that sunset, and all that walking, all the way up to Chambers Street, and this stupid red skirt, never should have put it on this morning. Never, never.

When she opens her eyes again, it's morning and the sun is up, flooding the tiny bathroom with light. She's confused, wondering where she is. Then, with a sinking sensation, she remembers, and she knows it's real. She can't move past this. The only good thing is that he hasn't come back yet, and she thinks, wishes, maybe he never will. But in that case, how will she ever get out of here?

And her poor mother going out of her mind, worrying because she never came home. How it all swirls around for her—her mother, her father, and Muddy, and now none of it matters, not Muddy and not Jinx. And if her father ever showed his face again, would her mother take him back or would she kill him?

The sun is up, but she doesn't know if it's one day or two that she's been here. Was it only yesterday Muddy was playing the shell game? Only yesterday the ferry? And then all the horror and insanity. She doesn't even know where she is, some street off Marcy Avenue, some old factory, holes in the floor where the machines had been bolted down, making things that even God never imagined. And she hears the ghosts of those old machines, thumpety-thumping, grinding on—and knows it isn't the machines, it's just her headache again. So crazy. Crazy window, crazy floor she's sitting on. Crazy toilet, crazy mirror stained and blotched, what good is it? Crazy headache. Crazy me. Am I the one—me? Am I to blame?

The headache grows and builds. And then she feels it, the spasm rising in her stomach, and she's up, leaning over the sink, retching, spewing up yellow bile, dizzy with the stink of it, and she turns on the water, the cold trickle, washing it away, and wets her mouth, cleaning out the bad taste. The headache is softer now, almost gone but still there, lingering at the edge.

She's all day there, locked behind the narrow door, paint peeling and the wood showing underneath. Out of patience, and out of hope. Hearing whistles and sirens, and planes low overhead, rumble of heavy-duty trucks passing by. Through the window she sees an empty alley below, and the tarred roof of the neighboring building. No birds, no pigeons or gulls. By noon she's sure he isn't coming back. By one, her headache has swollen again, throbbing front to back. She closes her eyes, tries to ease it away, wets her head, nothing helps. If he comes back, she'll try to get the knife from him, that's what. Take it and stab it into him. Hungry, so hungry. Why did he say he'd be right back when he never meant it? Why did he lie to me? That's what he did—he lied. Feeling it as a betrayal, an act of faithlessness, a special meanness in it.

Late afternoon, she feels pity for him again, thinking he needs help. She could take care of him, could turn him around. She thinks of the enormous loneliness he must feel—such desperation, grabbing girls on the subway and scaring them half to death, then running away, fleeing.

The day stretches on, and she does things to divert herself. She stands up and reaches toward the ceiling, trying to get the blood flowing. Up on her toes, up and down. In the dust on the window, she plays tic-tac-toe. She's both the Os and the Xs, so she can't lose. Yeah, some joke. Because what is she if not a loser?

She plays patty-cake, clapping her hands together, then clapping them to her knees—patty-cake, patty-cake. How good it was, when she was young and easy, free, unthinking, and now already she feels old, as if a whole lifetime has fled. And then she's praying again, trying to, thinking that's why this is happening to her, she never prayed enough. Hail Mary full of grace, the Lord is with thee. Blessed art thou among women. God, God, why am I so bad? Why is everything so wrong for me? Why don't this headache go away?

She sits on the floor, leaning her back against the door, and closes her eyes, the headache like a steady beam passing through her forehead and radiating through her brain. She thinks of birds, their wings, birds in flight, birds taking her headache and flying away with it. But still the headache lingers, shifting in intensity, moments when it eases off, but moments when it's simply unbearable. If only I could eat something, bread, banana. Her eyes are closed and she tries to sleep it away, telling herself to doze off, saying the word *sleep* over and over.

She passes into a dream, then out of it, in and out, dreaming of home, the el on Jamaica Avenue, the street full of shadows. Then, with a tremor, she wakens out of a dream of her father holding a knife—startled awake, as if dashed with cold water, because she knows it isn't a dream but true. She was five years old, her mother and father quarreling in the kitchen, and her father lifted the bread knife in anger, waving it around, by the sink. And her mother facing up to him, holding her own, not backing off—and she spat at him. It so provoked him, he raised the knife, to plunge it into her, and Yesenia, terrified, thought that he would. But he turned away, trembling with rage, and bent over and stabbed the knife into the floor, again and again, and the linoleum had those scars in it as long as they lived there. Which wasn't long, because less than a year later her father was gone, and her mother didn't want that apartment anymore. So they moved to Jamaica Avenue.

"Don't never marry black," her mother said, and it was the first of many times that Yesenia heard her say that. Years later, when she was casting her eyes around at the boys, her mother was still saying it, drilling it into her. "Ain't worth the time of day, no way. Stay away from them, honey. Your daddy was black and look how no-good he was." And Yesenia thinking, if he's my father, then don't that make me black too? And her mother staring into her eyes, knowing exactly what was in her mind: "Don't never contradict me, girl. You hear? Don't never do that." And Yesenia hovering, not knowing what to think, because her mother, flaunting her Latin blood, had, as well, a swatch of black in her, from a dead grandfather, and a few drops of Chickasaw too.

She tries praying again, Hail Mary full of grace, but the prayer falls apart on her, disintegrates, and she takes it as a sign of how hopeless her situation is. She wishes she could float away. Wishes the roof would open and she could float right up to the sky.

And then it's her mother's voice again, inside her, urgent. Time be movin', girl, you gotta move with it. Just do it, honey. Do what you gotta do.

And Yesenia, on the floor between the sink and the toilet, knows what it is that she has to do, and she hates it, isn't sure she has the strength for it, but it's the only thing, because there is nothing else. She's up on her feet now, moving her shoulders, flexing her waist, stimulating the blood flow, and sees exactly how it will unfold. She will stand against the wall, wedged between the wall and the toilet bowl, out of sight when the door swings open, with her hands high above her head, holding the heavy porcelain cover from the toilet tank, waiting to swing it down. And he'll come, unlocking the padlock, and not seeing her, he'll lean in, looking for her, and she'll slam the cover on his head.

That's how she sees it, how she knows it has to be. And she waits. Past five and six and seven, sitting on the floor and waiting, studying her wristwatch. When will he come? Will he? When? Looking through the window at the changing sky, and then the sun is down and she's frazzled with the waiting, her brain screaming with the headache. She closes her eyes, concentrating on the pain, trying to soften it, dissolve it, persuade it to go away, and then she's in and out of sleep again, people talking in her dreams, she doesn't know who, can't hear what they're saying.

And then, nerves jumping, she's jolted to wakefulness by the sound of the elevator, the grumpy groan of the machinery as the big cage rises from downstairs, and she's up off the floor, heart beating wildly, putting herself to the side of the door, between the wall and the toilet, and, awkwardly, she lifts the porcelain cover. The lightbulb is off, the only light is moonlight filtering through the dusty window.

The elevator creaks to a stop, and a moment later she hears the snap of the light switches. Light from the fluorescents seeps in through the crack under the door. Then silence, unbearable silence, and she stands there, tense, back against the wall, hearing her heartbeat, and her headache mounting.

Then she hears him at the door, fumbling with the padlock, inserting the key, and with fear and panic she lifts the cover high over her head. "Come on, my sweetmeat, my butter pie," he says, unhooking the padlock, "time for supper, darlin'. Went all the way Louisiana and

135

brought you back some crawfish and a pot of gumbo. You gonna love this, honey. You do like crawfish, don't you?" He pulls the door open and, not seeing her, puts his head in and extends an arm, reaching for the pull cord, and as he yanks it the light comes on, and she swings down with the heavy porcelain, catching him on the side of his head, the blow partly deflected by his upraised arm.

He goes down, dazed, fumbling backward, away from the door, and she's out after him, raising the lid and swinging again, bashing him in the back, on the spine. His head twists around, eyes turning up and looking at her with an odd mix of surprise and acquiescence, a weird innocence, as if begging for forgiveness. She sees the knife in his left hand, already open, but he makes no move to use it, it's just there, held in a loose grip. And, pushing herself, exerting what little strength she has left, she lifts the cover one more time, high up, and brings it down, the full weight of it, onto his head. When it hits, she hears a queer cracking sound and sees his body flatten out, a faint quivering in his right arm. One leg jerks a few times, like a child's when twitching during a dream, then it goes still, and she sees him as in a photograph, the maroon T-shirt, tight jeans, dirt-smeared sneakers, the knife still in his hand, the watch cap on his head. And on the floor nearby, a bag from McDonald's.

She doesn't know if he's dead or not, and doesn't care. She moves past him, toward the elevator, but takes the stairs instead, rushing down, almost tumbling, fast as she can, down the long flights of metal stairs, and at the bottom she confronts the big steel door, fumbling, in a panic, wrestling with the chains and the bolt, and finally she's out, onto the street. A heavy mist has moved in, and the sidewalk is wet, the moon a white blur.

She's cold, hungry, numb, just walking, moving toward the lights and the shops, not thinking, not knowing what she'll do or not do. Feeling nothing. Even the pain in her head is gone, though she doesn't notice, doesn't reflect that the headache has lifted. At the el, she pauses on a corner, looking up and down, seeing the flower shop, the laundry, the hairdresser. The mist has thickened, and the lights drift and float garishly. She's walking again, slowly, through rifts and folds of neon, veils of fluorescent fog sifting and bending in front of the storefront windows. A few cars, not many. The double yellow line down the middle of the street seems a long, luminous scar. She passes a bodega. *Comidas Criollas. Jugos Tropicales.* A tuxedo rental, a Jewish market.

She continues down the block, under the el, and pauses by a candy store, thinking right now there is nothing in the world she wants more than a chocolate bar. Newspapers on the wooden stand out front, *El Vocero, El Diario, Der Yid, Das Blatt.* Inside, a man smoking a cigar, and a woman in a long dress, with a shawl over her head. A gray man buying cigarettes. And she's outside, on the sidewalk, thinking chocolate, imagining it, conjuring it up, the smell of it, the taste, as if it were in her mouth. She turns away, not a penny on her, and for a while she lingers there, corner of Broadway and Marcy, feeling the mist, the touch of it on her face and hands. Then she walks again, under the el, and if she walks all night she may finally get home.

A patrol car cruises by, passes her, then turns and comes back, pulling up at the curb, and the officer climbs out, approaching her as she comes along. He has a moustache, that's what she notices about him. He's brown and hefty, with big hands and a black moustache.

"You need help?"

She doesn't answer. She feels a pain in her left shoulder and remembers the weight of the porcelain cover, how she held it above her head and swung it.

"I'll take you to the hospital."

"No," she says.

"You sure you're okay?"

"Just take me home. I got no money for the train."

"The one that did that to your face—that all he did, or did he do more?"

"I don't want to talk about it."

137

"Well let's have you checked out at the hospital first, make sure you're all right. Then I'll take you home."

"No," she says.

"You sure?"

"Yes."

"Don't you want to at least file a report? This guy shouldn't be on the loose."

"Just take me home," she says.

When her mother opens the door, she knows right away what happened. "I told you," she says. "Didn't I tell you? Why you not listening? Some boy did this to you? I been such a wreck, worryin'. Where were you, honey doll? Who did this? Look at you, what they done to your face. Who will want you now? Tell me. Who?"

Yesenia locks herself in the bathroom and runs the hot water in the tub. Her mother knocks on the door, calling to her, but she doesn't let her in. She rolls her clothes into a ball and sticks them into the hamper and sits in the tub, soaping herself, her breasts, and down between her legs, her whole body, wherever she can reach. She hears the sound of a train going by, on the el, and it isn't a sound she wants to hear. She goes on soaping, then she leans back, sliding down deep, the water up around her neck and chin, the cut on her cheek smarting, and she lies there, soaking, more than an hour. She falls asleep, wakes up, and sleeps again, the water touching her lips. She dreams she's on the ferry, in the cooling breeze, standing by the rear gate, the boat's wake spreading out like torn lace. Dr. Tattafruge is out there, on the water, in his canoe, paddling hard to keep up. And the others are with her, on deck, Mrs. Sowle in a rocking chair, with needle and thread, making a quilt, and Mr. Vogel on the floor, tinkering with his toy trains, which run everywhere under the chairs. Muddy Dinks is doing his shell game. Smoke is smoking, and Chase is reading a comic book. Even Oscar is there, talking to Yesenia, telling her not to worry—if she drops one of the vases it won't break, the rug will save it. But there at her feet is a broken vase, in pieces, and she's weeping, and everyone is telling her not to cry, but she can't stop. "If only I hadn't worn that red skirt," she says through her tears. "If only I hadn't done that." The sun is going down, crimson on the water, and when she glances about, she sees they're all gone, Oscar, Mrs. Sowle, all of them. Even Tattafruge in his canoe, no longer there. And then it's the boy in the woolen watch cap, standing in front of her, holding the bag from McDonald's, offering it to her. She wants to know his name, but he doesn't talk, says nothing, just hangs there. Then he too is gone, and she feels so alone, the only one on the ferry, nobody else. And her mother knocking at the bathroom door. Knocking and calling to her, frantically.

The War Against
the Ants

Some years ago, when Luther Rumfarm considered a move to Echo Terrace, he desperately wanted the penthouse, but Harry Falcon had it, and he was not about to sell. After a great deal of coming and going and rethinking, Rumfarm bought the three-bedroom Susan B. Anthony on the twelfth floor, and the four-bedroom Amelia Bloomer directly below, and merged them into an overly ample two-floor unit linked by a sumptuously designed S-curved staircase made of chestnut and bird's-eye maple. And since the Susan B. Anthony and the Amelia Bloomer had ceased to exist, the new unit became, at Rumfarm's request and with the board's approval, the Grandma Moses.

Rumfarm and his wife, Lyssa, have for many years had a growing attachment to the work of Grandma Moses. Two of her paintings hang in their living room, and Rumfarm has one in his office at the Trade Center, where he handles investments. For quite some time he's been having a problem with his blood pressure, and he claims that a few moments of gazing at a Grandma Moses does wonders for his numbers. The one in his office is a winter scene, snow-covered houses on a snow-covered hill, trees with bare branches, people in pink and lavender coats moving in and out of their homes. A horse-drawn sleigh, a man chopping wood. A wisp of smoke from a chimney. This keeps him calm, he says. He likes the snow, the smoke, the church steeple. At home, his wife uses bathroom towels with a Grandma Moses design, and she has a tea set ornamented with Grandma Moses barns and Grandma Moses children with long, red scarves. And in the evening, when Rumfarm returns from the office, it pleases him no end that he will finish the day by going to sleep in an apartment that bears the Grandma Moses name. A lot gentler, he thinks, than sleeping in the Sitting Bull unit, or in the William Tecumseh Sherman. Born in Georgia, Rumfarm still hasn't forgiven Sherman for burning Atlanta. And now that he's become a member of the board, he thinks that after he puts the waterfall in the lobby, he will take a look at the names and organize a complete reevaluation. Sherman, for God's sake. And Ulysses S. Grant. Time to turn everything on its head and start over, change the charter if necessary. Let's think about that.

Farro Fescu, at the desk in the lobby, does think about it and doesn't like it at all. The new names coming in, Mae West, Grandma Moses, don't feel right to him. They fail, somehow, to convey the right tone. And now Rumfarm wants to change everything? Farro Fescu can see it coming—the Ginger Rogers, the Donald Duck, the Lois Lane, the Carmen Miranda. Will Rumfarm name one for Jesse James? Or Richard Nixon?

Farro Fescu has been there, at Echo Terrace, from the start, when the building first opened, nine years ago. He knows the pace, the tempo, the rhythm, the vibrations in the lobby walls. Without looking up, he knows the tap of Ravijohn's cane, the scent of Maggie Sowle's cologne, the click of Lena Klongdorf's heels. He is tuned to the swoosh of Lillian Soo's satins, and the squeaky bravado of Knatchbull's three-hundred-dollar shoes. Mrs. Wax in her mocha pants, and her teenage daughter in jeans. And young Abdul Saad, studying to become a mortician. He knows them all—their eyes, their chins, the slant of their lips as they nod hello, the angle of the hand raised in greeting. The twitch of the nose, wrinkles in the forehead. The limp, the hobble, the strut, the swagger.

He knows their ailments too and their favorite colors,

141

where they swim and where they work. Food preferences, vacation spots. Who is unfaithful to whom, and with whom. And there are times when he feels he knows so much about each of them that it seems he is inventing them, creating them out of whole cloth. The condominium, Echo Terrace, does not exist. He is making it up. Dr. Tattafruge performing sex changes, Vogel on his long walks, and Mrs. Abernooth in her coma—all of it unreal, coming to life only in his mind. No elevators, no lobby, no crack in the subbasement, no mail in the mail room. And he too, he himself, Farro Fescu. How to be sure that even he is real, that he and Echo Terrace, and West Street, and the island of Manhattan, and beyond that, the world itself, all of it, has a pulse, a heartbeat that can be measured and scanned, and the heart itself genuine, not just some shadowy image in an echocardiogram. How to know what is solid, what is real, what is mush, what is fog, what sinks, what floats, and where, where, is the cream that rises to the top?

The cream, this moment, is the cream-colored telephone, blinking and buzzing, wrenching him from his reverie— and this, the phone, is what he never doubts, because it's always there, factual and annoying, like a leaking roof that needs attention. And already his hand is reaching out, automatically.

It's Mrs. Marriocci, who has lost her rosary beads again, asking him to look for them on the black couch, where she had been sitting, holding them in her hand. Yes. No. No. I will. Yes, you too, have a good day. And when he goes to the black couch and searches about, the rosary beads are not there, and now he must call her back and give her the disappointing news.

In a drawer behind the desk he keeps Band-Aids, shoelaces, cuticle scissors, and stain remover. A concierge must be ready for anything. He keeps shoe polish and tiny screws for eyeglasses. If he isn't ready, then what? That's why he's there, to handle the little emergencies that arise. The big emergencies he leaves for the paramedics and the police. The police were quickly there after Kapri Blorg shot himself, and only months ago, when the Knatchbull boy started a fire with his chemistry set, a company of firefighters went up with fire extinguishers. Quite a mess it was, and still is.

Today, a Monday, late afternoon and overcast, Farro Fescu is in a state of distress, because what he knows now, and did not know last month, is that the building is infested with ants. He found them two weeks ago, in the large, unused room in the subbasement—a dense swarm of ants oozing and seething in the great crack that zigzags across the floor. So many of them, like a dark ribbon of water, ebbing and flowing in the crack, black and gleaming, every one of them unpleasantly large. It struck him, at a glance, that they were not ordinary ants, nothing like the ants that he knew. He blamed Mrs. Abernooth. Her husband, the insect specialist, had brought in ants from South America, and, after his death, she had continued to keep them, in a formicarium. These were her ants— had to be. They had somehow got loose—long before her accident, perhaps—and here they were, now, breeding and multiplying in the slowly widening crack in the foundation. Poor woman, she was sick in a hospital, in a coma, and it seemed wrong to blame her—but he felt, nevertheless, that it was better to put blame where blame belonged. Otherwise life becomes intolerable.

On the day that he found them, he crouched down and measured the crack at the point where the wall meets the floor. The crack was a quarter of an inch wider than it had been a week earlier. He poked the end of the steel tape into the crevice, and the ants were deep, layers of them, moving busily. They swarmed onto the tape and he shook them off, not wanting to touch them. Abernooth ants. It pleased him to think of them that way. The fortunate thing was that they seemed to be localized in this one area, in the crack in the subbasement, and if only here, in this one spot, he could control them. And he would do it himself, without Oscar and his crew, for fear that rumors would fly and the residents would become upset.

The following day, he came in with several cans of insecticide, and the spray seemed to have an effect. But a day later, he noted that the swarm was more vigorous than ever. He applied a powder and set out generous amounts of a poisonous gel, and did more spraying, and he quickly understood that the little beasts were more resilient than he had imagined. Again and again he sprayed. They would disappear for a while, and then return. And the crack was widening. Were the ants creating the crack, or was the crack creating the ants, affording them a point of entry into the building? And were they Mrs. Abernooth's ants, or someone else's? Nothing matters, he thought. And yet he knew, painfully, that everything did. Life is up and down, dark and light, soft and hard. You wrestle with what comes, win what you can, and swallow your losses. And still he hasn't been to a doctor about the pimple on his penis—pimple or whatever, turning now an obnoxious shade of purple, the color of Kadota figs when they are overripe. And he hates figs, because he had once eaten a whole bagful in a single sitting, and they had made him desperately ill.

After all the spraying he had done, he thought, for a while, that he had finally beaten the ants off, but he knows now that he has merely driven them off to safer places. Mrs. Wax was the first to call. Then urgent messages from Rumfarm and Rabbi Ravijohn. And Aki Sato. The ants were in the walls, nesting in the nooks and crannies, increasing and multiplying. They were crawling along the pipes, making their way into bathrooms and kitchens, into cupboards, pantries, closets, and medicine chests. Finding their way into vest pockets and shoes, into bath towels and toilet paper. Mrs. Sowle found them in her jam. Ravijohn found them in his bathtub. Oscar found them on the palm tree in the lobby. Muddy Dinks found them in his locker in the basement. Rumfarm found them in his slippers and his wife found them in her underwear.

"They are only ants," Vogel says to Farro Fescu, pausing at the desk and trying to calm Farro Fescu's anxiety. "You want ants? Real ants? Go to Texas. One day, when I was test-flying there, in 1955, millions of ants swarmed across the tarmac. The field had to be shut down. But these ants here, in the palm tree, in Mrs. Sowle's jam, they are nothing. Nothing."

Farro Fescu hears but doesn't listen. Because an ant is an ant, and Rumfarm complaining is not nothing. And Mrs. Saad is not nothing. And Tattafruge. And Mrs. Knatchbull. There is a lot of unhappiness, and Farro Fescu understands now that the exterminators will have to be called in and the building will be filled with the reek of the toxins. And if it kills the vermin, who's to say it won't give you lung cancer or a tumor in your brain?

Sitting there, at the desk, doodling on a pad, he chides himself for fussing and worrying. Vogel is right—he takes things too much to heart. But that's his job, he is paid to worry, and he wonders if it may be time for him to quit and try something else. But what? A taxi he could never handle, and a library would drive him insane. Construction he is too old for. And selling shoes in a department store wouldn't be him. So? Therefore?

He spots an ant moving with cautious deliberation across the wide expanse of the lobby floor. He leaves his chair and takes a closer look. This is an ant on the move. He's left the nest and is exploring, making a journey, the Columbus of his race, crossing the Atlantic of the lobby in search of some new world for the ants to conquer. He watches, following the ant as it travels, and is struck by its daring, out there on the marble floor, alone against the universe. Determination like this is rare, among ants as among humans. For a moment, he thinks of picking the ant up and examining it under a magnifying glass, to see if he might detect in the eyes or the mandibles some clue that would lend an insight into the ant's audacity. But instead, he lifts his foot and steps on the ant with great vigor. His foot, coming down at an awkward slant, twists painfully, and he knows, with a flash of anger and regret, that he will be suffering from this for many days to come. And what, he wonders, would Karl Vogel say about it? Foolish? Careless? Too old to step on ants? Get a grip? Would he pull out one of his oranges and offer it as a cure?

The Persistence of Blue

Come on, my silly Lesbia, let's do it—
because once our small day is over,
an unending sleep folds over us.
So give me a thousand kisses, right now,
and a thousand more—and more!

                    —CATULLUS

About a year after the opera singer, Renata Negri, fell
dead of a brain hemorrhage in her tenth-floor apartment,
Kapri Blorg, the book publisher who lived two floors
below, in the Meriwether Lewis, put a pistol to his head
and pulled the trigger. It was Black Thursday, the day the
stock market spun out of control and went into a nose-
dive. He stood fully dressed in the shower stall, wearing
a white dinner jacket and his newest pair of black shoes.
The shower water was running, and dye from the blue
silk carnation in his lapel ran down all over his jacket.
No one quite understood why he had turned on the
water. Perhaps he expected the noise of the rushing water
would cover the sound of the gunshot, though it was
hard to understand why, at such a moment, that should
have been of any concern to him. Perhaps he was thinking of the children, not wanting them to hear, not wanting
them to live with the sound of the gunshot echoing
through the rest of their lives. But in that case, as even his
wife noted, bitterly, why hadn't he just gone off and done
the deed somewhere else, away from the apartment? She
put him quickly into the ground, and, with the two
children, she quit New York and returned to Vermont,

where she had grown up, and left the apartment in the hands of an agent. The agent worked hard to sell it, but it remained empty for more than a year, because, as was generally known, an apartment tainted by suicide was a hard thing to sell. Death, violent death, had a way of drying up the market.

When a buyer did finally turn up, it was Karl Vogel, who had been a fighter pilot with the Luftwaffe during the war. He had flown the Me-109, and then the Me-262, which was, at the time, the world's first jet fighter deployed for combat. What a plane that was, so fast, the fastest thing in the war. They called it the Schwalbe. In the 1960s, he wrote a book about his war experiences, which was well received, and he was active on the university circuit and on the talk shows. He wasn't tall, barely five and a half feet, and that had been an asset, enabling him to fit comfortably in the cramped cockpits of the fighter planes. Short but good-looking, with piercing blue eyes, a high forehead, firm jaw, and a brisk but friendly manner, the hint of a German accent rippling through everything he said.

He found it remarkable that he, who had shot down so many American and British planes, should be lionized by American audiences. They thrilled to his stories of aerial combat, the shooting, the bombing, the dogfights, and listened with a special delight when he spoke of Hitler as a nitwit and a fool. Still, it wasn't always easy, out there on the circuit. One night, uptown, at City College, a girl, a student with a long braid tumbling over her shoulder and down across her breasts, stands up and asks why he flew for Hitler if he hated him so much. The braid distracts him. He fumbles, meanders. How to explain? You fly for your country, you fly for your home. You do your duty. But how to clarify it for her—how to help her understand? As he stands there, on the platform, groping for words, someone hisses, someone groans. There are people in the audience, elderly people, who had relatives in the camps. They murmur and stamp their feet. A gray-haired woman in a black dress rises, shouting "Nazi! Nazi!" and throws a tomato that splatters against the wall behind him. Someone throws a magazine, and someone throws an egg that breaks on his shoulder. Someone throws a shoe. A security guard moves him quickly backstage and hurries him out of the building, the back way.

"But they're right," Vogel says to the guard. "They're right to hate me. I shot down all those Flying Fortresses. I want to go back—I want to talk to them."

The guard, a husky black man with a puffy face, grabs him by the shoulders and stares down into his eyes, ferociously. "Are you crazy? Where's your car?"

"I came by subway."

"Come on, then." He takes Vogel by the arm, clutching the arm just under the shoulder, and hurries him along, not leaving him until he's down in the subway, on the other side of the turnstile.

All of that was many years ago. Now, in his late sixties, the hint of an accent is still there in his voice, and he is still trim and active, a vigorous walker, though his hair has gone white and he's a trifle slower in his thoughts, with incipient cataracts and none of his own teeth. And, much to his disappointment, he's been forgotten by the media and ignored by the World War II buffs who had fawned over him in the past.

When he moved into the apartment in which Kapri Blorg had committed suicide, he had all of the walls painted blue. For the living room, he selected a bold cerulean that played off nicely against the cornflower blue of the dining room. One of the bathrooms was done in aniline blue, and the other in indicolite. He chose robin's-egg for the foyer, Brunswick for the kitchen, and *bleue lumière* for the master bedroom. For the den he picked a shade of blue so pale as to be almost white, and for the guest bedroom a shade so dark as to be almost black.

It was an odd thing, this persistence of blue, and it wasn't until the painters were gone that he understood, with a surprising immediacy, that it was related to the years he'd spent as a pilot, flying for the Luftwaffe. Day after day he'd been up there in the sky, making it his home, nesting in it, diving out of the sun to make the kill. The war became, eventually, a bitter thing—but at the start, before it all went sour, nothing thrilled him more than to be aloft, banking and weaving, soaring birdlike, with a sense of freedom he'd never felt on the ground. It was a feeling of wholeness, of being in charge of his own time and existence, and the blue of the sky was an intimate part of that feeling. And there was also his awareness of his own mortality, the color blue attaching itself to the knowledge that at any moment he could be shot down and killed. The sense of peril gave him an edge, a fierce alertness as he tangled with the bombers. Days and nights of blue washed over him, rushing through him like a river, noon blue and midnight blue, tired blue and angry blue, and now, fifty years later, when death was again much on his mind, the sky was coming back to him, reasserting itself, pushing up into his consciousness, unfolding the way a blanket unfolds when you pull it out of a drawer where it has been left unused for a very long time.

He'd been born in Pforzheim, on the River Enz, at the edge of the Black Forest. It was a small city of some fifty thousand, with a paper mill, a chemical plant, and many small manufactories where expensive lines of jewelry were crafted and prepared for shipment to the big cities at home and abroad. Karl's father worked not in jewelry but in decorative porcelains, having inherited the business from his father, who had died of a stroke. Karl was three when they buried his grandfather and had only the dimmest recollection of him, but of his own father he had vivid memories—he was tall, taller than Karl would ever be, with blond hair slowly turning gray, and assertive, with vigorous views about everything. He went daily to the factory that he owned on a commercial street close to the railroad and he brought home pads and pencils bearing the company logo, a bird in flight and the name VOGEL in gothic lettering.

150

"We should be in Meissen," Karl's mother said often, "or Dresden. That's where they do porcelains. Here, in Pforzheim, it's all jewelry." She'd been born in Meissen and resented that her husband had brought her to Pforzheim, which she considered a provincial town, with little of any importance going on. She'd been trained as a librarian, and in Karl's earliest years she read to him from the fairy tales of the Brothers Grimm, and many poems, some by Heine, some by Schiller.

At the secondary school, he followed a course of studies designed to prepare him for admission to a university. He was smart, quick, and a good athlete, despite the fact that he was short, and he won his share of medals, though he was not terribly good at throwing the javelin. People moved away when he threw, because he was considered dangerous. Like most of the boys that he schooled with, he was a *Hitlerjugend,* wearing the brown shirt and leather shoulder strap, and the knife with the inscription BLUT UND EHRE.

At thirteen, he was introduced to Latin, which he resisted, but after a slow start, he became deeply fascinated, learning the words and making them his own. *Puer, puella. Amo, amas, amat.* At fourteen he came under the spell of a young classics teacher, Johann Wirklich, tall and brown-haired, with a goatee, who guided him through hundreds of lines of Ovid in the Latin. The part about Daedalus and Icarus was his favorite—the image of Icarus flying with wings that his father had fashioned out of wax and feathers, soaring higher and higher, too close to the sun, and the wax melts and he falls into the sea. He wished it had been a happier ending. The idea of flying, lifting up off the ground and roaming about in the air, was too exciting for such a miserable finish.

And Catullus—him, yes, the best of all, sounding the mood of love.

> *Vivamus, mea Lesbia, atque amemus . . .*
> *nobis cum semel occidit brevis lux,*

151

nox est perpetua una dormienda.
Da mi basia mille, deinde centum;
dein mille altera, dein secunda centum . . .

Yes, yes, he thought, feeling the power of the Latin
words, it's true, so true. Once the sun goes down on your
life, it's over, nothing but unending night, so enjoy it
while you can. Love is the answer—a thousand kisses,
then a thousand more! He was fourteen when he
memorized those lines, and he was hopelessly infatuated
with a girl whose name was Effie. She was blond, with
dark eyebrows, gray-blue eyes, a dimpled chin, and juicy
lips ripe for kissing. She was from Munich, her family
arriving in Pforzheim only two years earlier. He found
her irresistible. They held hands and went for long walks
along the Enz, and sat on an old pier, watching the boats,
gazing across at a low stone house on a hill across the
river. They put their arms around each other and kissed,
long, soulful kisses. They shopped together, buying
sweaters and scarves, and had ice cream at a counter
where the man who served them wore a straw hat and a
peppermint-stripe shirt. They went to the movies, and in
the dark, as they watched Marlene Dietrich and Emil
Jannings, she let him fondle her breasts.

And then, suddenly, she was gone. Her parents hurried
off with her, gone from Pforzheim, and, for all he knew,
gone from Germany. It was 1938, November, right after
Kristallnacht, when there were attacks against the Jews
throughout Germany. Synagogues were burned, people
were beaten and murdered. Effie left a brief note, no
explanation, simply a heartfelt good-bye. "I'm sorry," she
wrote. "So sorry! I shall always love you!"

He was devastated. He asked around, trying to deter-
mine what had happened—where they went, and why.
Why such suddenness? He spoke to her girlfriends, to the
mailman, the greengrocer, to the family above the shop
where her father, a clock maker, had kept his business.
No one knew anything. The mailman shrugged, the
greengrocer shook his head. Finally, it was the Latin

teacher, Johann Wirklich, who told him. They went off, he said, because the mother was Jewish. That, in fact, was why they had left Munich and had come here two years ago—in Munich it was known she was Jewish, but here they managed to keep it a secret. In nearby Dresden, they found a printer who prepared new identity papers for her. But still it was difficult, with the growing violence and the laws against marriage between Gentiles and Jews, and the father, fearful that their secret would be uncovered, decided it was time to leave Germany. The plan was to cross through to Belgium, and from there to England, and perhaps to America.

"How do you know all this?" Karl asked.

"I know," Johann Wirklich replied. "Trust me, I know."

Karl's head was spinning. I'll find her, he thought. Someday, it will happen.

He plunged ever deeper into his schoolwork, reading the *Iliad* in translation and developing an interest in Greek drama, especially Sophocles. And he began to think that he might like to become a teacher, like Wirklich, reading the great authors and passing them along to students in a classroom. Sophocles and Homer, so powerful, he thought of them as vast forests tossed by rain and winter winds, with patches of sunlight filtering through. But already, as he turned fifteen, he understood that teaching was, for him, an unlikely future. The country was at war. Moves had been made in Austria and the Sudetenland, and now there was heavy action in Poland. The world was exploding all around him.

His friends, Otto and Franz, were elated. They couldn't wait to be out of school and into the fighting.

"War is good?" he wondered.

"War is better than a girl in her underwear," Otto said. "Bombs. Artillery. Blitzkrieg. Where the hell you been? Lost in the woods? In your silly *amo, amas, amat*?"

Karl's father, at home, at the dinner table, in the family, expressed considerable unhappiness with Hitler, thinking him bad for business. If he plunged the nation into all-out war, who would be buying porcelains? Or anything else? Only the war industries would prosper. And what would happen to his factory on Güterstrasse? The workers would be recruited for military service, and he would have to shut down. He complained about Hitler and spoke against the Jews too, and the Slavs, though he thought some of the things that were being done were excessive. Burning the synagogues, that wasn't right. And barring the Jews from the parks and the national forests seemed merely ridiculous.

On weekends, when his father's friends visited, there was little talk about Hitler but a great deal of vehemence against the Jews. "Throw them out of Germany," said Hermann Hölle, a neighbor, a man with skinny arms, a long neck, and ears like dead leaves, saying it over and over, a kind of chant, "Get rid of them, rid of them—clean out the stable!" And it made Karl wonder—could the Jews be so terrible? Throw them all out of Germany? Where would you put them? And would they want to go?

And still he thought of Effie, couldn't forget her, he still had feelings for her. Where was she? In England? America? Or had Wirklich merely been making that up? And all the anger and the violence, everywhere now, the marching, the shouting, the torchlight rallies, the broken windows, the rage and the craziness. He saw a gang of toughs throw a bearded Jew to the ground, and they kicked him. He saw two policemen taking tomatoes from a vendor's stand, laughing, throwing them at a Jewish woman passing by, making her run. What was happening? There was a tree where he'd carved a heart with an arrow through it, and their initials, and he went back there and climbed into the branches, all the way up, and looked out across the countryside. It seemed so peaceful, the trees, the steeples, rooftops and open fields, and the winding curve of the river. Such a quiet scene. Hard to believe that under all that serenity there was so much anger and muscle. The push and shove. The cursing and the spitting, and the hissing. And the snorting motorcycles—stay out of the way!

At school, his teachers railed openly against the Jews,

but the classics teacher, Johann Wirklich, was strangely silent. The Jewish issue didn't set him on fire. Some of Karl's friends whispered maliciously that Wirklich was a Jew. But Karl had seen him in church, at the Lutheran service, and when he mentioned that to his friends, they considered it a joke, saying Wirklich was a Jew in disguise. And then, with gleeful malice, they turned on Karl for defending Wirklich and accused him too of being a Jew, chasing after him as he headed home after class.

> Vogel's a Jew, Vogel's a Jew,
> He eats Jewish stew,
> Has Jewish teeth and a Jewish nose
> And his feet are Jewish too!

His closest friend, Willie Stichel, had an uncanny knack with these rhymes, pouring out new ones every day, some of them blatantly obscene, passing them around furtively during class and scribbling them on the lavatory walls. He was taller than Karl, had red hair, a freckled face, long white teeth, and a devilish grin. On the grass by the cinder track, Karl confronted him and punched him in the nose. Willie went down, bleeding profusely, and Karl took out a knife and cut away a lock of hair above Willie's forehead, and Willie had to live with that sign of humiliation until the hair grew in again. It put an end to the rhymes, and to the friendship too, but only briefly, and in a few weeks they were friends again.

A month before they graduated, they sneaked into the school one night and, on the stage in the auditorium, amid the benches, bottles, flasks, stacks of books, and other props, including swastika armbands and swastika flags, all to be used in the annual spring production of Goethe's *Faust*, they sat on the floor and shared a pint of brandy, passing the bottle back and forth, and smoked Turkish cigarettes that Willie had filched from his uncle. The brandy warmed them, making them heady, and they sang all the verses of the Horst Wessel song, screeching and groaning, making it sound as wretched as they could, because they hated it, this song written by Horst Wessel, a young SA leader, murdered in a Berlin slum and considered, now, a Nazi martyr.

> *Raise high the flags! Stand rank*
> *on rank together!*
> *Storm troopers march with*
> *steady, quiet tread!*

As they sang, they threw darts at a picture of Adolf Hitler. It was a large poster, black and white, five feet high, showing the face of Adolf Hitler at a moment when he was delivering one of his wildly impassioned speeches. Only the face, in close-up. The nose, jaw, moustache, the piercing eyes, light reflecting off the forehead, and the mouth open, a gaping black hole. One could almost hear the fierce, angry words raging from the darkness of that hole. The poster was mounted on thick cardboard and had been left standing against a wall, waiting to be hung. They threw darts at the eyes, the nose, the teeth. Then, inspired by the brandy, Willie Stichel went up to the picture, removed the darts and tossed them aside, and, dropping his pants, rubbed his groin rapturously into the Führer's open mouth. He writhed and moaned, breathing heavily, and Karl stood amazed, watching as Willie's hips pumped into the picture, as if the black hole were a real mouth into which he had inserted his organ. Then, drawing back from the mouth but still facing it, a few feet away, he wriggled wildly and launched a heavy flow of semen, great globs of it spurting out, all over Hitler's face. He hovered for a moment, legs and buttocks twitching, and then, perfunctorily, grabbed a flag and wiped himself off, and pulled up his pants.

"They'll throw us out of school," Karl said. "We won't graduate."

"Who'll tell? You?"

"Me?" Karl said. "No—not me."

"Then what's the problem," Willie said. He looked at

Hitler, whose eyes were smeared with oozing slathers of jism. "Him? He'll tell? He can't see a thing. And besides, he enjoyed it!"

The war had leaped forward with astonishing speed. The invasion of Poland in September of '39, and then, in the following spring, the blitzkrieg attacks into Denmark, Norway, and the low countries, climaxing in the flight of the British at Dunkirk in May, and the occupation of Paris in June. It was riveting, the movements of large armies and the swift victories. The invasion of England failed to materialize, but in the spring of '41 there were victories in the Balkans, and then, in June, the launching of the second front, in Russia. Slogans and watchwords swirled dizzily: *Lebensraum . . . Drang nach Osten . . . Ein Reich, Ein Volk, Ein Führer . . . Juden raus . . . Der Übermensch . . . Tausendjährige Reich . . . Sieg Heil! Heil Hitler!* The history teacher, who, many months ago, had been hit in his left buttock by a javelin Karl had thrown, wrote in bold letters on the blackboard: WAR IS THE GREAT PURIFIER. He read passages from Hegel and Nietzsche, warning of the dangers of peace and extolling the virtues of war. He read from *Mein Kampf*: "Mankind has grown great in eternal struggle . . . The stronger must dominate and not blend with the weaker . . . Those who want to live, let them fight, and, in this world of eternal struggle, those who do not want to fight do not deserve to exist!"

In the spring of 1942, when the class graduated, they all went into military service. Willie Stichel, after playing the wiliest, sauciest, most lecherous Mephistopheles the school had ever seen, went into artillery, and another friend, Otto Verrückt, went into submarines. Karl chose the air force, not knowing exactly why. It simply seemed the right place for him. The thought of fighting on the ground, in mud and rain, part of a herd that groped through thickets and scrambled up hills, dodging artillery shells and small-arms fire, none of that appealed to him. It seemed a darkness, a primitive ugliness from which he recoiled as from a bad dream. But when he thought of combat in the air, it seemed to him there was a cleanness in it, a freshness, a clarifying simplicity.

They trained him to fly the Messerschmitt 109, and he and the plane seemed made for each other. At the start, he'd been uncertain, thinking he would never make the grade. But very soon he found that flying came easy for him, and his instructors saw it at once—he had a knack and a freedom in the air, climbing and diving, looping and weaving. Maneuvers that others struggled to learn seemed no problem for him. Closing on a target, he had, at forty meters, a deadly eye.

He was eighteen when he went into training, and still eighteen when he saw his first combat in France. He flew against the British bombers that came in the night and the American bombers that came in the day. The war had been good, with the victories in Poland and the lowlands and North Africa—but suddenly, toward the end of '42, when he was commissioned as a flight officer, there were reversals, and in 1943 there were major losses. In January, the Sixth Army was crushed at Stalingrad, and in May, the army in North Africa surrendered, and soon afterward the Allies were in Italy. And the bombers, now, were striking hard into Germany, hitting Schweinfurt, Regensburg, Hamburg, Berlin. His squadron was shuffled around, sent in to meet the pressure points.

Over Hamburg, he shot down three B-17s and four British Lancasters. Over Ploesti, he knocked down two B-24s. In the months of battle in the sky over Berlin, he accounted for nineteen Lancasters and seven Flying Fortresses. The bombers were easy prey, but the fighters that accompanied them, coming in relays to protect the bombers, were harder to deal with. Early on, a Spitfire had shot up his tail section, but he brought the plane down safely. Later, over Germany, a Mustang shot off one of his wings, and, falling in a slow spin, he managed to climb out of the cockpit and parachute down. He flew and flew, some days going up five or six times—down to refuel and reload, then up again. He was exhausted. The war in the sky, which had begun with such zest and excitement, was now filled with dreariness and fatigue, and loneliness. Too many were being killed. He saw planes—flown by people he knew, people he'd eaten with, smoked with and joked with, and been drunk with—exploding in the air, or veering over and plunging, blowing up on the ground, and he was sure he would soon be one of them. Where was Willie, he wondered. Where were Otto and Franz? Effie was a blur. He hoped, deeply hoped, that she was far off, away from all this. And he began to understand that she was simply an event in his past, and it was pointless to think of the future because all there was now was the field where you took off and the field you flew home to, and the things you wore in the cockpit, your boots, your pants, your shirt, your flying jacket and the leather helmet, and tomorrow was a bad joke you didn't want to think about. At the porcelain factory in Pforzheim, the only workers now were women and old men, as his father had predicted. And who, these days, was buying porcelain?

In his apartment at Echo Terrace, on a pedestal in the living room, he keeps a statue of Venus, dating from the first century A.D. It's the most precious thing he owns, something he found in an antiques shop in Oranienburg, in the final year of the war. The legs are gone and one arm is missing, but the torso and head are intact, and, even in its mutilated form, there is an aura of perfection—the face, the midriff, the breasts, and the slender neck and delicately formed ears, the white marble not stony or hard but warm, seeming soft and alive. He had lugged it with him to the many places where he lived—all the way to America, to New Mexico, Nebraska, California, and now, in his retirement, to New York. She was beauty, sex, fertility, and who among the gods was more deserving of worship? He remembers the words of Lucretius that Wirklich had made them memorize—Venus, the delight of gods and men, wandering across the seas and mountains, putting passion and desire into the hearts of all creatures. Without her, nothing joyous, no new life, nothing coming forth into the light of day.

But where was she in those awful years of the fighting? Where was joy and daylight, and desire? And the heart, where was it? The hearts of all creatures.

In the massive confusion when the war came to an end, he made his way back to the town he grew up in, Pforzheim, and saw the destruction there, wrecked houses, bomb craters, shattered streets. More than three-fourths of the city was gone—it had happened in a single raid in February, a storm of bombs falling, destroying churches, homes, the jewelry shops, the chemical plant, the paper mill, the factory where they made radios. Both of his parents were killed that night, though he hadn't learned of it until weeks later, and he was still numb from the loss. The house he'd grown up in was gone. Effie's house too, and the shop where her father had made clocks out of oak and walnut. It was springtime, flowers pushing up from the debris. And the factory on Güterstrasse, his father's place, a heap of rubble. And the bakery where he'd gone with Effie for pastries. The streets they had walked on, and the movie house where, in the back row, he had put his arm around her and they kissed. He felt a bitterness, a sour taste rising inside him. So much devastation, the roots and vines of his past torn away, blasted out of existence.

But the school was still there, the secondary school, untouched by the bombs, empty, unused for years. He found an unlocked door and went in, it was all dust and cobwebs. Pictures of Hitler still hung in every room. He found the room where he'd studied Latin under Johann Wirklich—the desk that he sat at, in the third row, with the initials he'd carved, his own and Effie's. The blackboard on which Wirklich wrote the verses of Catullus and Horace that they had to memorize. A stick of chalk on the ledge, and an eraser. A map of ancient Rome filling the back wall.

He walked the debris-laden streets, and on the steps of a house on Wolfsbergallee, he found the history teacher, Hans Stumpf, who had been the leader of the *Hitlerjugend* at the school. Just sitting there, in a daze, staring emptily at the bombed-out row of houses across the street. He was in a torn army jacket, his face covered by a growth of beard. One of his arms was gone. Karl spoke to him, but Stumpf had no idea who he was and didn't seem to care. He'd been in the tough fighting in the east. He had shot two Russians, he said, before a grenade took his arm off.

He was broken, worn out, yet there was a lingering feistiness in his eyes. When Karl asked him about the Latin teacher, Johann Wirklich, Stumpf twisted his face and let out a sardonic laugh. "Wirklich," he said, "that sly one, Wirklich." He'd been caught fooling around with a young boy, corrupting his morals, and was arrested. For that, and for painting anti-Nazi slogans on the brick walls of the police station. He was sent to a work camp and died there. "Sanctimonious bastard! Diddling a boy! A mere boy!" He clucked giddily, madly, and Karl allowed himself to think the man crazy, and his story a lie.

Karl left him, and he left Germany. There was nothing there for him. All he knew about was flying, and the Luftwaffe was defunct. He went to the Americans, and when he told them he had flown the jet fighter, the Schwalbe, the Me-262, they wanted him. They flew him to England, then on to New York, and then to a base in New Mexico, and he gave them everything he knew about the Schwalbe, how it handled, how it performed under battle conditions, the rate of climb, the speed in a dive. They used him as a consultant for several months, then they offered him a position as a test pilot, but he didn't want it. He was burnt out. His feeling, at the time, was that he never wanted to fly again.

"Think about it," they said. "Take your time. You've had a long war."

A month later, after wandering around New Mexico, trying to figure out his life, he went back to them, and they took him on. But instead of using him on the new jets that were coming along, they put him into helicopters, about which he knew nothing. They were tricky, and he crashed quite a few. Once he went into a lake, and another time into a tree. He crashed into a mountain, and a week later he collided with a barn, which burst into flames, and he was several months in a hospital, recovering from the burns. When he healed, they took him out of helicopters and put him into the new bomber, the B-52. He crashed one of those too and spent more time in the hospital, this time with his leg in traction. And it was there that he met a nurse, Lucille, a girl from Abilene, and he married her. And that was good, really good. They were a match, they got along and they were right for each other. In the years that they had together, they fumbled through the usual squabbles and disagreements, but they mended and bonded, and he couldn't have asked for better. But she had hated the marble Venus, thinking it a silly, broken thing, one arm off at the shoulder, the other with a chipped elbow, both legs gone—and what was so pretty about her anyway? In the places where they lived, she pushed it off, keeping it half hidden in dark corners, where it could hardly be seen.

The Bench by the River

When you move to a place like Echo Terrace, fifteen stories high, you don't get to know everyone, not right away, and probably never will. That's what he thinks, Karl Vogel. Like Theo Tattafruge, he's been there three years. He knows Tattafruge, knows Maggie Sowle, knows young Abdul Saad, who wants to be a mortician. And Nora Abernooth, in the hospital. He doesn't know the Sandbars, the Krutterhouses, the Klongdorfs, the Coyles. Should he? Must he? He's tired. The board members he knows, but would rather not, he didn't vote for them. The heavy one, Rumfarm, in investments, getting richer by the day, and the one with the moustache, Noelli, in shoes. And Knatchbull who made it in plumbing supplies and ships toilet bowls to Spain, and has this annoying kid that hits all the buttons on the elevator, making it stop at every floor. Takes you all day to get to the mail room.

Sometimes, simply for the exercise, he uses the stairs, up and down. But today, a Monday, on his way out for his morning walk, he takes the elevator, and on the way down he's with Aki Sato, who is so rich, this Japanese merchant, he owns the entire seventh floor, keeps live-in help, and owns a house in Tokyo as well. Karl figures he's seventy at least, probably older, and lucky too, a pretty girl with him, young, with gray eyes and auburn hair.

He nods, and Aki Sato responds with a nod of his own. "Your daughter?" he asks facetiously, with unkind intent, conscious that it would have taken nothing less than a genetic miracle for Aki Sato to have produced this Aryan beauty.

"My protégée," Aki Sato answers tersely.

"Ah, yes," Karl responds, nodding again, thinking protégée indeed. The girl stares straight ahead at the elevator door, as if Vogel weren't even there.

"A good day for flying," Aki Sato says, referring obliquely to Vogel's days in the Luftwaffe.

"And a fine day for sailing," Karl answers, remembering that Aki Sato had shipped with the Imperial Navy.

They had met before, at a New Year's gathering for the residents, but only briefly, long enough to learn that they'd both been in the war. Karl felt no inclination to know anything more about him than he already did, and he had a strong sense that the feeling was mutual. Their only encounters now are these random moments on the elevator and in the lobby.

When the elevator doors slide open, Karl steps into the lobby but hangs back, slipping on his blue windbreaker and watching as Aki Sato and the girl go through the glass doors and approach the chauffeured car at the curb.

Not bad, he thinks, catching a last glimpse of the girl as she disappears into the Lincoln. And what he feels, as the car pulls away, is a muted sense of desire, jealousy, resentment—but, stronger than any of these, a good feeling, better than he's had for days, a sense of uplift, because only now, from this short ride on the elevator, has he become aware that, short as he may be, he's a shade taller than Aki Sato, and that has to count for something.

One night, late, a few months ago, browsing through the channels, he saw himself on television. It was an interview—a portion of an interview—that he'd given some fifteen years ago. The recent war in the Gulf, pushing the Iraqi army out of Kuwait, had stimulated a renewed interest in World War II, and the producers were digging into old interviews and splicing them together into new formats. The interviewer, a woman, was asking about fear—had he ever thought he might not survive? And he watched, seeing himself as a stranger, on screen, himself but not himself, responding briskly.

"The fear, yes, but I didn't dwell on that," he said. "I was too engrossed, too involved in what I was doing. There was a rush of adrenaline, everything intensely focused. It was kill or be killed, and if you thought of anything else, you might well be a loser."

It was odd to hear himself say that. Other things that he'd said, qualifying things, had been cut, and there was only this bald hardness, yielding the impression of a cold, unfeeling killer. Could that be me, he wondered. Is that who I am?

Soon afterward, there was again a flurry of interest in him, requests coming from journalists wanting to hear his story. He was, after all, an ace, he had shot down more than ninety planes. And he was, too, an antique, a rare item, a survivor from the long-ago war. One of a dying breed, fewer and fewer of them still around. The calls came in, but he turned them down, wanting no part of these hungry young journalists. I'm in vogue, he thought, with some amusement. Back in style. Fifteen, twenty years ago, they all wanted me, then they forgot me. Now they're after me again. And he noted, whimsically, and sadly, that it was all a matter of fashion, with people as with clothes, and with just about everything else. Fashion rules, and he'd had enough of it, and didn't want to be part of it again.

Then, only yesterday, returning from a morning stroll along the river, he sees Farro Fescu giving him a signal—someone's waiting for him. He glances about and there she is on the couch by the palm tree, dark blue pants flared at the bottom, and the matching jacket folded on one of the chairs. Her blouse is white, plain, with half-sleeves and blue buttons, and as he steps toward her, she rises, greeting him warmly. "I've been waiting for you," she says, as if she's known him for years. Her hair is dark and full, pulled back over her left ear, and, on a silver chain, a sapphire pendant, dipping down toward her breasts.

He places her in her early to mid-thirties, fleshy in the arms and face but still with a fine figure, and, to his eye, not at all unattractive. Her name is Anna—Anna Harte. Lovely, in her way, and with an obvious charm, but not exactly his type, he thinks, even if he were young enough for her. Still, she's caught his eye.

She writes for a national magazine and is planning a series on veterans, which will develop, she expects, into a book. She's already interviewed a colonel who led a tank column under Patton, and a U-boat commander who sank fourteen freighters in the Atlantic. And she's just returned from Yokohama, where she met with a Japanese kamikaze pilot who suffers, yet, from a guilt complex because the war ended before he had a chance to fly his mission.

Karl thinks of Aki Sato, who dates back to Pearl Harbor, and is about to mention him, but doesn't, because, disliking him as he does, he isn't eager to share her with him. And recognizes, with hidden amusement, that he suddenly feels he doesn't want to share her with anyone.

"Would you like that," she asks. "To be in a book?"

"But I'm already in a book," he answers. "In two. And I'm working on the third."

"And it's wonderful, what you've published," she says, floating a rapturous smile, "or I wouldn't be here. But this—this is different. In your books, it's you writing about your experience—but this now, it's somebody else writing about you, and it brings a whole different dimension, another angle. And it will actually enhance what you've written."

"Well," he says, "the truth is, I'm losing confidence in books. In Germany, when I was a boy, they burned the books, and the students loved it. They burned Sigmund Freud—did you know? And your famous Jack London, and that blind girl, Helen Keller."

"But that was Hitler," she says. "Hitler is dead."

He raises an eyebrow. "You don't think he's in South America, planning a comeback?"

She smiles at the fantasy. If Hitler were alive, he'd be over a hundred.

They sit on the sofa, her briefcase between them, and he quickly understands, from the things she says, that she's done her homework well. She knows where and when he was born, where he flew, and what units he had belonged to. She knows of his youthful fascination with the Roman poets, and the names of his high school friends who died in the war, Otto, and Franz, and Willie Stichel. Like so many who had come before her, she has a bagful of facts—names, numbers, and dates—and it bothers him that the particulars of his life, even some of the intimate details that he's never discussed in his books, are available to anyone, and with those facts a clever writer can construct an image that seems alive, walking and talking, singing and dancing, as if it were you. But the facts are not you, there is always so much that is left out. The inner doubt, the uncertainty, the unspoken dreams, the confusion. The darkness.

He glances slyly. "I suppose you know, do you, what color toilet paper I use?"

"No," she says, smiling, "but I will when you tell me. Will you? Tell me?"

"You should be so lucky," he says, flashing a sardonic grin.

"You live alone?"

"I do, and I enjoy my privacy."

"There's no one in your life?"

"My wife died long ago. But surely you know that."

She does. "I'm sorry," she says, "sorry about your wife. Tell me about her."

He draws back, surprised by the question, and resenting it. His marriage to Lucille is a matter of record, but in his books and articles, and in the interviews, this was a part of his life that he never discussed, feeling it was too private, too precious—not wanting to commercialize it. Not wanting to put it out there as if it were a piece of merchandise.

But now, to his surprise, he finds himself opening the door ever so slightly, saying things, a few things, and then more. "She was from Abilene, a Texas girl. A nurse. I met her in the Carlsbad hospital, that time I broke my leg. In my test-flying days." He hesitates, hovers. But, having come this far, he goes on with it, about the cancer that brought her down, and the radiation therapy that seemed to help, but then, on a Saturday, he lost her. She was thirty-two when she died. He was thirty-five. It was that long ago. Nine years of marriage they had, but no children, though they'd tried. Nevertheless, it was a good life for them, he says. They saw movies, played cards, hiked, they rode horses. She liked pickles on her hamburgers, and onions in her scrambled eggs. And popcorn with plenty of salt and butter. But she didn't like the part about not having a child, and she wanted to adopt, but he wasn't comfortable about that. Even this he's telling, even this, it's pouring out of him. And when he finally came around and said yes, we'll adopt, it was too late, because that was when they found out about the cancer.

What am I telling, he wonders, trying to hold back, trying to stop. Is it old age doing this? Senility? Talking now about the traveling they'd done, to the canyons, and up to Canada, and to Hawaii once. It was good money he made, test-flying the new machines they rolled out for him. Up to Yellowstone they went, and many times to Vegas. She enjoyed the slots, and blackjack, she got a kick out of gambling. Telling too of the time in Tucson, in a classy motel, they peeled the sheet back and there was this jumbo-size scorpion in the bed, and Lucille screamed and ran to the car in her night clothes. Why am I saying this? Why? And when he crashed the jet that he was testing for the navy, she was so mad at him, wanting him to quit—angry with him, because he made her worry so much. Right there in the hospital—scolding him, and he all bandaged up, unable to say a word, and she vowing that she would divorce him if he didn't quit. And it wasn't long afterward that they found out about the sickness spreading inside her.

Then he stops, quiet, thoughtful, leaning forward, hands clasped together, remembering, gazing down at the white marble floor with veins of blue and gold running through. And above them, the spreading foliage of the palm like a green cloud, and he is half expecting rain.

She tries to lure him back. "Have you eaten? May I take you out to lunch?"

He never takes lunch, he says. "Very rarely."

"But you'll make an exception?"

He purses his lips. "Not today," he answers, putting her off.

"Tomorrow," she suggests, aware that she's losing him.

"I'll be busy," he says, which isn't entirely true.

"Wednesday?"

He looks at her bluntly. "You need more? It isn't enough, what I gave you?"

"Much more. I'm putting a lot of energy into this piece."

"Wednesday, then," he says, and as she rises to leave, he sees something wonderful in her eyes, a kindness, sincerity, a quiet longing. She wears only one ring, a garnet, on the small finger of her right hand. And those interesting eyes. He wonders if she's ever been married, but doesn't ask.

On Wednesday, at one, they meet in the lobby, and he brings her to a nearby eatery on South End, next to the food market. They sit at a table by a window, people on the street stepping along at a quick pace. She orders the elkburger, and he takes the shrimp, which are served on a bed of mixed lettuce leaves. She has a tape recorder, but he won't allow her to use it.

"You're making it hard," she says.

"Life is hard," he answers.

"I'll take notes," she says, drawing a yellow pad from her black nylon carryall.

"What can I tell you that you don't already know," he wonders, lifting a shrimp with his fingers and dipping it in the sauce in a small side dish.

"You were a flier," she says. "An ace. You must have had many women?"

"That's what your readers want to know? Look—I shot down over ninety planes. Men died. And you want my sex life?"

"Well—anything," she says, backing off, reaching for the ketchup but deciding against and using, instead, a generous dose of salt. "Do you keep a dog? A cat?"

"Not even a bird. I had a parakeet once, but it was such a messy thing, I opened a window and encouraged it to fly off. It wouldn't. Many days I went through this ritual, opening the window, telling it to go. Finally, I took it in my hands and threw it out. And then, when it was out there, flying, it seemed very pleased with itself. It never came back."

"Tell me about your father," she says.

He doesn't want to talk about his father and speaks instead about his mother. She had red hair, that's what he remembers most. When he left for the war, her hair was still beautiful, not a strand of gray in it. She read poetry, and he recalls how she sat by the window with her books. She worked at the local library, two days a week, but she would have preferred being a teacher. "I felt bad for her. Few, very few, get what they want out of life."

"Did you find what you wanted?"

He glances at the remaining shrimp on his plate. "I hardly know," he says. "What do I want? What does anyone want?"

There is something about her that draws him out. She is easy to talk to—precise in her questions—yet there is also a vagueness about her, a welcoming softness. If he were younger, he thinks the two of them might have made quite a pair.

Through the window he notices the sun is gone and there's a threat of rain. An ambulance rushes by, and a police car.

She wants to see his apartment, but he isn't keen about that.

"How can I write about you if I don't see how you live?"

"You want to dig out all of my secrets?"

"I want to see your Venus," she says.

"You know about that?"

"I know a lot of things."

"You frighten me," he says, taking his credit card out of his wallet.

"Sometimes I frighten myself," she answers. She insists on paying, and she does.

Two days later, a Friday, they meet at midafternoon, and he brings her to his favorite bench on the walkway that runs along the river. Behind them, where they sit, there are low plantings of juniper and other evergreens, and young maple and locust trees. Across the river it's Jersey City, with Hoboken and Weehawken spreading to the far right. Directly across is the big Colgate clock, facing New York, the hands and hours in black against a white background. It has always puzzled him why a company famous for toothpaste should have such a pronounced interest in time. Off to the left are the Statue of Liberty and Ellis Island, and, farther left, a low hump of land rising from the water, a portion of Staten Island.

"Tell me where you flew," she says.

"But you know all that."

"Tell me anyway. I want to hear it from you."

"Poland I was too young for," he says, leaning forward, elbows on his knees, lacing his fingers together. Several yachts are on the water, one with its sails up. "I was still in school when they blitzkrieged all the way to Warsaw. The London Blitz, the same. I wasn't into the action until 1942. I flew in France, and after that I was raiding Malta from Sicily. When Rommel was in trouble after Alamein, they put me in North Africa, and when the Eastern front collapsed, they sent me to Russia. Always they were moving me around, back and forth."

"You liked it?"

"The flying? I reveled in it. I was good. Sharp. But in the end, you know, when it turned sour, it was a bitter time. I was twenty-one when the war ended, but already, I think, I was an old man."

"When did it go bad for you?"

"When the cities were burning and it was clear the war was lost. They had me up day and night. They put me in the new plane, the jet fighter, the Schwalbe, and that was exciting, yes, flying that plane. I shot down many bombers with it. But it meant nothing, because the bombers kept coming. I blamed Hitler, hated him for keeping the war going, and hated the British and the Americans for all the death and destruction. And I hated myself for just being alive."

She wants to take his picture—she carries a camera with her, in the carryall, an Olympus. She always takes her own photographs to accompany her stories. She wants him to pose by the railing, with the Statue of Liberty in the distance, but he declines.

"No pictures," he says.

"How can I do a story without pictures? I always use pictures."

"No," he insists.

"You're a hard man. You know that? Do you?"

"I have a right," he says. "When you lose a war, you gain certain privileges."

"If you had won, Hitler would have ruled Europe."

"That megalomaniac," he says. "That idiot corporal. I was happy when he shot himself. But still, you know, it hurts to think that I risked my life, day and night, and it was for nothing. A waste. Can you understand that? My life—that part of it—was meaningless. I killed the wrong people. But they were killing my people, the German people, so what choice did I have? You see? It's a vicious circle. I've never been able to sort it out."

They are still on the bench, in the sun. It's the very end of October, but the day is warm. She has taken off her jacket, and he's unzipped his windbreaker, letting it hang open. Two gulls hover low over the water, then sweep away, toward New Jersey. Far to the right, an empty freighter, high in the water, is coming

172

downriver. They hear the drumming of its engines.

"You're an interesting man," she says, with a slow, inviting glance. "I like you." And then she surprises him. Moving close on the bench, she touches a hand to his face, and kisses him on the mouth. It's a quiet, dreamy moment, all the more special for being so unexpected. He puts his arms around her in an embrace and feels her warmth, her breasts pressing against his chest. It's a long time since he's been with a woman, and he has almost forgotten what it was like. The softness, the tenderness.

"What are we doing?" he asks.

"Don't you know?"

"You're seducing me. But I'm too old for this."

The freighter, large and gray, with rust on its hull, passes in front of them, moving with a powerful slowness.

"Last week," she says, "for a few days, I followed you. That's how I work, I have to know who I'm writing about. How you walk, how you dress, where you go. You went to supper at the Brauhaus on Third, and I followed you in and sat at a corner table. You ordered the sauerbraten, and halfway through you had a horrible fit of coughing. You never noticed me?"

He studies her, trying to remember. "You spied on me?"

"I do it for a living. That's what we are. We're all spies, aren't we?" Then he's holding her again, and they're kissing, not with a fierce passion but gently, with a restrained eagerness, as if young again, at the beginning of everything, learning the art of the kiss for the first time and needing nothing more. Lips touching lips, subtly sensuous, pleading, wanting, puckering and rumpling, pressing close. Sitting there, on the bench, he feels that's all she wants, the kissing and the holding, and for the moment it's all he wants too.

A red speedboat comes along, off to their left, the high whine of its engine cutting the air like a buzzsaw. Fast, knifing through the water. A one-seater, the person at the wheel wearing a yellow life vest. When the boat hits

173

the first wave in the wake of the freighter, the front end rises high out of the water, as if riding up a ramp, and thumps down on the other side, and the same again with the second wave and the third, a wild ride, up and down, the boat leaping and thumping, never cutting its speed. Then, on the fourth wave, it all goes bad, the boat hitting the wave at a wrong angle, twisting as it rises into the air and coming down on its side, capsizing. There is a slow moment, the boat resting upside down on the water. Then it slips away and goes under, nothing there, just a lazy swirl on the surface. Then, a moment later, the yellow life vest breaks through the surface, bobbing around out there, a yellow spot on the water.

They're both up, off the bench and leaning against the black rail, watching. She's troubled, distraught.

"Isn't there something we should do?"

He rolls his shoulders, loosening the tightness. "They already know. They know everything that happens on the river."

And in a moment they see, to their right, a police launch breaking from shore and speeding toward the yellow life vest. An officer on the launch tosses a life preserver, and, after some cautious maneuvering, they pull the man aboard.

Vogel shrugs. "See? It was destiny his boat should sink, and destiny that he would survive. Good luck to him. There will be times when he will wish he had drowned."

"Destiny?" She grabs at the word, as if it were a clue, a key. "You believe in destiny?"

"Actually," he says, still watching the launch, "I don't. Destiny suggests some sort of plan—a purpose, a design. But life, I think, is mere craziness." He turns, looking at her with great intensity. "Do you know about the madness? I'll tell you. I've seen it, too much of it." He puts his hand on the back of his neck, briefly, as if touching a pain there. "Long ago, before the war, in 1938, there was an ugly night, they called it *Kristallnacht*. People were beaten, raped, killed. Do you know of it?"

She does, but faintly.

"It started because of this boy, Herschel Grynszpan," he says. "He was seventeen, a German Jew living as a refugee in Paris. His father was picked up and sent to Poland, to one of the camps, and the boy, wanting revenge, took a gun and went to the German embassy, intending to kill the ambassador. But by mistake he killed, instead, the third secretary, Ernst vom Rath. And here is the kicker—not only had vom Rath never been an anti-Semite, but the Gestapo actually had him under investigation because of his anti-Nazi sentiments." He claps his hands together and laughs. "Isn't it delicious? How do you like that for crazy? Life is ironic. There is no limit to the idiocy."

And then he tells her the worst of it—how Berlin bent the Grynszpan story to its own purpose and launched a pogrom. In retaliation for the death of vom Rath, Jewish homes were ransacked and burned, and the synagogues too. Thousands of shops were looted. Jews were raped and murdered in the street. A lot of glass was broken, and that was why they called it *Kristallnacht.*

"I was fourteen years old. My father, who felt no kindness toward the Jews, was shaken. I remember him saying that this time things had gone too far. And the interesting thing was that the Nazi bosses put on a show of being high-minded. They expelled from the party the ones who committed rape, because sexual intercourse with Jews was forbidden by the racial laws. But the ones who did the killing were sent home with a handshake and a pat on the back. See? See how madness prevails? It has a logic all its own, its own cranky rationale. In such a world, the wrong people are assassinated."

"I'm hungry," she says, taking her jacket and slipping it on.

He puts his face close to hers. "How can you be hungry? A man nearly drowns, and I tell you about *Kristallnacht.* Bad news makes you hungry? We'll go to a shop and eat donuts."

But she has to return to the magazine. There are things to do, phone calls, more work on another article she is busy with. "I hate donuts," she says, and hangs there a moment, her eyes lingering on his. And then, with a whimsical shrug, she turns and walks off.

And as she goes, he watches. The firm motion of her legs, the blue jacket snug to her waist, the black nylon carryall hanging from her left shoulder. The swing of her hips, and her ravishing dark hair alive in the sun. Why do I want this, he wonders, with a vague shiver of gratitude. At my age? Do I need this? Do I? Do I deserve it?

The Mournful Sound
of the Train,
Folding Over Him

They meet again two days later and they stroll by the river, watching the river traffic, a few tugboats pulling barges. She had him talking again about his youth, his early years in Pforzheim, by the Black Forest. He had never seen Hitler, not even once, only in the newsreels. Göring, in charge of the Luftwaffe, he'd seen three times—a fat, self-important man, pompous in his powder-blue uniform, with his silly baton studded with diamonds. This was the man who'd been a hero, a flying ace, in the First World War, but then he became entangled with Hitler, and what a mess.

They walk and walk, leisurely, the air brisk but the afternoon sun warming them. They reach the World Trade Center and sit a while in the plaza, by the fountain. Then back, along the walkway by the river, back toward Echo Terrace. And then, against his better judgment, he brings her up to his apartment.

In the living room, he shows her the Venus that he'd come upon during the last year of the war, in a shop in Oranienburg, when everything fell apart and you could buy things with cigarettes, with a half pound of coffee, or a pair of nylon stockings. The antique marble, yellow with age, glows warmly. An arm was broken off, both legs gone, but the head and torso remain undamaged, alive with feeling. The man who sold it to him said he had picked it up in Ephesus.

"Isn't she remarkable?" he says. "The lines, the slope of the shoulders. She's the only god I worship anymore. It must have been an incredible time when the gods came down and mingled with the mortals."

She walks around the statue, seeing it front and back. It stands by a window, on an oak pedestal, the legs cut off above the knees, halfway up the thighs. "But they caused so much trouble, the gods."

"True, true—yet they brought pleasure too. Zeus himself, think of it, disguised as a swan, making love to Leda."

She turns, glancing at him over her shoulder, an odd, slanting look. "I'm not sure I'd really fancy that—sex with a swan."

She touches the statue's face, running her fingers across the cheek, the lips, the chin, down the neck and across the breasts, and again he notices only the one ring, the garnet set in silver.

"You never married?"

"Oh—marriage. Yes, I did. Long ago, and it ended long ago too. He wasn't a bird of paradise. More, I'd say, like a porcupine."

"And you?" he says, eyeing her whimsically. "What's the truth about you? Are you one of the immortals, from Mount Olympus, or just a girl from Brooklyn?"

She lifts her head coyly. "That," she says, "will remain my secret. All my own."

He puts up a pot of coffee, then brings her to another room in the apartment, a bedroom converted into a hobby room, and shows her what he had never mentioned in any of the interviews. His trains. They are model trains made in prewar Germany, by the Bing company, very like a set of trains his father had bought for him when he was young, at Christmastime, with markings on the cars, VIEH and SCHAFE and MILCH and PETROLEUM, sliding doors on the boxcars, and lanterns hanging from the caboose, the locomotive throwing an intense beam from the headlamp, and the mournful sound of the whistle. And rare too, not many of these had survived the war. He found this set in a catchall junk shop in Omaha, after he had stopped with the test-flying and was traveling as a consultant for Northrop.

The trains are on a large tabletop that a carpenter had made for him, filling most of the room—the tracks running through a papier-mâché landscape ornamented with miniature railroad stations, trees, houses, churches with steeples. There are lights in the houses and blinking signals at the railroad crossings, and tiny automobiles at the crossings.

He turns a knob, and the locomotive sets out on its journey, drawing the long train of cars, moving through straight runs and turns, over a bridge, through a tunnel, and past a small Alpine village.

"See?" he says. "See?" The trains brought him back to his childhood, to his father, that extraordinary time of life when so many moods and feelings were opening up for him, when everything seemed ripe with promise, before the war broke everything apart.

"The trains," she says.

"Yes, the trains."

"Boxcars," she says. And the way she says it, he understands what she means, that the Jews had been put in boxcars when they were transported to the camps.

But he doesn't, at the moment, want to think about that. "These are my toys," he says. "They give me pleasure when I'm tired. Don't spoil it for me."

"Boxcars," she says again. "You knew? You knew what they were doing?"

"Of course I knew. Everyone knew. They were relocating the Jews, putting them in the camps. The Slavs and the Gypsies too, and others who were considered undesirable. But the other camps—the extermination camps—I didn't know about those until the end of 1943. It was Hitler's madness. Hitler and Himmler."

"It made no difference to you?"

"Of course it did. But still I had to fly, didn't I?"

He turns off the switch, stopping the trains, and they return to the kitchen, where he pours the coffee into large mugs and opens a can of almonds. Then, leading the way through the living room, he brings her onto the terrace, where there is a view of the river.

"At first," he says, "I didn't believe, I dismissed it as enemy propaganda. The stories were too fantastic. But then, when people, reliable people, told me it was true, I did what the others did, I set up a partition in my mind. What Hitler and Himmler did, the Gestapo, the SS, that was their own perversion, I wasn't part of that. When I flew against the bombers, I flew to protect the German people. My own people—my mother and father. The bombing was terrible. Cologne was devastated. And in Hamburg, the firestorm—fifty thousand dead. We had a word for it, we called it the *Katastrophe*. In a firestorm, the streets catch fire, and the heat creates hundred-mile-an-hour winds that tear up everything. In the shelters, people die of suffocation. If I shot down one plane with its load of bombs, I was saving lives on the ground. But in the end, I couldn't save my own parents. One night, in February, the British sent their Lancasters, and one of the bombs hit the house where they lived. They were killed, just like that," he says, snapping his fingers. "It was the house I grew up in. The town itself, Pforzheim, was demolished, thousands killed. Why? Tell me. It was the jewelry center of Germany. They bombed people who made bracelets and gold watches. The war was winding down, almost over. This was the same month they bombed Dresden, that beautiful city."

He falls silent, and for a long while they sit motionless on the wrought-iron chairs, gazing at the river. A tugboat passes, hauling a barge loaded with bricks. A white yacht motors upriver. High in the air, nearby, a seagull hovers, then it moves closer, and it settles on the railing. They watch it in silence—the head, the beak, the legs, the feathers gray and white. Eventually it flies off, catching a thermal, sailing on a long arc down toward the river, and they're up now, leaning against the railing, watching its descent.

When it's gone, out of sight, she turns toward him, and again they are kissing.

"I want to be good to you," she says.

"Why?"

"Must there be a reason?"

"There is always a reason."

She puts her hand to his mouth, not wanting him to talk. Then, withdrawing her hand, she touches her lips to his and leans against him and they linger a long time. That was all it was, the kissing, the clinging. She seemed satisfied with that, and so was he.

There are things that he hasn't told her, many things, which he doesn't speak about not because he wants to keep them hidden but because they were long ago and too complicated and strange, difficult to explain. One of the things he never told her was that toward the end of the war, during the Ardennes offensive, in deepest winter, something snapped inside him, and his mind went into a downward spiral. He got hold of a bottle of whiskey, took to his bed, and refused to fly anymore. For a whole week he stayed in his quarters, his radio tuned to a station that played old love songs, and when the others went up, he remained behind, on the ground. After the first bottle, he located another, the whiskey lifting him, tilting him into moods of defiance he hadn't imagined himself capable of. What could they do to him? Shoot him? He to whom they had given the Knight's Cross with Oak Leaves and Swords? The way the war was going, he would be dead soon enough anyway.

His squadron leader pleaded with him, and the base commander cursed him roundly. The Lutheran chaplain knelt by his bed and prayed, and when he was done praying, he helped himself to the bottle, finishing it off, then left and returned with another. They drank, and the chaplain sang his favorite hymn, "Come to Calvary's Holy Mountain." The squadron leader stopped in, and he too drank, and so did the base commander, who came with a bottle of twenty-year-old Scotch the British had left behind at Dunkirk, on the beach, when they evacuated mainland Europe in 1940.

The next morning, wobbly and disoriented after so much drinking and too little sleep, Karl left his quarters wearing only his pajamas and his flying boots, and a scarf around his neck. He climbed onto the tail section of his plane and urinated on the swastika that was painted on the rudder. It was so cold, his urine merged with the film of ice on the metal, leaving a yellow smear on the swastika. Half the squadron saw him do this, along with the squadron leader and the commander—but not the chaplain, who had walked off the base and was still walking, on his way home to Hamburg, which didn't exist anymore, most of it, because it had been leveled in the saturation bombing.

After breakfast, when Karl returned to his quarters, the base commander went to him and talked to him about the new plane, the Messerschmitt 262. It was the first jet fighter in the war, and his for the asking. A transfer to Oberstleutnant Niemand's group could be arranged, JG-7, where they had the 262s. "It's the fastest plane ever, you'll love it, it hums like a Dresden whore when you give it to her backwards. They went operational last October. Knocking down a hundred bombers a month!"

It was a generous offer, yet Karl understood that the base commander was not doing him a kindness—he was merely trying to get rid of him because he had become an embarrassment.

"No," he said.

"It's powered by two jet engines," the base commander said. "It flies faster than the wind."

Karl was unresponsive.

"I'll throw in a promotion. Go to Niemand, at Achmer, and you'll be a Major. You'll like that, won't you? No longer a mere *Hauptmann*. Welcome to the higher ranks!"

"I don't think so," Karl said. He was on his bed, his head propped up by three pillows, still in his pajamas and still with the flying boots on his feet. "There has to be—something," the base commander said, and Karl saw in his eyes, and heard in his tone, that he was begging.

His face was twisted, as if Karl were a canker sore that was driving him out of his mind.

"Something, yes, there is something," Karl said.

"What?"

Still on the bed, Karl grabbed a scrap of paper from the floor and wrote Effie's name. "Find her," he said, passing the paper to the base commander.

"You're joking."

"Find her."

"The country is in pieces. You think I, an *Oberst* in the Luftwaffe, can go to the Gestapo and get a straight answer from them? Or from anyone?"

"Then forget it," Karl said, putting his hand on a bottle of cough medicine he'd liberated from the pharmacy, because, that morning, he'd been unable to locate any more whiskey.

The commander's face swelled with rage. "No—I won't forget it," he roared. "I'll do it. I will. But there won't be an answer today. Or tomorrow. Or next week. Or next month. I'll do it—but first you go to Achmer and report to Niemand."

Karl didn't trust the base commander as far as he could throw him. "How about another bottle of the twenty-year-old stuff?" he said.

"And you'll go?"

"Make it two."

"Agreed," the base commander said, and left for his office to arrange the transfer.

Karl put on his clothes, gathered his things, picked up his new orders and the two bottles from the commander's aide—the commander refusing, now, to see him or bid him farewell—and by the end of the day, having hitched a ride with a supply truck, he was all the way to Achmer, where JG-7 was based, with the 262s. Achmer was the perfect place for them, lying athwart the main approach route used by the Flying Fortresses as they crossed into Germany.

He trained for a week, learning the ins and outs of the new plane, its moods and subtleties. It had searing speed, close to five hundred and fifty miles an hour—more than a hundred miles faster than anything else in the sky. Four cannons in the nose, and two Jumo turbojet engines, each with two thousand pounds of thrust. It could climb to twenty thousand feet in six minutes and soar beyond that, up to seven miles high. He loved that plane. It was a fantasy, a leap beyond anything else in the war. Fast, so fast, beautiful to fly and beautiful to watch from the ground. They called it the Schwalbe—the swallow.

The 262s were lethal against the bombers, but hard too on the pilots who flew them. More went down from pilot error and mechanical failure than from enemy fire. When Karl reported to Niemand, it was the last day of January, cold, and Niemand, sitting in his office with a fur hat on his head, warned him of the risk. "It's a hell of a plane," he said, "but it's cranky and it will yank your nuggets in the lower altitudes. Don't get killed."

"I won't," he answered, surprised by his own confidence.

Three days later, it was Niemand who was killed. Karl watched from the ground as his plane went out of control and crashed into a wooded area and burned. Niemand was replaced by Schnuller, who crashed into the squadron's fuel depot, touching off a round of explosions that destroyed three 262s and a 109 that were parked nearby. Schnuller was replaced by Major Axel Schutz, who didn't crash but was arrested by the SS and shot for complicity in the July 20 attempt on Hitler's life. In the general chaos that prevailed, it was no longer clear exactly what complicity might mean. If you were somebody's cousin, that could make you guilty, and Schutz had many cousins. The execution took place in the open, on the airfield, a warning for any other Luftwaffe officers whose thoughts might be running along treasonous lines. At dinner, after the three o'clock execution, what the pilots expressed among themselves was a certain surprise that Schutz had stuck his neck out as he had, for he'd seemed, to most of them, a man without a political thought in his head. Surely the SS had shot the wrong man. Nevertheless, they preferred to think that Schutz was the right man, because it seemed an honor to have served under a squadron leader who'd had the guts to put his life on the line in a plot to kill Hitler. And they felt a special pride in the fact that he'd escaped detection until now, long after most of the conspirators had been rounded up and butchered. They began to think of him not as the stupid man they knew him to be but as a genius of subterfuge, stealthy, cunning, a hero of the fatherland, a knight, a prodigy, a saint, a martyr.

After Schutz, they had Oberstleutnant Sinzer, who stayed alive for a while. He was lean and leathery, with a bony forehead, a slack jaw, and smoky eyes that looked as if they had come straight from hell. In the air, in his cockpit, he stared across at Karl, in his cockpit, and Karl stared back. They disliked each other, and they did so with great intensity. There was no reason in it, it was instinctive. Karl was short, Sinzer was tall. Sinzer was from the north, near the Baltic, and Karl was from the south, between the Rhine and the Danube. Karl had blue eyes, Sinzer had brown. Sinzer liked butter on his toast, cream in his coffee, mustard on his wieners, and girls with thick legs and plump bottoms. Karl liked his coffee black, and his women slim. Sinzer had the Knight's Cross, but Karl, younger and only a *Major*, had the Knight's Cross with Oak Leaves and Swords, and Sinzer never forgave him.

Once, on the way home, cruising after hitting the bombers, Karl was bounced by a Mustang, cannon fire blazing past him, inches away from his cockpit. He turned on the speed, evading, but had a hard time of it, the Mustang putting a patter of machine-gun fire into his wings. The 262 spun out of control, losing altitude, but after a few harrowing moments, Karl pulled the plane out of its dizzy plunge and, circling in a wide arc, came up above and behind the Mustang. But he was out of ammo, and the Mustang, which may also have been dry, lit out, vanishing into the safety of a cloud that stretched out for miles like a long gray sleeve. And all the while, Sinzer had been right there, circling at a distance. But he did nothing, no help at all.

On the ground, when Karl confronted him, all Sinzer said was, "I just wanted to see how good you are."

After the failure of the Ardennes offensive in January, it was perfectly clear that the war was lost. By the end of February, the Americans and British reached the Rhine, and less than a month later, they held the entire west bank and were pouring across the Rhine in two places. The Russians were plunging ahead from the east, sweeping across Poland, and it was only a matter of time before Berlin would be overrun. Karl thought, occasionally, of the base commander who had negotiated the transfer to Achmer—he had promised to locate Effie, but the day after Karl's transfer, he was blown to pieces during a night bombing-run by British Lancasters.

For the 262s, it was a losing battle, and they all knew it. There was a crescendo in the air war, streams of bombers filling the sky, huge caravans of a thousand and more. What if you knocked down ten? Or twenty? Or a hundred? There were still all those others dropping their bombs. Every time Karl went up now, he felt impotent, little more than a pesky fly buzzing around the hindquarters of a gigantic elephant.

As the Americans and British advanced from the west, the squadron abandoned Achmer, moving to Parchim and Oranienburg. But this only brought them closer to the Russians, who were advancing from the east. And still they flew, answering the alarm when radar spotted the incoming bombers, and Karl was as sharp as ever.

In the few months that he flew the Schwalbe, he scored more shootdowns than in all of his previous flying time. When Major Schutz was still alive, before the SS shot him, he was so impressed by Karl's performance that he recommended him for the Knight's Cross with Diamonds, sending up the recommendation a few hours before the SS dragged him out of his office. For one reason or another, the medal never came down from Luftwaffe Command, and Karl never forgot that, feeling a ripple of bitterness whenever he thought of it.

The long winter had been a nightmare, and April was

worse, a taste of hell. The British were sweeping toward Bremen and Hamburg, and the Americans surrounded Field Marshal Model's armies in the Ruhr. On the eleventh, an American unit reached the Elbe. So? What to do? Move east? Move west? Destroy the planes and surrender to the Americans? Wait to be bombed off the face of the earth?

On the afternoon of April 30, in the bunker in Berlin, Hitler shot himself. On the following day, at ten in the evening, a radio station operating from the ruins of Hamburg announced that the Führer was dead, and played Bruckner's Seventh Symphony. Karl was in the rec room when the announcement was made. Some were playing cards, some writing letters, a few throwing darts. Almost everyone was drinking and smoking.

Karl, by a lamp, was browsing again through the Roman poets, the same collection he'd used when he studied under Wirklich. He was tired, eyelids drooping, the Latin lines easing him toward sleep. When the brief announcement came over the radio, scratchy, interrupted by static, nobody said a thing. The pilots sat in a spongy silence, the lugubrious tones of the Bruckner symphony oozing over them like engine grease. Then, quickly, they were themselves again, the ones with the darts throwing at the target, the ones with beer lifting their glasses. And Karl, drowsy, wishing Hitler had passed from the scene long ago, turned the page, going on to the next poem by Catullus, the one about Lesbia's sparrow, but before he was half through, his head sagged and he floated off in a dream. He was at home, in bed, in the house on Pelikanstrasse. The railroad ran through town, and as he lay there in the dark, he could hear the train rumbling across the tracks, and then the whistle, a dreary, mournful sound that folded over him, wrapping itself around him, enclosing him as in a cocoon, and the steady chug-chugging of the wheels on the rails.

He was awakened from his dream by Sinzer's aide, standing over him and tapping him on the shoulder. "He wants you," he said. "Right away."

"Now?"

"Now."

Groggily, Karl closed his book and left the rec room, making his way across the field to Sinzer's office. There was a mild chill in the night air, the full moon painting the trees and the hangars with a pasty light. The aide didn't accompany him, going instead to his quarters and turning in for the night.

In his drowsiness, Karl was thinking hopeful things. Maybe his medal had come through, the Knight's Cross with Diamonds, recommended by Schutz. Yes? Could be? Or perhaps they were moving to Austria, to elude the approaching armies. Or better yet, Sinzer wanted him to supervise the destruction of the planes, and then they would surrender to the Americans. But that, he knew, was too much to hope for.

Sinzer was at his desk, which was cleared, not a paper on it. His jacket was open, his glasses off, his eyes smokier than ever, a strange and troubling expression on his face.

"You've heard about the Führer?" he asked.

Karl nodded that he had.

"A great man," Sinzer said.

Karl didn't answer.

"We never saw eye to eye, you and I. True?"

"True," Karl answered.

"You do despise me, don't you?"

"Only if you think so."

"I do think so. Yes. Indeed I do. And I despise you," he added. "Make no mistake about that. And because I dislike you so much, that's why I summoned you."

He opened a drawer, took out his service pistol, and waved it about loosely. Karl felt the floor shifting, sliding away from under him.

"I want you to see this," Sinzer said. "I want you to imprint it on your memory and have nightmares about it the rest of your useless life."

Swiftly, he swung the gun around and put the barrel in his mouth, and, leaning forward over the desk, he pulled the trigger. The bullet exploded through the back of his skull, spraying blood and brain matter high on the wall behind him.

Karl stood trembling in front of the desk, the report of the gun ringing in his ears. Sinzer was crumpled forward on the desk, his head blown open, thin rivulets of blood running slowly down the wall. Bending close, Karl studied the wound, a mess of blood and hair and bone and tissue. This is what we are, he thought, staring into the dead brain. This is where it begins and ends. A few hours earlier he'd seen Sinzer at supper, eating what they all ate, potatoes and canned meat. Now his head was on the desk, and the meat was still in his belly. He wanted to touch him. All hatred gone. Poor man. Poor senseless fool. Not having to worry anymore about the Americans, the Russians, the bombers, the fuel supply. He reached out, to touch the shoulder, but his hand pulled back, and he looked again at the wound, a splinter of white skull sticking up out of the morass. Life was so dear, so precious, yet in the end it was so cheap. He left the office and walked out onto the field, into the night, and kept walking, to the end of the field and onto a road. The road led to another road, and still he went, numb, not wanting to think. Hitler was dead, and Sinzer was dead. The war was lost, but it had been lost a long time ago, and now it would go on for a while until someone figured out how to stop it. The moon halfway up the sky, chalky white. A cat crossed the road. A dog howled. The sudden wail of distant sirens, and the long finger of a search beam probing the sky for enemy planes. It was not until he saw a sign for Hanover, a hundred kilometers away, that he realized he was walking south, and it was then that he understood where he was going. He was heading home, all the way to Pforzheim, pushing on as if in a dream, and, one way or another, he would get there. There were buildings he remembered, steeples and bridges, the school where he had studied Latin, and he was thinking home, home, and he could taste the memory. But that, he understood, was all it was, a memory, because the house he grew up in had been bombed, and his parents were dead. He knew all of that, but it hadn't yet fully sunk in. He was making his way into a past that no longer existed.

All of that, so much of it, far off, and he doesn't tell Anna about any of it. Nothing about that day in January when he stood in the cold and did the unthinkable, urinated on a swastika, and instead of punishing him they promoted him and gave him the new plane, the Schwalbe. And nothing about that sad, desperate creature, Sinzer, who made him watch as he put a pistol in his mouth and blew out his brains. Those and other things. How could he? The memories too painful, too layered with darkness, and how to pull them up and find words for them? How do you explain a dream at the point where it turns from good into bad and runs downhill into a nightmare?

The morning after that Sunday afternoon when he brought her up to his apartment and they kissed on the terrace, he calls and invites her to dinner, but she declines, she's too busy, swamped with work for the magazine. A day goes by, two days, and when he does see her again, it's past noon, and they take the short walk down into Battery Park. They buy hot dogs from a vendor and find a bench by one of the memorials. Where they sit, they don't see the water, they see trees, sycamores, and the plaques with the names inscribed on them, the names of wireless operators who went down at sea, many hundreds of names. And the sparrows, the pigeons, people on a path, and on the grass, going this way and that, and squirrels up in the trees.

And as they sit there, with the hot dogs and the coffee, he tells her about the girl he was in love with when he was a boy in school—Effie, sweet, young, irresistible Effie, with her vivacious smile, the blond hair and gray-blue eyes, the one whose mother was Jewish, but only the family knew. And Effie's father, who was not Jewish, had tried to take them out of Germany before their secret became known.

"I was infatuated," he says. "Bewitched. It was delicious! She was Jewish and I didn't know—but even if I had known, it would have made no difference to me. My father would have gone berserk, of course, but he would have come around."

"Young love," she says, lifting her coffee mug. "So innocent, gushing with hormones."

"Don't be cynical," he says.

"I didn't mean it cynically. Hormones are a gift."

"I looked and looked," he says, "asking everyone who might have known. But nothing. If anyone knew where they'd gone, they weren't saying. Even later, when I was flying, I made inquiries. I worried they might have been sent to one of the camps."

He hasn't touched the hot dog. He takes a sip of the coffee.

"In some ways," he says, "you remind me of her. Not the hair, she was blond. Something in the manner, the temperament—the way you move your hands when you talk."

"I'm not fifteen," she says, with a wry smile.

"I know."

"Not Jewish, and not in Nazi Germany. Does that make me more desirable, or less?"

"It makes you an enigma. Why are you writing this story about me? I was an ace, true, one of the *Experten*, but there are many who had more interesting lives."

He takes a bite of the hot dog, then sets it down, on the bench, on the wrapper. She has finished hers and has torn open a bag of chips.

"You're disappointed with your life?"

"I wouldn't say disappointed. Perplexed, possibly. Skeptical. Curious."

"You're not eating."

He shrugs, waves a hand vaguely. "About disappointment. Look—I don't go often to church, but when I do, I go to Grace, on Seventy-first, and I sing the old Lutheran hymns. 'O Lord, Look Down from Heaven,' and 'Jesus, Refuge for the Weary.' I try to recapture the old confidence, but it seems, somehow, to have slipped away."

"You still think of her," she says. "You never found her?"

"Sometimes it's better not to find what you're looking for."

She purses her lips, neither agreeing nor disagreeing.

"But I did find her father," he says. "He was killed in one of the camps, at Mauthausen. After the war, when the records became available, I searched the lists, and there, at Mauthausen, I found his name. It was one of the smaller camps, they didn't have the gas chambers and crematoria that they had at Treblinka and Auschwitz. At Auschwitz, you know, at the height, they gassed six thousand a day. It boggles the imagination. At Mauthausen, they just took them out and shot them. That's what they did to Effie's father. He was a clock maker. They threw him in a camp, and killed him because he'd married a Jew and tried to take her out of the country."

The list of the dead at Mauthausen—the *Totenbuch*—contained some thirty-five thousand names, but it was, he found out, incomplete. At Nuremberg, the camp commandant, Franz Ziereis, admitted that the total was more like sixty-five thousand. It was possible that Effie and her mother had been there with the father and had simply not been listed.

"But I prefer to think that they escaped the horror and fled Europe," he says.

"Perhaps they did."

"California," he says. "I like to imagine that when the father was picked up, Effie and her mother somehow slipped through. All the way to San Diego, or Santa Barbara. That would be good, if she is still alive out there, in the sun, among the orange trees. That's what I wish for her."

The following day, and the day after that, they don't meet, and he's glad about that. He needs space, time, separation, a few days to absorb and digest what is happening between them. Better, he thinks, not to see her for a while. Several days pass, some rain, some sun, and then, on a Monday, she finds him again, in the lobby, after his morning walk, and they go down to the river and sit on his favorite bench, by the black iron railing. The day is overcast, clouds stretched across the sky like gray laundry. A few gulls wheeling lazily, hovering over the water, mewing eerily. The big clock across the river is lost in mist.

"Were you at Schweinfurt?" she asks.

He's silent, thinking back, pulling it up from the shadowy places of memory. "Yes, yes," he says, recalling. "The Americans were going for the ball-bearing plants. I remember that. Over two hundred bombers they sent, B-17s. August, the middle of August. In 1943. They did a lot of damage, hitting the plants, but we knocked down many bombers. It was catastrophic for them. Ten men in a bomber—think of it. And then, in October, they tried again. Sixty bombers we destroyed that day. I shot down four myself."

"October fourteenth," she says, naming the date.

"You know about this?"

"It was the day my grandfather was killed."

"He was there? At Schweinfurt?"

"In a B-17."

"How terrible."

"My father was four years old. He remembered when they received the news, how his mother cried. Weeks and weeks, she wept."

"You knew," he says. "You knew I was there at Schweinfurt."

"Yes."

"That's why you sought me out."

"Yes."

"I didn't kill your grandfather," he says.

"How can you know?"

"I know it. There are some things you simply know."

"But you were there," she says. "Even if you weren't the one, you were there."

193

"And you blame me."

"No," she says, drawing back, "I don't blame you."

"But you do. That's why you're here, because of your grandfather."

"I had to see you and get to know you, I don't know why. You lived, he didn't. I had to see for myself what kind of a person you are."

"It was the war that killed him," he says.

"No," she says. "It was someone in a plane, shooting at him. That's what killed him."

Layers of mist hang above the river, and he understands now how different they are, he and Anna, the way they think, the way they feel. For him, the killing had nothing personal in it. It was simply the war. If he were to take it personally, how could he live with it, the burden of all those lives, the ones that he killed? War is a thing, a process, a momentum, a madness that doesn't explain itself. That's how he thinks of it, and, seeing it that way, he's been able to accept it and live with it.

But for her, it's all personal, and that's why she has sought him out. She is making peace with the enemy. Closing the loop, as it were. And for him this is a disappointment, because he'd thought her interest in him was for himself alone, uncomplicated by extraneous reasons. And he'd even begun to think, foolishly, that their relationship was something that might take root and last, longer than mere weeks or months.

But it was the grandfather. She carries a wound and she needs to heal. And he respects that, honors and admires it. Still, he is tired of the war, and tired too of the ones who, so many years later, are still bleeding from it. And here they are, the two of them, on the bench by the river, in the thickening fog, and he knows that somehow, through him, she is connecting with her grandfather, whom she has seen in photographs but has never known. It's her grandfather that she is in love with.

He puts his arm around her shoulder and she leans into him, and they sit that way a long time, watching the gulls diving through the mist. Across the river, the shore is wrapped in fog, and off to the left, Liberty Island is fog-bound too. And they sit there, silent, not talking, in this gray space by the river, locked together in the groaning of foghorns and the mewing of the gulls.

The next day, in his mailbox, there is a note from her, not sent through the mail but delivered by hand, telling him she is on her way to Somalia. Her editor wants a story on the drought there—the political anarchy and the famine, people starving to death, shipments of food from the relief agencies not getting through to the ones who need them.

A ripple of resentment wanders around inside him. Why couldn't she have told him this herself, if only over the phone? Why had it been necessary to do it in a note? He holds the small sheet of pink paper, the handwriting clear but hurried, and this, he knows, is the last of her. He will, in all likelihood, never see her again. He feels a stab of pain, and even some anger, but also a sense of relief, because why, after all, at his age, had he been fooling around like this, kissing on a park bench a woman half his age, who blamed him for killing her grandfather? Could he really have been that fatuous?

He goes up to his apartment and putters around for a while, stacking old newspapers, cleaning the kitchen. And then he goes to the room where the trains are. He's thinking of his high school friends. Willie Stichel, killed on a road just south of Brunswick. And Otto Verrückt, who went down in a U-boat in the North Atlantic, and Franz Albern, blown to pieces by a shell from a howitzer soon after the Normandy invasion. There were others—a boy named Lumpig, who was put in charge of one of the death camps, and Ludwig Hosen, who was among the first to be executed during the purge that followed the July attempt on Hitler's life in '44. When Karl first heard news of the failed plot, how he wished it had succeeded! That sour, puffy-faced goblin, destroying Germany and leading it into ruin. The punishments after the failed coup were swift and vicious. Hosen, with whom Karl had

195

once played a game of chess, was strung up on a meat hook with a noose of piano wire around his neck.

The room with the trains is dark, the window covered over, keeping out the sun. The only lights are from the layout itself, from the trains, the houses, the miniature lampposts. He works the controls and wonders about Effie. Is she in one of the mass graves at Mauthausen, or, through some fanciful twist of fate, is she alive and well, eating plums in California? So good, if that were true. So wonderful! And Anna flying to Somalia, how that rankles. Yet he wishes her well, hopes she will have only good things. But her sudden departure has taken his breath away, and, in his disappointment, he doubts he will ever see her again. And that saddens him, leaves him feeling adrift. Disoriented.

He turns a knob and moves the train faster, the locomotive pulling a long string of cars, a coal car, an oil tanker, a flatcar, cattle cars, and boxcars in many colors, with sliding doors and black wheels. Behind the locomotive, a tender with a mournful whistle, and at the tail end, a fancy caboose with lights and lanterns. He sends the train across bridges, past trees and houses, schools and parking lots. He throws the switches, shifting the train from one track to another. In the darkened room, in the dim light from the houses and steeples, the boxcars seem loaded with people, heavy with them, the ones being transported, bodies packed inside, no room to move an arm, a leg. He presses a button, sounding the whistle, and in the low moan he hears the drift of their misery as they pass into the long tunnel. It was sorrow and more than sorrow, a lingering despair. Again he sounds the whistle, the foggy, forlorn sound, and still he hears them, the ones in the boxcars, the terrible echo of their grief, and it requires all of his attention to slow the train at the turns and keep it from running off the track.

The Return
of Renata Negri

At the desk, in an idle moment, Farro Fescu is thinking about importance—what is of value and what is not. Is life important? Death? Time and memory? Dream? Is Luther Rumfarm important? He with a smile as fake as a paper flower and a nose that would make a good paperweight? And Mrs. Wax with her bichon frisé that took best-of-breed at the Westminster last year, is she worthy of notice? And what is importance anyway? Does it have a scent, an odor? Can it be touched? Can it be put under a microscope and examined in its separate parts?

He thinks of Nora Abernooth in the hospital, in her coma, and her niece from California, the only relative, who flew back and forth during the summer, taking care of her aunt's affairs. So worried, going again and again to the hospital. And now she is here, living in her aunt's apartment, having made the move late last October. Angela. A pretty girl, trying to make it as an actress. Is she important? And the dying aunt? Are the sun and the moon significant? And the far stars at the edge of the universe, which have been photographed in living color and shown on the evening news? Vogel's bad back—is that of consequence? Mrs. Marriocci's arthritis? Harry Falcon's cancer?

And Yesenia, the housemaid on Oscar's cleaning crew, raped on the subway. Never went to the hospital for a scraping, and now, foolish girl, she's pregnant, and won't have an abortion because it's against her religion. In such manner does life tumble along. What if the baby grows up to look like the rapist-father, same eyes, same face, same evil bent in the brain? How will she live with that? And Abdul Saad, studying to become an undertaker—is that meaningful? A bright young man, but such a morbid choice. A life of funerals. Driving his father crazy. His father rich in the spice trade, but him, the son, he chooses death. And Mrs. Sowle, who makes quilts—she too. Important? Rare? Someone to notice?

In the morning, before breakfast, he puts himself on the floor and does ten push-ups. At night, before flopping into bed, another ten. That's his exercise for the day. Occasionally, on a weekend, a long walk. He eats lightly. A small breakfast, a banana and some cereal, a sandwich for lunch. Supper is a fried cutlet or a chop, and beets from a can. Frozen peas. He's plump on ice cream, that's his vice, this little paunch that he's growing, another notch in the belt. Pistachio, chocolate fluff, vanilla snuggle laced with honey.

When the lobby becomes dreary and boredom sets in, he rides the elevators. Up and down on the east, then up and down on the west. He likes the sensation of near weightlessness as the elevator, rising to the top, comes to a sudden stop. He feels it in his gut, his organs still floating ever so briefly even though the elevator has quit. Good for the arteries, he thinks. Good for something. To be in motion, up and down, down and up. The hum of the machine. Sometimes a dozen times, then back to the desk.

On the holidays, he comes in extra early and works the lobby. Having no family of his own, no wife, no children, rather than sit alone in his Seward Park co-op at the corner of Grand and Clinton, he hangs out at the desk, greeting the residents as they come and go. Answering the phone, fetching cabs, taking deliveries of cakes and flowers. And that's what he is doing now—Thanksgiving Day—a gray morning, the street wet from an early rain, the lobby buzzing with activity. Some rushing off to grab a good viewing spot for the parade—the Knatchbulls and their boy, the Dillhoppers, Mrs. Wax and her daughter—

and others setting out on long drives to visit friends or family. The Rumfarms to Scranton, the Saads to Greenwich, the Klongdorfs to Philadelphia. Vogel goes for his usual long walk by the river, and Juanita Blaize, with her pink hair and two Dalmatians, taxis to the downtown heliport. Rabbi Ravijohn gropes stiffly into his Audi, going God knows where.

Usually, for Farro Fescu, this is a stimulating time—but today, as the lobby traffic thins, he sits pensive at the desk, troubled by what he learned only a few days ago about Renata Negri, the opera singer who had lived here at Echo Terrace, on the tenth floor. What a splendid woman she was, vital and saucy, winking at him as she passed through the lobby, blowing kisses, making him feel that there was, between them, a subterranean emotion, an unspoken sense of connection. And that's why the information that reached him only days ago— from a doorman who knew a chauffeur who knew a maid who knew a makeup assistant at the City Opera—is so upsetting.

It's been five years since Renata Negri died, that long ago, from a cerebral hemorrhage, and only now has he learned that in the final year of her life she was having an affair with the book publisher, Kapri Blorg, who was living at the time on the eighth floor, with his family. He put out cookbooks, almanacs, and how-to manuals, but specialized in pornography, which he published in great abundance—women with dogs, men with sheep, women with women, men with boys, pubescent girls, other men.

For Farro Fescu, it's too painful. If he'd heard that Renata Negri had been sleeping with Pavarotti or Domingo, or José Carreras, he would have understood, and would have been happy for her. But to bed down with someone so second-rate, a sleaze who made his money selling pictures of women and men exhibiting their genitals—it was a disappointment, and even, in a way, an affront. The only small comfort is that Blorg himself is dead, shot himself at home, in the shower stall, when the stock market plunged. But this? This is comfort?

Five busy years since her death, and still his memory of her is so vivid. Her black hair and eager hazel eyes, and her thick, fleshy body, top-heavy because of her wonderfully ample breasts. Yet how nimbly she angled across the lobby, from the elevator to the front door, in her silk dresses and high heels, and so whimsical, the way she would purse her lips and coyly wink at him. She of the gleaming, miraculous voice, treating them, at a Christmas Eve celebration in the lobby, to a few arias, singing by the tall Douglas fir that he had decorated with his own hands, with ornaments from Bloomingdale's. She gave them a few moments of Puccini, a morsel from Verdi, a small excitement from Rossini, and finished with a heartrending "Silent Night," flavored by her lilting Maltese accent. And two weeks later she was dead, having just turned forty-two.

But Kapri Blorg? Him? That lump? That seedy merchant of flesh? If him, Farro Fescu thinks, then why not me? She could have had me! And only then, as this thought erupts into consciousness, does he realize that all this time, these many years, in a mysterious and hidden way that he can hardly understand, he has been in love with her and haunted by her ghost. And it's this new knowledge, about her affair with Kapri Blorg, that has brought all of these feelings to the surface, desire and bitterness, passion, need, and a terrible sense of the futility of human longing.

For days now, she's been alive in his mind. He's tried to put her out of his thoughts but can't. She looms and hovers, urgently present. Again and again he tries to shut her out, but the more he resists, the more she imposes, filling him with cravings that can never be satisfied. What has he done to deserve this? To be punished this way, strapped with such feeling for someone gone and unreachable.

It's a phase, he tells himself. A passing weakness. It isn't love, or passion, nothing so grand, merely a deception. A confusion in the glands.

By the clock in the lobby, on the high marble wall

where the doors to the elevators open, it's ten minutes to nine. Half of the residents have gone on their way, the other half are settling in. Vogel is still out on his marathon walk and won't be back for another hour. No mail today. No cleaning crew. And Farro Fescu sits at the desk, remembering, and trying to forget.

With an odd suddenness, the doors of the east elevator snap open, and when he looks up, it's as if lightning has pierced his brain. It's her—Renata Negri—coming from the elevator and stepping toward him, crossing the marble floor. Her thick black hair like black fire, her face, lips, and the bold, saucy eyes with a kind of laughter in them. She herself! Her! But how? The sound of her high heels clicking on the marble, and the swish of her garments, and in a moment she will be near, with her perfume, passing him as she goes for the front door—in a moment she will wink, and in a moment she will put her hand to her lips and toss a kiss. It's too much for him. He breaks into a sweat and hears his heart thumping like a drum.

Then, blurry, his eyes begin to refocus—and, of course, it was a delusion. What's wrong with me, he wonders. What's happening? The woman approaching, on her way to the door, is not Renata Negri but Mrs. Marriocci, in her red vinyl coat, blue pants touching the tops of her heavy brown shoes, and a flamboyant knit scarf thrown carelessly around her neck. An umbrella under her arm, because the sky is so threatening. Looking at her, he's embarrassed with himself, amazed that imagination could so easily distort what he saw. Mrs. Marriocci's hair is not black but light, colored a pale shade of blond, and wispy, in disarray. And even in his disturbed state, he can't resist thinking she should try another hairdresser.

He manages a smile. "You're going to the parade?"

"No," she answers. "Just up to the corner, for some aspirin."

He opens a drawer, rummages briefly, and comes up with a bottle of Bufferin.

She shakes her head. "I use Aleve," she says.

He shrugs. She answers with a shrug of her own and goes out the door, and what he knows now, more than anything, is that he has to get a grip on himself. He takes a deep breath and, coming out from behind the desk, goes to the door and steps outside, breathing the moist November air. He looks to the left, toward the river, gulls wheeling in the mist, then turns and looks to the right, up the block, where Mrs. Marriocci is making her way toward the convenience store on South End.

But now, again, it isn't Mrs. Marriocci that he sees but Renata Negri—and again he is flushed with delight, seeing her, the jaunty stride, wide hips, black hair bouncing off her shoulders, moving away from him, far up the block. And as he watches, he hears a church bell, not a bell from the neighborhood but something from long ago, a bell he remembers from the village where he grew up, in the Balkans. The sound fills him with a good feeling, as if he were young, before the war, before his grandfather and his uncle Grigor were killed in the bombing. And still he watches, far up the block, his eyes on Renata Negri, studying her every move. Such a woman, such charm. So much energy and vigor, and such finesse. And now, gracefully, she lifts her arms, a lazy, sweeping motion, and rises up off the ground, walking on air. He is not surprised by this. It seems completely natural that she should leave the ground and lift toward the sky. He needs her, wants to run to her, but doesn't, because he knows there is nothing there, only a phantasm, a trick in his brain, and he stands rooted, watching as she rises, high up, above the buildings—glad for her and grateful for this moment, watching until she slips into the low clouds and fades, and the street is empty, and he's alone. The bell that he heard has stopped ringing. He hadn't noticed just when it stopped, but it's gone, and now nothing, only the rumble of a helicopter, and a distant siren flattening out, thin and gray, like the sky.

He goes inside, back to the desk, and, wishing he had a pint of whiskey, he opens the Bufferin and swallows two tablets, and another two, then he goes to the men's room and runs the hot water, warming his hands, only now aware of how cold it had been out there on the street. Letting the water run and thinking, as the steam rises toward his face, that the ants that had infested the building are finally gone, and this, yes, is good. As the mice before them are gone. But what will come next? Worms? Moths? Lice? Microorganisms so small they are invisible to the eye, entering through the nose and the pores of the skin?

Think positive, he tells himself, returning to the desk. Hope for the best. But why? Why live in delusion? Better, he thinks, to be on the alert, ready for whatever comes, for when, and who, and how, and wherever. Better a feet-on-the-ground realism than to live in a mirage. And he is thinking too of the crack in the subbasement, wondering if it has grown much since he last saw it, deeper and wider, and perhaps it is now so large he could fall into it and, God help him, disappear.

The front door swings open and Abdul Saad, returning from a trek to who knows where, drags himself in and slumps across the lobby toward the east elevator. Looking tired, worn. Depressed. Studying too hard, and for what? To bury the dead? He too, Farro Fescu thinks, he could fall into the crack in the subbasement and vanish, and perhaps be better off. But that isn't what he says. "Sometimes," he says, as Abdul waits for the elevator, "sometimes it's better to forget about it all and laugh it off."

And Abdul, nodding, inclines his head toward the desk, offering the barest hint of a smile.

God Gives the Rain

At the very end of October, when Angela Crespi came east and moved into her Aunt Nora's apartment, she hired the cleaning service to scrub the kitchen and bathrooms and had all of the walls, which were in terrible shape, painted white. Many of her aunt's things—old magazines, frayed scatter rugs, a broken chair, the tired old throw pillows—she gathered up and deposited in the storage space in the subbasement. She didn't touch the clothes in the closets and the bureaus, except to make room for her own things, which weren't many, because she wasn't planning on a very long stay. Nora was still at the Cabrini Center on East Nineteenth, with the brain injury she suffered when she was hit by a taxi in July. She had stepped into the traffic, witnesses said, a hot, sunny day, not looking, as if walking in a daze.

Angela had flown in from Los Angeles as soon as she learned of the accident, and visited again in August and September. Early on, Nora went into a coma, and now she was lingering in what the doctors spoke of as a vegetative state. Occasionally she opened her eyes, but there was no indication that she recognized anyone, and when asked to move a hand or a foot, she was unresponsive. She never spoke, and it was painful for Angela to see her that way, on the hospital bed, in a tangle of tubes and wires. The feeding tube, the urinary drain, the cluster of wires connecting to the machine that monitored the erratic rhythms of her heart.

Angela moved into the apartment after the play that

she'd been in, in L.A., had completed its run. The director there had recommended her for a part in New York, and when she auditioned for it, they took her on. It was a small role at an off-Broadway theater, but still it was New York, and someone, she hoped, might notice. In any case, she was closer to her aunt now and could visit more often, sitting by the hospital bed even though Nora was adrift, closed off in some nebulous dream.

The theater was on Christopher Street, and the play was Marlowe's *The Jew of Malta*. Angela had the part of Abigail, the daughter of Barabas, and there were a few good moments for her—when she recovers her father's gold and, in the middle of the night, from a balcony, tosses it down to him, and later, her anger and torment when she learns that her father was responsible for the death of the man she loves, Don Mathias. But then, in Act Three, that soon, she dies, poisoned by her father, and she has to hang around backstage through the remaining two acts, waiting for the curtain call. Rehearsals were to run through the month of November, with an opening scheduled for early December.

When she arrived at her aunt's apartment, a few days before rehearsals were due to begin, Farro Fescu was helpful, putting her luggage on the elevator and bringing it up to the ninth floor. A week earlier, he'd sent Oscar and his crew in to do the cleaning and painting, for a rate that was, Angela thought, high but not unreasonable. Soon after she was in, as she came and went through the lobby, she met Mrs. Wax and Mrs. Marriocci, and Maggie Sowle. And Dr. Tattafruge, from whom she'd had, through the summer, several phone calls about her aunt.

And then she met Abdul Saad, who lived on the tenth floor with his parents. When she first saw him—he was waiting in the lobby for the elevator, and she had just come in with some groceries—she became aware that, in a powerful way, she'd caught his eye. But she wasn't, at the moment, in an eye-catching mode, because there was too much to do and think about, and the eye-catching things, the grooving and the sparking, would simply have to wait. But he hurried over to her, introducing himself, and for a few moments, by the palm tree in the lobby, they exchanged small talk about the rain. His thick black hair was combed straight back off his forehead, and, though he spoke fluent English, there was a distinctly foreign look about him, Middle Eastern, she thought, Iranian or possibly Syrian—but as she eventually learned, his parents were from Iraq, and he'd been brought up in Passaic. The elevator came and went and arrived again, but he ignored it, still talking, and when he did finally board, she stepped away, moving toward the mail room, not wanting to be alone with him all the way to the ninth floor.

Less than an hour later, he was at her door with a brown bag full of Chinese food. "My parents are away and this is too much for me," he said, "so why don't we share? It's from the Lotus. They're Szechuan, the best in the neighborhood."

She was tired and had wanted to be alone that night, and as she let him in she felt miffed at his forwardness and annoyed with herself for not having the strength of mind to turn him away. She felt she was being invaded.

They ate in the kitchen, on her aunt's white dinnerware. Steamed dumplings, vegetables with prawns, and *mu shu*. He prepared the *mu shu* for her, wrapping it in a crepe that he smeared with a thick brown sauce.

"You've done this before," she noted.

"*Mu shu?* It's your first time?"

"My very first."

"Your aunt was a nice lady. I helped her with her packages a few times. She's been too long in that hospital. Is she going to make it?"

"I hope so, I do hope. But the doctors aren't terribly optimistic."

"What do doctors know?"

They talked for a while about her work in the theater. She wanted to be in film, but nothing had happened for her yet, and she was keeping herself active, taking whatever stage parts came her way.

"Being up on stage," he said, "that must be hard, in front of people. I don't think I could do that. And all those lines to remember."

She had made a few commercials, one for toothpaste, two for aspirin, and hated it, but at least it paid. The toothpaste piece was still running. When she was an undergraduate, she had played Ophelia and Desdemona, but she didn't see a future for herself in Shakespeare. Her graduate courses were mostly in film and television, working in front of a camera, adjusting to the lights, the sets, the technicians, the intimacy of the camera lens.

"And you?" she asked. "You spend your life bringing *mu shu* to the new women in town?"

"Cute," he said. "Touché. I'll send you my résumé."

He'd been a psych major at LIU, and then he was with his father for a while, in the spice trade. His father specialized in cloves. He dealt with other spices too, but mainly cloves, buying in the Moluccas and selling in London and New York, and Hamburg. Abdul did that for a while, but it wasn't what he wanted, so now he was at school again, on his way to becoming a mortician.

It surprised her. She'd never met anyone who was studying to become an undertaker. "That's a leap, isn't it? From psychology to corpses?"

"Actually," he said, "there's a lot of psychology in the death business. It's more complicated than people think."

He'd already finished most of the program—Embalming Theory I and II, Pathology, Restorative Art, History of Funeral Practices, Information Systems for Funeral Management. Now he was taking Anatomy for Embalmers and Embalming Lab I.

"More *mu shu?*" he asked.

She took more. She didn't care for the dumplings, though. They were too doughy. And the mixed steamed vegetables were bland.

"You like it? Handling corpses?"

"The dead have nobody," he said. "Somebody has to take care of them."

"But still—" she said.

"You're squeamish about death?"

"Not about death but about bodies. Messing with them."

"Embalming is an ancient art," he said. "The Egyptians and the Assyrians used it. The Persians. The Incas. The Chinchorros in Chile were doing it a thousand years before the Egyptians. In Papua, the embalmers used to smoke-cure the dead. You know, it's good to be close to death, it reminds you what life is all about. Yesterday, in lab, we worked on that girl who was killed on the Interboro Parkway. She was just twenty-seven, a singer with a rock band, with a great future, but cut short like that, and her face was a wreck. But we fixed her up, and now, at the wake, they can have an open coffin. Do you know what Walt Whitman says about death? He says 'All goes onward and outward, nothing collapses, And to die is different from what anyone supposed, and luckier.' "

"You like Whitman?"

"When I was an undergraduate, my last year, they had a Whitman festival. All these poets came and read, and they all had fancy things to say about Whitman. He's okay. Sure. Yeah, I like him. Such a strong belief in life and the future. I wish I had half that much confidence."

He took another dumpling, and she watched as he cut into it and lifted a portion on his fork. He was good-looking, in his way, with a high forehead, a straight, slender nose, and a well-defined chin. His eyes were large and dark, and his skin had a faintly olive texture. There was a friendliness, a gentleness in his manner, yet he was, she felt, too eager. She didn't like the urgency, the obvious show of desire. And anyway, it was bad timing for her, not only because she'd just arrived from the opposite side of the country, but because there had been a boy she'd been involved with for more than a year, and it had fallen apart—and now she wanted to move on with her acting before starting up again with somebody else. And in any case, beyond all of that, there was, with Abdul, all this embalming stuff, putting people into coffins, and how could she possibly become involved with somebody who was going to spend his life doing that? And what did he know about death anyway? Had he ever lost anyone? When she told him about her parents, that they were both dead, he was sympathetic and made a show of concern, taking her hand—but could he know what it was really like? He was outside of it, an observer, a witness, going to make big money off of death, but he didn't know it from the inside.

Three days went by and she didn't see him, and she thought, happily, she might never see him again. Then came a phone call, and an invitation to dinner and a movie.

"I can't," she said. "I'm horribly busy."

"How busy?"

"Too busy."

"So we'll skip dinner and do lunch instead. How would you like that?"

She hung back, full of caution.

"Hamburgers," he said. "On the ferry. Ten minutes to Staten Island, ten minutes back. It passes close to the Statue of Liberty."

"Ten minutes? Are you kidding?"

"Maybe fifteen. And I promise it won't rain."

"You're an animal," she said. She was thinking dog, lizard, pest.

"Tomorrow," he said.

"Maybe," she said, refusing to commit. "Call me in the morning."

But when he called the next morning, to confirm, she begged off—canceling, she said, because the director needed her for yet another rehash of the third act.

"This director," Abdul said. "Is he any good?"

"He's very good."

"Do you sleep with him?"

There was a long silence at her end, and when she answered, she was all ice. "You never stop, do you."

"When you stop, you're dead," he said, "and the only one getting rich is the undertaker. Which will be me, I suppose, when I have my license. You'll be glad you know me then. I'll give discounts to all of your friends."

It amazed her, the things he dared to say. It was, she thought, because they lived in the same building. It gave him a freedom. If they weren't in the same building, she would have told him to buzz off and get out of her life.

"Do you practice?" she said. "Or does it come naturally?"

"Practice what?"

"This thing that you do."

"What do I do?"

"Well, you push. You know that, don't you? You're a pushy guy."

"Really? That's what you think?"

"That's what I think."

"Well, I'm sorry," he said. "I'm sorry you think that. I was just joking, about the discounts for your friends. I'm sure your friends are wonderful like you, and I hope nothing sad ever happens to them."

"See?" she said.

"See what?"

"You're doing it again."

"I don't think I understand," he said.

"I guess you don't," she said.

It had been a lie that she'd told him, about going to rehearsal. She just wanted to be alone. And if not alone, certainly not with him.

Mornings, after breakfast, she did her voice exercises. She hummed, and then she sang scales, flexing her vocal cords. She spoke rapid-fire tongue twisters, sharpening the enunciation and expanding her tonal range: "Peter Piper primped and preened, parading proudly with his plumply purple penis." Said it over and over, turning the words from sweet to sour, angry to soft, dumb and sullen to smart and dangerous. She had other lines too, about Beastly Barbara and Naughty Nancy. She growled. She purred. She whined. She barked. She sputtered. And most of all she remembered something her acting coach had told her. "Live for the unexpected," she had said. "The unlooked-for move, the unforeseen gesture. Surprise is everything." And, while she tripped along with her Peter Piper repetitions, a quiet and lonesome part of her brain was wondering if Abdul, arriving with his *mu shu*, was the kind of unpredictable thing that her acting coach would have considered worthy of notice. What a drag.

She liked pistachio nuts and raisins, and cookies flavored with cinnamon. A few times a week she jogged, and occasionally she jumped rope. The music she liked best was old American jazz, Charlie Parker and Stan Getz, and Coltrane. It had been her father's music, he had filled the house with it. He was in his late forties when he died, and she held on to his jazz tapes and recordings, carried them with her from city to city. The cool, rich, complicated sounds simmered in the background while she did sit-ups and yoga stretches and studied her lines, and memories of her father floated out of the far past—how he had held her wrists and swung her in a circle, making her dizzy, and pushed her on a swing, and lifted her onto his shoulders, high up, on top of her three-year-old world.

What she knew, but didn't want to think about, was that her breasts were small. Was that why the film parts weren't coming her way? "More chest," her agent, Appeltooker, had told her, when she'd been passed up for yet another role in a film. "It's as simple as that. You got a scrawny chest." He told her to see a doctor for an enhancement, but she held off, refused, not wanting any part of her body to be something that wasn't really her. The mere thought of implants made her squeamish. And there was so much talk now about the health risk and the long-term problems.

"Think about it," Appeltooker said. "You're good, you're young. You can go places."

What places? She was getting nowhere fast. A few more inches of breast—that would do it? That's all it was about? She didn't want to believe that. Others had made it with scrawny chests, so why couldn't she? She would wait, hang in and struggle, and bide her time. And hope. But what if Appeltooker was right? What if she missed her chance and had to spend the rest of her life making toothpaste commercials?

Abdul was wooing her now with flowers, leaving bouquets at her door, and small boxes of chocolate in gold wrapping paper. He didn't see her or call her on the phone—just the flowers and the candy, waiting for her every day when she came home from rehearsal. Didn't he know she couldn't take chocolate? It would thicken her out, and then where would she be? And the flowers were more than she could manage—there weren't enough vases in her aunt's apartment. One bunch she put in a water pitcher, and others she left in the kitchen sink. Poor boy, he was out of his mind, wasting all his money.

The foyer outside her door was covered by a Persian carpet. There were two straight-backed chairs, and between them a marble-top table with a mirror above it, in a gold frame. There was the door to the elevator, and the door to the neighboring apartment, where the Dillhoppers lived, and the entry to the stairs. One morning, as she was leaving for the theater, she opened her door and found the foyer covered with rose petals, red and pink, an inch deep on the carpet, the air thick with their wild aroma. She was too astonished to be annoyed. She knelt down and ran her fingers through them. Impulsively she tossed a handful high in the air and watched the petals fluttering back down. One settled in her hair. He's daffy, she thought. Over the edge. And what an embarrassment—what will the Dillhoppers think? She pulled the lone rose petal from her hair and held it to her nose. And couldn't help but smile at the cushion of petals across the floor, the dreamy softness, the color, the heady scent. Nothing like this had ever happened to her before.

Soon afterward, he was leaving messages on her phone. One night, it was a passage from the Koran.

God gives the rain—
gives the grapes and the fresh vegetation,
the olive and the palm,
the thickets, the fruit trees, and the green pasture.

Just that, nothing else, and it was lovely, she thought. The olive and the palm, the fruit trees. But she hardly knew him! Couldn't he see that it was mad and unbalanced, and out of control, his pursuing her with flowers, chocolates that she couldn't eat, and passages from the Koran? She was tired, exhausted from the move east. The travel and all the arrangements, taking with her only what she could carry, her clothes and some books, and more than enough to worry about. Her aunt in the hospital, and now problems with the play, the rehearsals ragged and not coming along fast enough. And the one who played her father, such an unpleasantness, putting his hands on her in the first act in a way that was more than fatherly, grabbing a good feel of her ass. The things to put up with!

The next night, on the answering machine, it was the Persian poet Rumi—

What's to be done? I don't recognize myself.
I'm neither Christian, Jew, nor Muslim.
Nor anything else!
The circling heavens mean nothing to me.
I am not earth, or water—not air, or fire.
I am intoxicated with love.
If once in this world I win a moment with thee,
I will dance the dance of joy, and never end.

She knew about Rumi, she had read some of his poems in a world literature course. He was a religious poet, a Sufi and a dervish, and the love that he talked about was a love of God. But this, now, the way Abdul read it over the phone, was not about God, and the dance of joy, the weird way he lingered over that, had nothing to do with divine ecstasy. It crossed the line, she felt, and alarmed her, making her wonder, even, if he might be dangerous. He was coming on too strong, and it was time, she thought, to be as plain with him as possible.

But before she could speak to him, there was yet another message on the phone. This time, a piece from the poet Sadi—

> This summer breeze—is it a garden,
> Or is it the fragrance of friends meeting?
> Your eyebrows, like beautiful writing,
> Take hold of my heart.
> O bird, caught in the heart's net,
> This is where you belong, your home, your nest.

There was no doubting what that one meant, and it worried her. Too serious, much too intense. What had begun in apparent playfulness—the flowers, the candy— had progressed, now, to a level of earnestness she didn't think she could handle. And she blamed herself for letting it happen, for not having been more firm. When the first flowers appeared at the door, she should have phoned and told him to crawl off. But she hadn't— because, she now understood, she had probably wanted the attention, even while telling herself that she didn't. There was so much uncertainty in her life, the move, the play, adapting to New York, and not knowing if she would make the cut for another role here. And her aunt, her poor Aunt Nora, and that was the worst, the hardest. Every day waiting, hoping, for some sign of improvement, but nothing. So much up in the air. She should have been firmer with Abdul. Meaner. Tougher. Should have nipped it in the bud. What's wrong with me, she wondered.

That night, the night of the Sadi poem, she called him on the phone.

"Abdul, it's lovely, it really is," she said. "But don't you see? This isn't going to work."

"What won't?"

"All of it. It has to stop."

214

"Why?"

"Because it's wrong."

"Why is it wrong?"

"We hardly know each other."

"But we do. I know you. I see into you. I know your feelings. I know what you want and don't want."

"No you don't."

He was quiet for a moment, then he said somberly, "You don't like it that I'm going to be a mortician."

Exasperated, she spared him nothing. "Yes, that too," she blurted out. "Especially that. You're handling dead bodies all day, draining the blood and embalming. I mean, look at your hands. Look at them. These are hands that were just handling a corpse. How am I supposed to feel about that?"

"In the embalming room," he said, "we use gloves."

"Gloves?" It was almost a shout. "That changes it? That makes a difference?"

"It does. It does. With gloves, there is no chance of infection. You know you are safe. But everywhere else, look—people handle money, it's filthy. Someone with the flu sneezes, he opens his wallet, pulls out a twenty, and you take his germs. That's better?"

"Abdul, don't do this."

"Don't do what?"

"What you're doing."

"What am I doing? I adore you."

"You don't adore me. You have a crush and you'll get over it."

"I worship your eyes," he said, sounding like one of the poems he'd left on her voice mail. "Your lips, your feet. I want to be your shoes so your feet could be inside me."

"Abdul, that's just . . . silly."

"I am not silly," he protested angrily. "Never say that. Love is not silly. It's sublime. You, with your fancy words on stage, don't you understand sublime? Love is flame, passion, ardor. It is pain and it is agony."

"You make it sound so hard," she said. What she didn't say, because the words and the thought were only half formed, was that his allusion to her on stage suggested, somehow, that—what? That he was following her to rehearsals and somehow, from some hidden spot in the theater, watching and listening? Was he stalking her?

"Love is hard," he answered. "It's devotion. For better or worse."

"Abdul, I'm not ready for this."

"No one is ever ready. When it strikes, you are stuck with it. If you haven't felt the lightning yet, give it time."

Lightning? Had he actually used that word? My God, she thought, and regretted that she'd made the call. She had wanted to create clarity, to be resolute and determined, to close the door, but he wasn't listening, and it was clear to her now that he wouldn't be shut out. She felt a spinning confusion, a sense of panic, as if in a plane, flying through turbulence and suddenly falling, a quick drop, not knowing if the engines would grab again or if this was it. Life was too mad, too hard and harsh and complicated. Her mother and father both dead, too soon, and that, it seemed, was more than enough. Moods, memories, miscues. Phases of the moon and hormonal tides. In a kind of rage, she rushed though the apartment, gathering up all of the flowers Abdul had sent, dahlias, sunflowers, giant zinnias, stuffing them into a trash bag, and dropped them down the garbage chute.

Years ago, when there were things in her life that she couldn't resolve, more often than not she would talk them over with her father. She missed him—more, even, than she missed her mother, though she missed her too. Both of them so swiftly gone, her father eight years ago, when she was seventeen, and her mother the year after, as if some hideous curse had swept down and carried them off, leaving her to figure out the rest of her life on her own.

Her father had been born in Florence, and his family came over when he was nine. After college, he settled in California and made a living in fabrics, buying wholesale from mills in Florence and selling to tailors in Los Angeles who did custom work for the film industry. And he went outside of L.A. too, up to San Francisco and Sacramento, to Seattle and Eugene, the car loaded with his sample cases of Florentine cloth.

He loved fabrics, and he also loved jazz, having a sizable collection of recordings that he kept neatly stored in an oak cabinet that he'd picked up at an auction. Home from the office, he mixed martinis, and on came the jazz, booming over the speakers, tense and subtle, rough and sometimes gaudy, or silky-smooth and intricate—Bird's saxophone, soaring and searching, and Armstrong's cornet, brash with quick-toned breakthrough rhythms. He liked Tatum and Fats Waller, and Billie Holiday. And Angela, hearing the same pieces over and over, felt they were constantly fresh and new, reinventing themselves every time they flowed over the speakers. When her father was away, off to Reno and Phoenix, her mother turned up the volume, filling the house with Mulligan and Mingus and Monk, and it was as if her father was still there with them, easing into the sound, the martini glass held loosely in his long, lean fingers.

Then, on a Friday, a police officer was at the door, telling them about the accident on the interstate, a six-car pileup. Angela's father was in a hospital in Fresno, and they rushed off to see him. Four days he lingered in intensive care, showing small signs of improvement, but then they lost him. Angela was in her last year at high school, about to go on to UCLA.

"Be a star," he used to say to her. "Don't let anything stop you." In the high school productions, she had played Laura in *The Glass Menagerie*, and Hermia in *A Midsummer Night's Dream*. He was always there, and she could still hear it, the sound of his clapping, louder than anyone else's, and sees him yet, in memory, with his pencil-line moustache and iron-rimmed eyeglasses, rising from his seat, standing, his face flushed with excitement. Clapping so hard she thought his hands would fall off.

"Be the best," he told her, many times. "You're good, you can do it. You know that—don't you?"

Her poor mother, she grieved terribly after the funeral. She had breast cancer and didn't know it. Not till she had the intense pain in her abdomen did she see a doctor, and then it was too late. The surgeon removed both of her breasts and sent her into chemotherapy, which wasn't helpful, and Angela, still reeling from the loss of her father, lost her mother too, little more than a year later. She was desolate, torn apart, but something inside her, a mysterious hopefulness inherited from her father, kept her going.

Toward the end, her mother's sister, Nora, had come in from New York and she was a help, doing what little she could. Her husband, an entomologist at NYU, flew in for the funeral but left immediately afterward to teach a summer course. Nora stayed on a few more weeks, urging Angela to return to New York with her, but Angela had no enthusiasm for that. Her friends and her memories were there in Los Angeles, and she'd already started at UCLA and wasn't eager about making a change. Nora went home without her, and somehow Angela got through the summer, working with the family lawyer, signing papers and transferring accounts. She gave the house to an agent and sold it, and took a room close to the university.

And now, years later, here she was, in New York, in her aunt's apartment, rehearsing for an Elizabethan play that she liked less and less every day. It was full of hate and melodrama—duels, stabbings, strangulation, death by poison. When the Christian governor, Ferneze, seizes Barabas's wealth—intending to use it to pay the tribute demanded by the Turks—Barabas is enraged over the way he's been wronged and sets into motion a plan for revenge that quickly outgrows itself, producing one death after another. And in the end his stratagems backfire, leading to his own horrific demise in a boiling cauldron that he had intended for someone else.

It was Christians, Jews, and Muslims at each other's throats, and the director, Fritz Kovner, had picked it for its timeliness. Old as it was, the play spoke to the chaos of the Middle East. The Gulf War was over, but the region was still in a ferment. The Israelis were in Lebanon, the Americans were in the Saudi desert, Saddam Hussein still ruled in Baghdad, the Palestinians were throwing rocks, Syria and Iran were supporting Hezbollah, and Hamas was raising hell at every opportunity. And the Turks, hovering at the edge, watched it all nervously. In Egypt, Islamic militants were trying to bring down the government by shooting at buses that were carrying tourists.

When the play opened, the first week of December, Angela was surprised to see Abdul in the audience, in the fourth row. She was so disturbed, seeing him, that she stumbled over one of her lines. After her death scene in the third act she was backstage, and, looking through a peephole in the scenery, she watched him. He was engrossed in the play, turning his head to the left and right as the actors moved across the stage. He wore a dark gray suit and a tie that seemed, through the distance, a blend of midnight blues and grays. Properly funereal, she thought. Even when he's out to theater, he dresses for death. Why couldn't he be a trapeze artist, or a blackjack dealer? Or a New Orleans blues pianist, bleeding his soul out on the black and white keys?

She expected he'd be waiting for her after the play, but when she came through the door with Kovner and the others, he was nowhere in sight. Kovner treated them to a Third Avenue bar that offered beef sandwiches on rye, pseudo-Tiffany lamps, and a waitress in black lace leotards. Delighted with the opening performance, Kovner drank gin, and the Russian Jew from Williamsburg, who played Barabas, took vodka. Angela asked for a beer, which she only half finished. She had a headache, a low, humming thing, nothing unbearable but enough to let her know it was there. She did her best, smiling and nodding, but felt none of Kovner's enthusiasm for the production. The one who played Ferneze was too stiff and wooden, and the lead, Barabas, too much of a ham, upstaging at every opportunity. The tall Haitian who played Ithamore should have stuck to basketball.

As she subwayed home, she was thinking again of Abdul and felt an odd swirl of emotion—so bold of him to show up like that, and yet, despite her annoyance, she was puzzled, if not put off, that he hadn't stayed to greet her. Had he been disappointed? With the play? With her? Perhaps, seeing her on stage, he had come to his senses and changed his mind about her, and, for all she knew, he might never bother her again. Thank God! It was over. But something inside her twisted doubtfully, a queer uncertainty, an ambivalence that she didn't want to think about, or confront.

At the next performance, Abdul was again there, in the same seat, wearing the same gray suit, and, this time, a pair of dark glasses. Very dark. Her first thought was that something might have happened to his eyes, but then she felt he was simply trying to annoy her. Well, of course. She had rejected him, and now he hated her. Two weeks ago he'd been sending flowers every day, and now that she was a star, on stage, poisoned in the third act by her own father, not even a daisy.

The third night, he had a seat in the second row, off to the left. Again the dark glasses, but now he also wore a moustache. A big one. He was clowning—mocking the play. Making a joke. She was furious. She wanted to throw something at him, and nearly did, wanting to fling the pot of poisoned porridge in his face. But then, after the first rush of anger, she felt, despite herself, a prickle of amusement, because he really did look funny with that dumb moustache. Could it be that was all he was after—trying to make her laugh?

The reviews appeared sporadically during the first week, and they were mixed. The *Times* praised the energy of the production but questioned the wisdom of resurrecting this particular Marlowe play, which was, the reviewer felt, interesting but not Marlowe's strongest. *Newsday* thought the role of Barabas had been brilliantly interpreted, but the *Village Voice* thought not, asserting that the Haitian who played Ithamore had stolen the show. The *Post* gave Angela a mention, praising the elegance of her death scene, but thought it was out of character, earlier, when she winked at the friar who brought her to the nunnery.

A monsignor from the cardinal's office complained that the play put Christians in a bad light, and a spokesman for the PLO protested that the play was blatantly anti-Muslim. Hadassah issued a brisk statement, declaring the play to be an insult to world Jewry, and an affront to peace-loving people everywhere.

Kovner reveled in the publicity. In an interview with the *Times*, he went out on a limb, arguing not only that the play was not anti-Jewish, but that Marlowe himself was probably a Jew. His statement sparked a fiery debate among scholars, starting at Yeshiva and spreading as far south as Baton Rouge, and west to Pepperdine. In a letter to the *Times*, a spokesman from the Malta embassy wrote that Marlowe had the story all wrong—in the sixteenth century, the Turks did much worse than attempt to exact tribute from Malta. They sent an armada and invaded the island, but were repulsed by the heroic efforts of the Knights of St. John and the Maltese people. The Turkish embassy wrote a quick response, arguing that the invasion had been provoked by corsairs from Malta who had been interfering with Turkish shipping. After that, the two embassies traded letters every day, until the *Times* simply stopped printing them, and it was shortly after that, on a Saturday, that a chauffeur from the Turkish embassy was found badly mauled in an alley on Bleecker Street, behind the church of Our Lady of Pompeii. And a day later, an aide from the Malta embassy was discovered in the cemetery by Trinity Church, barely alive, with a knife in his back. The police considered the incidents to be unrelated.

On the evening of the fourth performance, Abdul had been there yet again, with dark glasses and moustache, and the same suit, somberly gray, but now he was without a shirt, bare skin under the jacket, the tie around his neck hanging down over his chest. And she finally understood what he was doing. Not mocking but provoking, getting her goat, trying to force her into a reaction. Wanting her to confront him—call him on the phone, knock on his door—anything, as a way of reestablishing contact, even if only in anger. I won't do this, she vowed. Won't, won't, won't. Never. As she died in Act Three, she stared right at him, as if to say death was better than to live in the same building with such a banana brain. But as she stared, in her death throe, an uncanny thing happened. He disappeared. He was sitting there, the jacket, the tie, the dark glasses, and suddenly he began to disintegrate. There was a fuzziness, and then the chair in which he'd been sitting was weirdly empty.

Backstage, when she looked out, he was there again, exactly as he'd been. Unchanged. It was her, she thought, a momentary spasm. Something with her eyes, a dizziness. A trick of the lighting. Or was it him—could he really do that, vanish and reappear? No way, she thought, not possible. It was her, she had done it, a simple wish fulfillment. She had wished him gone, and he went.

But was it, she wondered, what she really wanted? That he be out of her life? And she understood, painfully, that in some altogether subtle way she had, over the weeks, grown used to his fatuous attentions, and she might very well be at a loss without them. On the way home, she wondered if there would be flowers at her door—and saw, when she arrived, with a twinge of disappointment, that there were not. He was death, she thought. That's what he was, and she felt, eerily, that she was being drawn into a darkness.

Monday afternoon, she went to the hospital and spent some time with her aunt. Nora lay on her back, motionless, eyes closed, her breathing slow and regular. She was covered by a white blanket. Her brown hair was spread out against the pillow, and her face, in repose, without makeup, had a quiet serenity that belied the seriousness of her condition. Her left foot stuck out, dangling off the bed, and Angela moved it back in under the covers. The monitor by the bed, with its weaving green lines, showed the peaks and valleys of the motions of her heart.

Usually, when Angela visited, she read to her, thinking—wanting to believe—that despite her condition, she could hear the words and take some comfort from them. She read from Nora's Bible, passages that Nora had marked, and from a book of poems that Nora had left on her dresser, the love sonnets of Edna St. Vincent Millay. But today, instead of reading, Angela sat by the bed and, leaning close, spoke into her ear, telling her about Abdul. She told her about the Chinese dinner he'd brought to the apartment, and the flowers and the chocolates, and the rose petals in the foyer. And his silliness at the theater, with the dark glasses and the fake moustache.

"I no longer know what to make of him," she said, with some urgency. "Is he spooky or is he wonderful? Tell me, Auntie. Tell me what to think. He wants me so much. What right does he have to want me like that? Have I been foolish?"

She told her how he was studying to become an undertaker, and wasn't it hateful? But he was hardworking and bright, and good-looking too, and he was going to make something of himself. But a mortician?

And then, as she lapsed into silence, Nora opened her eyes. Her face had a sadness in it, a sense of confusion and uncertainty, but in her eyes there seemed, strangely, a hint of brightness, and it appeared, for a moment, that she wanted to say something. Her lips parted, but there were no words, just the lips, barely open, and her gleaming eyes, gazing into Angela's eyes.

Angela was amazed. Nora was awakening, coming alive. She'd heard every word. Angela hurried out into the corridor, to the nurses' station, and not finding a nurse, she returned with an aide. "Come—come! She opened her eyes and looked at me. I was talking, and she heard it all."

But as they came into the room, Nora's eyes were closed and there was again that odd serenity in her face. Her head was on the pillow, and she was very still.

"But she looked at me. She did. And she was about to speak. I think now she's going to be all right."

She took it as a sign—not just of an impending recovery but of something else as well. Nora had been trying to say something, and whatever it was, it was something good. There was so much life in her eyes, and such warmth, and feeling. Yes, yes. That's what she'd been trying to say—she had opened her eyes and Angela was now convinced, she had been trying to say yes, emphatically *yes*.

There was no performance that evening, it being a Monday, and at suppertime Angela whipped up an omelet, throwing in some chopped onions, chunks of cheddar, leftover peas, plenty of basil, and a few sprigs of parsley. She watched the news as she ate—a one-legged Santa Claus arrested for pushing drugs, and a bank thief in the Bronx whose getaway car wouldn't start. Twins born on a Metro-North train coming in from Connecticut. The plight of the Kurds in northern Iraq, and more than a thousand dead in the riots in India. Killings and starvation in Somalia.

She put on some music, Billie Holiday, then turned on the gas jets in the fireplace, and for a while she just sat there, on the large bearskin, watching as the small flames curled and bent around the ceramic logs. She remembered how her aunt had loved the bearskin. It was from long ago, from Nora's grandfather. The thickness of it, and the rich cinnamon color, lit by the flickering flames—it seemed alive, soft and dense, full of hidden memories, and the voice of Billie Holiday floating dark and lonely, feeling its way into the corners of the room. "What a Little Moonlight Can Do" segued into "Strange Fruit," which stretched and turned with its stark mood, and melded into "God Bless the Child." Angela was up off the bearskin and standing by the door to the terrace, swaying with the music and gazing at the lights across the river. So many separate lives out there, in the high-rises, yet it was as if no one was there, only the lights.

Moonlight on the water, and chunks of river ice floating down from up north, and as she stood there, mesmerized by the magic of the lights, the door chimes rang, yanking her from her reverie, and she knew it was him.

This time he brought her a pie. It was a peace offering.

"Friends," he said, standing in the doorway. "Is that all right? We'll just be friends."

She simply stared at him. A dumb, vacant stare, the door open and Abdul standing there, holding the pie with both hands. It was on a pink dish.

"Are you all right?" he asked.

"Yes, yes," she answered vaguely.

"It's an Arab pie, they call it Pie of Paradise. My parents use the Arabic name, I can never remember."

"You found this at Abouti's?"

"This? I made it myself."

"You bake?"

He shrugged. "My mother made it, I put it in the oven. She made it for you. I shopped for the apricots and the almonds."

"How nice," she said, "your mother bakes."

"You don't?"

"Carrot cake is as far as I go. Anything more complicated, I leave it to the experts."

He put the pie down on the small table by the door. "I can't stay," he said. "I have to set up a VCR for my father. Next time I'll bring homemade baklava."

"Abdul, I'm not sure there should be a next time."

"Shush. Trust me. Take the pie. We'll be friends."

"Just friends," she said, and as the words escaped her, she felt she had conceded too much.

"I understand, I understand," he said. "We have our separate lives and you're not happy that my business is with corpses. I understand about that. So now, if we're just friends, it won't matter." But then, unable to restrain himself, as if the words had been stored up inside him and he could no longer hold them in, he let it all out. "And you too," he said. "You have to understand. Look at you. You're in a play where you are killed every night. It's a play filled with death and violence. Your father kills you and all those others. He connives, he cheats, he murders. That's a better world? At least I have respect for the dead. I fix their faces. I give them a smile if the family wants one. I fix the hair, I put makeup over the blemishes. But you, on stage, it's kill, kill, kill. Is that human? You can live with that? With make-believe murder? Yet you can't live with death itself, the real thing? So even though I understand, I don't. I'm trying. See? But it doesn't make sense to me."

She watched as he spoke, but hardly heard a word. She was looking at his eyes, his mouth, the lips, seeing the intensity, the conviction. He believed what he believed, and she admired that. Under the silliness, there was a seriousness.

"Where did you find the moustache?" she asked.

"I used to wear it on Halloween, when I was a kid."

"You dressed up for Halloween?"

"Of course. All Iraqi-immigrant children dress up for Halloween. How else can we become good Americans?"

Something changed in his face, and she saw it, a softness after his passionate outburst. He was reminiscing, thinking back. Remembering his youth.

And then, to her own amazement, she did something which, even as she did it, she knew it to be implausible, if not, in fact, unthinkable. She went close up to him and kissed him on the mouth. It felt good, her lips on his, and she lingered there, still not believing she was doing this.

And then, for both of them, the kissing turned serious, and she knew it was lunatic. She was letting herself go, losing herself in the heat of the moment, and, still kissing, she drew him into the apartment, into the living room, across the carpet and toward the fireplace, pausing along the way to turn out the lamp, the only light coming now from the hearth. It was deep, hungry kissing, the two of them on the bearskin, standing, her tongue in his mouth, and they were under each other's clothes, touching and holding. And then they were down on the bearskin, and she opened herself to him, and there was only the feeling, the tense, mounting sensation, the passion and the movement, all of her pores alive to the moment—and it was, for her, like being part of the ocean where it runs against the sand, the rippling and churning, silvery waves spending themselves toward a feverish exhaustion on the dunes.

And then they were just lying there, on the bearskin, gazing at the ceiling and breathing hard. The gas-fired flame in the fireplace still flickered, the ceramic logs glowing dim and crimson.

"You think your aunt ever did this?" he asked. "Here on the bearskin?"

"My aunt did everything."

"She was wild? Frantic?"

"No, just outrageous. She kept animals. She had monkeys and snakes, right here in the apartment. She would have kept a giraffe if she could have squeezed it in."

Abdul knew about the animals. He had seen them, those times when he helped Nora with her packages.

"I liked the macaw," he said. "And the finches."

"Poor Aunt Nora," she said.

"She'll be all right."

"Will she?"

"It's important to have hope," he said. "Hope makes everything right."

Then he surprised her by quoting from the play. The lines were Ithamore's, to Bellamira, the courtesan. Ithamore was a slave from Thrace, brought up in Arabia, and there was nothing appealing about him, except that he had some good lines, and Abdul knew them by heart. He was still on his back, gazing at the ceiling, watching the undulations of light and shadow cast by the fire.

> *That kiss again!—She runs division of my lips.*
> *What an eye she casts on me! It twinkles like a star.*
> *O, that ten thousand nights were put in one, that we*
> *Might sleep seven years together afore we wake!*

Then it was just the silence, the words lingering invisible in the air, ten thousand nights, and the glow from the low flames in the fireplace.

"What will your father say?" she asked.

"I didn't do his VCR," Abdul remembered. "I'll do it tomorrow."

"I mean about us."

"He doesn't know about us."

"When he finds out," she said. "That you've been with a Christian from California who plays a Jewish girl who becomes a nun."

"He'll disown me. He's very serious about Islam, every day he says his prayers."

"And you? You don't pray?"

"He'll want me to move out of the apartment. My mother will weep, and my sister will celebrate because she'll have my room, which is bigger than hers and has a view of the river."

"See?" she said. "That's what I mean. This is not going to work."

"But it will. We will make it happen."

"I'm the infidel," she said.

"Yes, that's what you are. But God and my parents will have to understand. I can't be bound by the old ways."

"And I really can't handle it that you're a mortician."

"It's hard for you, I know. And for me?" he said. "You think it's easy? Watching you on stage touched and fondled by other men? This is good?"

"See? It's bad for both of us. We shouldn't see each other."

"But we must. It's fate."

"That's what you think? You believe in fate?"

"I believe in death. Death is fate. And the best that we have against death is each other."

They were both up now, standing on the bearskin, and she felt with her bare feet the bristly thickness of the dead bear's fur. A helicopter passed low over the river, the roar of its engine creating a tremor.

"Life is good," Abdul said.

"Is it?" she wondered.

"We can be together."

"Maybe," she said, feeling doubt, uncertainty, a blissful confusion.

"Why not yes?" he asked.

"There's too much against it," she said.

"If you want something to happen, it will," he said.

She was afraid of permanence. Permanence seemed too much like a locked door, and she disliked locked doors, even when she had the keys to open them. She preferred to be floating, drifting from possibility to possibility. She thought of Nora in her hospital bed, and her mother dead and her father dead, and so many wrong things everywhere. And what was life really about anyway?

"We have to be sensible," she said. "We'll have to think about it, and we'll see."

He had her in his arms again, and they were kissing, not greedily, as before, but with a quiet ease, a softness, and despite her doubts and refusals, she felt an impossible desire that she couldn't understand, and for the moment, at least, could not deny.

A Wish List, a Hate List

At the desk in the lobby, in his high-backed leather chair, Farro Fescu has been working on the puzzle in the *Times* and has just set it aside. This was a hard one, yet he's done well with it, filling in most of the blanks, though several of the answers remain elusive. He feels mildly frustrated, as he often does when he leaves a puzzle unfinished. A mountain in Tanzania ... a Stravinsky ballet ... the name of a troubadour at the court of Eleanor of Aquitaine. And, among some others, the Provençal word for love. Yeah. Sure. Fine. Good luck. Thank you very much.

He pushes the paper off to his left, and on a yellow pad he jots down a list of things for Oscar to attend to. There's a dead lightbulb in the west foyer on the tenth floor, and water from somewhere on the sixth is seeping into a unit below—a broken pipe? Need a plumber? Mrs. Marriocci's bedroom window is stuck again. And no more flowers, please, in the foyer on Mrs. Wax's floor, her daughter's allergies are active again.

He keys the list into the computer, dates it, prints it off, and leaves it in the basket, where Oscar will pick it up when he's done with the morning's chores.

Then he works on a list for himself. The Christmas tree is up, standing in front of the wide wall between the two elevators, but many of the lightbulbs and ornaments are broken. Knatchbull's kid did it, the boy, eight years old, taking target practice with his pistol, shooting pellets. Broke six lights and nine ornaments before Farro Fescu emerged from the mail room and saw what was happening. So off to Bloomingdale's for replacements, where he purchased the originals nine years ago.

What else he needs is bananas and feta cheese at the market, milk, an avocado, coffee beans, and a tea kettle—he burnt the one he has. The water boiled away when he fell asleep watching the news, and what a stink. Socks too he needs, and new underwear. And there's this homeless woman turned up yesterday near the front door, just lying there on a piece of cardboard, with a blanket. He told her she could use the bathroom and then she would have to move on. She used the toilet, then went outside and stayed where she'd been, slept the night out there, on a piece of cardboard, wrapped in a blanket, and hasn't moved yet. What to do? Call the police? Talk to the board? The residents will go crazy. Her too, he puts her on his list, folds it, and slips it into his pocket.

Lists and lists—one list after another. He loves them, needs them. Likes nothing better. If you put it on a list, somehow it will get done. Lists are the way the world runs. Adam in the garden, naming the trees, he was making a list. Noah putting the animals aboard the ark, pair by pair, he too was preparing a list, making sure he had them all with him, the geese, the hawks, the zebras, giraffes. And God himself, thinking up the commandments, one to ten, what a list, still around after all these years. Without a list, where are you? How do you remember things? How do you know what's important? Lists everywhere—menus, directories, bank statements, the alphabet. The calendar, the almanac. The five-day weather forecast. Without a list, how would you know who you are?

The morning rush is over, no calls, no footsteps on the marble floor, and in the crisp aroma of the Christmas tree he relaxes at the computer and browses through his files. The files contain lists attached to other lists that lead forward and backward to still other lists—hotels, restaurants, limo services, food shops. Electricians and plumbers. Contractors for kitchen alterations. A wish list. A hate list. A complaint list. And Knatchbull's son, the eight-year-old, the one who shot up the Christmas tree, he's a list all his own. Just yesterday he left a wad of chewing gum on the black couch, and Rabbi Ravijohn sat on it and ruined a fine pair of trousers.

He opens his file on Rumfarm, and this is a long one, longer than most. The shoes he wears, the brown suede, the alligators that he brought back from last year's trip to Guanabara. And his hand-painted ties with bold images of palms, dahlias, hibiscus, even in winter his ties are hot summer. The cufflinks are onyx, ruby, jade, and a pair with diamonds set in polished steel. He still has all of his hair, and once a month he uses LaBosco in the Trade Center, for the three-hundred-dollar cut, though one would hardly know.

From chatter in the lobby, Farro Fescu has gleaned a list of his favorite meals—the lasagna at Gattopardo, the luncheon salads at Houlihan's across from St. Paul's, the two-inch steak fillets at the Windows on the World, the escargots at Jean Lafitte. And he has, too, a runaway appetite for old-fashioned pancakes drenched in maple syrup, and he's been plumping out, too many calories, too many carbs. He swims once a week at the club, but it's hardly enough.

Years ago, green out of Stanford, he did novice work at Bangkok Metropolitan. After that, he moved over to Deutsche Bank, and then he was with Nikko Securities for a while. For the last eight or nine years he's been with the Sukabumi Investment Group, which was, for a while, loosely connected to the Bank of Indonesia. And that's where he still is. Ten in the morning, four days a week, he strolls over to the South Tower and rides to the office on the ninety-sixth floor—and even there Farro Fescu tracks him, from afar, digging through the stories, the news items, the gossip good and bad.

"The nifty nineties" is the phrase Rumfarm used with a reporter from the *Wall Street Journal*, and there it is, scanned into Farro Fescu's file, Rumfarm predicting a bull market the likes of which nobody had ever yet seen. The Dow is up over 3000, which only a short while ago had been unthinkable. "The sky's the limit," he said in the interview. "It's a new kind of world. Get used to it."

He markets a sliding-scale investment instrument that he calls the Multiple Modified Reflex Money Magnifier—MMRMM—a computer-driven money tool that moves your investment in and out of stocks, bonds, real estate, and gold. The point was to keep the money moving to the places where it worked hardest. "We don't want your money sucking on a dry tit" is the way he's explained it. And an integral part of the process is the buying up of bond issues from companies heading into bankruptcy, picked up for pennies, and when a company emerges from bankruptcy, your pennies come back a thousandfold. It can happen, of course, that the company doesn't emerge, but if you don't want risk, why get out of bed in the morning?

When Farro Fescu thinks of Luther Rumfarm, he thinks of the large nose, the broad, beefy face, the washed-out eyes pale as dishwater, and mostly the hands, pudgy, with short stubby fingers. He dislikes the man, yet he respects those hands. Thick they may be, but they are clever hands, nimble hands, sleight-of-hand hands that are making money hand over fist.

The perception in the building is that Harry Falcon, in the penthouse, is the wealthiest man there, with Aki Sato not far behind—and Rumfarm pushing hard and closing in, on his way, and getting there fast. This tall, heavyset man with his fixation about a waterfall in the lobby—and now, too, his talk of a casino in the basement, and, at big expense for the residents, a flashy new pink granite skin for the building. Farro Fescu sees him as not just a problem but, in his bland, calculating way, a menace.

And the answer, he thinks, the solution to it all, is to plant Rumfarm in a brass urn, like the urn that holds the thatched palm by the couch. Rumfarm and all his restless, intrusive, topsy-turvy ideas, with his money, his dentures, his colorless busybody eyes, his junk bonds, his smooth arrogance, his glaze, his gloss, his velvet-gloved pushing and shoving. Plant him and watch him grow, right there in the lobby, the Rumfarm tree, with Rumfarm leaves and Rumfarm branches. But, in the way of things, this tree is a tree that is all plastic, right down to the roots. Plastic leaves and plastic branches, and a few plastic birds that make squeaky plastic noises.

Nobody loves this tree, and why should they? Even the kid who delivers from Poppo Pizza hates it. Every morning, Lillian Soo's Afghan pauses, lifts a leg, and gives the tree a warm welcome. Muddy Dinks tries to carve Yesenia's initials into it, but the bark is too tough and the blade breaks. Chase lights up and blows smoke on it, expecting the leaves will wilt, but plastic is forever. It's an obstinate tree, an unflappable tree, too smart for anybody's good, and nonbiodegradable. In the lumpy geography of its bark, Farro Fescu sees the Rumfarm nose, the bovine neck, and a lot of jaw. And all those thick, pudgy leaves, too many to count and green as dollars. It's time, he thinks, to get rid of this tree, to remove it from the lobby and leave it out by the curb, and watch how it copes with the traffic and the weather.

At this moment, snowflakes are falling, Farro Fescu sees them through the glass doors. And, bravely, he returns to the crossword and gives it another try. A few answers light up for him right away. The mountain in Tanzania is Kilimanjaro. Simple, he should have known that, the highest, yes, in Africa. The Stravinsky ballet is *Firebird*, and that too he should have known. But the troubadour? It begins with B-E-R-N, but that's all that he gets. And even more irritating is the Provençal word for love, four letters, and he doesn't have a one of them. Love? Love? It haunts him. It lingers and is still with him when he finds Mrs. Marriocci's sunglasses—they were on the couch— and brings them up to her. What is that word? And even when he rides down on the elevator and thinks, fleetingly, of Renata Negri, even then it tortures him, this word that he does not know. The word for love, which he can't solve, even with hints from the surrounding words.

And why does it bother him so? Is he lonely? Disappointed? Unhappy with his life?

The homeless woman stayed around by the front door for three days. Knatchbull's boy gave her a chocolate bar, and Louisa Wax's daughter gave her a box of cookies. Maggie Sowle gave her a bowl of soup and an extra blanket. Farro Fescu tried to explain to her that the homeless are like pigeons: if you feed them, they will hang around for more. Maggie gave her more soup. And then, for reasons of her own, the woman picked up and left one night, and when they went down in the morning, they saw she was gone. Farro Fescu was pleased that the episode had ended without involving the police.

"The soup," he said to Karl Vogel. "That's what drove her off. That Mrs. Sowle, she makes famous quilts, but soup she should leave to others."

The End-of-the-Century
Memorial Quilt

Maggie Sowle's apartment, on the fourth floor, was named for Helen Keller, who'd been born blind and deaf, yet she had accomplished a great deal in her life, as a writer and lecturer. Maggie admired her, but the blindness—the idea of blindness—was something that frightened her, because if anything were to happen to her own eyes, her career as a quilter would be over. She would much have preferred living in the Emily Dickinson, because she greatly admired those crisp, poignant poems, so alive and gleaming, so intensely felt. But alas, Louisa Wax lived in that one—the Dickinson— with her dogs and her teenage daughter, and when it came to poetry, Louisa was hopelessly tone-deaf.

At the moment, Maggie was at work on a quilt that was to hang at the UN, in the entrance hall at the north end of the General Assembly building. The piece had been commissioned in May, and she was already well along with it, working in her living room, which she'd been using as a studio ever since Henry had passed away, four years ago. They had lived together for fifteen years, though they had never married. He was a Bonheur and she was a Sowle, and she had used, always, her own surname. And somewhere along the way people had begun to address her as Mrs. Sowle, which made her feel old, but she accepted that.

The quilt was to be a large one, fifteen by thirty feet, larger than anything she'd done before, and since she didn't have a wall that large in the apartment, she had to create the piece in separate panels that would be stitched together at the very end. She had the overall design in her head, and in sketches on paper, but it was, in a way, like laboring in the dark, not knowing exactly what the piece in its entirety would look like until it was fully assembled and hanging on a wall—and that wasn't going to happen until she installed it at the UN. She moved restlessly among bales of scrap cloth and fat spools of thread, measuring, stitching, cutting with a large pair of scissors. Some sections were spread out across the floor, others were pinned to the walls. She had removed the couches and easy chairs, putting them into a spare room, but kept the stereo where it was, and always, while she sewed, there was music—Copland or Gershwin or Kurt Weill, and much of Carl Orff, whose pounding rhythms stirred something elemental in her.

She was forty-nine, with a dreamy intensity in her dark hazel eyes. Her hair was paper-white and she wore it shoulder-length, drawn back from her face and kept in place by amber barrettes. Her face was smooth, little marked by wrinkles, and even in moments of fatigue it was suffused with a quiet energy that made her seem younger than she was. After years of toil and little recognition, she was now enjoying a belated success. Her quilts were works of art. One hung in the Whitney, and another in the Hirshhorn, and there had been showings abroad, at the Wallraf in Cologne and the Beuningen in Rotterdam. It was the exhibition at the Beuningen that led to the commission for the quilt that was to hang at the UN. An aid of Boutros Boutros-Ghali, the new secretary-general, had seen the show while he was traveling through the Netherlands and was so impressed that he passed her name on to the appropriate committee.

Her earliest pieces had been made of square patches forming geometrical patterns, but she had abandoned that style and worked now in the tradition of the crazy quilt, using patches of differing shape and size, with a rich array of color—and somehow, out of the jumble, there emerged, here and there, images of trees, clouds, swans, and helicopters. She used silk and burlap, satin and polyester, whatever she could put her hands on, cutting large, swirling designs, brisk and daring, or small intimate forms that teased the eye with subtle allusions. And she sewed, she sewed. She played ovals against squares, rectangles against circles—everything deliciously unbalanced, and yet, trickily, there would be, in the whole, a mysterious sense of harmony, a sense that the pieces, no matter how unrelated in color or contour, all fit together. "Like life itself," she wrote one night in her journal. "We're all so terribly different, every one of us—yet we connect, we belong. No matter how much we may hate each other!" Even as she wrote it, it struck her as perhaps overly optimistic, the part about connecting and belonging. Nevertheless, given the bleakness of the alternative, she favored optimism, thinking it better to hope and believe than to succumb to a darkness that had no meaning.

The striking thing about her quilts was that she stitched into them a wide variety of familiar objects—buttons, zippers, cufflinks, beaded necklaces, and even, at times, wristwatches and old fountain pens—and her quilts became, in effect, a form of collage. For the United Nations quilt, she had solicited items far and wide, and was much helped by Aki Sato, the Japanese businessman who lived a few floors above her. He was an avid collector, with influence among other collectors, and in the end she had more things—relics—than she could possibly use. Among them, a scarf that had been used by Mao Tse-tung on the Great March from Jiangxi to Shanxi province, sunglasses that had been worn by Lawrence of Arabia, one of Winston Churchill's silk handkerchiefs, and a pair of stockings that had belonged to Golda Meir. Also a leather tongue from one of Charlie Chaplin's shoes, and a strip of cloth from the prison uniform of Nelson Mandela. From his own collection, Aki Sato gave her a sleeve from the shirt that Charles Lindbergh wore when he flew across the Atlantic, and a button from the jacket worn by John Kennedy on the day he was assassinated.

And, at Aki Sato's urging, a collector in Bonn contributed a silk tie used by Adolf Hitler during his first year as chancellor. She worried over that, wondering whether to use it or not, and finally did, thinking that anyone who had caused so much trouble and death should never be ignored or forgotten. The quilt was her memorial to the twentieth century, and she was trying to fit in as much as she could. But there was too much. How, in a single quilt, to allude to the bombs, the planes, the high-speed trains, the skyscrapers? The Model T and TV. Aspirin and penicillin. And what about Joseph Stalin, where to put him? Or should she leave him in his grave, with his turbid memories of the millions he killed?

When Henry was still alive, he had always been urging her to rent a loft in SoHo, to give herself the space she needed. But she liked working at home, and the thought of going elsewhere made her uncomfortable. It would have been too formal, like going off to business—to an office, or a bank. She liked to sew or not sew as she pleased, early or late, getting up even in the middle of the night if a special idea woke her.

Henry had been in pianos. He went around the country buying up old Steinways and had them shipped to his shop in Tribeca, on Worth, where he reconditioned them and brought them back to life. There were old Steinways in Mississippi and Nebraska that people were eager to be rid of, but in New York there was a huge demand, and he made a good living at it. At home, in their condo apartment in Echo Terrace, what he had was just an old upright, on which he pounded out some Gershwin tunes, and some Kurt Weill.

When he traveled, she sometimes went with him, but mostly he traveled alone and she stayed home, busy with her quilts. He would be gone for two or three weeks, moving from city to city, and when he returned he brought back scraps and odd pieces for her to cut up and work with. A kimono from a second-hand shop, an old gown, a silk petticoat. And it was as if they were young again, gazing at each other, flirting, into bed and tearing eagerly at each other. Absence made them greedy, it stoked desire and stimulated their lust. He was eight years older than she was, and she liked that, he older and she younger. Even when she turned forty and he was pushing fifty, still they had this strong feeling for each other. She baked cinnamon cakes and corn bread, and he brought her wine and perfume and licorice, and made bread for her in the bread maker. He was not a great dancer, but when she put Sinatra on, or Lena Horne, they did slow dancing on the rug in the living room, and with the lights low, the feeling was as smooth as it had ever been.

And now here she was, in the same large living room, on the same rug, but she had removed all of the furniture and turned the room into a work space, and Henry, in his vague way, lingered in the shadows, looking on as she stitched the patches together. In the lower left corner, she had used Hitler's tie to make a dead tree, and beside it a dead horse. Through the broad middle, she had been inserting hints of skyscrapers, power lines, helicopters, though she was not entirely happy with this part, the middle, feeling that something was missing. In the upper right she had just finished with a gabardine patch that was the sun. It was emerging from behind a cloud, and that, she thought, was just right, because she liked the sun, believed in it, its lazy warmth, the way it nourished trees and growing things.

But the sun, she knew, was dangerous. Henry had always been warning her, insisting that she use sunblock and dark glasses when they went on their long walks, and the hateful irony was that it was Henry, always so careful about these things, who developed the skin cancer, and by the time the melanoma was discovered, it was too late for him. In three months he was gone, and she was devastated. They had been good for each other, and suddenly there was this emptiness, an enormous gap. They had got along. They'd had, each of them, their quirks and eccentricities, but they had managed, through the years, to amuse each other, teasing, annoying, entertaining, sleeping with each other in the big four-poster she had inherited from her grandmother. And he was still there for her, in memory, four years after his death, like an old habit, and somehow, she knew, she had to find her way past him. A few times she'd been out with other men, and became intimate with one, but nothing lasted, because the men she was meeting didn't seem right enough, or engaging enough, for her to make the effort.

After Henry's death, she had plunged more than ever into her work, and now it was still the work, more than anything else, that sustained her—planning, designing, using scissors, and needle and thread, picking and choosing from among the scraps of cloth that stood in heaps in the corners of the apartment. Her hands roving deep into piles of cotton and denim, taffeta and brocade, touching each piece. For her it was a tactile thing, as much as visual. The feel of the cloth had to be just right, or she wouldn't use it. And if she found a piece that evoked something special, it might change her whole idea of what she was doing, and she would alter her design.

She gathered the scraps from tailors who saved their throwaway pieces for her, one on Broome, and another on Seventh Avenue, in the Twenties. And there was a bridal shop on lower Madison, where gowns were made by hand, and there they passed over to her pieces of silk and lace and satin. Once a month she made the rounds in her hatchback, returning with plastic bags stuffed with everything she needed, each scrap unique, with its own mood and texture, like a song or a poem.

"Everything is love," she had said in a telephone interview that was aired on radio, on NPR. "Without love, I don't think I could have made any of these quilts. But love, genuine love, the love that moves and motivates, is so painful," she said. "So difficult."

They sent her a tape, which she occasionally replayed, and it always felt strange, listening to herself. How on earth had she ever wandered off into talking about love?

Suddenly the words had sprung to her lips, and there it was, love, love, love. The interviewer was miscued into thinking that she wanted to make some grand confession about her love life, but that wasn't it at all. "No, no," she said, and now, replaying the tape, she heard herself saying again, "not sexual love, not plowing around in bed, that's not what I mean at all, but something . . ." And then she was wordless, unable to come up with the phrase for exactly what she meant. "You mean something spiritual?" the interviewer asked. But she was confused, uncertain. "Yes. Yes—in a way. And yet—no, not exactly." She went on for a stretch, rather meaninglessly it now seemed, and realized she had made something of a fool of herself.

She was methodical in her routines, shopping at the food market on Tuesday, gallery-hopping on Thursday, and swimming at the Y on Friday. Every morning she was up at seven for breakfast and at work by eight. At ten she went down to the lobby to pick up the newspaper and her mail, and by eleven she was back at work again. If she swam or shopped, it was usually in the afternoon.

On a Wednesday morning, back in November, on her way to pick up her mail, as she stepped off the elevator, into the lobby, she saw Muhta Saad sitting on the black couch by the palm tree. He rose to greet her, and she sensed that he'd been waiting for her. He was from Iraq, having come over years ago to study for an MBA. It had been expected that he would return to Baghdad, to help in the oil industry, but he liked New York so well that he stayed and raised his children here. And now, instead of oil, he was in spices, working not for Baghdad but for himself, buying from growers around the world and selling to packagers here and abroad. He had cargoes of cinnamon and cloves in the holds of ships, moving from port to port, Ceylon to London, Zanzibar to New York.

"We have something to celebrate," he said, speaking in his slow, casual manner, a welcoming friendliness in his small brown eyes. His hair was thick around his ears but thin on top and black, no hint of gray.

He wore a dark worsted suit, and black-rimmed glasses.

"And what might that be?" she asked.

"I've just been to that gallery in SoHo, where they hang your quilts. I bought one."

"You did? Really?"

"The blue one. *Blue Feathers and Memory.* You will have to explain it to me."

She remembered laboring over that one, the trouble it had been, but in the end she had liked it very much and was sorry now that it was passing into Muhta Saad's hands. She would have hoped for someone with a greater feeling for the art, someone who didn't need to have it explained to him.

"They gave you a good price, I hope."

"I mentioned I knew you, but I think that only sent it up a notch. Still, anything for art—yes?"

She raised an eyebrow. Anything? And she had, dimly, a sense that there was more on his mind than a bit of small talk about her quilt. Something inside her was putting on the brakes, saying no, move on—but something else inside her was hovering, watching, waiting to see what might develop.

They had met several times before, once at Aki Sato's, and another time at the Rohrs'. She'd met his wife, a short, dumpy woman, and the son, Abdul. The wife dressed well, in subdued silks, but seemed tired and confused, if not depressed. But then Saad himself had struck her as depressed, and she wondered if it might simply be a cultural thing, the manner that middle-aged Iraqis adopted when they were in public. She didn't know any other Iraqis, and had been to the Middle East only once, on a tour of the holy places, where she had met no one but other tourists.

He invited her to dinner, to the St. Moritz, and she understood, now, exactly what was happening. He was using the purchase of the quilt as a hook to drag her into bed. Should she? Dare she? And something inside her whispering "Why not? Why not?" She'd been, in recent months, too much nose-to-the-grindstone and needed something, a diversion, something to lift her away. Too much needle and thread, and not enough simple abandon. She had never been involved before with anyone from the Middle East, and, since Henry's death, there had been only that one other man she'd been serious with, a musician, and it had lasted only a few months. So yes, she needed something, wholesale, though she did wish, at that moment, that it were someone else extending the invitation, because, pleasant though he seemed, Muhta Saad did not strike her as someone who was deeply interesting.

She was in motion, drifting past Farro Fescu's desk and stepping into the mail room, and Muhta Saad was close beside her.

"Do you enjoy your life?" he asked.

"Which part of it?"

"Being a genius."

"I'm not a genius," she answered, amused that he would use that word.

"But that's what they say about you at the gallery."

"Oh, them," she answered with a shrug, "what do they know?"

"Much too modest," he said, summing her up. "It's very attractive in you. It's admirable."

He was smooth, too smooth, and she wondered if that too might be an Arab trait. Or was it just him?

He looked at her now very earnestly, with softness and generosity in his gaze. "We could have, you know, a very good time together."

She was surprised by his directness, but not altogether put off by it.

"We can?"

"Why not?"

"I'm not aware that I was looking for a good time," she said, politely firm and maintaining her distance. And, reaching into her box, she took out what was there and saw that it was nothing but junk mail.

"But you owe it to yourself," he said. "It must be lonely, living alone."

"I owe nothing to anybody," she answered, annoyed now at his presumptuousness. And then, taking him all in, the tailor-made suit and the silk tie with tiny red circles against a field of gray, and his somber face, eyes with a drowsy remoteness, the jaw heavy, she saw how undesirable he was, his skin like old newspaper that had been in the sun too long, yellowing, on its way to a pale shade of brown. "You're a married man," she said. "You have a wife, and a son and a daughter at school, and I have to tell you—I am not a home-breaker."

"But you would not be breaking up my home," he answered, with restrained zest. "I am Muslim, and Allah is much more friendly about these things than Jesus and the Pope. And Muslim wives, you know, are very understanding."

She wondered if that was true, about Muslim wives. Weren't they jealous? Didn't they watch their husbands, like everyone else? She did know, though, that he was right about Allah, because years ago, in college, she'd read passages from the Koran, and now she remembered the Muslim vision of paradise—the men sitting around at an endless feast, being served by fancy young women who offered wine and sherbet and anything else they might desire. That, at least, was how she remembered it.

"I'm sorry, forgive me," he said, retreating in a way that wasn't quite a surrender. "I think, perhaps, I may have been too forward. I did not mean to offend."

"Oh, no offense," she said, a little too quickly, realizing, as she said it, that she was offering an encouragement she wasn't sure she wanted to give.

With his fingers he brushed some lint off his sleeve, then he tilted his head, looking at her with the barest hint of a smile. "The St. Moritz," he said. "They have a new chef. He's quite good, from Milano. Shall we? This evening? We'll talk about your blue quilt."

Do I need this, she wondered. Is it really worth the time of day? One by one, she dropped the pieces of junk mail into the wastebasket, not a single thing among them that

245

she cared to look twice at. And there he was, standing before her, waiting for an answer.

They met at the hotel, in the lobby, on Central Park South, at seven, arriving separately. She wore a black silk dress and pale lipstick and had made up her face, applying blush and mascara, but still with the amber barrettes in her brilliant white hair. He brought her into the dining room and the waiter sat them at a table by the wall, under a painting of the Matterhorn. She lingered over the menu and selected a rice dish, the risotto Milanese, with an artichoke on the side, and he ordered the marinated chicken breast on a bed of polenta. She drank Pellegrino, and he took Hennessy on the rocks, replenishing twice through the meal.

He ate slowly and spoke slowly too, a relaxed simplicity in the way he turned his words, and she noticed that his hands were large and thick, with stubby fingers. There was a puffiness about him, and she sensed that he was not a man who denied himself any of the comforts. Something oozy and thick in his manner, like heavy cream, yet there were redeeming moments when he exhibited a droll sense of humor. "I have a wife who watches the talk shows and the soaps," he said, carving into the chicken, "and a son who has decided he wants to be an undertaker. You see how it is? He can't wait to put me in the ground. But I'll fool him—I'll outlive him. And then what will he say?"

They talked about Yesenia, the girl on the cleaning crew who had been raped on the subway. Word was around, now, that she was pregnant. And they spoke of Mrs. Abernooth, still in the hospital after her accident and not doing well. Happily, he didn't bring up the quilt that he'd bought at the gallery, and she was glad to be spared the agony of having to explain it.

He had left Iraq long before the time of Saddam Hussein and considered himself lucky, at the moment, to be in America, rather than in the terrible mess that Iraq had become. Saddam was a distant cousin—"We're all related, you know, one way or another"—yet he deemed him a megalomaniac and a fool. "Nevertheless, he's devilishly clever," he said. "Bush won the war, but Saddam lives on. Already he has nerve gas and rockets, and now he wants the bomb."

"You visit? You go back?"

He laughed. "No, I don't return. They consider me the black sheep of the family. The government sent me over to study, and I was supposed to return but I didn't. So they think of me as a traitor. Two of my cousins are colonels in the Republican Guard. We used to throw rocks at each other, that's how we played. And now, if they had the chance, they would like nothing better than to strap me in a chair and pull out my fingernails."

He had handled, over the years, a wide variety of spices—nutmeg, cinnamon, mace, cardamom—but cloves remained his specialty, and much his favorite because of their history. He told her about the Portuguese, and the Dutch in the Moluccas, how they enslaved the natives and treated them brutally. But the Dutch wanted it all for themselves, so they drove out the Portuguese, and to guarantee their monopoly, they destroyed all of the clove trees in the Moluccas save those on the one island of Amboina. It sent the price sky-high. And there was a death penalty for anyone trying to break the monopoly. But a gutsy Frenchman, Pierre Poivre, smuggled some seedlings to Mauritius, and within thirty years, Dutch control of the clove trade was broken.

"Slavery, torture, death," he said, his fork hovering above the polenta. "In those days, they thought nothing of it."

"And us," she said. "We're more civilized?" She was thinking of the wars, and the millions of dead in the camps and the gulags, and in Cambodia, and so many in Africa.

"People are people," he said, with a wave of his hand. "It's unwise to expect too much."

Then he was talking again about the spices, the big

trading centers in New York and Hamburg and London. If the price dropped in New York, he diverted his shipments to London. If London dropped, he diverted to Hamburg. It was a daily grind, monitoring the markets. Only three years after he'd been in the business, he made a small fortune. When the clove trees in Zanzibar were hit by a disease, he rushed to the growers in Pemba, bought up all of the cloves he could find, and sold at a huge profit because of the scarcity. The following year he lost it in mace but made a comeback in cardamom.

"With cloves, there is this thing they call sudden death. It's a virus that attacks the trees without warning. Well, sudden death. We all worry about that, don't we."

"You find the thought of death troubling?"

"Only," he said, "when it interferes with business."

It was hard for her to imagine trees, whole acres of them, dying suddenly. One day full of leaves and flowers, and the next day gone.

"Do you use cloves?" he asked. "I have a shipment coming in from Zanzibar. There are some wonderful recipes, you know. Blackberry clove cake, and spiced beef tongue. And hasenpfeffer. Have you tried hasenpfeffer?"

After dinner, he led her through the lobby to the banks of elevators and brought her up to a room that he had on the twenty-first floor. It was a room that he kept on a long-term basis, for his business associates. When his contacts came in from India and South Africa, this was where he put them up, and he made the arrangement economical by time-sharing the room with a Syrian who ran a business in carpets.

And now me, Maggie thought, as she rode the elevator with this man she hardly knew, and for whom she had no special feeling. My turn to be time-shared. She had a sense that he went through many women, trying them out, the way one might try out different cars at a dealership. She didn't dislike him, but had no urgent need for him either. If she had been looking for a lover, on the hunt, Muhta Saad would not have been the one. But he was the one who had presented himself, wanting her, and as the elevator rose she felt unbalanced and at a distance, not just from him but from herself, as if she were outside of herself and looking on, uneasily.

Why, why, she wondered. Why am I doing this? And she thought again of the quilt in her living room, the section in the middle that she couldn't make right, that she had done and redone, tearing it apart and starting over, and wondered if her frustration with that was the thing that had brought her to this. Self-doubt and desperation, leading her on. Float with it, she thought, let it happen. But she couldn't, and, off the elevator, walking down the corridor, she was thinking crazy, wrong. Forget it. And in a kind of panic, she was about to turn and rush back to the elevator, but suddenly they were there, at the door, and she watched as Muhta Saad slipped the magnetic card in and out of the lock, and turned the handle.

And there it was, waiting for her, a spacious room with beige walls, with a desk and a wet bar, and the bed, a big one, king-size, covered by a spread of heavy brocade, blue and rose. The drapes were open, and after lingering by the door, she drifted over to the wide window and looked down at the park, the leafless trees lit by lamps and the headlights of cars sweeping through. The room had a faint aromatic smell, a hint of vanilla and something else, cinnamon, or was it cloves, and the sense of panic that she'd felt began to dissolve. She was calmer, less troubled. And somehow, as he drew close to her, it was easier for her than she had expected, as if they had done this with each other before, many times, and there was an old familiarity.

In bed she emptied her mind, turning physical, no thoughts, no words, and, closing her eyes, she thought of a forest, a warm wind racing through the trees, and she wasn't there, in the room, on a bed in a hotel, but somewhere of her own imagining, among the trees, transported. And a secret part of her was still wondering what it was that had brought her here, curiosity, or loneliness, or whimsy, or a latent, lingering fatalism. Or simply, in the strange way of things, a need for change, distance, something different.

Afterwards, he asked her if she would mind if he smoked, and she said that she didn't, and then he asked if she would like to try one, but she did not. "A new brand," he said. "I've never tried one of these before. Let's see. Here, look. Would you like to light the match for me?"

On a Friday, early afternoon, in her russet coat, she walked to Rector Street and took the N for a few stops, then switched to the J and rode to Queens, to visit the housemaid, Yesenia. She wore gloves and had her hood up, and carried a vinyl shopping bag.

She had always liked Yesenia and had enjoyed the times when she came to do the vacuuming. They would have juice and cookies together, and she'd show Yesenia what she was working on—and Yesenia, amazed at the colors, would shake her head in awe. "I could never do nothin' like that," she would say. "Never." And Maggie, passing the plate of cookies, would tell her she could do more than she imagined, if she trusted herself. And Yesenia would tell her about the apartment on Jamaica Avenue, by the el, and the trains going by, and how she looked down from her window one afternoon, when she was seven, and saw two men on the street shooting at each other. "You can't let that bother you," Maggie said. "Don't let it haunt you and slow you down." And Yesenia, shaking her head, looked away, through the window. "It don't slow me down," she said. "It's just there, like the other things." And then she was into the vacuuming, and Maggie never got around to asking what the other things might be.

And now it was December, bitter cold, and Yesenia hadn't been in since mid-October, because of what had happened on the subway that night in July, a sex maniac attacking her and dragging her off to a warehouse. She was so traumatized she was afraid to leave her apartment anymore. So Maggie, now, was going to her.

The J crossed the river into Williamsburg and, high on the el, grumbled along between Bushwick and Bedford-Stuy, then on through Woodhaven, heading toward Jamaica. Maggie got off at 111th, coming down the steep stairs into the avenue traffic, trucks and cars and buses, gut-roar of a motorcycle, slashes of sun and shadow under the el like something in an odd-angled dream. Sewer smells and car horns, no snow on the ground, but cold. Puddles frozen into black ice. Past the shops she went, pizza, video, linoleum, flowers, a bar and grill. Christmas decorations in the windows, blinking lights and plastic poinsettias. A dog lifted his leg, urinating on a parking meter. A blind man, black, with a white cane, lingering by a newsstand, and at a bus stop, a woman with a red scarf around her face. Two Hispanic girls walking, talking, warm breath from their mouths blossoming like white smoke, and across the street a tall, gangly boy with dreadlocks, the boom box on his shoulder thumping out a rap song.

Yesenia's place was above a hardware store. She lived there with her mother, who was at work, at the phone company, in the complaints department.

"I'm having a baby," Yesenia said, when she opened the door for Maggie. She was in jeans and a pullover sweater, and Maggie saw the long scar where the rapist had run his knife across her cheek.

"I know," Maggie said.

"Someone told you?"

Maggie had learned of it from Oscar, Yesenia's supervisor, who had visited Yesenia a few times already, and Yesenia had told him everything.

"Well, just imagine," she said calmly, putting her hand flat on her stomach. "Pretty soon I'll be big as a boat."

She showed Maggie her room, which overlooked the el, and she took Maggie's coat and laid it on the bed. On one wall there was a poster of Michael Jackson dancing on a car, and on another wall, Paula Abdul performing a lively gyration. Over the bed hung a crucifix, with a dried-out sprig of palm looped over it, which she had taken home from church on Palm Sunday, last spring. On the bureau was a small vinyl Christmas tree, and a picture of herself when she graduated from high school. And a Buddha, with a place on his lap to burn incense.

They went to the kitchen, and Yesenia put up a pot of coffee. It was a small room, with a gas stove that Yesenia lit with a match, and a small table with two wooden chairs. The checkerboard linoleum, gray and blue, was faded, cracked, worn through in front of the sink and the stove. There was a vase of artificial flowers on a ledge above the sink, asters and black-eyed Susans.

"You want to have it?" Maggie asked.

"Yes," Yesenia answered, with no uncertainty in her voice. "I do."

"You've thought about it? You're very sure?"

"It's mine," she said, touching herself again, putting her hand low on her abdomen. "And besides," she added, "I owe him. I took his life, and I owe him. That's why."

It took Maggie's breath away, hearing her say that. "Honey," she said, "he was bad to you. Real bad. You don't owe him anything. How can you think that?"

"It's how I feel," Yesenia said. "I hit him so hard, right on the head, with that heavy lid from the toilet."

Maggie put her hand on Yesenia's arm. "I'm sorry," she said. "I'm sorry you have to live with that. But don't dwell on it, try to let it pass. It will go away."

"I don't think so," she said.

"Yes, it will, it will become less important."

"I hope so."

Yesenia poured the coffee into white mugs and set out milk and sugar. She took out a crumb cake her mother had picked up at the supermarket and sliced a few pieces.

"What did your priest say?" Maggie asked.

"He said what I did was self-defense, so it was no sin. But he give me a whole rosary to say for penance. I think it was just in case."

"In case of what?"

252

"In case he was wrong and maybe it really was a sin."

"Don't think that," Maggie said. "You mustn't. You did what you did because it was what you had to do."

"He told me to go to the police and tell them everything what happened, but I didn't. If I do that, they only make a big fuss and bother, and I already got more fuss than I ever need."

Maggie nodded, accepting the wisdom of that. What could the police do for her now? Just bother her and make her life more complicated than it already was, with questions, reports, an investigation, and all the publicity in the news.

There was no living room in the apartment, just the kitchen and Yesenia's room, and her mother's room in back, and a tiny room off the kitchen, with the TV and a pile of laundry waiting to be folded.

"I brought you these," Maggie said, taking from her shopping bag a box of cookies, the same that she'd always had for Yesenia when she came to vacuum. Almond cookies, a whole almond on top of each one.

"You always so nice," Yesenia said.

"Save them," Maggie said. "Have them with your mother."

Then, from the shopping bag, she took a quilt that she'd made, vibrant blues and pinks. "This one is to put on your bed," she said. "It will keep you nice and warm." She stood up and let the quilt fall open and held it up for Yesenia to see.

"Can't put that on my bed," Yesenia said, rising to look at it, touching it. "It's too pretty."

"I'll make you a prettier one for the wall, if you want. This one is to sleep with." And then, letting go of the quilt, letting it fall, she reached out and took hold of both of Yesenia's hands.

"You mustn't bury yourself here," she said.

Yesenia stared blankly, as if she hadn't heard, or didn't want to hear.

"You ever coming back?"

"I don't know. I just don't know."

"What happened doesn't matter. You understand that, don't you? It wasn't your fault. You can't let it eat at you and ruin your life."

Yesenia stared at the floor.

"It's important to dress up and put on some lipstick and go out. You mustn't let the darkness close in on you."

Yesenia looked at her as if she were a stranger. "Is that why you come? To tell me that?"

"I came because I wanted to see you."

Yesenia put a hand up to her face, to the scar, where the man had cut her with his knife. "My face, you mean. You wanted to see my face."

Maggie put her hands on Yesenia's shoulders. "The scar doesn't matter, honey. It really doesn't."

"That's what you think?"

"It's what I know. You can move past this. You have to try."

Yesenia took a step away, to the kitchen window. The shade was up, and there were fly specks on the glass. The window looked across to the brick wall of another tenement.

"How much do they pay you?" Maggie asked. "When you do the vacuuming."

Yesenia told her.

"Look," Maggie said, "I need somebody to sew for me. I'll pay you twice that amount."

Yesenia rolled her head, left to right. Then she straightened. "I don't want no charity," she said.

"It isn't charity. Sewing is hard work. I'll expect you to do it right."

"I don't know how to sew," Yesenia said. "Never sewn nothin' but socks."

"I'll teach you."

"That Mrs. Wax—don't she sew for you?"

"And Mrs. Marriocci, yes. But they only come once a week, for a diversion. I need someone I can rely on all week."

"I don't know," Yesenia said doubtfully.

"You can work here at home, if you want. I'll bring the patches and show you what to do."

"I'll talk to my mom," she said.

"Yes, do that. That's good. Talk it over with her." And then, as she prepared to leave, "Did you see a doctor yet about that baby?"

"I went to the walk-in."

"The doctor examined you? They gave you an ultrasound?"

"They give me a book to read about how to breathe when the baby come."

"They tell you when to go back again?"

"Next week," she said.

"Well, you do that. You hear? A baby is a wonderful thing." She looked long and seriously into Yesenia's eyes and felt a kind of jealousy, because she'd never had a baby of her own. Twice she'd miscarried, the first time early on, but the second time in the fifth month, and it had been too much for her. She told Henry she didn't want to try again. She didn't have the strength for another disappointment. And now she regretted that, wished it hadn't been so, and blamed herself for not having had the strength and the energy.

Against her better judgment, she continued to see Muhta Saad, once a week and sometimes more, meeting always at the same room in the hotel at the park, usually in the evening, but often in the afternoon. He was a comfortable lover, attentive and slow, helping her, and she helped him. She liked him, and yet she didn't. Didn't and did, and it troubled her, being intimate with someone about whom she had ambiguous feelings.

His thick wrists and short, stubby fingers, and the thickness of his knees and ankles. She thought she would become used to him, but she hadn't. The hair on his head was thin, combed right to left, with a bald spot at the back, and his pubic hair was sparse, going bald down there too. His genitals, in repose, had a flabby, tired look, and she saw them as an image in a crazy quilt, off in a corner somewhere, made of burlap. That's what his genitals were, tired burlap, a muddy mix of yellow and brown, with the barest hint of blue for the vein. She wondered if his wife still loved him, if they still pleased each other, or did they play games of avoidance, merely putting up with each other?

This is wrong, she thought. So wrong. Yet she was caught up in it, drawn on by the strangeness, the uncertainty, the knowledge that sooner or later it had to end and she didn't know how, or when.

One morning she watched as he shaved. Half of his face was clean and smooth, the other still white with shaving cream. He held a straight razor with the fingers of his right hand, gripping it lightly and maneuvering deftly, as if it were an artist's tool, or a scalpel. She thought it quaint that he shaved that way. Henry had always used an electric shaver that buzzed warmly and lustily against his cheek, clearing the stubble.

His breakfasts, which he had sent up to the room, were ambitious—scrambled eggs, toast, orange juice, half a cantaloupe, coffee overwhelmed with sugar and cream, and double portions of bacon. What kind of a Muslim was he, she wondered, into the pork that way, and so thick at dinner with gin and brandy? She had never seen him pray. Five times a day the call to prayer for Muslims, but did he even own a prayer rug?

One night he had to leave early, at ten, to catch a plane to Houston, and she stayed, sleeping there, in the hotel room, and woke after midnight, the television on but the sound turned down. It was the end of a movie, two people in a car driving on a long, open road out west, a man and a woman, past cactus and Joshua trees, rain falling on the desert, the windshield wipers going. Long and somber, driving in the rain, and then it was over. The news came on, and still she didn't turn up the sound. People rioting on the streets of some foreign city, and police throwing tear gas. Then the anchor again, a woman, in a green blouse and pink jacket, talking, the lips, the eyes, and Maggie, only half awake and hating herself for being in this hotel room, thought it was better this way, the image but no sound, not having to hear the words.

In the morning, early, she stood by the window, barefoot, looking down at the park, the grass white with frost and the near pond iced over, seagulls wheeling in the air, and somewhere out there, among the evergreens and leafless maples, the joggers and walkers, and the statues she'd passed many times, Shakespeare and Schiller and Beethoven and Mother Goose. And already the heavy traffic nudging east and west, north and south, and she knew the trees and the grass were only ornaments, a disguise. The reality was the cars and the buses, the trucks, and the trains underground, and the cranes and the backhoes, the city a great engine coming awake and already in motion. Grinding, churning.

Even the skyscrapers were a deception—so tall and solid and motionless, but nothing standing still inside them, elevators rising and plunging, memos in and memos out. Money changing hands. Movement. Here to there, and there to anywhere. Taxis. Trucks carrying Muhta Saad's spices and Harry Falcon's frozen foods. Gas in the tank was the only true thing, and power in the third rail. Farro Fescu and Oscar and Muddy Dinks and the others on their way to Echo Terrace, starting their day, and why is she here, in this hotel where she has never felt comfortable, despite the paintings, the rugs, the marble, the studied elegance, the potted plants and the flowers.

A week later, when they went up to the room, Muhta Saad collapsed into one of the upholstered chairs, leaning back and stretching out his legs. His trip to Houston had not gone as well as he'd hoped. "Sometimes I become so tired," he said. "Do you grow tired?"

"All the time," she said.

"Life is heavy, it weighs."

She saw in his face a vulnerability that she hadn't seen before.

"When I'm busy," she said, "handling the quilts, I'm fine. But when I'm not working, that's when it weighs."

"For me too," he said. "When I'm closing a deal, time races. But then the weariness sets in."

He lit a cigarette. He was smoking Rothmans. A week ago it was Bima, from Indonesia. She noticed that he switched brands often. He inhaled deeply and, tilting his head, let out a long stream of smoke, sending it toward the ceiling. It seemed to relax him.

"Sowle," he asked. "Sowle. Is it an old name?"

"Very old," she said, settling into the other cushioned chair and slipping out of her shoes.

"Tell me," he said.

And she did, telling him about the Sowles who had crossed the ocean to Virginia, and soon there were Sowles in Maryland and New Jersey. One had died at Valley Forge, and there were Sowles who fought in the Civil War—one for the North, and two for the South. Sowles and Sowles, so many of them. Sometimes it was spelled with a *u* instead of a *w*: Soule. There had been a Soule on the *Mayflower*, but she was sure that her branch of the family had not descended from him.

"Did they all make quilts?"

"The women, yes, many of them."

"But not as fine as yours."

"Some were better." She told him of a Civil War quilt by a Sara Sowle, hanging in the Smithsonian. It had been used as a signal for runaway slaves making their way through the Underground Railroad. When it hung outside, on the line where Sara hung her wash, it was a signal the house was safe, but if it wasn't out, that was a sign to stay away. "It's rather weatherworn, as you might imagine. But a relic, priceless. She was good with a rifle too—shot a poor Confederate soldier who was trying to steal her nanny goat."

"Killed him?"

"Shot him dead. One of my great-great aunts."

"I'm glad you don't own a rifle," he said.

They didn't meet again until four days later, and not in the hotel but in a coffee shop in SoHo. He was much recovered from the gloom he'd been in after Houston, and she assumed that, one way or another, he had resolved whatever it was that had been causing a problem. He was cheerful, elated, and tried to persuade her to smoke one of the new brand that he had, Mild Sevens from Japan, but she hadn't smoked since she was a teenager and wasn't about to start again now.

This time, it was she who was experiencing gloom. Their relationship had begun in the early days of November, and now, in late December, it had reached a point where she was feeling the strain.

"I can't go on this way," she said. "This morning I passed your wife in the lobby, and we chatted. It made me feel so terrible. I don't thrive on deception."

"But my dear Maggie," he said, reaching across the table and putting his hand on hers. "It's not deception. If she knew, she would understand. As I told you. She would not be unhappy."

"Then why don't you tell her?" she said in a challenging tone.

"To spare her the concern," he answered calmly. "She would have to adjust, and I don't want to put her through that."

"You mean, in other words, that she'd be furious."

"No, no, not at all. Good Muslim women are brought up that way. Things are changing, I know—the younger ones, some of them, are different. But she was brought up the old way."

Maggie pursed her lips, giving him a look that cut deep.

"Maggie," he said, "you are putting trouble. Why are you like this today?"

Trouble? she thought. Am I trouble? She wanted to tell him he was trouble. Life was trouble. His Darshan cigarettes from India were trouble, and the Sweet Aftons from Ireland, and the Gauloises from France. The plain truth was that her quilt was not moving along very well, and she was beginning to panic. She should have been done with it by now, yet there was more to do, parts of it giving her trouble, especially toward the center. And she was feeling again the pains in her legs that she used to feel, years ago, and the only help was to soak in a tub of hot water, very hot, and when she did that it left her depleted and ready for sleep. So the bottom line in all this was yes—she was, and wanted to be, trouble. Testy, on edge, and she had a lot more to say. But there was no time to say it, because he had to rush off to a meeting at City Hall. He finished his drink, and they agreed to see each other the following afternoon, at the hotel. And by then she had made up her mind to break it off.

This time, she didn't spiff up for him. She wore a plain denim dress, no lipstick, no eye shadow, and didn't use the Chanel he had given her.

When she entered the room, he was lying on the bed, on top of the brocade spread, on his back, head on the pillow and hands clasped behind his head. His jacket and shoes were off, but he was still in his shirt and tie, and the sharkskin pants.

She sat on the edge of the bed.

"I have to get back to work," she told him.

"But you work every day. Don't you?"

"It hasn't been going well. I arrange the pieces, and then, when I look again, it's all wrong."

"It's a bad time?"

"A very bad time."

"What does that mean?"

"It means, I think, it's time for us to stop."

"Yes? You think so? Isn't that—a bit radical?"

"It's what I think."

She noted that he didn't seem particularly troubled by her decision.

He pushed up and swung around, sitting on the edge of the bed, beside her, a small space between them. He took a cigarette from the night table and tapped the end against his thumbnail, packing the tobacco, but he didn't light up.

"You're a complicated woman," he said. "Perhaps too complicated."

"I don't think of myself that way," she said, glancing toward the window.

"You know," he said, "I never did understand that quilt I bought at the Griffin. Even if you were to explain it, I think it would still escape me."

"In that case," she said, "I won't try."

"If you did, I would listen. But, as I think you know, I am wiser about spices than I am about art."

He put the cigarette down on the night table, and then, after a moment of silence, he stood up, facing her, looking down at her, and, much to her amazement, in a firm voice he pronounced the Islamic formula for the separation of husband and wife. "I divorce you, I divorce you, I divorce you," saying it first in English, then in Arabic. "See? Now it's over," he said, with a seriousness that seemed almost whimsical, "and the good part of it is that we can remain friends."

"But we were never married," she said, looking up at him, astonished.

"In your mind, perhaps not, but in mine we were. How could I, a religious man, make love to a woman to whom I am not married? I say the prayers five times every day, the *salah*. I don't always use a prayer rug, but in my heart I say them. I expect, soon, to make the journey to Mecca. My son doesn't consider these things important, but perhaps, when he is my age, he will begin to understand."

She looked up at him with bemused sympathy. "I think you're balmy," she said in a not unfriendly tone.

"I think so too," he said, with composure. "And of course, I shall return your quilt to you."

"But you purchased it at the gallery," she said. "You paid for it. I can't take it back."

"You must. I've been hiding it in a suitcase. If my wife saw it, she would begin asking questions and she would go crazy."

"She suspects?"

"About us? No, I don't think so. But there are other things, and I don't want to add to them." He stepped over to the wet bar and poured a Scotch, and returned with it, sitting again beside her on the edge of bed. "It's my son,"

261

he said. "He's taken up with that girl, the actress. Mrs. Abernooth's niece. You've met her?"

"She's a wonderful girl. And beautiful on stage."

He put the Scotch down on the night table, beside the unlit cigarette. "You saw the play? I couldn't bring myself to go. In any case, you know how it is. Only a Muslim can marry a Muslim. And my wife is losing her mind over this."

"Does she see a therapist?"

"She talks to her imam. But to what good, I don't know. This is America, where everything is permitted. My son the mortician, he's going to embalm non-Muslims and bury them in heathen cemeteries. And now he wants to marry an actress and beget children who will worship rock music and make television their bible. And still, he tells me, he thinks of himself as a good Muslim, even though he doesn't say the prayers." He looked at her. "Do you pray?"

"I don't know," she said. "I think living is a prayer. Working is a prayer. I know people who think looking at a cloud is a prayer."

"We all have our way," he said. He picked up the cigarette, and now he lit it, the smoke rising and vanishing into the ventilation grille.

"I'm thinking of moving," he said. "When there's a family crisis, I think it's always helpful to pack things up and make a move. There's a house on Long Island, on the north shore. I want you to see it and tell me what you think. Would you do that for me? I'll hire a car."

"Muhta, I don't think so."

He seemed weary, leaning forward, elbows on his knees, the cigarette in his left hand.

He shrugged. "As you wish," he said, in a way that seemed to suggest that he expected to see her again.

That night, she felt a cleanness, as if she'd been to a spa and had a body scrub and a soak in a hot tub, and had been anointed with holy oils from an herbal shop on

Mott Street. Washed clean and blessed, and free, able to think again and hope, and find her way.

She went back to the unfinished quilt, and she was on fire, full of ideas, and working swiftly. It was all opening up for her now, the part in the center that had been such a problem. She had tried putting FDR there, but that was wrong, and then an airplane, and that was worse. She had thought of many things, each less interesting than the last, but now, finally, she had it right, filling the center with a pair of hands. Her fingers flying in the night, busy, restless, racing—her fingers making fingers, and they were Henry's fingers. His fingers that had repaired old Steinways that he found in Cleveland and Pittsburgh, Denver and Kansas City, fixed them and made them new again, and made them sing. His long, tapered fingers that played so well, snatches of Gershwin, portions of Copland, zesty doses of Kurt Weill, pounding pronouncements from Carl Orff.

No one would know whose hands these were, and they would be talked about, by the people who talked about these things, as symbolic hands, the hands of workers and doers, the hands of humankind, but they were her Henry's hands, more precious to her than any hands she had ever known, right there at the center. And as the sun came up, flooding the room with its brightness and igniting the quilt, she felt tired, so tired, and went to the kitchen for a glass of warm milk before going off to bed.

PART TWO

I hear robins a great way off, and wagons a great way off,
and rivers a great way off, and all appear to be hurrying
somewhere undisclosed to me.

—EMILY DICKINSON, LETTER TO LOUISE
AND FANNIE NORCROSS, 1873

And so it was I entered the broken world
To trace the visionary company of love, its voice
An instant in the wind . . .

—HART CRANE, FROM "THE BROKEN TOWER"

The Blood Purge
of 1934

For many cosmetic surgeons, a liposuction is just a liposuction, but for Theo Tattafruge it's a work of art. Before
he operates, he spends a great deal of time getting to
know his patients. What kind of music do they prefer,
what kind of weather? Do they follow baseball?
Basketball? Read poetry? Several of his patients are
actors—he wants to know the kinds of roles they hope to
play. If someone has lost a husband or a wife, or a child,
these are things he must know about. Before he can start
a procedure—working on a nose or a jaw, a buttock or a
breast—he has to understand the personality. Is the
patient garrulous or shy? Witty or ponderous? For him,
all of these things matter.

He handles everything, from face-lifts to breast
enhancements, though increasingly he's been focusing
on sexual reassignment surgery—SRS—changing male
anatomy to female, and vice versa.

The simple procedures, nose jobs and cheek implants,
he handles in the office, on East Sixty-ninth, but the
more complicated things, like the sex-change operations,
he performs at a surgical center or at a hospital. The costs
are staggering. For a full female-to-male procedure,
including hysterectomy, mastectomy, penis construction,
and hormone treatments, more, much more, than the
price of a high-end imported luxury sedan. And try to
find an insurance carrier that will cover it. Yet it isn't
only the rich who come to him but waitresses, postal
clerks, and school teachers too, struggling for years to

come up with the money, and at the very least it's a mark of how desperately they want the change.

After his morning shave, he looks at himself in the mirror and wonders—would he do it? Change his sex? Give up his penis and live with a vagina? Lunacy, he thinks, feeling no such need or desire. Still, he wonders what life would be like as a woman. His hair long, eyebrows plucked, mascara and rouge on his dark skin that he's inherited from his Nubian grandmother. And breasts, the weight of them on his skinny chest. To exist in a woman's body, thinking a woman's thoughts. Would he flaunt his sexuality, bold and insolent, or would he hide it, cutting his hair, wearing pants and mannish clothes?

Touching his face, turning left and right, what he knows about himself, what he sees in the mirror, is that he's tired. The lines, the bloodshot eyes, drabness, down-turned lips, the frown lines etched into his forehead. It's the stress, the involvement. Some days he loves it and can't imagine living without it. He carves, shapes, brings beauty out of ugliness, and that, to him, is a pleasure like no other. But other days it tries his patience. A ballerina complaining because her new nose is half a centimeter shorter than what she wanted, and she goes away miserable. The cheekbone implants on an aging dentist shifting ever so slightly, giving his face a lopsided look. Fix it, fix it. One patient wants his penis lengthened, another wants it removed. A woman, a postal clerk, wants her breasts cut off and her vagina blocked, but she can't afford a penis, so she will live in a strange limbo between male and female. Having turned fifty a few months ago, he begins to wonder how long he will go on. Should he continue till he drops, or should he pack it in while he still has his health and energy and retire to the islands?

The music of Vivaldi continues to please him. At night he relaxes on the couch, enjoying the cantatas, the violin sonatas, the motets. He has a special attachment to two of the flute concertos, *La Notte* and *La Tempesta di Mare*, and there is a piece for the bassoon that he never tires of.

Around Christmastime he acquired a cat, an old thing that he found at a pound, a patch of fur missing from its forehead, and a scar there. Afflicted, no doubt, with traumas and bad memories, but friendly, affectionate, and needing attention. When he's on the couch, lying down, she rests on his chest, purring. When he sits up and reads, she's on his lap, bothering him. Sometimes, whimsically, he imagines the cat must be Nora, who is still in the hospital, in a coma, her body hooked to tubes and catheters but her spirit wandering free, and now it has taken up residence in this lonely creature that demands so much of him. She sleeps on his bed. She wakes him in the morning, complaining strenuously, wanting to be fed, and then wanting to be brushed. Often, when he returns from the office, or the hospital, he finds her asleep in the canoe, as if she understands about it, that it's something special, a water hearse that had ferried the dead to another world.

His reading, these days, is still focused on Teddy Roosevelt. It was Nora who started him on this path, and he's still there, browsing through the diaries, letters, biographies. Teddy with his high-pitched voice and clenched fist, gritting his teeth when he smiles. Heavy moustache and pince-nez with thick lenses, and a poetic eye for sunsets. And his gun, his cowboy boots, his small feet, his gargantuan appetite, his San Juan Hill, his speak-softly-but-carry-a-big-stick. And the bad times that he had. The worst was a day in February, in 1884, when his mother and his wife both lay dying in the same house, at 6 West Fifty-seventh Street. His mother was on the second floor, suffering from typhoid, and his wife, Alice, on the floor above, dying of Bright's disease. A day and a half earlier, she had given birth to their only child, a daughter. And Teddy going back and forth between them, up and down, his mother passing on in the early hours of the morning, and Alice at two in the afternoon. A day of fog, rain, and muddy streets, St. Valentine's Day and warm for February, the temperature soaring into the high fifties. He was twenty-five years old.

After the double funeral, he sold the house, thinking it cursed, and returned to Albany, where he immersed himself in work and finished out his term as an assemblyman.

In June, he left New York and went off to the Maltese Cross, a ranch where he owned some cattle, in the Dakota Badlands. He roped cattle and branded them, handled horses, and wore himself out on the range, the stark drama of the Dakota landscape matching the loneliness that he felt. There were days when he rode more than a hundred miles, and nights when he had no sleep at all. Once he was in the saddle for forty hours, and five horses went down under him.

In August he rode off to the Big Horn country of Wyoming, with a Colt revolver, a No. 10 choke-bore shotgun, a Winchester repeater, a Sharps, and a double-barreled Webley express. He killed whitetail bucks and blacktail bucks, and sage hens, prairie chickens, jack-rabbits, elk, and grizzlies. In all, more than a hundred and fifty kills in less than seven weeks. One morning he put down two bucks with one bullet, at four hundred yards, and remembered it, years later, as the best shot he ever made.

An unusual life, Theo thinks, a man of paradox and contradiction. He's soft and hard, tough and gentle, filled with thought and reflection but restless, with a gnawing hunger for rugged adventure. He has a profound involvement with nature, writing again and again of "the hidden spirit of the wilderness ... its mystery, its melancholy." But despite the visionary drift of these reveries, he remains a hardheaded realist, a tough, roughriding cowboy, eager with a gun. And Theo is unable to put the two Teddy Roosevelts together—the melancholy contemplative who feels the power of moonlight, and the one who has a passion to hunt and kill.

On the morning of the battle for San Juan Hill, while the regiment moved into position, what he saw from the top of El Pozo was, he wrote, a "lovely morning, the sky of cloudless blue, while the level simmering rays from the just-risen sun brought into fine relief the splendid palms which here and there towered over the lower growth." But then, after that moment of sun and tall palms, he plunges into a fierce day of fighting, July 1, 1898, rushing about, organizing his men and urging them on, shells bursting overhead and bullets from the Spanish Mausers whizzing past his ears. As he leads his men against a line of trenches, two Spaniards, retreating, fire at him and run, and he fires back, emptying his revolver, missing one, who gets away, but hitting the other, who doubles over, in Teddy's words, like a jackrabbit.

And Theo, reading that, wonders about himself. Could I do such a thing? Kill a man? Aim a pistol and shoot him dead? He has never fired a gun, never been in a war, and it amazes him that Teddy, who could write so beautifully of sunrises and sunsets, could speak of the soldier's death so offhandedly, shooting a jackrabbit, that easy, just like that.

In the operating room, during a long surgery, he talks, bantering with Marie, his surgical nurse, and Sharlene, his anesthesiologist. The chatter relieves the tension, and he finds too that it heightens his alertness. And today, working on a female-to-male transsexual, he pulls up the story about Teddy that he likes best—Teddy as a boy, visiting the Nile with his parents, sailing from Cairo to Luxor, on to Aswan, and back to Cairo, some twelve hundred miles, the dahabeah gliding dreamily between the muddy banks of the river.

The woman on the table is fully under, with general anesthesia. The hysterectomy had been performed a month ago, and Theo is now constructing a penis, using skin taken from the patient's forearm. It's tedious work, manipulating the skin, with its veins and arteries and sensory nerves, converting it into a penis shaft with a urethra and glans. It used to take him six hours to do this, but now he does it in four, largely because of Marie's help.

She's fast with the instruments, knowing what he needs without his having to ask, and she's quick to apply clamps, and deft with the forceps, gripping portions of tissue as he bends close, cutting and shaping and linking and tying.

"Teddy Roosevelt is fourteen years old," he says, not lifting his eyes from his work. "His parents take him for a two-month journey up the Nile. Question: This entire trip, what does he have his eyes on?"

"The belly dancers," Marie says, handing him the ribbon retractor, and adds, coyly, because she knows her answer can't be right, "Do I disappoint you, Dr. Tattafruge?"

"In a thousand ways."

Marie glances at Sharlene, the anesthesiologist. "I just don't know how to please him," she says, in her faux-naïf manner, then reaches across the table and, with a swab, wipes the beads of perspiration from Theo's forehead.

"He was looking at the birds," Sharlene says.

Theo, intense, working on the forearm skin, is amazed. "How did you know that?"

"I went to Luxor during my junior year in college. The Nile was full of birds."

"And what did Teddy do to the birds?"

"He took their picture," Marie says.

"Hopeless, hopeless," Theo says, handing the ribbon retractor back to her, and she puts into his gloved hand the hooked knife. "What he did is—well, he shot them dead," he says. "And how many do you suppose? Ten? Twenty?"

"Thirty-seven," Marie says.

Theo, working on the glans, putting the sensory nerves in place, still doesn't look up. "More like two hundred," he says.

"With his mom and dad looking on?" says Sharlene.

"His dad gave him a brand-new double-barreled shotgun. It was Christmastime. He killed kestrels, doves, herons. Egrets. Cranes."

"What's a kestrel," Marie asks.

"An eagle," Sharlene offers.

"Well, more like a falcon," Theo says. "He stuffed them. Every night, after supper, on the boat deck. He disemboweled them, cleaned them, washed them with chemicals, and stuffed the ones that were dried out and ready. He was bringing them home, creating his own natural history museum. A few wild ducks, and kingfishers too."

He uses the labia majora to construct a scrotum, and in the final hour of work he puts the penis in place, attaching the urethra and connecting the artery and veins to their proper links in the groin. The nerves that had given sensation to the clitoris he connects to the penis, where they will grow and, in time, with luck, they will furnish the sensation of orgasm.

And then, with everything in place, the connections made, the penis is done. It's long and thick, and, as Theo steps back, giving himself a breather before starting on the breasts, Sharlene moves in for a close look.

"Beautiful," she says. "I think she's going to have a swarm of happy orgasms."

"He," Theo says. "She is now a he."

"What a lovely piece of work," Marie says, admiring the penis through a large magnifying glass.

"Would you like one for yourself?" Theo asks.

"Not quite yet," she answers. "But I'll think about it. I really will."

"On that trip up the Nile," Theo says, "when they reached Luxor, Teddy saw the temple of Karnak by moonlight, and he was awestruck. Those gigantic, ancient columns. He said it took him back to the time of the pharaohs, giving him a glimpse of the ineffable. Isn't that impressive?"

Marie was still using the magnifying glass. "Fourteen you said he was? Why did he kill all those birds? What was wrong with him?"

"Well, they didn't have television," Sharlene says.

"There's plenty of things they didn't have," Marie says. "Isn't that right, Dr. Tattafruge?"

"Well, they had books. And horses. And bonnets. And

273

snake oil. And ice cream, plenty of ice cream." And then, rolling his shoulders, loosening up, "Now for the mastectomy."

This is the part he hates, the cutting away of the breasts, especially when they are young and beautiful, as these are. The patient on the table is an exotic dancer whom he's seen in performance in a sex den in the East Village. She's looking for a new life. She wants to go home to Wyoming and work in rodeos, riding wild horses and roping steers. Such a waste, he thinks. He puts a hand on each breast, getting the feel of them. The weight, the heft. He has, he knows, a romanticized view of breasts, and why not? Fountains of milk they are, sources of life and full of magic, stirring up a rich hormonal surge in adolescent boys and their brothers, and in some who are not so young. The maracas, the jugs, the nay-nays, the TNTs. The cakes, the jujubes. The lollies. The gazongas. And this lovely pair, about to be lost to history because the silly girl wants to be a rodeo cowboy in Wyoming.

The procedure will take an hour. "Let's go," he says, and Marie is ready, handing him the surgical scissors.

That night, after a light supper, he sits for a while in his living room, in the canoe, relaxing, elbows on his knees and chin in his hands, thinking he should move out of Echo Terrace because too many of the residents have used his services, and he has never considered it sensible to live close to his patients. He has worked on Ira Klempp, giving him cheek implants, and on Luther Rumfarm, lengthening his penis and adding to its thickness, and now he wants an implanted pump, to improve his performance. For Mrs. Dillhopper, a breast augmentation, and for Mrs. Marriocci, a breast reduction because she suffered so much from the weight and the sweating, breaking out in rashes.

For Juanita Blaize, the pop singer, he performed a buttocks enhancement, and quickly after that her popularity soared. She became the Bad Girl from Bahama, the

Naughty Nuisance from Nassau, the Saucy Sister with the Swivelling Bottom, the Toothsome Thunder from out of Tomorrow. A few pounds of transplanted fat did it all.

Should he move? Go elsewhere?

Vivaldi is on, a new CD, the "Primavera" section of *Le Quattro Stagioni*, and his mind slips away, floating, and when the phone rings, he doesn't hear it until there is a pause in the music. He climbs out of the canoe, feeling a kink in his back, and grabs the phone from the table by the couch. It's Maggie Sowle, on the floor below.

He likes her, likes her voice, thinking how pleasant it is, as he returns to the canoe. She's calling, she says, for a special favor, and apologizes for bothering him like this at the end of the day. It's about the maid, Yesenia, she still has this awful scar on her face, from the assault last October, on the subway. It would be wonderful, she says, if something could be done.

"Could you?" she asks, with a gentle urgency. "Would you?"

"But does she want it?" he wonders. "I haven't seen her, she hasn't spoken to me." The cat is in the canoe with him, toying with his untied shoelaces.

"Oh, she wants it," Maggie says.

"You asked?"

"Of course not. How could I bring it up without first knowing you'd be agreeable?"

"I see," he says, feeling, for a moment, that the canoe is in cloudy water, drifting. "But you know," he says, "there are many who prefer to keep their scars. When a trauma occurs, it changes the personality. Not everyone rushes into restorative surgery. Some feel that to erase the scar would be a way of denying the event that caused it—so they hold on to it, it's part of their identity."

"Theo," she says, with a touch of exasperation, "all I'm asking is if you'd be willing to do it. She has no insurance."

"Who's paying? You?"

"No. You. That's why I'm calling. But sure, I'll pay for it."

"Well, in that case," he says, fumbling, feeling dumb for having, in his obtuse manner, missed the point, "since you put it that way, of course, yes. I'll do it. I will. As a favor to her. And to you. But talk to her first. Find out if she really wants it. Is she still at home, afraid to travel?"

"Oh no, she's past that," Maggie says, and adds that Yesenia was coming in now and sewing for her, working on the quilts.

He's out of the canoe now, walking around the apartment, with the cat on his shoulder. "You mean she's quit the maid service? Really? Is she any good?"

"She has a knack for sewing. I think she'll do very well at it."

"Well, if she's going to be a seamstress instead of movie star," he says, a bit too brashly, "why does she need the scar removed?"

There's a silence at Maggie's end, and then, simply, "You don't want to do it."

"But I do. I do. I'm just upset she doesn't do my rooms anymore. They send that awful Hungarian woman, Zegroba. She looks so angry and unhappy, it's depressing to have her around."

"Did you have a thing about Yesenia?"

"What kind of thing?" he says, surprised at her forwardness.

"She said you took her picture. Did you have sex with her? Is that why you don't want to fix her face?"

Not just forward, he thinks, but bold and more interesting by the minute. "Is that what you think? God help me, no, how could you imagine such a thing? I only have sex with my special woman, and I pay her well for it. She'd be very upset if she thought I was playing around with the help. I took Yesenia's picture to use with my patients, to show the possibilities. She has terrific nose and jaw alignment."

"She *was* pretty, yes, before the scar," and he hears the change in her tone. "I'm sorry," she says, "I never should have asked."

276

"Why?"

"We're neighbors, and neighbors shouldn't impose. And this is, I realize, a big imposition. It was wrong of me."

He understands, now, that she's fearful of being in his debt, doesn't want to be obligated in any way.

"But I'll do it," he insists. "I want to."

"I'm not sure you do."

"I would have made the offer myself. But, stupid me, it never crossed my mind."

"It's all right," she says, "it really is. I'm to blame."

"If I'd told you that I did have a thing about her, would that be better?"

"It would be worse."

"And if I'd said I had slept with her?"

"That would be unspeakable."

The cat leaps from his shoulder to the slate ledge above the fireplace, landing deftly among the framed photographs—his mother, his father, the Nubian grandmother, his son in Seattle, and the Belgian grandfather who died in Cairo many years ago, the victim of a spirochete that entered his body while he was swimming in the Nile.

After another long pause at her end, Maggie's voice is soft and reluctant, like a voice in a darkened room, where nothing is certain, and every step is precarious. She says, simply, with a kind of fatigue, "Will you do it?"

"But first we must talk," he says.

"I thought we just did."

"I mean Yesenia," he says. "And no matter what you think, I will want her picture, before and after."

The cat leaps back onto his shoulder, claws gripping hard, and he hates the pain.

Occasionally, for relaxation, he shoots baskets in the park. Just stands there at the foul line, sinking one after another. Ball through the hoop, ball through the hoop. He has never played on a team, always too slight for that and never quite good enough. Just likes the feel of it, holding the basketball in his hands and aiming for the hoop.

Completely meaningless, he's aware, yet it reflects, in many ways, what he sometimes feels about life, about time and destiny. The universe expanding forever, thinning out, no purpose in it, simply playing itself out. Ball through the hoop, ball through the hoop. Everything moving farther and farther away. But he can still score, shooting from the foul line, and when he's had enough of that, he goes home and showers, washing himself clean.

The big secret in his family, when the members of the family were still alive, was that his grandfather, on his mother's side, had been a brownshirt, one of the rough, brawling group, the SA, that had helped to catapult Hitler into power. But the brownshirts, opposed by the army, quickly became an embarrassment, and Hitler got rid of the leaders, including his friend Röhm, in the Blood Purge of 1934. It was fast and ruthless, morning to night on a Saturday, the thirtieth of June, with Göring and Himmler in charge of the dirty work, and by noon of the following day it was mostly over. Hitler announced that sixty-one had been shot, though a postwar investigation in Munich put the number at over a thousand. Among the dead were not just the leaders of the SA and some of their followers, like Theo's grandfather, but many who had nothing to do with the brownshirts, people who had opposed Hitler in the past, old enemies, as well as former friends and aides who knew too much and had loose tongues.

Theo didn't learn about it until he was a junior in high school, at a time when his mother was about to undergo a gall-bladder operation. She was in great pain, and fearing she might not survive, she told him many things that she'd never spoken of before. The story about her father was something she had agonized over, thinking it would be better if it died with her. But then she decided to tell him, saying it was too important to keep hidden and he should know about it, because it was useful to know such things, it might have a bearing on how he lived his life.

"He was so young, my father, he hardly knew what he was into. It was the craziness of the time, he was swept up into it. The brownshirts, they thought they were doing something for Germany. The marching, the singing, the clashes in the street. They had guns, uniforms. But my father was just a carpenter. Why did he let himself become involved with that rowdy crowd? What did he know of Hitler? How could he foresee what Hitler would become? And then, that awful day, he was arrested and brought to the Prinz Albrechtstrasse jail, where they killed him. He was thirty-one. My mother was so distraught, she gathered our things and we left Germany and went to live with her aunt in America, in New Haven. And when I met your father, he brought me to Cairo with him, where his parents were living. And there, as you know, you were born."

She survived the gall-bladder operation, though it was a hard recovery for her, and it was quite some time before she was herself again. And Theo, stirred by what he now knew, spent a great deal of time in the library, learning everything he could about the purge that killed his grandfather.

One brownshirt, Karl Ernst, was taken while on his way to his honeymoon. The bride and the chauffeur were shot and wounded, and Ernst, severely beaten, was brought back to Berlin, put against a wall, and shot. He died crying *"Heil Hitler!"*—never suspecting that it was Hitler himself who had unleashed the Gestapo.

An army general, Kurt von Schleicher, was shot at his villa on the outskirts of Berlin, with his wife. And Erich Klausener, the leader of Catholic Action, was killed in his office. Franz von Papen, vice-chancellor of Germany, protesting to Göring about the killings, was put under house arrest. His chief secretary, Herbert von Bose, was murdered at his desk.

When he had exhausted the resources of his school library, and the Muhlenberg library at Seventh, next to the YMCA, he went to the Forty-second Street library and found a copy of *The White Book of the Purge*, which had been put together by a group of émigrés in Paris, listing the names of the dead. And there, on the yellowing pages, he found the name of his grandfather, Hans Tort, but no explanation of why he had been killed. And still he read, searching, roving through pamphlets, scouring the indices of heavy tomes, finding chapters and whole books on the purge.

Gustav von Kahr, who had suppressed the Beer Hall Putsch in 1923, was found in a swamp, his body ripped apart by pickaxes.

Bernhard Stempfle, the Hieronymite priest who had helped in the editing of *Mein Kampf*, was found in a forest near Munich, his neck broken. He knew things about Hitler's affair with Geli Raubal, who had committed suicide, and he'd had a way of talking too much. Geli Raubal was Hitler's niece, the daughter of his half-sister.

Schneidhuber, chief of police in Munich, baffled by what was happening to him, called out to the firing squad, "Gentlemen, I have no idea what this may be about—but please shoot straight."

And Röhm, infamous Röhm, against him too Hitler turned. Boss of the brownshirts, whose friendship with Hitler had survived fourteen turbulent years—for him too, the thirtieth of June, it all fell apart. Fleshy, muddy-eyed, brutal, his face scarred from the Great War, part of his nose gone— without him, Hitler would never have gotten off the ground. But him too, his time was over and he had to go. In Munich, in Stadelheim prison, he was offered a pistol and given the option of suicide, but he declined. "If Adolf wants me dead, tell him to shoot me himself." At that, two SS officers entered the cell and fired their pistols at him.

And there were others, innocent bystanders, caught in the storm and killed by mistake. Willi Schmid, a music critic, was at home with his family, playing a Beethoven sonata on his cello when the SS broke in. They took him away, and a few days later they sent him home in a sealed coffin, with apologies. He was the wrong man. The Willi they'd been looking for was Schmidt, not Schmid, and now both of them were dead.

All of that Theo read about. Page after page, book after book. But nothing about his grandfather, just the name on a list. Had he, like the music critic, been simply a mistake? Or had he done something, said something? But he came to understand, painfully, that there were to be no answers, because the past was like a faraway country that you could never visit, sealed off at the border, and though you might read about that country and learn certain things, you could never see it for yourself, and the things you wanted to know were lost in fog and rain and mud and bad weather. When he pestered his mother, urging her to dig deeper into memory, all she could say was that her father had been a simple man, a carpenter, and had let himself be caught up, stupidly, with the wrong people.

"That's what they did, the Nazis, they were killing everyone. They put in jail, into concentration camps. And they killed. See? That's to learn," she said. "There are bad people. One must stand up to them and not let them have their way. The Hitlers, the Himmlers, the Görings. Your grandfather, poor man, he was nobody, but he became mixed up with them, and look, the price he paid."

Foolish he may have been, but Theo, sixteen, wished he had known him and tried to visualize him, imagining the touch of his hand, the sound of his voice, the smell of his cigarettes. There were no photographs. What color was his hair, he asked. And what color his eyes. How tall? How long his fingers, his arms. Did he wear sweaters? A hat? And it turned his stomach that they had grabbed hold of him one day and put him against a wall and shot him.

"What kind of cigarettes," he asked his mother.

She didn't know, couldn't remember. "German cigarettes," she said. "And my mother hated them, they smelled awful."

At six in the morning, he lies half awake, his body too sluggish to move but his mind in motion, looping through problems, new data, unresolved questions. The

German report on the high incidence of depression among female-to-male transsexuals, and the Italian report on infection. The French report on hormones. Estrone lowering the metabolic rate, robbing the body of energy, making the patient feel cold. Estinyl hardening the body lines, removing fat and raising metabolism, making the patient feel overheated. Progesterone in synthetic form causing leg cramps. Maximum breast size achievable from hormones alone is a size A. For anything larger than that, implants are necessary.

What, he wonders, would Antonio Vivaldi have thought of all this? Would he have composed an Estrogen sonata? A Provera concerto? His music still pleases. It charms, warms, makes life bearable. When the morning wake-up sounds, Vivaldi comes on automatically, piped into his bedroom, and he lies there, listening, letting the music sweep through him, giving himself over to the rushing notes, the crisp rise and fall, the swift crescendos, preparing himself for the moment when he will move off the bed and plunge into the new day.

In his travels, he's run into several Vivaldi hotels and restaurants. One in Leipzig, where he stayed two nights, on his way to Munich, and one in Belgium, in Westerlo, where he stayed for a week. And an Osteria Vivaldi near the Campo San Polo, in Venice. Several months ago, he discovered the Caffè Vivaldi in the Village, on Jones Street, where he goes for the lobster soup and the chicken Trieste and the espresso doppio. He brought Nora's niece there for dinner. Angela. When he first saw her, in the lobby at Echo Terrace, he was astonished at how much she resembled Nora. The nose, the eyes, the chin, the way she held herself, and the way she tilted her head when she spoke. But younger, of course, and prettier, with a refreshing liveliness, and none of Nora's remoteness. Still, it was that laid-back quality in Nora that had made her interesting, and he had always liked that in her.

He wishes he had known Nora when she was Angela's age, with youth and energy and everything good going for her. He might have married her instead of Estelle, and everything would have been vastly different. Different for Nora, and obviously for him. But as he thinks this, he wonders if it's true. Would things have been better, really, or simply other, not the same? And, possibly, worse?

He continues to visit Nora, once a week, and with his stethoscope listens to her heart. At first, he'd thought her long coma came of a refusal to heal, as if she were choosing death, wanting it, and it was coming on too slowly. But now he suspects that she was, in fact, struggling to stay alive, using the coma as a way of resisting the death that would have taken her long ago, if she hadn't had such a strong desire to live. Life continues to baffle him, life and death. He doesn't understand any of it. The more he knows, the less he understands, and that, he thinks, is the whole meaning of birth and existence, a leap into the unknown, with the allegros and andantes of Vivaldi lending a comfort along the way. The unknown and the unknowable, and for all the brainpower that he has, he is not, he realizes, a quick learner.

Angela's play has been on since December, but he doesn't have a chance to see it until the very end of January. And then, when he goes, on a Tuesday evening, he loves it. Christopher Marlowe, full of violence and treachery and hate, a perfect metaphor for life—the cheating, the killing, the grabbing for money and power. When he listens to Vivaldi, he's lulled into imagining that it's possible to grow beyond the hate, but when he takes a hard look at Somalia, Bosnia, Zaire, and the boil and simmer of the Middle East, there it is, plain as mud—life is a mess. He thinks of his grandfather killed in the purge, in Germany, and here, just last summer, Yesenia raped on a subway. And Estelle, how she robbed him of his son, taking him to Seattle. People will do wrong things. It's in the architecture of the brain, hate-love. But this is news? History, too true, is the history not of paradise but of paradise lost. Who said that? Somebody? And here, now, the bloodiest century of them all, more killing, torture, bombing, and destruction than ever before. So yes, why not, *The Jew of Malta*. Marlowe with his garish, manic, black-humor vision of hell on earth, still cooking. And yet, passionately, he clings to Vivaldi and wishes the Creator had listened to "La Primavera," rather than to Marlowe, before rushing into let there be light.

During the play, he's in the fifth row, center, attentive through the first two acts, following the plot and the character development. But then, as often happens when he goes to the theater, his mind wanders and he's thinking of the women in his life, reflecting that, by and large, he's been lucky. His mother giving him Vivaldi, and Nora giving him Teddy Roosevelt and those peaceful hours with her animals, which made such a mess of her apartment. And María Gracia giving him sex, and wonderful sex it is. His women so good to him, except of course for Estelle, who gave him a son and then took him back, carrying him off to the other side of the country. And how he feels that pain, wanting a son that he could see and touch and lift up and carry around, and help, and watch grow. But how? He's spoken to María Gracia about it, pleading with her, but she was right—for her, plainly, it was impossible, and he was wrong. How could he have imagined such craziness anyway? Yesenia is out of the question, already pregnant, carrying a rapist's child, and Angela, young Angela, there on stage, eager for a career—she needs the burden of a pregnancy? Juanita Blaize was never possible, and Mrs. Wax and Mrs. Marriocci, well, sadly, over the hill.

And then, remarkably, while he sits there, fifth row center, when he sees Barabas raising a hand, making an obscene gesture, it strikes him that if María Gracia won't give him a child, then it will have to be Nora. It comes to him with such force and clarity that he's astonished he hasn't thought of it before. An egg could be taken from her, and an embryo could be formed. Claudio Nascita will do this for him. Nora, yes. It could be done. And he will find a woman, someone suitable, to grow the fetus. Already there were rent-a-womb listings in the yellow pages. He feels lofty, lifted beyond himself, because this, surely, is the answer, and it continues to amaze him that he has only thought of it just now.

His mind returns to the play at the moment when it's discovered that the nuns, after partaking of the poisoned porridge sent by Barabas, are all dead, except Abigail, who says, in a failing voice, "And I shall die too, for I feel death coming."

The moment, for Theo, is so real that he wants to cry out—*No, no, don't die!* Angela, as Abigail, is lovely, soft. Too beautiful, dying. A madonna, full of pathos. But then, cutting across the emotions that he feels, a practical thought intrudes, a crass, professional awareness that Angela would be even more lovely with a breast enhancement. Nothing too large or gaudy, but something, because clearly she needs more than she has. He will speak to her about it. Or he'll ask Maggie Sowle to talk to her. And he will do it for her, as a favor to Nora.

A few days later, he has lunch with Claudio Nascita at Bruno's, a bar and grill on Third Avenue. Theo goes there often, liking the leaded glass windows down front, the long bar, and, behind the bar, the tall, beveled mirrors framed in oak. A high tin ceiling, hung with fans that rotate slowly, moving in reverse, sucking away the cigarette smoke. They sit at a booth in the back, Theo hovering over a Reuben stacked with corned beef and sauerkraut, for which he has little appetite, and Claudio working on a chopped steak sandwich on rye. They've been through medical school together, and, early on, Theo had worked on Claudio's wife, removing heavy scars on her arms and legs after she took a bad spill on her Harley, skidding in sand while exiting from a highway.

Claudio had specialized in gynecology, and as new technology came along, he moved into in vitro fertilization, and then into cryogenics. He's now affiliated with a privately owned commercial lab in the vicinity of Columbia University, and, as he's proud to say, he's making money hand over fist. Within a decade, by his best estimate, there will be over a million cryogenic children in the country, and in two decades, maybe five times that many, or ten. At the moment, only sperm and embryos can be frozen, whereas eggs have to be put to immediate use after being taken from a donor. Soon, though, they will figure out how to freeze and thaw eggs safely, and the field, already booming, will mushroom. Claudio envisages supermarket laboratories where clients—couples and singles, fertile or infertile—will shop for eggs or sperm, or embryos, from donors they want their children to resemble. Giving their kids the genes of a movie star or a fashion model, a Phi Beta Kappa, a CEO, or a star quarterback. There is no guarantee that quarterback sperm would produce a quarterback, but it improves the odds. Maybe a linebacker, or a tight end. Pick the color of the hair, shape of the nose, height, dimple on the chin. Claudio works with students from several of the city's more prominent universities, and faculty members too, paying fifty dollars for each deposit of undergraduate sperm, more for faculty. An M.A. is worth two-fifty. A Ph.D., a thousand. The stipends for women are higher than for men because of the inconvenience they go through—injections to stimulate egg production, and the harvesting of the eggs. High stipends too for the star athletes, star actors, star dancers. The debaters and chess players.

"I need a favor," Theo says.

"Tell me."

"It's complicated.

"You want me to rob a bank."

"Something like that, yes."

And then he lays it out, about Nora in a vegetative state at Cabrini, and what he wants Claudio to do.

Claudio says nothing, just looks at him, long and hard, and Theo knows what his silence is saying—it's a silence that worries about medical ethics, malpractice suits, loss of license to practice, maybe a jail sentence, and other unspeakable possibilities. And Theo answers his look with a look of his own, a long silence that speaks of loyalty, friendship, remember when, and what about this, and what about that.

Claudio swallows down a stiff belt of Jack Daniel's and gazes bleakly. "It takes time, you know."

"How long?"

"I have to put her on Lupron first, then FSH, to make sure there's good egg production. We want as many eggs as possible. Depending on where she is in her cycle, it could be a month, more or less."

"If she were awake," Theo says, "I know she would want this."

"But she's not awake."

"I know. You're a friend."

"I'm a sap."

"It can be done? You'll do it?"

"Look," Claudio says, "I can set you up with some of the finest eggs on the market. Blue-eyed eggs, Ph.D. eggs, English-major eggs earning straight A's. Virgin eggs. D-cup eggs with wide hips or narrow hips. Spare yourself, Theo. Do yourself a favor."

"How could I use a stranger's egg?" Theo says. "It has to be someone I know."

Claudio lifts both hands. "Why? What's the difference?"

"The difference is, it has to be personal."

"So old-fashioned?" Claudio says. "I never guessed that about you. You need it personal?" And then, motioning the waitress for another drink, "Look, if you really want this, this is how it happens. You give me semen and I freeze it. When I aspirate the eggs, I thaw the semen and make the embryos, which I freeze, and you can do what you want with them. Put them in the bank, or carry them around for a good-luck charm."

"I'll come to Cabrini with you when you give her the injections."

"And we both get arrested?"

"I know the night nurse," Theo says. He looks at his Reuben, untouched. He's eaten the pickle on the side and the fries, and is still nursing his beer. "You want this?"

Claudio has already disposed of the chopped steak sandwich loaded with onions and ketchup. "Yes," he says, reaching for the Reuben, and eats ravenously, as if it were his last meal.

Snow Falling, Eighteen
Minutes Past Noon

A few weeks later, Friday, the end of February, it's cold and dreary, a grimy cloud cover hanging over the city like gray cement. Theo wakes with a headache, which persists through breakfast and lingers long after his third cup of coffee. Before leaving for the office he takes an aspirin, and when he arrives he takes another. From nine to eleven he sees patients, evaluating one for a liposuction, one for cheek implants, and examining three that have had breast enhancements. Having no afternoon appointments ahead of him, and with the headache returning, he swallows another aspirin and starts for home.

As he makes his way to the subway, snow flurries are falling, melting on the pavement. He goes underground, through the turnstile, and takes the Lex to Canal Street, where he switches to the N, two stops to Cortlandt, and he comes up on Church Street, at the World Trade Center. The flurries have gone to sleet, and he puts up the collar of his London Fog. He turns the corner onto Liberty and passes under the immense, upward thrust of the South Tower, its top, like that of the North Tower, lost in a low cloud. He crosses left and heads down Washington, and a block away, on the corner of Cedar, he stops to pick up a sandwich at the Amish Market. It's his favorite place for a takeout, a huge deli counter, wide bins of fruit and vegetables, and hanging plants with long tendrils of ivy and fuchsia. They sell hero sandwiches by the foot, sausages by the yard, cheese from everywhere, and loaves of bread molded into every conceivable shape. Above the front door, spelled out in tiles, the words IN GOD WE TRUST.

He orders turkey on a roll, with sprouts and cranberries, and picks up a cantaloupe, a few oranges from Jaffa, bananas from Ecuador. And a pound of Jarlsberg. All of it going into a brown grocery bag, along with the white deli bag containing the sandwich. The clock on the wall by the door shows a quarter past twelve, but he knows it to be unreliable, always a few minutes too fast or slow.

As he goes through the door, cradling the bag in his left arm, he glances up at the vastness of the South Tower, in front of him, only a block away, the topmost floors draped in mist. It's still sleeting. He moves along on Cedar, toward West Street, but before he's taken more than a few steps, he's brought up short by a thunderous, ground-shaking roar that shudders right through him.

He looks up and sees both towers swaying, ever so slightly, and thinks it must be a trick of his eyes, a dizziness, from stopping short and lifting his head so suddenly. Then he sees the other people along the street, all dead-still and looking. And others coming out of the Amish Market, staring at the towers—shoppers and workers too, a stock boy, two of the deli men in white aprons, one of the checkout girls. A woman in a red coat, with a woolen hat pulled down around her ears. He knows they're all thinking the same thing, a bomb, but nobody says it. A young woman in sneakers, carrying a bag, starts running, around the corner and down Washington, away from the Trade Center, as if the towers might fall. Then others start off, hurrying away, walking fast. The stock boy, the checkout girl. A woman with a child in a stroller, going quickly down Washington. And Theo too is in motion, turning back, not away from the towers but toward them, lugging the brown bag, and already he hears the sirens of approaching fire engines. As he draws near to Liberty Street, throngs of people are coming from the South Tower, coughing, choking for air, holding scarves and handkerchiefs to their faces, and he sees the tower's lobby windows are gone, blown out, shards of glass littering the street. And smoke, volumes of black smoke, but no visible flames.

He enters the plaza, passing through the area between the South Tower and the Vista Hotel, toward the North Tower, into more smoke, people rushing through the doors, vacating the towers and the hotel.

Glass crashes down not far from him, and his first thought is that it's ice from the upper floors, like the ice that fell last month, when the plaza was cordoned off because of the danger. But, glancing up, he sees that people high up are breaking windows, desperate for air.

He comes to a stop near the middle of the plaza, by the bronze sphere, the large Koenig sculpture, away from the falling glass. The sleet has changed to flurries again, it's that kind of a day. People are pouring out of the towers, into the weather, some with coats, some without, faces twisted with doubt, fear, anger. Annoyance. One with a bloody nose. One limping on a sprained ankle. One, a three-hundred-pounder, out of breath, struggling for air. Many of them soot-laden, soot on their clothes, in their hair, smeared across their foreheads, gargoyles drifting across the plaza. Some rushing, dashing, but most dragging, exhausted from the long trip down, heading toward Vesey or Church. "Is Andy out? . . . Where's Julia? Still up there? . . . It was a bomb—had to be . . . Ain't it crap? They're giving us snow too . . . Watch the glass! Watch the glass!" Another slab of broken glass sails down and crashes, splinters flying wide, but again, implausibly, it's good luck, no one is killed.

Theo just standing there, middle of the plaza, both towers pumping out smoke and the crowds surging, sweeping past. A woman with white hair brushes against him, her forehead bright with blood—grazes against his left shoulder, and a little farther on she stumbles and falls. He goes to her, and, setting down his bag of food, he looks at the cut on her forehead, which is nothing terrible. She has a hard time breathing.

"Dizzy?"

"A little. But I'm all right. I am."

"Your legs okay? Your arms?" He feels for fractures.

"I'm fine," she says.

The emergency vehicles are pouring in now. Fire equipment, police. Firefighters moving rapidly into both towers and into the hotel.

She makes a move to get up. But stops, closing her eyes.

"Where does it hurt?"

"Everywhere." And then, "I'm just—dizzy."

He takes her wrist and finds her pulse. It's racing, skipping around.

Gradually the dizziness goes, and she opens her eyes again.

"You work here?"

"I'm from Oklahoma," she says.

"On tour?"

Her face is full of weariness. "We're all of us on tour. Aren't we?"

"I suppose we are," he answers. "Enjoying your trip?"

"Until today," she says. "I so much wanted the view from the top, but it was all clouds. And now this. I think I can get up now."

"You're sure? You feel strong enough?"

"I think so. Yes."

He helps her to her feet and, stepping slowly, walks her to the nearest ambulance, where he borrows a stethoscope from a paramedic. He listens to her heart and picks up an arrhythmia.

"Are you on medication? Coumadin?"

"That, yes."

"What else?"

"Sotalol. Sometimes it works, sometimes it doesn't."

"I think you should be looked at," he says.

"If you think so."

"I do."

He leaves her in the hands of two paramedics, they'll bring her to St. Vincent's.

"Get home safe," he says.

"I will, I will," she answers. And, tilting her head, "Thank you. I'll remember you."

He wanders back toward the bronze sphere near the center of the plaza. The low cloud that had hung over the towers has lifted slightly, and the upper floors are now visible. On the roof of the North Tower, he sees people waving coats and jackets, and behind them, the tall television mast rising like a long white finger, the tip of it lost in mist.

And only now, looking up, does he realize that the lights in the towers, in the offices, aren't on. The power is gone. Which means the elevators are down too, and the heat.

He talks to a police officer, then a paramedic. To an intern from Cabrini Medical Center, and a priest from a nearby parish. Before long, word spreads that the explosion had occurred in the underground garage, beneath the five-acre plaza that stretches out between the towers, on the second level down, B2. Several levels have collapsed, all the way down to B6, and there's a huge crater down there, some two hundred feet wide. Just the worst place for it too, the blast knocking out the power plant for the entire complex and touching off a spate of fires. Everything is off, not even the emergency backup systems are working. People are stuck in elevators, calling for help on cell phones, others trapped on floors where the exit doors are locked or jammed. Ninety-nine elevators in each tower, somebody says. That many? Yeah? Right. Somebody says ninety-three. Somebody says ninety-five. Somebody says move it, move it, before the whole damn plaza caves in. Police officers at the doors are hurrying people out, urging them off, away from the towers, away from the possibility of more falling glass.

A helicopter comes in, just under the gray cloud cover, and puts down on the roof of the North Tower, where the coat-waving people are waiting. It lands, and some moments later it's up again. A second helicopter arrives to pick up more.

Standing there, in the plaza, the crowds rushing and stumbling past him, Theo feels, strangely, more alive than ever before. Nothing, for him, has ever been so large and intense, so vivid. People coming at him in waves, from both towers, swarming past him, coughing, gagging, lungs seared by the sooty smoke. It seems some old fresco come to life, in motion, an end-of-the-world doomsday catastrophe, the dead arriving for judgment, the sky dark with finality. But the people coming toward him are not dead, they're alive, as if they had died in there, in the black smoke, and now they are breathing and walking again, resurrected from some bleak enigma and pressing on, looking for a subway, a cab, a place for a sandwich and coffee.

The PATH station for the train to New Jersey has been wiped out by the blast, and the city subways under the plaza have been shut down. Thousands of people, tens of thousands, heading east to Broadway for the 1 or the 6, or to Nassau for the J, or north to Chambers Street for whatever comes along. It's midday, past noon and going on one, but it has the feel of night. The sleet, the heavy clouds, the gray darkness that seems like dusk. This alone is real, he thinks, this moment, the darkness, nothing else as genuine as this. Everything else vapid, irrelevant.

From the upper stories, how long to walk down? An hour? More? Less? Down is easier than up. Moving fast, maybe a half hour? He imagines detours, locked doors. Stairwells leading to corridors that lead to other stairwells. People tripping, stumbling. And finally down, coming through the lobby, spilling into the plaza, sweeping past him. Some break into a run, others are slow, out of breath, gasping. And always more of them, coming through the doors. And he's thinking of the ones who can't make it, the ones who are hurt, unable to move. And now, instead of standing there, letting them flow past, he walks toward them, into them, heading for the entrance of the North Tower.

A fireman in full gear, helmet, axe, smoke equipment, blocks his way.

"Where you going?"

"I'm a doctor."

"So?"

"People need help in there."

"Don't I know it. Wait in that rescue station," he says, pointing to ambulances lined up on Vesey Street. "Anybody needs help, we'll bring them there."

Theo hesitates, then turns and ambles toward the rescue area. Before he's there, he looks back and the fireman is gone. Bothered by the smoke, he wets his handkerchief, dipping it into a puddle, and drapes it over his nose and mouth, knotting it behind his neck. Then he retraces his steps and enters the tower, against the tide, making his way through the surge of bodies in the lobby.

He finds his way to a stairwell and starts up, holding to the right, but it's tough going against the throngs coming down. The stairs are in the building's center core, windowless, and the lights are down. The backup system is out, and the only light is from battery-operated lanterns the security people have set out on some of the landings, and from flashlights and cigarette lighters that some are carrying. The effect is ghostly—faces and bodies descending toward him out of the looming shadows, not a stampede but a steady, deliberate flow, shoulders and hips pressing against him as he pushes his way up, one flight after another, past the fourth, the fifth, the sixth floor, up through the smoky air wafting from the climate-control vents. He breathes through the wet handkerchief, the smoke's stink catching at the back of his throat. The firefighter who had stopped him was right— this is insane. Yet it's something he feels he must do, be part of it, enter it, in some way make it his own. But not smart, no.

On the ninth floor he quits the stairwell, entering a corridor that leads him into a wide space filled with computer stations. Here the smoke seems milder than in the stairwell, with hazy light filtering through the windows on his left. To his right, a row of windowless cubicles, doors open, everyone has fled.

He turns a corner, then another, and realizes he can lose his way in here. The smoke thickening now, burning his eyes, then down another corridor, where the light is fainter and the smoke denser, and on the floor by a water cooler he sees, thinks he sees, someone lying there, at the base of the wall. Small, very small, and even before he bends for a closer look, wincing, peering through the gritty dark, he's sure it's a child. He touches a finger to the neck, and the pulse is strong. Dimly he's aware of blond hair, a sweater, the shirt collar open at the throat. A boy, young, how did it happen that he was left behind? Passed out from the smoke, but breathing. And where is the parent, or the aunt, the uncle, who brought him here? How did they become separated? Seven or eight, or nine, he thinks, lifting him, like his own son, but he can hardly see him in the faint light, lifts him and cradles him, the face against his left shoulder, and starts back, searching for the exit, down one corridor, lit by a battery lantern, then another, into a dark dead end. Then, choking in the smoke, he enters another corridor and stumbles into the wide room with the computer terminals, snow pelting the windows, and quickly, then, he goes to the door that takes him into the stairwell. And now he is traveling with the crowd, down, not up, every step clicking in his consciousness.

Outside, in daylight, dim as it is under the winter sky, he sees that it isn't a child he's holding, it's a man, a midget, limbs and head and torso perfectly proportioned, but small. The hair blond, as he'd thought, but the face, as he wipes the soot away, wrinkled, mapped with age.

He carries him to an ambulance on West Street and puts him on a gurney, and as he attaches an oxygen feed, the man opens his eyes and fumbles into wakefulness.

"You're going to be all right," Theo says.

He watches as the midget's large gray eyes take in the interior of the ambulance. Tubes, oxygen tanks, mysterious vials and containers. The back gate is still open. The snow has changed to a mild, misty rain.

"What happened," he says groggily.

"It was a bomb," Theo says.

The midget stares emptily.

"They blew up the underground parking garage. I found you on the ninth floor, you had passed out."

"All that smoke," he says, remembering. "I couldn't breathe."

"How old are you?" Theo asks, checking the blood pressure.

"Thirty-six."

He seems older. His face wrinkled, puffy, his skin stained by sunspots. The blond hair is gray-black at the roots.

"You work up there?"

"I'm an accountant."

"Your heart okay?"

"You tell me."

His heart is running close to a hundred, and his blood pressure is on the high side.

"Any health problems?"

"They took my appendix out last year."

"You married?"

"No."

"Anybody you want to call? They have a phone hookup in one of the trucks."

West Street, six lanes wide at this point, is filled with emergency vehicles. Fire engines, rescue trucks, ambulances, police cars. Utility people working on gas and electric lines.

After a pause, all the midget says is, "I'm okay."

"I want you checked out at the hospital," Theo says.

The midget stares out through the open tailgate. "Can you get me some coffee?" he says. "Black."

Theo goes to a vehicle parked nearby, and when he brings the coffee, the midget takes the plastic cup and holds it a long time, warming his hands.

"You're cold."

"No." He sips the coffee.

"Did you have a coat up there? In the office?"

"And an umbrella too."

He takes another sip of the coffee, then drinks it all down, swiftly, and hands the empty cup to Theo.

"I'm going to leave now," he says.

"It's cold out there."

"Yes, it is," he answers, slipping down off the gurney, and at the back of the ambulance, with some difficulty, he negotiates the drop down to the street. And Theo, grabbing an orange slicker from a rack by the oxygen tank, follows him out.

"How about this?" he says.

The midget takes it and slips it on. It's far too large for him, like a long, oversized coat, falling all the way to his shoes.

"That should help," Theo says.

The midget, rocking his head, skeptical, walks off into the gray afternoon, and Theo, hands in the pockets of his London Fog, watches as the orange slicker disappears up West Street, into the crowd of fire engines and police cars, lights flashing as in some brain-damaged fever dream of a midwinter hell. Small flakes of snow still falling, flurries, nothing on the ground but puddles and slush.

Theo returns to the plaza, thinking he might push on and go home, but instead he approaches a rescue station set up near the Calder stabile, where a sizable crowd is waiting to be looked at. There are other doctors on hand, interns from the hospitals, and many who, like himself, just happened to be there. All doing the same thing, checking the ones who need help. A few with broken ribs, some with broken fingers, sprained ankles. Cuts from shattered glass. But mostly it's respiratory stuff, wheezing and coughing because of exposure to the smoke, hard on the asthmatics. The bad cases they dispatch in ambulances, to the nearby hospitals, and for the others they do what they can and send them home.

When he looks at his watch, it's well past three. He'd lost all sense of time. It's as if it's still only a moment since he heard the explosion, when he was coming out of the Amish Market on Cedar Street. He continues to treat the injured, but by now the towers are emptied out, except for some people stuck in the elevators, and a few still trapped behind locked exit doors on the upper floors.

At the rescue station, he examines so many he loses count. One face after another. Strangers, yet he seems to know them, they are oddly familiar. A woman with an arm in a cast from a skiing accident, and a janitor with a patch over his right eye. A girl with her hair dyed green. A middle-aged man, a stockbroker, with a braid hanging down his back, and a younger man with his head shaven clean. People on business from Hamburg, Brussels, Kyoto. A hunchback. A woman with an artificial leg.

Firefighters are still in the underground garage, working on the fires, and word has filtered up about the mess down there, the wrecked cars, rubber tires burning, utility rooms blown open and in flames. Four Port Authority employees have been found dead in their belowground office, killed by the blast while eating lunch. And word too of a man who died of a heart attack shortly after the explosion. Five dead. But it is, in the peculiar way of things, good news, considering the thousands who might have been lost if the explosion had done more damage.

When dark sets in, just after five, deep dark, metallic winter dark, Theo is sitting in an ambulance on Church Street, trying to warm himself. His shoes are wet and he feels a chill coming on. He's taken a few more aspirin from the vial he brought from home this morning. Off to his left, the plaza is lit by banks of emergency lamps. The great throngs are long gone, the tens of thousands who walked down the stairwells, but the ones stuck in the elevators are still waiting for deliverance. He had hoped to hang in until the last of them were brought out, wanting to see it through to the end. But he's exhausted. The day has worn him down, and he's hungry and cold, and even though he wants to stay, he knows it's time for him to go home. He's done what he could. Some six hours have passed since he left the Amish Market and heard the blast, and now he remembers the grocery bag he'd been carrying. He recalls putting it down somewhere, and slowly it comes back to him. That old lady who fell, and he helped her. That's where he left it, where she fell, somewhere in the plaza. The lady from Oklahoma. She was coming out of the South Tower, so disappointed it was snowing and no view at all from the observation deck.

He leaves the ambulance, collar up around his ears, no hat, and returns to the plaza, tramping through puddles of slush, fragments of glass, fire hoses snaking everywhere, the firefighters still struggling belowground, the site not yet under control, but they're on top of it, and at least the people are out. He sees the Calder stabile, bright orange-red in the glare of whirling emergency lights. Police everywhere. The ATF and FBI in their marked slickers hustling around. And as he moves across the plaza, the area lit by high-intensity floodlights, he spots his market bag, soaked, torn open, the cantaloupe several yards away, crushed, and the oranges and bananas beyond redemption.

But, still in the bag, in its own white deli sack, is the sandwich, unharmed, sealed in a see-through plastic wrapper, turkey on a roll, with sprouts and cranberries, and he takes it, accepting it as a gift from the sooty hands of this dismal day, and walks home with it, leaving the plaza the way he came in, through the area between the South Tower and the hotel, both still venting smoke. Then on to West Street and across to South End. And soon, walking snappily, he turns toward the river and he's home, at Echo Terrace, which is still there, safe and intact, this mini-tower where he lives, the lights in the lobby casting their brightness through the high, glass doors and flooding the street with welcoming light.

Nora Dancing

After the blast, there were, within the first twenty-four hours, nineteen phone calls from parties claiming responsibility. Most of the callers identified themselves as members of various Balkan groups—Croatian militants, the Serbian Liberation Front, Bosnian Muslims. One caller said he was a member of the Iranian Revolutionary Guard, and another, phoning from Europe, said he was with the Black Hand, a Serbian group that hadn't been heard from for more than a decade. Progress was expected to be slow. The explosion had ripped through four floors of the underground parking lot, and there were tons of debris that had to be sifted for clues. The force of the blast ripped steel fire doors from their hinges and hurled them hundreds of feet, and scores of cars and vans had been blown to pieces.

For Farro Fescu, who had heard the sirens and had seen the smoke in the gray, snowy sky, it's a bad time, hauling him back to his early childhood, when German planes bombed the village where his family lived. So much devastation, houses and stone buildings blown to pieces. His uncle and his grandfather dead. And now here? In New York? Crazy people are doing it here?

It's the next morning, he's in the mail room, putting the mail in the pigeonholes. Something for Rosen. Something for Ravijohn. Something for Tattafruge and a bank statement for Mrs. Sowle. A bill for Mrs. Marriocci. Then, like a flock of crows, before he's finished, they're already there, descending for the mail, hungry, summoned by instinct.

When the bomb exploded, Neal Noelli had been in his office in the South Tower. And Muhta Saad was in the North, worrying over a freighter loaded with cloves, due in from Zanzibar but running late. Knatchbull too was there, in the North, negotiating for a truckload of plumbing supplies, buying from Pennsylvania, shipping to Nevada. And today, in the mail room, he is still upset, a tall, solid man, big-voiced, but in a flutter, worried about the lost revenues during the cleanup period. The mess. The soot and grime. How to do business? When, if ever, will they be able to access their offices?

Rumfarm, concerned but unruffled, agrees it's a bad time. He had been in the South Tower, ninety-sixth floor, in his office at Sukabumi, and endured the long hike down through smoke and soot. His suit, handmade by Mandragola, was a total loss, clotted with grime. Insurance will cover it—but the bother, the annoyance. He thinks the bombing had been a joint venture by Iran, Iraq, and Libya, and suggests, calmly, that it may be time for all three to be carpet-bombed.

Even Harry Falcon comes down for his mail, having a fair-to-middling day despite the cancer. He arrives in suede slippers and silk pajamas, which look snappy and sensible compared to the Krazy-Kolor pants that Ira Klempp wears.

"Libya?" Falcon says to Rumfarm. "Did you say Libya?" His voice is nasal, with a dark resonance, as if he were speaking from beyond the grave. He knows Libya, he's done business there, sending them frozen desserts that they can't get enough of.

"Well, let me put it this way," Rumfarm says. "It wasn't a bunch of bad-boy Irish kids from the Bronx that did this."

Harry Falcon has his own notions about the bombing, but he's too weak, too tired. He collects his mail, and, clearing his throat and drawing up phlegm, he shuffles off toward the west elevator.

Knatchbull thinks Sudan may have been involved, and Noelli thinks a new generation of Black September may be on the scene, but neither of them says anything.

And Aki Sato thinks Shining Path, the guerrilla group in Peru, may be expanding its operations, but he too, like Harry Falcon, shuffles off to the elevator.

Rabbi Ravijohn blames Hezbollah, and Ben Rosen blames Hamas, and they keep their opinions to themselves. And Muhta Saad, angered to hear Rumfarm indicting three Muslim countries, is convinced that a right-wing Israeli group is responsible, blowing things up in the expectation that the Palestinians will be blamed. But he says nothing, and in his heart he blames American policy makers for getting into bed with the wrong people. In effect, he thinks, America has bombed itself.

Farro Fescu has his own ideas, and he too keeps them to himself. He thinks there is a new breed of revolutionary out there, international, mixed, a whole generation of malcontents, organizing, flexing their muscles, and probably some Americans with them too.

Muddy Dinks comes into the mail room with a ladder, to replace a dead fluorescent. He too had been at the Trade Center during the bombing. After picking up a VCR at Radio Shack for Mrs. Marriocci, he was eating a hamburger in the underground concourse by the PATH escalators. When the blast hit, the people high in the towers felt only a mild tremor, but Muddy, so close, felt the huge shake and rumble and almost fell off his chair. "It wrenched my nuts," he says, on top of the ladder, inserting the new fluorescent. "Not gonna be the same after this. Scary business, a bomb so close. In the PATH station there was chunks of ceiling fell down all over."

Rumfarm, still scanning his junk mail, dropping flyers into the waste basket, tries, in his creamy-smooth way, to put a positive spin on it all. "We're lucky, lucky," he says. "Only five or six dead, a small price to pay. And those five dead people, they're only five in a city of how many million? We don't even know them. Nobody from here, not one of us." As if, somehow, in the calculus of existence, in the swirl of human history, they simply don't matter.

Rabbi Ravijohn feels uncomfortable with that. "Well, I don't know," he says, fingers to his jaw. "In the end, everybody knows everybody, is what I think. We don't escape each other. The world is small."

"Not small enough," Noelli says.

"Too small," Knatchbull answers.

"Small is smaller than you think," says Farro Fescu, daring to interject an opinion as he puts the last piece of mail, a flyer for Angela, into her mailbox.

Not even Farro Fescu, who knew so much, was aware that yesterday, before the bomb exploded, Karl Vogel, on one of his extended late-morning walks, marched up Greenwich to where it becomes West Broadway, and then, in Tribeca, when he angled left onto Hudson Street, he came up short in front of a flower shop, pausing to admire the display in the window. On impulse, he decided to send flowers to Nora. Not much point in it, he knew, she being in the condition she was in, but it's the thought, the feeling. The nurses, they like flowers. And Angela, the niece, would be grateful.

Cut flowers in a vase he asks for, and the girl in the shop, in her late twenties, shows him the flowers she'll put in the arrangement. Some of these, and a few of those. She's pleasant enough, though she doesn't strike him as particularly pretty. They chat, small talk. He sees how into the flowers she is, so knowing and caring, and asks if she had studied botany at school. No, no, she says. She used to be into insect behavior, very heavy into that, but she found that she didn't like the warrior ants and the damselflies half as much as she liked flowers, so she quit the program and here she is, now, hands-on with the sweet williams.

No, he thinks, not particularly pretty. There is a round-ness in the chin, and a blandness, a kind of apathy, in the eyes. The eyebrows too thick and close together, and her hair short, brushed back behind her ears, and she wears drop earrings that do nothing for her face. Yet there is something about her, physically, that somehow appeals, some kind of raw earthiness that she projects as she moves about, working on the flowers.

The flowers and the vase, plus delivery, come to seventy-five dollars. The young man who delivers is there, waiting, same age as the girl maybe, and Vogel, watching, senses something between them—they're a number, a pair, a go-together, something in the manner, the casual touches, they've been to bed together.

"Busy day?" he asks.

"Too busy," the boy says. His face clean-shaven, the chin angular and well defined. He's good-looking. Crisp blue eyes, dark blond hair combed flat, straight nose, and a small inch-long scar at the corner of his left eye.

The van is loaded with corsages and small bouquets for the Towers. Some of the bosses give flowers when a secretary has a birthday, he says. You can buy flowers in the Trade Center, but many call here because it's cheaper, and better. The ones who know, they know that. He'll deliver to the hospital first, get that done right away, then down to the Trade Center. "Don't worry," he says, "she'll get these right away."

He takes the flowers, carries them to the van, and Vogel, out on the street, watches as the van pulls away from the curb, moves up Hudson, then takes a turn at the corner and is gone.

And that part of it, that much, is all he knows.

When the young man in the van reaches Cabrini, he delivers the flowers to the room himself. If you leave them at the desk, the wrong person gets the flowers. It's happened. To him. Besides, he likes to see the sick ones, how they react when they see the flowers. It adds some life to the job.

"But she's—really very out of it," the aide on the corridor says.

"I just want to be sure she gets them," he says.

In the room, when he sees Nora, she's a sad sight. Lying there on her back, covered by a white blanket, eyes closed, her dark brown hair like strings on the pillow, streaming down on both sides of her ashen face. And all the tubes and wires, and the green monitor tracking the peaks and troughs of her beating heart. For a moment she opens her eyes. But only briefly. And in that moment, her eyes seem to fasten on him, as if she sees him, knows him. Then the eyes close.

He stands there at the foot of the bed, struck by the sorry state she's in. Poor woman, he thinks. The lousy things that happen. The things people go through. Like, end-of-the-world lousy. Well, she has her flowers.

Then slow, through heavy traffic, the van filled with the heady fragrance of gardenias, and at the Trade Center he turns into the underground parking garage, around and around, finding a spot next to a beige van, on the B2 level. His watch reads a quarter past noon, but it's always a couple of minutes off.

He takes out a carton full of corsages, each tagged for a different floor, locks the van and, as he steps away, notices the van he's next to has a big dent in it and a New Jersey plate. There's music in his head, something old, from the Beatles, not the words, just the tune, the rhythm, beating away, wishes he knew the name. His head is locked on that tune, stuck on it, enjoying it, but in a furious bright instant the tune vanishes into a high, piercing whine and a hot-cold shiver flashes through him, and he feels he's wrinkling, shriveling—shrinking to an infinitesimal white-hot point, and as the point itself vanishes, all sound is gone and there is only the scent, the aroma of roses, and a fading hint of lavender, sliding away.

In her bed at the Cabrini Center, Nora Abernooth lies on her back, under a sheet. Some things she knows, and some she does not. She knows nothing about the bomb in the Trade Center, and has only the faintest awareness of the flowers by her bed, sent by Karl Vogel. She is afflicted with bedsores and doesn't know about those either, a deep one on her left thigh, and lesser ones on her back and arms. Sometimes she hears Angela's voice, and there is something familiar in that, but she's never sure what

Angela is saying. She hears Louis's voice too, and Louis has been dead a very long time. She doesn't know about the rose that Maggie Sowle sends every week, nor does she know that Yesenia is pregnant. She doesn't even know Yesenia—never met her. It was someone else, a different maid, who came to vacuum, and not often, because of the animals and the birds, so many of them, everywhere. In the dim recesses of her mind, there is a filmy uncertainty, a dreamy darkness, slow images that draw themselves into living shapes and then dissolve into a mist. And often there is nothing, as in sleep there is nothing when there are no dreams.

A nurse, passing by, checking on her, notices movement down by her feet. She pulls the sheet away, and it's her toes, all of them moving, wiggling, and what could that be about? She calls in the Russian doctor, the new one on Nora's case, who had been born in Novgorod but did his medical work at NYU and now lives in Forest Hills.

"She's trying to tell us something," the nurse thinks. "Getting our attention."

"Could be," the Russian says, "but maybe something else," and he studies the toes, bending close and drawing away, observing from the left and from the right. "Do you know what I think? I think she's dancing. She's having a dream and she's dancing."

"In a coma? She's having a dream?"

"My grandmother in Novgorod used to say even the dead have dreams."

And it was true. Nora was dreaming. She was in a field of grass, feet bare, and she was dancing. And at a distance from her, dancing with her but not touching, was this young man, good-looking, clean-shaven, the chin angular and well defined. And she remembers now, he's the one who brought the flowers. Crisp blue eyes, straight nose, and a small inch-long scar at the corner of his left eye. He dipped this way, then that, and she did the same, this way and that, and she turned and leaped, lifting away from the grass.

There are young almond trees in this field, with pink blossoms, and as she weaves in and out among them, the dance that she dances is a dance of hate and a dance of love, a dance of joy and of rapturous despair. And what she feels, as she dances, is freedom, deliverance, because this is the dance of the great escape, she is slipping off, out of her bed and out of her body, and, with any luck, out of the world.

But not quite. No. It isn't working for her.

She is still there on the bed, moving her toes.

And the Russian doctor, whose voice she doesn't recognize, bends close to her. "Keep dancing," he tells her, close to her ear. "It's important you do that. Can you hear me, Nora? Keep dancing."

She hears, but she doesn't want to hear. Her toes have stopped moving, and the doctor, who was born in Novgorod, doesn't know if this is a good sign or a bad.

When the bomb went off at the Trade Center, Yesenia, pregnant, was home in her bedroom, reading a book that Maggie had given her, about babies. She had the television going, not watching, just something in the background, and became aware, suddenly, that the picture had turned to fuzz. She left it like that, thinking it would come back, but it didn't, so she fiddled with the knob and found it was all like that, mothy snow. Then she found one channel that was working and there was news about the bombing, which scared her because it was so close to Echo Terrace and all the people she knew there. She worried for Muddy and Chase and Blue, and Oscar, and Farro Fescu, and especially Maggie, and she knew there were a lot who worked in the Trade Center, and she hoped they were all right.

The TV had gone off because the power was down at the Trade Center, and most of the stations transmitted from there, but she had this one channel transmitting from somewhere, and she was riveted, watching all the smoke and the people coming out of the buildings, and she thought it was too strange and mystifying, the way

God lets certain things happen, bad things. She knew there had to be reasons, but the reasons were sometimes hard to see. She had been busy looking at pictures in the book Maggie gave her, showing a baby as it grows in the womb. At five weeks, it's the size of the fingernail on your little finger. At two months, it's one inch long and already has fingerprints. At three months, it has hiccups. At twenty weeks, you can feel the kicking. And that's where Yesenia was at right now, feeling her baby moving around inside her. And this too, she knew, was something that was beyond her. And the part about the hiccups was really wild, because how does a tiny thing like that, in your belly, get hiccups, of all things?

The Whiteness of the Fields— No Crows, No Deer

Two weeks after the bombing, on a Sunday morning, shortly after seven, Theo Tattafruge is awakened by a call from the concierge. Two FBI agents are in the lobby, wanting to see him. Theo yawns, moans, clears his throat, doesn't open his eyes. He's hung over with deep-dream images of a nightmare in which he was climbing the stairs in a tall building, trying to get to the roof, feeling a need, an urgency to get there, but with no notion why. Then he was going down, not up, yet he was still aiming for the roof, and didn't know why he was moving down rather than up.

Still foggy, bothered by that dream, he tells Farro Fescu to send the agents away. But they insist, and Theo, sitting up now, on the edge of his bed, in pajamas, understands grumpily that he doesn't have a choice.

"Ten minutes," he tells Farro Fescu, and gropes his way to the bathroom. Urinating, he looks through the window, and the day is as crummy as he feels. Overcast, a threat of snow, but it will probably rain. He splashes his face with cold water, brushes his teeth, combs his hair, and pulls on a white terrycloth robe over his pajamas. In the kitchen, he puts up a pot of coffee. By then the agents are at the door, and, glancing at their credentials, he lets them in.

The tall one, Korn, is jowly and sour-eyed, a heavyset black man with a fleshy nose and a scar above his left eyebrow, his winter-lined raincoat open, showing a gray double-breasted underneath. The other one, Bowditch, is a woman, raincoat over her left arm, in a blue suit with a striped tie, red hair cropped so close it's almost a crew-cut. Good-looking, in her way, handsome nose and lips, but Theo, at a glance, sees the bone structure is all wrong, narrow hips, broad shoulders, thick wrists, hands like hammers and a jaw like an anvil. She too is tall, though shorter than Korn, and there is an off-putting hardness in her eyes. He's sure, certain, hundred percent, she's had the male-to-female change. Well, ninety? Ninety-five? Out of a purely professional interest, he would like to put her on a table, in stirrups, for a good look, to see if there are surgical scars.

"We have a problem," Korn says, the smooth baritone of his voice a queer mismatch for the blunt features of his face. He's a rich, dark brown, unlike Theo, whose skin is darkened only by the shadow of his grandmother, and among those who don't know, it passes for a suntan.

"This is about the Trade Center?" Theo asks. "The bombing?"

"No, not related," Korn says.

They're in the archway that opens onto the living room, Theo with his hands in the pockets of his robe. They have a man in a witness-protection program, someone important, valuable, they want to give him a new identity.

"Who?" Theo asks.

"You don't want to know," Korn says.

"Where from?"

"You don't want to know about that either."

"Look," the woman says, Bowditch, taking a step forward, "we've come to you because you're really very good, we know that. And we know you're the sort of person who would be willing to lend a hand." There's a throaty hoarseness in her voice, as if she's been shouting for hours at a football game. "And besides," she adds, "we're giving you twice your usual fee, for the inconvenience." The words sound a wrong note for him—the sort of person, lend a hand, and besides. If, by their idea of him, he's the right sort, then maybe

311

he'd rather be the wrong sort and send them packing.

"He needs a face change?"

"And a sex change," Korn says.

Theo's eyes lift with surprise. "A sex change? For witness protection?"

"We want to give him maximum protection," Korn says.

Theo hangs back, his eyes roving across the living room. The fireplace, the canoe, the shelf of books, the stereo. The cat is asleep on the couch.

"When?" he asks.

"Right away. Today."

He laughs. "I have to see the patient—evaluate, discuss. A patient is not just a piece of meat, you realize." He laces his fingers together, cracks his knuckles.

"Dr. Tattafruge," Korn says, "the man is at risk. There are people want to kill him."

"But you're talking about a sex change. How do we know he can live with it? My patients work a year with a therapist and they take hormones, building up to it. The surgery is irreversible."

"We're aware of that," says Bowditch, putting a hand on his elbow. "The man knows what he's doing. You don't have to worry about a malpractice suit."

"What does his wife think? He has a wife?"

"The sex change was her idea."

"Sounds like a happy marriage," Theo says.

The aroma of coffee drifts from the kitchen, thick, inviting, but Theo doesn't offer. He tries to imagine Bowditch in a dress, with long, thick hair tied back with a ribbon, and wonders if she would be pretty. Then he imagines her with no clothes on and doesn't find her appealing at all.

"The blood tests," he says. "The CBC, the BUN. Has he had an EKG? Urine analysis?"

"We have it all," Korn says, drawing a sheaf of photocopies from his briefcase.

Theo glances at the reports, running his forefinger down each page.

"Is he HIV?"

"Him? Not him. No."

"Did he kill somebody? Why's he so important to you?"

"Trust us," Korn says.

"Yes?"

"You're in good hands. It's all arranged."

"Where is he?"

"We'll take you."

"A sex change is no joke," Theo says, the reports in his left hand, hanging down at his side. "You have an anesthetist? A nurse trained for the procedure?"

"We have a facility all prepared for you. Everything you'll need."

And only now does he become aware of the way it has turned. They're no longer asking, they're telling—and his own drift has changed too, from resisting to accepting, and he feels unbalanced, because everything inside him is telling him this is no good, something simply not right about it.

So why, at that moment, is he going to his room and taking off his robe and changing into his street clothes? This is sensible? He grabs his black medical bag, an oversized computer case with a shoulder strap, in which he keeps his surgical glasses, stethoscope, sphygmo-manometer, some spare instruments if there should ever be a need, a few emergency medications, and licorice-flavored cough drops for when his mouth runs dry. Is he out of his mind?

In the kitchen, he turns off the coffee and, hungry, grabs a muffin. He hasn't had breakfast yet. And when he returns to the living room, with the muffin and the medical bag, he says grouchily, "Let's go before I change my mind."

It's mid-March, cloudy, the remnants of a week-old snowfall lining the curbs, the snow blackened and muddied from car grease and soot. The streets are clear, but there are patches of ice. Theo is in jeans and a flannel shirt, in a gray parka that reaches to his knees. They put him in the front seat of the black Taurus, with Bowditch behind him, and Korn driving. And Bowditch, in an appeasing tone, explains about the blind he'll have to wear, that it's for his own good that he not know where they're taking him. He doesn't understand that, doesn't want it, hates it, but smothers his resistance, thinking if he's come this far, what the hell. As the car turns a corner, Bowditch, behind him, slips the hood over his head. It's a cloth sack, black and thick, impossible to see through, from the top of his head down to his shoulders, but cut away at the mouth and nose.

"I hope it's not too uncomfortable," she says. "Can you breathe?"

He can breathe.

The last he saw, they were approaching the FDR, and, even blind, he knows they boarded northbound, because he's done this so many times, his body knowing the approach, the entry, the turns, the feel of the road. The bumps and the potholes, and the construction slow-down near Fourteenth, and, up in the Forties, the way the sound of the traffic changes in the underpass by the UN. Then they're beyond that, passing the Upper East Side, and before long they climb the up-ramp onto the Willis Avenue bridge and cross the Harlem River into the lower Bronx. But then, coming off the bridge, Korn confuses him. There are stops and turns, and, at one point, a U-turn, and he's scrambled, not knowing, when they enter another highway, if it's the Major Deegan or the Bruckner. He doesn't like it. Doesn't like to lose control of where he is, what he can see or not see—as if, in a way, he has lost control of who he is. He has a name, an address, a body that he inhabits, and his body is him. But his body has been taken away from him, carried off, and he is no longer who he was. Under the hood he is restive, thinking this is too much like being dead. Driving, driving, no radio, no music, no sound but the engine and the hum of the tires on the road. Blind.

The wipers come on, a swishing sound, back and forth, back and forth.

"Is it rain or snow?"

"A little of both," Korn says.

Then, after a while, the wipers are off, and Theo wonders if the sun has broken through.

"That Jordanian," he says, "you think he's guilty, or was he just in the wrong neighborhood?"

"Guilty as sin," Korn says.

The Jordanian had been picked up a week ago, a week to the day after the bomb went off at the Trade Center. A twenty-six-year-old Islamic fundamentalist, Mohammed Salameh. He was the one who had rented the van that held the bomb, at a car rental in Jersey City. And the bomb, it turns out, hadn't been anything terribly sophisticated, nothing but ordinary dynamite. Well over five hundred pounds of it, stuffed into the van and parked on the second level of the underground garage.

"And the others?" Theo asks. "You think you'll get them?"

"We always get them. Even if they're dead."

The PATH train to the Trade Center is operating again, but other than that, things are a mess, the towers and the hotel full of soot and needing a top-to-bottom cleanup. Plenty of broken windows, and the belowground garage needing reconstruction where the bomb had blown through four levels. The FBI still sifting through the heaps of debris that had piled up on the sixth level. And another victim had been found in one of the offices, bringing the death toll to six.

They drive on in silence, a steady speed, in cruise control. Then the car slows and comes to a stop.

"Traffic?"

"Looks like a semi jackknifed up ahead. We're merging into a single lane."

It's slow, stop and go. Tedious. Then the pace picks up, and soon the car is up to normal speed.

"Anybody hurt back there?"

"Sure looked that way," Korn says.

Theo squirms around in the seat, getting the blood flowing, turns his head left and right, easing the stiffness in his neck, rotates his shoulders. He's lost all sense of time—have they been an hour in the car, or is it two?

"How much longer?" he asks.

"Fifteen, twenty minutes," Korn says.

And as the car moves along, speeding, then slowing, switching lanes, and speeding up again, it seems like a lot more than twenty minutes. And having lost all sense of direction, he has no idea where they might be—upstate, into the lower Catskills, or maybe northeast, into Connecticut. Or west into Pennsylvania. Or just wandering around in some nearby part of New Jersey. They're off the highway now, traveling what seems a state road, slowing behind the slow traffic, then pulling out and passing, and back into the lane again. And then the same thing all over again.

"Almost there," Bowditch says.

He doesn't believe her. But the car turns off onto a steep uphill road, makes some slow turns, then a final turn onto crunching gravel, and the ride is over.

She removes the hood, and he rubs his eyes, getting used to the light. The clouds are gone and the sun is out and there's snow on the ground. Korn is wearing sunglasses. They're parked on gravel, in front of a white cottage, next to an old jeep with a snowplow attached to the front. Wherever they are, it's country, the road clear, but more than a foot of snow in the fields. No other houses in sight. Behind the cottage it's all woods, and to the right and left it's open fields, and beyond the fields, more woods. In front of the house the land slopes down to the main road, and beyond the road it's another field, bordered by snow-filled woods.

And when he sees all of this, the land, the woods, the small house in the middle of nowhere, a doe leaping across a field and disappearing into the trees, he feels he's been lied to and tricked. This is no place for surgery. And who are they anyway? Are they really FBI? He feels a hole has opened under him and he's been sucked out of existence. Everything he knows, the condo where he lives, his office, the hospital, the Amish place on the corner of Cedar and Washington, where he shops, and Alfredo's, where he likes the atmosphere—all of it gone, no longer his. They've delivered him to this other world and somehow, in his desolation, he feels lost, and he blames himself, his own stupidity and gullibility.

In the cold air, out of the car and looking at the house, he realizes he's hot, perspiring. Time is a fever, that's all it ever was, fever and a bad dream. It sends a shiver through your bones, and when the fever is gone, time is also gone. And where are you then?

The cottage is just a couple of rooms on the first floor, and there's another room up. The largest of the rooms, with a stone fireplace, has been turned into a surgery, very basically equipped. There's a gurney for an operating table, two high-intensity lamps on adjustable stands, and a sterilizing unit containing a tray of surgical instruments. Retractors, forceps, clamps, surgical scissors. A stack of towels and surgical gowns sealed in vinyl, and an array of medicines and disinfectants on a table. The suction apparatus, and the anesthesia equipment.

"I can't operate in here," he says.

"Why not?" Korn asks.

"It's primitive. That's not a proper operating table. And the suction machine is outdated, it could break down. The place isn't scrubbed—it's not sterile."

Bowditch points to the sterilizing apparatus containing the surgical tools.

"It's the whole place," Theo says, running a finger along a window ledge. "Dust and germs everywhere. This isn't a proper operating environment."

"You don't seem to understand," Korn says, stepping up to him, close. "This is something that has to be done. And it has to be done here."

"Then get somebody else," he says.

"It's too late for that."

"What do you mean?"

"I mean you're the one. We chose you and you came. Come on, now, you do it. We're on a timetable."

Korn is so big, and Theo feels so small. What he thinks

is that Korn could pick him up with no trouble at all and fling him against the far wall.

"And besides," Korn adds, "we seen the reports about how many doctors don't even bother to scrub up, so what are we being so fussy about?"

Theo looks him in the eye, his mind darting restlessly. How to get out of this? Why me, he wonders, desperate to close it down. How did I let this happen?

"The nurse," he says. "And the anesthesiologist?"

"I do the anesthesia," Korn says. "The Bureau trained me special."

"You're licensed?"

"That I am," Korn answers, drawing from his wallet a vinyl card with his picture on it. Waving it.

Theo looks to Bowditch, cross-legged on a wooden chair, filing her nails. "And you, I imagine, the nurse?"

"She's an R.N.," Korn says, "and a damn good one."

"You worked in surgery?"

"With the Twenty-second Surgical at Phu Bai," she says, studying her nails.

"Vietnam? You don't look that old."

"I take hormones."

"I bet you do," he says dryly, and she answers his sarcasm with a gritty stare.

"Nothing personal," he says.

But it's all personal, he knows it and they know it, and he knows that they know it. They've taken him from his home and put a blindfold on him and brought him here, to a godforsaken shack.

"We know about your grandfather," Korn says.

"Which one?"

"The one that was in that mess in Munich."

"Him? That's important?"

"No, not at all. Not unless it is to you."

"Then why do you mention it?"

"Just to let you know we check out all of our people before we use them. Don't feel threatened, it's routine."

But he knows Korn wouldn't be saying this unless he wanted him to feel threatened.

318

"The man is dead," he says. "It was very long ago."

"Yes, yes." Korn nods. "Long ago." But the inflection is there, a tone, a hint of ugliness, and Theo knows that if he pulls out now, there will be consequences, repercussions of one sort or another. They were that kind of people. Somehow, they would figure out a way of using his grandfather against him.

"Where's the patient?"

"Upstairs," Korn says. "I'll get him."

He goes up the narrow stairs and a moment later brings the man down, conversing with him in Spanish, and Theo is doubly surprised—that the man is Spanish-speaking, and that Korn can use the language so well.

The man is short, hefty, overweight, in black pants and a yellow shirt, the pants held up by suspenders.

He approaches Theo, not smiling. "You are . . . doctor?"

"I'm the doctor," Theo answers, noting the man's downbeat manner and the forlornness in his eyes. He sits the man on a stool and, taking the stethoscope from his bag, listens to the heart and lungs.

"You speak English?"

"*Poco*. A few words."

Theo feels something weirdly familiar about him. He knows him, has seen him before. Or has seen his picture. But where? When? He examines the eyes, touches the face, the skin, all the time wondering why the man seems so familiar.

He has the man stand and drop his pants, and when he sees the penis, how small it is, he's aghast. It's a long time since he's seen one so dwarfish. He pulls on it gently, checking the elasticity, wondering how he'll ever make a vagina out of this. He'll have to graft, and grafting will complicate the procedure.

He looks to Korn. "Are you sure he understands what's happening?"

"He understands."

"Tell him. I want to hear you tell him."

Korn talks to the man in Spanish, and the man looks

at Theo and nods. "*Si, si,*" he says, with conviction, gesturing toward his groin. "*Bueno.*"

Theo tells Bowditch to get him ready. "Shave the area, and paint it. The face too. And give him an enema."

"He had one this morning."

"Give him another. And scrub up," he tells her, and says the same to Korn.

He grabs a surgical gown and a pump bottle of anti-bacterial soap and goes to the kitchen, but before he scrubs, he opens the refrigerator and finds it loaded with deli sandwiches and bottled beer, imported. The sandwiches from Krug's Deli. He wonders if that's local—or far away, put there deliberately, to throw him off. He takes a ham sandwich and, eating, lingers by the window, looking at the snow and the line of trees. The sun beats down, slow drops of water slipping from icicles at the edge of the roof. The snow is crisscrossed by animal tracks, deer, dogs, foxes, rabbits, whatever. A few birds flying around, crows, big and black. Snow is in the trees, on the limbs, and some of the trees have a glaze of ice on them. Sunlight glints off the ice, flashes of ruby and sapphire. A cloud blocks the sun and the scene darkens, then the cloud moves off and the snow glares. A person could die out there, he thinks, in the snow. Wandering around, lost in the woods. Only the crows would know, and the animals. The sandwich not bad, plenty of mustard and sprouts, and a pickle in there too.

When Bowditch has the man ready, they put him on the gurney, and she hooks him to the heart monitor and the pulse oximeter. Korn starts the IV, a flow of propofol, and then, after an injection, he puts the breathing tube in place and makes an adjustment on the vaporizer.

Theo works on the genitals first, cutting into the scrotum and removing the testicles. Bowditch is right there with him, quick and precise, focusing the lamps, handing him the instruments, ready with the clamps, the retractor, the cutting scissors. Korn was right about her. She's good.

He's a long time working on the penis, removing the internal tissue but leaving the skin, which he will later push up into the inguinal cavity, where, inside out, it will function as a vagina. But first, because of the shortness, extra skin has to be grafted on. Normally he uses skin from the scrotum, but in this case he needs so much, he takes it from one of the thighs.

He moves deliberately, as quickly as he can but with great caution, because a wrong move can be ruinous. He could puncture the rectum, and when the man wakes up, instead of a vagina he has a colostomy.

The work is tedious—cutting, scraping, positioning and repositioning, and sewing. It's more difficult than he'd expected, because of the shortness. But he keeps at it, perspiring, wiping his forehead on his forearm. He wears his special glasses with the magnifying inserts at the bottom of each lens. There is a moment when he thinks none of it will work, the penis simply not long enough, not enough skin for a vagina—but he keeps at it, and eventually it all comes together. He takes a portion of the glans, with its rich supply of sensory nerves, and positions it as a clitoris.

He's four hours at this, removing the testes and scrotum, performing the skin graft, and inverting the penis and putting it up inside the body. Getting everything just right. Then, exhausted, and not happy with the readings on the heart monitor, he leaves it at that. He doesn't do the nose, the facial implants, the breast augmentation.

"We'll finish next weekend," he says.

Korn doesn't like it. "Tomorrow," he says.

"It would overtax his system." He's looking at the heart monitor, and at the blood pressure readings.

"Wednesday," Bowditch suggests, offering it as a compromise. "You're free on Wednesday, he should be strong enough by then."

"Where's his wife?"

"Not here," Korn says, and leaves it at that.

Theo takes from his medical bag a list of post-op

instructions that he turns over to Bowditch. The morphine IV stays in the arm five or six days, till the pain is gone. Sleeping pills at night, and ice packs day and night, to control the bleeding and swelling. He writes prescriptions for Estinyl and Provera, but not to be used for three weeks yet. And ten days of antibiotics.

"He stays in bed for six days. Give him plenty of cranberry juice, it will take the smell out of his urine. The stent in his vagina comes out in ten days, and no heavy lifting for six weeks. Douche the vagina twice a day with a splash of white vinegar in a quart of warm water. Explain to him he's now a woman. He can get trichomoniasis, yeast infection, cancer. All of it. He needs a Pap smear every six months."

And he notices, as he speaks, that he's referring to the transgendered man as a he. But he's now a she—yet strangely, this time, he can't think of him that way.

Bowditch stays behind, with the patient, and Korn drives Theo back to the city, again with the hood over his head. It's half past three.

"Is this really necessary," he says, hating the hood.

"I know, I know," Korn says. "But if the wrong people ask where you've been, it's better, isn't it, if you can't say."

"Who are the wrong people?"

"You'll know them when you see them."

Again, no radio, no music, just the sound of the road, and this time, Theo distracts himself by playing Vivaldi in his head. *The Four Seasons*, beginning to end. *Le Quattro Stagioni*. He's heard it so many times he has it all in memory. Misses a few notes here and there, a few bars, fumbles around, but basically it's all there for him, the violins, the harpsichord, the repetitions and inversions, the contrasts in mood and tone. He throws in instruments that aren't in the original, a trumpet, an organ, a bassoon, and he's heavy on the harpsichord in the second movement of "Autumn" and the first of "Winter." And the violins, always the violins, rich and sparkling, with contrasts and contradictions that weave and blend, resolving peacefully.

Home, he fries an omelet, throwing in scallions, morels, bits of pre-fried bacon from a jar, tuna from a can, chopped celery. He's still haunted by the man that he made into a woman. Had he seen him, somewhere, on the street? Had they sat opposite each other on a subway? Or was he in the news, on TV, too long ago to remember. It gnaws at him, and later, after supper, as he lies on the couch, close to sleep, it's still with him, running through his head. When? And where? Or was his mind simply playing tricks, creating a false memory of a moment that never existed.

He sleeps, but only a short while, and then he's awake again, and as he floats up out of sleep, suddenly it was there for him. The man—he's seen him in a picture, black and white, in a magazine. Not a newspaper, not TV. A clear, vivid recollection, the same man but in a military uniform, on the upper right-hand corner of the page. He's up now, hurrying through the apartment, grabbing the few magazines he has, flipping through and searching. But nothing, nothing close, not what he was looking for. And what was he expecting anyway?

He makes coffee and sits on the couch, obsessed. The picture so alive now, as if he'd seen it only yesterday. He wrestles with it, gropes, and then, grabbing his keys and wallet, and the parka, he boards the elevator and descends into the night, and takes a taxi to his office on East Sixty-ninth.

The office is on the third floor, he walks up. His junior partner, Lal Chakravorti, orders the magazines, and he can't get enough of them. Things come in from as far away as Bombay. A fine surgeon, Chakravorti, and a good man, but he lacks resonance—too fussy and precise, no sense of humor, and tone-deaf, no ear for music of any kind. He collects things, postage stamps and old coins, and post-cards, and, most of all, the magazines. When they pile up in the waiting room, the receptionist, Dawn, stores them in a closet next to the john, and when the closet is full, Chakravorti bundles them and brings them home, and his poor wife has told Theo she is losing her mind because they are simply running out of space.

Eight-thirty, Theo is there in the waiting room, setting aside *Art World* and *National Geographic*, and going through the news magazines, page after page. But nothing, the picture he's looking for isn't there. And the short nap on the couch at home had not been enough. Fatigue has set in, exhaustion from this long, unreasonable day, and he wonders why he had ever allowed Korn and Bowditch to enter his life and turn his world upside down. What weakness in him allowed him to be drawn into something that he really wanted no part of?

Finished with the magazines in the waiting room, he's down the corridor now, near Lal's office, at the closet next to the john, and digs into the high stack of magazines Dawn has put there. Slumping down onto the floor, onto the industrial-grade carpet that he hates and wants to replace, he races through, pell-mell, glancing at one glossy page after another. Tired, eyes heavy. Dozens of magazines, and when the picture does finally turn up, he doesn't see it, goes right past it, turning the page. But something in his brain, a flicker, a shadow, tugs at him, and when he flips back, there it is, as he remembered it, on the right-hand corner, at the top. The man not in black pants and suspenders, as he was this morning, but in a smart military uniform, a general, one of Augusto Pinochet's mob in Chile.

Chile, yes, it comes back, bits and pieces. All that grimy stuff about Pinochet and the junta, how they dealt with political enemies. Tying them up, loading them into planes, dropping them into the ocean. And the tortures, which some lived to tell about. Electric shock, with electrodes hooked to ears, noses, genitals. The women gang-raped and turned over to dogs, held by guards while the dogs had sex with them. These were the things that were coming out. Locked in a tiny room with rats. With snakes. And this man, Emilio Matoso, there in the magazine, his name in print, had been part of it, one of the team. They were rooting out Marxism, that's how they had talked about it, and in the end the victims were priests, teachers, social workers, students, factory workers, children. Getting rid of the long shadow of Salvador Allende, who had been killed in the coup.

Theo pushes the magazines back into the closet, and taking the one with Matoso's picture, he returns to the waiting room and settles into one of the leather-seated armchairs, facing, across the room, a painting of an autumn scene that he had picked up years ago at a gallery, yellow and scarlet leaves, blackbirds in the grass. And, on another wall, the poster-size picture of Teddy Roosevelt, twenty-five years old, skinny, wearing his cowboy outfit, buckskins, the ten-gallon hat, a holstered gun on his hip.

He feels eerie. Astonished. Only hours ago, he had Matoso on a table, worked on him, removed his testicles. The same man? He feels tilted, caught up in some reckless, roller-coaster fantasy in which nothing is what it should be. Matoso—the FBI is protecting him? Why would they do that? And as he thinks about it, he prefers, instead, to go back to what he thought before, that Korn and Bowditch are not who they say they are, not FBI, but mercenaries hired by Matoso to rescue him from whatever he was running from and deliver him into a new life. The two of them part of a network, an international combine servicing the huge numbers living an underground existence, gangsters on the lam, war criminals, terrorists, deposed dictators, drug lords, a vast subterranean fellowship in need of a safe house and a ham sandwich. He imagines a worldwide chain of such places, because where there is a need, there is always somebody eager to make a buck. Not just humble cottages like the one he's been to but deluxe retreats providing hot tubs and massage—Hideaway Hiltons, Shady Sheratons, Murky Marriotts simmering with opium dreams and Cherry Herring, sambas, safe sex, Cuban cigars, Perrier Jouët.

Should he call Flakk? Should he? He should. His old high school buddy Ray Flakk, who will or won't explain everything, or nothing. Will he?

They had been at the prep together, on Eighty-fourth, off Madison, and great days they were, his first cigarettes, first cigar, first pastrami on rye. First Amstel, and

Caesar's *Gallic War*, and Shakespeare with his too many words. First naked girls on stage at the All-in-One on Seventh. And first sex with a cousin of Roy Campanella, but she turned out to be a cousin of nobody at all, just a working girl from the Bronx who wanted to be paid. And the hunt for the right, even-tempered, couldn't-care-less priest who wouldn't scold too noisily in the confessional, for everyone to hear.

Flakk is with the Bureau, though how that ever happened, and what he might be doing there, Theo can't begin to imagine. They haven't seen each other for twenty years but keep in touch—by postcard, phone, and now e-mail. Skinny Flakk, tall and towheaded when he last saw him, and he wonders if he's still thin and still has the hair. Flakk sends him patients, a weird assortment of young and middle-aged men and women ranging in profession from key grips and best boys to grave diggers and skyscraper window-washers, though obviously they are all, one way or another, linked to the Bureau. Crazy world. Crazy Flakk. Crazy subway to crazy corner of Lexington and Eighty-sixth, on the way to school. Crazy long-term memories of trying to decipher the meaning of life while they cribbed their way through Virgil, parsing verbs and declining nouns, Theo wishing that all of the verbs, in all their moods and tenses, were pouty blue-eyed girls with long hair and Mona Lisa lips, and forever seventeen, never a day older. The school was for boys only, they wore jackets and ties. Run by the Jesuits.

He goes to the receptionist's desk and, sitting in her chair, dials the number. As often happens, he's forwarded to another number, where he's sent on to yet another exchange, and this time, on the seventh ring, Flakk, clearing his throat, picks up. They haven't had voice contact for more than a year, yet it's as if they are continuing the same conversation, though lurching off into another direction.

He asks about Korn and Bowditch.

Yes, Flakk knows them. Knows Korn, knows Bowditch.

"What do they look like?"

Flakk tells him, and the descriptions fit.

"They bothering you? What's the problem?"

"No problem," Theo says. "But tell me, what do you know about Emilio Matoso?"

"Never heard of him."

"In Chile. One of Pinochet's people."

"Oh. Those jerks."

"Is the Bureau protecting Pinochet?"

"Him? He doesn't need protection. Nobody in Chile will put a hand on him. They don't want him to be president anymore, but he still owns the army, and there are some who think he's a saint. If he leaves the country, though, he's had it. The Italians are after him. Can you believe—the wops? They have pictures of the prison ships in the water off Valparaiso. Got a bug up their ass about some leftist Italian nationals who were disappeared by the Pinochet people. What the hell's a bunch of leftist wops doing in Santiago anyway? You know what Matoso means, don't you? It means bushy, messy, full of weeds. Is he garbage, Theo? Who is this guy? A friend of yours?"

"A passing acquaintance."

"Not passing gas, I hope. You need Korn's number?"

"I have it."

"Then why you bothering me? It's Sunday night, Theo. Nine-fucking-thirty post meridiem, and in two hours I'm out of here and on my way to fucking Waco. Who did he kill?"

"Matoso?"

"Yeah."

"Nobody important."

After the call, he knows less than before. Korn and Bowditch are, it seems, who they say they are. But then, if Flakk never heard of Matoso, maybe this whole messy business isn't a Bureau operation but something that Korn and Bowditch are doing on the side, freelancing. Odd, Flakk not having heard of Matoso. Wouldn't he know? Or was he just covering? And what Theo suspects now is that he's been lied to all around, lied to by Korn, lied to by Bowditch, and lied to by Flakk, who was a friend but not a friend, because though there is this peculiar long-distance bond that holds them together, it had always been impossible for him to know what was really going on in Flakk's mind, or in his life.

And as he sits there, at his receptionist's desk, in this midtown office that needs fresh paint and new furnishings, the truth, he knows, is that Flakk had always lied. When they were in high school, in junior year, he boasted about going to fancy whores in the Village. Theo wanted to join him, but Flakk taunted him for being too young and never brought him along. They were in the same class, but Flakk was nine months older. On a Friday afternoon, after school let out, Theo followed him down to the Village and watched as he entered a walk-up on Commerce Street, across from Cherry Lane, where there was a small theater. He waited by the theater, and some twenty minutes later, when Flakk reappeared, he was almost unrecognizable, in lace leotards, high heels, and a red miniskirt, his face lit with lipstick and blush, and accompanied by a cadaverously thin, middle-aged creep wearing cowboy boots, and a bandanna around his neck. It was startling. Were they lovers? Or was Ray Flakk just playing at being a transvestite, out on a lark?

He never confronted him about what he had seen and simply accepted that there were aspects of Ray Flakk's personality that were elusive, misty, inaccessible. And that, he suspected, was probably why he eventually linked up with the FBI. In part to dodge the draft and avoid Vietnam, but largely, Theo thought, because he was in love with secrets, and that's what the FBI was mainly about, investigating, prying into the darkest privacies, accumulating vast archives of hidden things, levels and sublevels, archaeological layers, deeper and better concealed than the tombs of the pharaohs in the Valley of the Kings.

He has left the receptionist's station and is back in the waiting room, lying on the floor, on his back, on the blue and gray carpet that he hates, eyes closed and thinking again of the cottage where on Wednesday he will work on Matoso, changing his face, and he assumes if there is one cottage out there, there must be many. And again he imagines a network of shelters around the world, some in the mountains, others in cities, because there is such an enormous market out there, people on the run, and someone by now must have figured out how to get rich off of this. Korn, Bowditch, and whoever else. Flakk? Was he part of it? The boss? Theo puts nothing past him and can well imagine Flakk designing and running a whole empire of safe houses, Radisson Retreats and Holiday Inn Hidey-Holes. And as he slips off into sleep, the magazine with Matoso's picture under his left arm, already he can hear Flakk's voice in a TV commercial and sees him, in a glossy dream, in lace leotards and red miniskirt, fresh and chirpy, and skinny as ever—"Stop over with us, we do it all, haircut, manicure, aromatherapy. All you dirty dozens out there, if you're tired of running, tired of lurking in gritty places, tired of waiting for the bullet that will split your skull, come join us in Hidden Valley, where every tree is hung with mistletoe." He swivels into a groin-grinding dance, twisting and writhing, bending and leaping, and when he swings close, leering, he takes off his face, and there is nothing underneath, empty air. Puts his face back on, and he's Bozo the Clown, in a polka-dot dress, and weeping.

Then, in the dream, he's gone, and Theo is alone. It's raining on him. Lots of rain, but he isn't wet. Perfectly dry. Why so much rain, he wonders. Then the rain is snow, and he's cold.

When he wakes, it's after two in the morning, and he's hungry. He's slept more than four hours, on the floor in the waiting room. His back hurts and his joints ache, and it's painful to move. He goes to the john, then washes, splashes his face, and then, by the closet, restacks the magazines, keeping the one with Matoso's picture.

Then he shuts down, grabs his parka and closes the office, and he's off, out of the building and into the cold early-morning air, no moon that he can see but plenty of light on the street—down the long stretch of Sixty-ninth, and he crosses Park, on past Hunter College, and across Lexington, hands in the deep pockets of his parka. He turns down Third, heading south, walking briskly, a long stride, and ducks into an all-night coffee shop, where he grabs a mocha and a bun and sits for a while by the front window, looking out at the avenue. Steam rising from a manhole, not much traffic, a couple of motorcycles grumbling by. A taxi, then a stretch limo. A hot rod racing noisily. Two guys in leather walking south, and three women going the opposite way. A police car cruising. Distant sirens and the hidden hot life underground, steam pipes, wires, sewers, subways.

He feels a numbness. Opens again the magazine and studies Matoso's picture, the eyes, the nose, lips like a firm, thin line across his face. Who is he running from? The ones who survived the torture and want revenge? Or the Italians? Or the Germans, who, like the Italians, lost some of their own in Santiago? Or perhaps he was perceived to be a weak link and his friends have turned on him? Was that it? He was running from Pinochet?

On Wednesday, he will give him breasts. Eventually, hormones and electrolysis will take away his facial hair. Estrone will change his emotions, making him feel graceful, feminine. It will soften the skin and add a thin layer of fat all over the body. Will he be a different person? Not himself? Less vicious? Should I do this, Theo wonders. Change this man's face and let him disappear into another life?

Still in the shop, hands wrapped around the coffee mug, he runs through it many times, trying to sort it out, but no matter how it plays, the bottom line is that Matoso has caused a lot of pain. He was part of it, giving the orders, permission to the sadists to do their worst. Electrodes on the scrotum, worms in the beans, hot metal into the anus. Teenagers found dead with their stomachs ripped open. And the ones who were disappeared—the *desaparecidos*—thrown into rivers, into the ocean.

He's read about the people on the Bulnes bridge over the Mapocho, which runs through Santiago, and on the Las Tejuelas bridge over the Ñuble, a mile and a half from Chillán—how they looked down and saw the bodies in the water, and the soldiers chasing them off the bridges, telling them to forget what they saw, they saw nothing. And Theo imagines himself on one of those bridges, looking down at the floating dead, the way they drift in the water, one with no arms, one with no head, and on Wednesday the man who did these things will be lying on a table, in a cottage with snow on the roof, waiting for a new face.

From the coffee shop he moves south on Third, past the bars, the videos, the high-rise apartments and hotels. Walking is good, it takes the edge off. When he doesn't know what to do, that's what he does, a long walk, with a relaxed stride. The closed shops are lit inside, flowers, a laundry, a deli, a Japanese carryout. The bars and some coffeehouses still open, but not the hair salon or the pet shop. Just walking, not thinking, because he knows, when the walk is over, everything will somehow have to sort itself out. He trusts his legs, the motion of his body, the rhythm of his breathing.

He moves past a cinema complex and a deli, a manicure parlor, a Duane Reade pharmacy and more movies, and the Eastside Playhouse, all closed but lighted. Gritty remnants from last week's snow still around, small patches, not much. Cigarette stubs and candy wrappers on the sidewalk, a sheet of newspaper lifted by a gust of wind. Street people asleep in doorways, cardboard boxes against the cold.

And to his left, now, the Lipstick Building, all lit up, red granite and bands of stainless steel, shaped like an oval tube of lipstick, no corners, a sleek elliptical form, reminding him of Vivaldi in a gaudy moment, daring and crisp, and all the right notes. He crosses Fifty-third, and before he's fully over, a white sedan zips through a red light and he has to leap to get out of the way. Too close, and for a moment he just stands there, at the edge of the sidewalk, adrenaline pumping, catching his breath, and he thinks good, good, reminds you you're still alive.

Up ahead, more glass palaces to the left and right, rising odd-angled in the electric night, and he plunges on, passing another pharmacy, and the Lebanese restaurant, the photocopy shop, the barber. He's in the forties, by Muldoon's, where he had his first martini with Ray Flakk, who was a student of martinis, going from bar to bar, comparing the quality. Then a Helmsley to his left, and Alonti's, his stride steady, and he savors the night, moving fast, arms swinging. His body has taken over from his mind, there is an ease, a cadence.

In the thirties, it's Nail City, pizza, and a string of bars and eateries, names in neon, or in fancy floodlit lettering, or spelled out in clusters of colored lightbulbs. Carney's, Black Sheep, Famous Chicken, Haruko, Back Porch, Kwak Deli. The names are a stream, a river of silent sound pouring over him, washing his brain. A photo shop, another barber. A public library.

Somebody on a bicycle comes whipping along, swings around from Thirty-first, miscalculates, hits the ice by the curb, and goes sprawling. A black kid, wide-eyed with pain, woolen hat pulled down over his ears, leather jacket torn at one elbow from the fall. A taxi swerves to avoid him. Theo goes to help him up, blood on the kid's face.

"Don't touch me," he shouts, eyes darting, looking for the bike.

"I'm a doctor."

"I don't give a fuck. Stay away."

Theo watches as the kid pushes past his pain, mounts the bike, and pedals off. A big canvas pouch lashed to the saddle over the back wheel. Drugs, he figures. Making a delivery. Or just picked up what he'll sell this week. Watches him pumping fiercely, vanishing up Third.

Then on the move again, a pet shop, the Ace Luck

wash-and-dry. And the Dakota bar, where, some years ago, he met a woman who was coming on to him, he'd thought, but she had Lyme disease and that was all she wanted to talk about, what to do for her Lyme disease. An ambulance sirens by, lights flashing.

As he reaches Twenty-seventh, he glances toward the Armenian church to his left, and then, up ahead on Third, it's the Rodeo Bar and Hug Joe Deli, and Caliban. The Abbey Tavern across from the frame shop, and another manicure. The names, the names. Keep thinking the names. The names calm him, ease him. And farther along it's Molly's, where he drank one night with Roberto Quattrello, and Roberto was so drunk he fell down twice. And Paddy Maguire's, and the Belissimo, where he brought María Gracia once and she had a bad reaction to the shrimp marinara.

Two blocks down he turns left, onto Sixteenth, past the church for the deaf, St. Ann's, and on through Stuyvesant Square, grass still covered by a thin layer of sooty snow. And slowing now, he moves toward the hospital where he performs most of his surgeries.

The building is old and familiar, and has, for him, the feel of a second home. On an upper floor, he opens his locker, takes off the parka, and dons his white hospital coat. And still he walks, as if walking were now as necessary for him as food and air. Wandering, cruising the corridors. Cardiology, angioplasty, electrophysiology. He turns corners, goes through doors. On the elevator again, up, then down, one floor after another. Quits the elevator and takes the stairs. Gastroenterology. Hazardous Waste. Hematology. The night staff mopping the floors. An aide pushing a white-haired man in a wheelchair. Someone on a gurney. Infectious Disease. Radiology. Up and down, the different zones and departments. Biohazard. *Peligro Biologico*. Oxygen Shutoff.

At Toxicology, he pauses and tries the door, knowing that at this time of night it will be locked, and it is. Toxicology is Roberto Quattrello's domain. They've been at bars together, drinking. He's obese and full of jokes,

Polish jokes, Jewish jokes, Catholic jokes, jokes about the poisons he stares at all day under a microscope, and Theo could use some of that humor now.

Again he walks, down the hall, past the women's, the men's, the chute for dirty linen, through swinging doors, up the elevator. And, strolling, he wanders into obstetrics, into the nursery, and behind the big glass window, in plastic bins, like fresh fruit in a market, are the infants, purple and asleep, only hours out of the womb. Everything he knows and can think about is in the past, but the infants, there in the bins, with no idea what's in store for them, are the future. One will be a bus driver, one a soccer star. One, perhaps, a plastic surgeon, or with the FBI. One will be Nora, and one will be María Gracia. None, he hopes, will be Luther Rumfarm. But whoever they are, whatever they do, it will be in their own way, with their own slant, entirely new.

He studies them, looking at one face, then another, then glances down the long corridor that leads to the bank of elevators. This is home, he thinks. This is where you're born and where you die. Where you come to get fixed when you aren't working right. Where you are probed and cut open and tinkered with and sewn back together. Where your heartbeat is on a screen for everyone to see, until it stops, and they start it up again with the paddles. Where you shit in a bedpan and pass urine through a catheter, and a gray old lady comes by, collecting for the TV. Somebody brings the newspaper. Maintenance mops the floor. An aide takes your temperature. An intern shines a flashlight into your eyes to see what can be seen in there.

He goes down again to Toxicology, and this time it's open. Sam, past fifty, from Jamaica, is in there, mopping the floor with disinfectant. He wears a green surgery cap on his head, green shirt and pants, the pants tucked into disposable plastic booties that he wears over his shoes. Dressed for contagion, in case it's around. Don't want none of them godforsaken bacteria in this here place, no sir. A surgical mask over his face.

"You nearly done, Sam?"

"Just about," Sam says. "Did over there but not over here. You come right in, it's dry that side. If you need."

Theo steps in and goes to the safe in the far corner. He's been here before. Roberto Quatrello has shown him around. He works the lock, knowing the combination because Roberto jokingly mentioned it one day, high on Hennessy and cocaine. Said it's the year of the first flight at Kitty Hawk, 1903, and who could possibly know or remember that?

He rotates the dial, clicking the numbers, and after a few tries, using the numbers in varying sequences, he gets lucky and the door clicks open. And there, nested in the fireproof safe, are the toxins, samples in vials, dozens of them, some less friendly than others. There is no anthrax here, no botulinum, no ricin, but plenty of others that could be a bother and more. He stands there, scanning the labels, a syringe in his pocket, and Sam calls over, "I'm done now, Doc. You lock the door when you go—huh? Okay?" Theo waves, assuring him that he will.

When he leaves the hospital, the sky is pale with pre-dawn light. He has patients scheduled at ten, but no surgery. Traffic is on the move, cars, buses. People coming up out of the subways already, this early. Trucks unloading bottled beer at the delis, vans bearing milk and juice. And the coffee shops ablaze with fluorescents, already busy with the croissants, the muffins, the coffee to go. He walks a few blocks, and then, with a vengeance, the lack of sleep catches up with him and he's hit by a fierce exhaustion, muscles limp and bones turning to mud. He stops, too weak to move on, lingering in front of a camera shop, at the curb, waiting for a cab. And when one comes, he gets in, and before they've gone two blocks, he's asleep.

Wednesday morning, early, Korn picks him up at Echo Terrace and drives him back to the cottage—and Theo, though hooded, is aware that Korn is taking a different

335

route. They don't board the FDR and don't go over the Willis Avenue bridge. They go through one of the tunnels—impossible to mistake the sound of it, the long downward slope and then the upgrade—across to New Jersey. He's trying to confuse me, Theo thinks. Wasting his time. Doesn't he know it no longer matters?

At the cottage, he finds Matoso on a cot that Bowditch has set up for him downstairs, in the surgery room, in a corner by a window. He examines him, checking the vital signs, and takes a close look at the site of the operation.

"How do you feel? Are you all right?"

Matoso understands the drift, nods groggily. The morphine and the sleeping pills have put him into limbo, he feels no pain.

"This work should be done in a hospital," Theo says.

"He's doing fine," Bowditch answers. "His vitals are good."

"Still, it should be a hospital."

Bowditch prepares Matoso, and Theo, after scrubbing, goes to work on the face, using local anesthesia. He modifies the nose, reducing its size and altering its shape, making it more feminine. He does a face-lift and, using implants, gives prominence to the cheekbones. The nose takes an hour. The face-lift, another hour. And after finishing with the face, he takes the syringe that he brought with him, in his medical case, and injects small amounts of the filmy liquid into the incisions.

"What's that?" Bowditch asks.

"A saline-vitamin mix. It expedites the healing process."

"You didn't use it on the vagina," she says, letting him know that she notices such things.

"It's different tissue down there. Here, on the face, it's effective against scarring."

He does the breast implants, using a brand that he gets from Canada. These too he's brought with him, like the cheek implants, and, at Korn's suggestion, he's selected a moderate size, nothing that would attract attention. He has some difficulty with the left breast, but

336

he gets past it, and in less time than he expected, he's done.

"Is he beautiful?" he says to Bowditch.

"I wouldn't know," she answers.

He's glad it's over. He feels a burden has been lifted. What he's done, he's done, and he doesn't want to think about it, or worry over the possible consequences. All of the confusion, the doubt, it's finished. He strips off his surgical greens, tosses them into a laundry sack, washes in the kitchen, and takes a sandwich from the refrigerator. This time the choice is between cheese and tomato on rye and liverwurst on whole wheat. He takes the rye, and it's a disappointment. No sprouts, no mustard, and he suspects Bowditch may have made this one herself.

When Korn drives him back, he closes his eyes and sleeps the whole way.

The rest of his week is uneventful. He performs a rhinoplasty in the office and two transsexual operations at the hospital, both male to female. He sees a foreign film at the Angelika, on Houston and Mercer, about a chess player, a Russian, who murders his chief rival, a Lithuanian, but in the world competition he loses anyway, to a newcomer from Latvia. After the film, he dines at the Caffè Vivaldi, alone. He'd thought of inviting María Gracia, but didn't, and had considered Maggie Sowle, but resisted. Home, he eats a bag of chocolates from the French place on South End. He brushes the cat. He tries not to think about Matoso. Puts him out of his mind. What's done is done, come what may, and what kind of pigs were they anyway, the soldiers in Chile, dumping corpses in the street, and when the families came to pick them up, arresting them and putting them to the torture. Emilio Matoso. Well, so much for him.

Saturday night there's a call from Korn.

"He's not doing well," he says. "He has an infection."

"Where?"

"The face. The whole left side, and the nose."

337

"She's giving him the antibiotics?"

"Yes."

"Fever?"

"Yes."

"Give it a few days. It'll clear up."

"It's spreading."

"These things take time."

"I want you should have a look. I'll pick you up in the morning. You be ready by six?"

"I'm on hospital duty tomorrow." It was a lie, rolled out with great ease.

"Then get somebody to cover."

"I can't."

"Of course you can. There's always backup. Do it."

"He isn't going to die overnight."

"I'm not so sure about that."

"Do I have to wear that damn hood again?"

After a pause, Korn says, "Don't press your luck."

In the morning, it's just him and Korn in the car, and despite the little sleep that he's had, he's alert, conscious of the road, aware of every turn. The toll-booths and the bridge crossings, and now, he thinks, he has it figured out. The cottage is not in Connecticut, and not in Pennsylvania, but in the lower Catskills, some-where in Sullivan County, or Ulster. He feels the hills, the rises, and it comforts him, imagining he knows where he's going. His mother used to bring him to a cabin in Liberty when he was a boy, up near Monticello. But then again, he thinks maybe this is Connecticut.

In the cottage, when he looks at Matoso's face, he sees what a mess it is. Matoso is still downstairs, in the surgery room, on a cot by the window. The skin on his nose and the left side of his face is violet. Several bullae have developed, liquid-filled blisters. The right side of the face shows redness around the incisions. The disease will develop there too. The fever is still up, his heart rate rapid, his blood pressure low. Theo holds up three fingers and asks how many. The man's eyes are empty, he's in a daze. Korn asks a question in Spanish, and still the slanting gaze and confusion in the eyes.

"It's the morphine," Bowditch says.

"That too, but mostly it's the disease. If it gets any worse, he'll go unconscious. It's a necrotizing fasciitis," Theo says, "from a nasty strain of streptococcus. It's killing off the tissue under the skin. Pretty rare, not many cases in this country."

"You did that," Bowditch says, standing close. "When you irrigated with the syringe."

He stares hard at her, thinking smart, smart. She knows. She's wearing the navy-blue pants and double-breasted jacket she wore when he first met her, not the hospital greens.

"No," he answers. "You did it. I told you—the place isn't sterile. It's the wrong environment for surgery. It's you—both of you. You botched this."

She doesn't blink. "Can it be fixed?"

"It's a thirty percent mortality rate. He needs a hospital. Massive antibiotics and round-the-clock monitoring. The infected area has to be cut away. If he survives, he won't have a face."

"Thirty percent?" she says.

Theo shrugs. "In his shape, the odds aren't wonderful. Right now, I'd say he's in the thirty percent."

She looks to Korn, long and intense, and Korn nods.

"Let's go," she says to Theo.

"Where?"

"Outside." And moving toward the door, she grabs her coat and her overnight bag.

She brings him to the car and they get in, he in the front, on the passenger side, and she in the back, behind him. A few moments later, even with the car doors closed, he hears the gunshot. Just one. Then nothing but silence, the whiteness of the fields, no crows, no deer, and eventually Korn comes from the house with a duffel bag, which he stows in the trunk. Then he comes around and gets into the driver's seat.

Theo gives him a dark, questioning look. It's a look that says, What about me?

"If anybody talks to you," Korn says, "just remember—you were part of this. Anything you say, it's your own neck."

"Who will want to talk to me?"

"You never know."

"Who knows I was here?"

"I do. And Bowditch."

"Who else?"

"You don't need to know."

"Don't I?"

"We'll drop you in New Jersey. You can train in the rest of the way on PATH."

He doesn't believe them. They killed Matoso, and now they will have to kill him too. They're taking him to some deserted spot where they will dump his body and drive off. In the strangeness of the moment, he accepts that, it seems clear and logical. It's even logical that they didn't shoot him at the cottage, because one corpse at that location was enough. If he were found there, dead, he'd be a link, a connection.

Logic keeps him calm. As if he were thinking these thoughts about someone else. Clear and simple, cold, dispassionate. If he can hold on to logic, he won't panic. But the hood is over his head again, and in the darkness, logic sags and goes limp, and anxiety begins to build.

They're on a highway, he feels the speed, the shifting from lane to lane. The roar of trucks, and boom boxes in the cars. He hears not the music but the heavy thumping of the beat. And still, hot in memory, the sound of that single gunshot back at the cottage. Had it been a decoy? A deception? Is Emilio Matoso still alive back there, the gunshot merely a way of tricking him into thinking he was dead? But why? The man was dying, the infection eating away at him. As the car shifts from lane to lane, threads of paranoia loop through his brain, weaving, twisting. He doesn't want to die. He isn't ready for that. Never will be.

"Where are we now?"

"Almost there."

"Where?"

"Where I said. Jersey."

And still the car plunges ahead. A quick swerve left, and another swerve, to the right. Then steady again, the hum of the engine, and Theo tries to empty his mind, blocking out thought, because thought is too terrible. Images crowd in on him, forcing their way in—María Gracia, and Nora, and that morning on the Sepik River when he first saw the funeral canoe that he brought home to his apartment. The chanting, the low prayerful moans of the natives on the river. He thinks of María Gracia, wanting her, needing her. Resenting her for not wanting to bear his child. Is she safe? Will they be after her too, thinking he told her something? He remembers that morning on the Sepik, when he saw the canoe carrying a dead woman into the mist, and when it came back, it was empty. Life is empty. Time is empty. And Nora, still in a coma, she too is empty. She had given him so much, those hours of peace and calm, sitting on her sofa, with the animals—the cockatiel, the macaw, the turtle, the monkey. The finches out of their cage, flying about. I'm going mad, he thinks. This is how it happens. Before you die, it's all scrambled, the system breaks down, the mind chokes itself.

The car slows and drifts to the right, going off on a long, slow turn. They're leaving the highway. A brief pause at the end of the ramp, at a stop sign, then they nudge slowly along, stop and go, in traffic. Bowditch, in the seat behind him, removes the black sack, and light assaults his eyes. He winces, blinks, as his pupils adjust.

"I'm dropping you here," Korn says, pulling over to the curb. "The PATH station is two blocks ahead."

He doesn't move. What will they do? Shoot him when he gets out and speed off?

"Go, dammit," Korn says, reaching across Theo's body and releasing the catch on the door, pushing it open.

Theo looks at Korn, thick eyebrows, small eyes, fleshy mouth, and as he pushes up out of his seat and steps out onto the sidewalk, what flashes through his mind is that

Korn needs work on his face. Get rid of the jowly look, do something with the nose. Bowditch is up too, out of the backseat, onto the sidewalk, and when he looks at her hands, they're empty.

"PATH is that way," she says, pointing, and climbs into the front seat and pulls the door shut.

Theo, heart racing, sets off with a quick step, the opposite direction the car is pointing in. He hears the engine start up, and with a slight turn of his head, sees from the corner of his eye that the car is backing up, approaching, and Bowditch's window is down. His gut twists, knotting up, and though he wants to run, he can't, unable to move, legs like lead weights.

He's facing the car now, the open window slowly approaching, and Bowditch's arm comes out. The hand is empty, no gun. Her finger is pointing. "Didn't you hear? PATH is that way," she calls. "But maybe you'd rather grab a cab." The arm pulls back in and the window goes up, and the car switches from reverse to forward and jumps out, into the traffic, and he's left standing there, heart pounding, his mouth dry.

And that's what he does. Grabs a cab. Out of New Jersey and under the river, through the tunnel. Down West Street, then turning again, and home to Battery Park, to Echo Terrace, home again to the seagulls and the pigeons.

In the lobby, Farro Fescu signals from the desk, saying there is a package for him. He goes to the mail room, and it's a cardboard carton containing a picnic bucket, and inside the bucket a stainless steel thermos with a note from Claudio Nascita. "The FSH worked like a charm. Harvested seven eggs. There are five embryos in here. Two of the eggs didn't make it. If these don't get you that son you wanted, try talking to God."

The Long, Happy Death
of Ira Klempp

It's Wednesday morning, the lobby busy, brisk with the comings and goings of carpenters, plumbers, delivery boys, wallpaper hangers. Everybody signs in, even the ones with whom Farro Fescu is familiar. No exceptions, because he knows how it goes—you let one by, then another, and before long you forget who's in and who is not. And then you're in trouble with the break-ins, the robberies, and maybe worse. So everyone signs, even the girl who walks the dogs, taking three at a time, each on its own leash.

This morning, toward ten, after the great rush and clatter, there is a pause, a gripping silence. Farro Fescu is alone, behind the desk, in his leather chair, and even the phone is quiet, a bird in its nest. He thinks of the pimple on his penis, which is no longer a pimple but a bluish-brown spot, a discoloration in the skin. Has the pimple healed, or has it turned into something worse? He feels a fullness, a pressure in his lower belly, and he leans to one side and quietly passes gas, the odor vanishing into the ventilation ducts. He runs a hand through his hair, feeling the thickness above the ears. It's time already for the barber, and he'll treat himself this time to a shave as well, the hot towel on his face warm, wet, welcoming.

He has needs, desires. And hatreds. Dislike is a wide spectrum, ranging from simple aversion to loathing and enmity. Toward Knatchbull and Noelli, he is merely neutral. Dr. Tattafruge he considers an enigma, a man tinkering surgically with genitalia and breasts—why would anyone want to do that? For Juanita Blaize, the pop singer, he has nothing but contempt, but wouldn't mind grabbing her hot bottom for a quick feel, and maybe more. And Rumfarm, that bothersome idiot, he should fall down a flight of stairs and live the rest of his life in a body cast. And Klempp? Ira Klempp? The same. If not worse.

He knows now what goes up to Klempp in the pizza boxes that arrive late afternoon and in the morning too. He's had his suspicions, but now he knows, having only yesterday stuck out a foot and tripped the delivery boy. As the kid went down, the keep-warm box hit the floor and tumbled open. No pizza in there, no pasta or manicotti, just small brown bags bound by rubber bands, and inside the bags, for sure, it wasn't jelly beans. The boy scrambled to retrieve the bags, glaring at Farro Fescu with a look meant to kill.

"You okay, kid? Hurt your knee? Gotta be careful on the marble, it can be slippery."

"Yeah," the kid says. "Sure." Then, lifting a brown bag— "Coffee beans."

He had a wiry body and a skinny face, an amber glaze on his Latino skin.

"No kidding," Farro Fescu said. "Poppo Pizza delivers coffee beans? Let's see." He bent and reached for one of the bags, but the boy snatched it away, replacing it in the keep-warm box, and closed the lid.

"Can't open the bags," he says. "Wouldn't be sanitary."

"Oh," Farro Fescu says.

"We got Mexican, Colombian, Peruvian, and Venezuelan. You want I should bring you some?"

"What's the toll?"

"It depends."

"On what?"

"Just depends."

"Maybe bring a sample."

"We don't do samples."

"Then maybe Mr. Klempp will brew some for me."

"Maybe."

There was in the kid's face a tense uncertainty, as if, instead of delivering the stuff, he might bolt and run. But just then the elevator arrived, and up he went, and Farro Fescu, back at his desk, didn't have to open any of those brown bags to know what was in them. He knew the names, having heard them on street corners and bars, the names jostling through memory like a subway train rattling through a tunnel. Nose candy, gonzo, snow, charlie, flake, toot, jam, blort, golden girl. And maybe some Chinese Number 3. Or tar. Or just a shabby pile of homegrown. All those bags, Ira Klempp wasn't buying only for himself. He was passing it around, selling in the building. To Juanita Blaize, no doubt, because all those pop singers were buzzbrains. And Rumfarm? Him? That snaky hypocrite? Wouldn't be surprised. Not Vogel, though, he had too much German discipline, and not Mrs. Wax and Mrs. Marriocci, they were just harmless aging air-heads. But Tattafruge, maybe, because he'd heard how doctors and nurses snorted, like movie stars and the tele-vision crowd. The Dillhoppers, he figured, and maybe that Saad boy, Abdul, who wanted to be a mortician. And the father, Saad himself, you never can tell about Arabs, never. Ira Klempp like a cancer in the building, spreading it around, whatever the shit was, hash, coke, Lebanese gold, black Russian, acid, mellow yellow, angel dust, strawberry fields.

He went to the toilet and urinated, thinking how good if he could piss away all the bad. His urine stank. What was it, he wondered—the asparagus last night? Or was it Ira Klempp? Get rid of him, rid of him. Piss him into the urinal and flush him away, the droop-shouldered junkhead. Into the sewer, where he belongs.

That was yesterday, Tuesday. Groceries for Mrs. Saad, UPS for Nora Abernooth's niece. The new chandelier for Mrs. Rumfarm, flowers for Mrs. Sowle, then the kid with the pizza box full of drugs. Gusty March winds making themselves felt in the lobby every time the front door opened. Today, in the lull after the early morning rush, Farro Fescu closes his eyes, trying to shut thought out, feeling a need to empty his mind. Behind his closed lids, first there is a darkness, then a warm, dim light. Not to think, not to remember. Not to feel. Everything quiet, even the wind has died down. He sits immobile, breathing slowly, hearing the sound of his breath, in and out. But still the hum, the buzz, the anger that owns him and won't let him rest. It's no good. Bad. He has to move past this. But can't. He stands and leaves the desk and goes through the glass door and, in the crisp, cold air, walks briskly to the river, in the sun, noting how few the ice floes are, compared to those of last month. Then a quick tour around the block, moving fast, hands in his pockets, jacket collar turned up around his neck, and, invigorated by the bracing cold, back into the lobby, to the desk, rubbing his hands together to warm them.

A few days later, toward noon, Angela Crespi, Nora's niece, is standing by the living room window, brushing her hair and gazing at the boats on the Hudson. It's a bright, sunny day, the air crystalline, and as she stands there, brushing, admiring the view, something falls past the window, going swiftly by. So sudden, she hardly knows what it was. It had seemed, strangely, like a person, yet she knows it couldn't have been, because how could it? Nine stories up? She thinks maybe a large bird swooping by—or, if not the bird itself, perhaps its shadow. She searches the sky, thinking a pelican, or a stork. Are there storks in New York? But sees nothing, only some gulls and pigeons, and feels cheated, because it had certainly been something, and she missed it.

On the floor below, Mrs. Marriocci is reading a piece in the *Times* about prairie dogs, the way their habitats are being encroached upon. Only two percent of their former habitat is still theirs, and if the prairie dog vanishes, what will happen to the hawks, eagles, badgers, and coyotes that feed on them? She's tired. She removes her glasses and massages her eyes lightly, then glances through the window, and in that eye-blinking moment she sees something falling. She thinks it odd, but concludes it must have been a piece of newspaper blown by the wind. It's March, famous for wild winds. Strange, though, a piece of paper this high? In her years here, she's never seen a single thing blowing past her window. But anything, of course, is possible, and she returns to the prairie dogs, reading how they were now being hunted for sport, and that was making them less of a nuisance and more of a curiosity. In the Dakotas, the Sioux are inviting hunters to come in and shoot all they can. In Texas and Nebraska, hunters are killing prairie dogs and having them preserved and mounted, putting them on the mantel, and those that don't have a mantel are hanging them on the walls.

A few floors below, Dr. Tattafruge is making love to María Gracia Moño. Usually, he goes to her apartment, but today her place is being painted, so she's here at his place and they're on the floor in the living room, on the deep-piled Kazak carpet he had picked up on a trip to the Caucasus a few years earlier. Only a few moments after he's reached his orgasm, he glances toward the glass door that leads to the balcony, and in that instant he sees Ira Klempp falling. It's a moment of tantalizing slowness, in which he observes Ira Klempp in intricate detail. His face, eyes, nose, his overly large ears. His spiked yellow hair. His black shirt. His colorful jigsaw-puzzle pants made of bright patches, red and yellow and blue. His feet, which are bare, and his hands, which are clenched. But most of all the face, blue eyes open, luminous with a sense of horror, the mouth agape, teeth whitely visible, lips at a crooked slant in an expression of despair. And what most impresses him is the slowness, as if, in its fall, the body is pausing, hovering briefly before resuming its downward rush.

In the room directly below, on the fourth floor, Maggie Sowle is in an easy chair by the window, relaxing, taking a break, time off from the new quilt she's been working on. She's reading a murder mystery. From the corner of her eye, she glimpses the barest flicker of a shadow falling past the window but pays no notice. She turns the page and reads on, drawn along by the fast pace of the narrative, the crisp dialogue and gory details, and no clear clue as to who the murderer might be, though she has a few hunches.

Oscar, the supervisor of the maintenance crew, is the one who reaches the body first. He's outside, with Blue, showing him how to polish the brass handles on the big glass doors. He had just applied a dab of pink paste to one of the handles when the body hit, making a sound like nothing he's ever heard. When he turns to look, he sees Ira Klempp on the sidewalk, some sixty feet away. He knows it's Klempp because of the pants, the Krazy-Kolor jigsaw pattern of bright patches. The legs and arms are twisted all around, and when he goes close, he sees the spurts of blood that have shot out in several directions. The skull is smashed, brain matter leaking out onto the sidewalk. He stands there, looking, and Blue comes up beside him, the two of them just standing there, saying nothing.

Oscar turns and goes inside, to the lobby. "Something awful," he says to Farro Fescu, who is stepping off the east elevator as Oscar comes in. "Better call 911."

"What happened?"

"Somebody fell. That young man, Mr. Klempp."

"Klempp? Really?"

"Fell off a balcony."

"He's all right?"

"He's dead."

Farro Fescu places the call, and an ambulance and a patrol car arrive in moments.

There hadn't been a death in the condominium since Kapri Blorg, the book publisher, committed suicide, shooting himself in the mouth while standing in the shower, fully clothed. The residents, learning about Ira Klempp, wonder if this too might have been a suicide. Had he jumped, or had he simply leaned too far over the railing? The autopsy report, released a week later, shows that he'd been loaded with drugs, high on cocaine and full of whiskey too, so more than likely, it seems, the fall had been accidental. Nevertheless, the police interview everyone, and a shiver of alarm runs through the building when it becomes evident that the investigators suspect Ira Klempp might have been pushed.

It's an unnerving thought, the possibility of a murderer in their midst, one of the residents, or one of the staff. But the idea is too preposterous to gain credence, and, as the days and weeks go by, the police themselves give up on it, concluding, in the absence of any clear evidence of foul play, that the death had been accidental and drug related.

"Good riddance," Farro Fescu says, confiding his feelings to Karl Vogel, who, like himself, had never been one of Ira Klempp's admirers.

"Yes, of course," Vogel replies. "I agree. But still, you know, he was so young. Twenty-nine? Is that what the paper said? When death strikes so young, it seems not appropriate to rejoice."

Farro Fescu calls a local florist and orders a wreath, which he places among the junipers, near the spot where the body had hit the sidewalk and broken apart.

And still he thinks, Good riddance.

The Chapel Near the Ferry

In her apartment in the East Eighties, María Gracia's walk-in closet is filled with tight-fitting pants and turtlenecks that hug her forty-two-year-old body and show it to advantage. She favors muted colors, earth tones and pastels, but has in her wardrobe some garish things too, strawberry red and aquamarine, for moments when garish is required. She has wigs and falls, and shoes in abundance, boots and pumps and spike heels, and a bottom drawer stuffed with coy silks and gauzy see-through extravaganzas. She doesn't do whips and chains, or mutilation, and nothing at all with guns or knives, or razors.

Some of her patrons she entertains in her apartment, but most she meets elsewhere—in hotel rooms, or in their condos, or, as sometimes happens, in other countries. One, a congressman, arranged a meeting in Montreal, to avoid attention, and another, a Brazilian architect, flew her, out of sheer bravado, to a palazzo in Venice. Her client list includes a judge, a brain surgeon, an IRS supervisor, a monsignor, the son of a Colombian drug lord, and a mayor from across the river, in New Jersey.

The one she's known longer than any other, some twenty years, is Harry Falcon, who lives in the penthouse at the top of Echo Terrace and is struggling now with a recalcitrant cancer. He's the wealthiest of her clients, and the one, of the many she's had, that she likes best. He had made his fortune in frozen foods, marketing bags of frozen blueberries and fancy gourmet dinners ready for the microwave. He's more than ten years older than she is, with a thin, spare body, dark hair, and a wry sense of humor. He was born in London about a year before the war against Hitler began, and he has memories of being with his mother on a platform in the underground, staying whole nights there, on a blanket, during the bombings. His father served in the army and saw action in France, and it was after the war that they came over, to Toronto first, where they stayed a year, then to New Jersey, where they moved into a large old house in Morristown.

Before his illness struck, Harry flew around a great deal, to plants that he owned in different parts of the country, and he often took María with him. They had met a few years after she finished her one-year tour in Vietnam, working as a Donut Dolly for the American Red Cross. She passed out donuts and Kool-Aid, and visited the wounded and helped them write letters home, and there were also times when she entertained the troops in the field with songs and card tricks, and clever little games that someone in the Red Cross had dreamed up.

Once, during a helicopter flight to Bien Hoa, a corporal sitting next to her was killed by a bullet from the ground. It was horrible. One minute he was alive, talking, telling her about the farm in Oklahoma where he'd grown up, and the next moment he was slumped over and dead. The other Donut Dolly in the chopper, a girl named Janelle, became hysterical, screaming and moaning, on and on. María sat in her harness, dumbstruck, listening to Janelle's wailing, and felt a kind of hopelessness. The helicopter rumbled on, cutting a straight line through the blue mist, low over the trees, and this, she thought, was how it was, this was life. In the next instant there could be another bullet from the ground, and it could take any of them.

That night, at Bien Hoa, she had sex with the pilot who had flown the helicopter. It was fierce, angry, defiant sex, and the intensity of it, the sweaty clutching and grabbing, was somehow, for her, an answer to the corporal's death and to the blind terror of Janelle's screaming. If it wasn't, then what did she have? How do you talk back to death and tell it that it is meaningless, hateful, stupid, a piece of chaos, and that you want to spit on it and forget it forever?

After Vietnam, instead of returning home to Rochester, she floundered around in Manhattan for a while and eventually found work at an escort service operating out of an office in midtown. And it was a month after that, toward the end of the summer, that she met up with Harry Falcon. He hired her and some other girls to act as hostesses aboard his yacht, a forty-footer, turbine-driven, during an afternoon excursion up the Hudson, as far as the Peekskill bridge, then back to the berth in North Cove. He was thirtyish, with gray eyes, a bony face, and a hairline that was already receding—and young, she thought, to be so rich. He owned a company named Arctic Swan and was trying to persuade a group of Slovenian middlemen to give his frozen brisket a try. He had already landed contracts with the Isle of Man, Togo, and Madagascar, but the Slovenians, who were at that time still part of Yugoslavia, were slow to come along and needed some persuading.

When he saw María in her blue and white sailor outfit, which she'd bought special for the occasion, something flickered in his eyes, and she noticed he was suddenly protective, keeping the Slovenians away from her. He brought her to the helm and showed her the controls, and let her steer for a while, though it proved not a terribly good idea. Unwittingly, she put the yacht on a collision course with a small sailboat, and when Harry saw what was about to happen, he grabbed the wheel and veered off sharply, avoiding the collision, but the small boat was swamped by the yacht's wake, and the man and the woman who'd been aboard had to be fished out of the water.

And on the yacht, there were injuries. In the sudden turn, one of the girls fell against the gunwale and broke her nose, blood spurting across the deck, and two others, falling, bruised their knees. They blamed María for everything. And the Slovenians, shouting obscenities in their native tongue, blamed Harry.

When the yacht pulled into North Cove, the Slovenians rushed off with the girls, leaving behind María and the one who was bleeding, and on the following day they signed contracts with Arctic Swan's competitor, Penguin Mist, never realizing that Penguin Mist, like Arctic Swan, was owned by Harry Falcon, who had learned early that the quickest way to grow his market share was by competing with himself. He ran commercials in which Penguin Mist and Arctic Swan warred with each other, each declaring its products to be tastier, richer, wholesomer, and altogether more flavorful than those of the other, and as the advertising war raged, profits for both brands soared. When the Slovenians discovered that he owned Penguin Mist, they canceled their contracts and signed on with Snow Cuisine, never suspecting that Harry owned that too.

And he owned other things—a cottage in the South of France, a cargo jet that flew his frozens around the world, a herd of cattle in Texas, which furnished the beef for many of the frozen dinners, and several herds of cows in the Catskills, providing milk and cream for the frozen desserts. And cars, many cars, a Gordon-Keeble, a 1938 Hispano-Suiza, a Ferrari, a freshly minted Lamborghini Espada. And, as time wore on and María learned more and more about him, she wondered if there was anything that he didn't own, and she sometimes imagined he owned things that he didn't even know were his.

"Vietnam?" he said, finding it hard to believe she had actually been there. "You? No kidding."

"Me. Yes."

"Yeah? Tell me."

She did. Told him. Telling him some of it, most of it, though not all of it. How she had flown out at the end of a mild July, on an air force transport, nine of them, in powder-blue dresses with short sleeves and knee-length hemlines, a Red Cross insignia on the left sleeve, and when they reached Saigon they were assaulted by hundred-degree heat and dense humidity, a thick purple mist looming over the palms and tamarinds. An army truck took them from the airport into the city, and she had her first glimpse of Saigon, its wide streets and boulevards crowded with bicycles and pedicabs, and the parks, the pagodas, vendors on the sidewalks selling cooked meat and cigarettes, and incense sticks.

One year, that's all it was, yet it's still very much with her, the rice paddies and bamboo, and the helicopters lifting off and returning with the body bags. She was at Cam Rhan Bay for a while, then at Cu Chi with the Twenty-fifth. The troops that she met were mostly young, like herself, and scared. Names and slogans scribbled on their flak jackets and helmets. TOMAHAWK, 7-ELEVEN, CROW, JANE FONDA. END OF THE WORLD. CHOP SUEY. HEAVEN HERE I COME. Some of them carried pets. She remembers one with an owl, another with a monkey. And one who burnt his mosquito bites with a cigarette. And there had been one in a hospital bed in Saigon, with no legs, how he put his hands on her one day and held her, kissing, such warmth and desire, his lips holding hers. Life is good, she thinks. Life is always beginning. If life is not good and not always beginning, then it's bad, and who needs that?

A year, only a year, and now it's twenty years later, so fast, snap of the fingers. And for Harry, poor Harry, time has been too fast, because now he's sick, and it's cancer. Just fifty-four, that's all he is, still lean and good-looking, and those gray eyes that have a way of drawing you in. And what she has always liked most about him is that he talks, he enjoys conversation, even when they're in bed.

He's told her everything—about his wives, his children, and his business, his doubts, his hopes, his confusion, his indecision. Even about the pains in his knees. And about his parents too, Mabel and Wyndham, endlessly at odds, shouting at each other in their noisy bedroom dramas, which Harry, as a child, could not help but overhear. His mother was an unreconstructed

Marxist, and it was a thorn in her flesh that the man she had married was a common capitalist whose only dream was to build an empire in frozen foods—and though he brought in good money, an empire it never was, because something was lacking in him, the skill, the intuition, the right kind of practical sense. And when he died, all of her confusion came into focus and she went crazy at the cemetery, sobbing wildly and tearing off all of her clothes as the coffin was lowered into the grave. She ended her days in an asylum, writing letters to the *New York Times*, extolling the genius of Karl Marx. Only one of the letters was ever printed.

And for Harry, poor Harry, it will soon be over for him too. In the time that she's known him, he's divorced three times. The last one, the horse lady who rode and won prizes in competition, had been a disaster. He was now supporting five children whom he rarely saw and didn't much think about, except when he signed the checks. He was not a model father, he knew that. But that was the way he was, not cut out, he would say, for the role of paterfamilias. And in the past, before his sickness, he used to joke about it, how he was wise in frozen foods but dumb in sex, having spent a small fortune on the three women he'd married, and very little, by comparison, on María, who had always been there for him, and much more fun.

"Don't laugh about such things," she chided when he talked that way. "A family is a precious thing. You should be ashamed, not seeing your children."

"I need this? You're my shrink?"

"I'm your whore, and you better listen to me. Since there's nobody else."

He had brought her to Panama, where he sold heart-healthy frozen chicken dinners to the Noriega regime. General Noriega paid him in cocaine, which he in turn sold to the CIA, which wanted the cocaine for reasons of its own, which he wanted to know nothing about.

After Panama, he brought her to Iran, where he personally delivered a case of his finest frozen blueberries to the

Ayatollah, who was partial to blueberries. This was the year when senior U.S. officials secretly traded arms to Iran in exchange for their help in gaining the release of American hostages held in Lebanon, and the blueberries were a way of sweetening the pie.

From Iran, Harry took her to Afghanistan, into the mountains of the Hindu Kush, where he had business with the mujahideen, who were fighting the Russians and winning. María liked Afghanistan, the cloud-draped mountains, ice-glazed cliffs, trees growing out of rock. But so much devastation from the long war. Over a million Afghans dead, and more than five million had fled the country.

Too fast, too fast, she felt, the way the months and years leaped by. When she turned thirty, it had seemed an earthquake. And then, when she turned forty, it was as if a tidal wave had swept over her. But she was adjusting, getting used to it. What she understood was that time, like a falling body, doesn't move at a steady rate of speed, but moves faster and faster as you grow older.

At Sloan-Kettering, on York Avenue, up in the Sixties, they gave Harry a course of chemotherapy, but it was clear that his body was shutting down. With more chemo they could slow the process and keep him alive for a while, but no promises. The chemo devastated him. He vomited. He had diarrhea. He had dizzy spells. He didn't smile anymore, but still, somehow, he saw the ironies, the hangnail humor of being moribund. "Just when the damn economy is picking up? They're throwing my switch? Now? When we're about to have the biggest bull market ever?"

It used to be that she saw him at her place, or they would go to a hotel, or an island. But now, because of the sickness, she comes to him. He's too weak for anything strenuous, and the medication leaves him impotent. He wants her to lie in bed with him and talk. He dozes for a while, and when he awakens they talk again. It had always been that way with him. He liked slow, rambling conversation.

"You know what bothers me?" he says. "It's that damn clock. Always out there across the river, staring me right in the face."

He means the big Colgate clock in Jersey City, enormous, in the shape of an octagon. Huge black hands creeping across the face. It stands fifty feet tall at the edge of the river, at 105 Huyden Street. Harry knows the address and everything else about the clock because he had tried, some years ago, to buy it from Colgate so that he could tear it down. And when Colgate refused, he attempted an unfriendly takeover and nearly succeeded, but the stock market went into a spasm because of trouble in the Middle East, and reluctantly he backed off, and he still doesn't forgive himself for failing to carry through.

"I should have grabbed that company by the throat and knocked their damn clock into oblivion." And then, touching María's arm, "You like clocks?"

"Some are pretty."

"I hate them all. Clocks are time, and time is death. Who needs it?"

The minute hand on the Colgate clock weighs twenty-two hundred pounds. It moves twenty-three inches every minute. Built by Seth Thomas, who had started making clocks almost two hundred years ago, in Connecticut. This one considered the largest single-faced illuminated dial clock in the world.

"Time is good," she says. "Take what you have, don't fight it. It's best to hold each moment. Just breathing, in and out, is good."

"You always were partial to that silly zen crap. Katerina was like that too. She was a bad influence on you."

Katerina was the woman who had set María up, telling her where to shop for clothes, and what books to read, what shows to see, and always to accept only the best clients, never anyone who does not come recommended. She showed her how to handle her money, and what kinds of investments to make.

"Breathe," María says.

"Fuck breathing."

"In, slowly. Then out, slowly."

"Yeah," he says, hating it, but does it. In, slowly. Then out.

"There, there," she says.

"The only problem," he says, "if I concentrate on breathing, all I can think is that the next one might be my last."

She slaps his wrist.

"That hurt," he says.

"I wanted it to."

"So mean. Why so mean? Be nice. Talk to me. Tell me everything."

"What else is to tell?"

"All of it. Everything. Leave nothing out."

She tells him about when she was seven years old and made her first communion. She wore a white dress and a veil, and carried white lilies. Her image of heaven, when she was seven, was that it was full of silver trees with gold leaves, and flowers that sparkled like glass.

"Sounds good to me," he says. "Are you booking reservations? Are these one-acre or two-acre plots that you're selling? Who gets the one high on the mountain with the best view?"

"Not you," she says. "You've been too bad."

"Me? Naughty?"

"Bad, bad boy. You're so wicked today. What's making you so disagreeable?"

"Don't hate me," he says.

"I despise you," she answers. "I loathe you. You're an abomination. Why did I ever let you into my life?"

"See?" he says, closing his eyes. "Finally she tells the truth. Does it make you feel better?"

"I don't know," she says. "How does it make you feel?"

"Makes me feel like shit. But it's good shit, it takes away the pain."

She leaves, goes home to her apartment, and the next day she returns. She's canceled her appointments with her other clients, telling them she has to be away, traveling. She's nursing him, bringing him juice, giving him his pills, calming him when he's fretful. He has a live-in nurse, sleeping over, but when María is there, she sends the nurse away, out to a movie, wanting to do these things herself, the juice, the pills, the rubdowns.

In the bedroom, in the rosewood wall system, he has seven television monitors. There are times when each of the seven is tuned to a different channel. But today, when she comes in, she sees herself on all seven. It's a video of her that he took when they were in Tierra del Fuego. She was naked, surrounded by a crowd of penguins, walking among them. Silly little tuxedo creatures all around her, checking her out.

She never lets her clients photograph her, it was something Katerina had taught her. No pictures, ever, they only cause problems. But with Harry she has never observed this rule. He's the only one.

Tierra del Fuego was in 1973, when Pinochet took over after the coup that brought down Salvador Allende. The State Department, which had supported the coup, was eager for things in Chile to calm down, and it was thought frozen pizza might help. Harry shipped thousands of pizzas to Pinochet, paid for by the CIA, which had appealed to his patriotism and humanitarian instinct, asking him to sell at cost because the pizzas were going to the widows and orphans in the barrios of Santiago and Valparaiso. Which he did, sold at cost, only to discover later that the pizzas went not to the widows and orphans but to Pinochet's army, which was so delighted with them that Pinochet placed another order. But this time, Harry, pissed at Pinochet and the CIA, sold instead to Guatemala, where there was a revolution brewing, and he hoped that now, perhaps, his pizzas would find their way to the mouths of the ones who needed them, though he wasn't entirely sure that would happen.

Images of María among the penguins were still on the seven monitors, all of them the same image, María naked and beautiful, her breasts, her thighs, the way she moved, hair tossed by the wind. Some of the penguins seemed shy, turning away.

"I should have invested in your body," Harry says. "Look how sensational you were. All seven of you. I should have bought MGM and put you in the movies."

Sometimes, late in the day, when the pain is worse than in the earlier hours, he asks about her other clients. This is something else she never does, gossip about her patrons, even with Harry. But now, in the shape he's in, what does it matter?

"Tell me about Muhta Saad," he says.

"The Clove Man? I only saw him twice. He wanted to pay me with cloves, but of course I refused."

"That's what you call him? The Clove Man?"

"He buys and sells cloves, ships them all over the world."

"That much I know."

"He had some kretek cigarettes with him, from Indonesia. They grind the cloves and mix them with tobacco, and when you smoke them they make crisp, crackling sounds. Very aromatic. Half the world's cloves go into kretek cigarettes."

"You shouldn't smoke," he says. "You'll die of cancer, like me."

"You didn't get it from smoking."

"I got it from sleeping with whores, like you."

"Don't be mean. You never had anything from me but fun."

"Are you mad at me?"

"No, I'm just pissed."

"Don't be pissed. Be nice. Tell me about the cloves."

"They grow on trees."

"Trees? I thought bushes."

"It's a tall evergreen, with flowers. They pick the flower when it's pinkish green, before it turns red. Then they dry it in the sun and it turns brown, and that's your clove."

"You saw one? A clove tree?"

"Of course not, I'm making it all up. That's what you pay me for, isn't it? To make things up?"

He tilts his head boyishly. "Was he better than me?"

"Nobody was better than you."

"That's a lie," he says.

It is, yet there was some truth in it, because even though others may have been, in bed, more vigorous and inventive, Harry had been the most pleasant, talking, telling her things, and wanting her to tell things to him—and that, she thought, was the best sex, when you talked and the sex was layered with the past, with memories, with jokes, with sadness, and the memories burned and fused, and when the release came, it was better and richer because there was so much more in it than just the physical bashing around. And now he was so sick, all that was left were the words.

"The best," she says again. "You really were."

He leans up on an elbow and puts his hand to her face, gripping the chin between thumb and forefinger. "Such a pretty mouth," he says. "But so full of make-believe."

Then his hand drops away, and he's studying her eyes. "Tell me," he says, "how'd you get into all this?"

"All of what?"

"What you do. Here, with me. And with the others."

She glances away lazily, then her eyes slant back to him.

"Let's talk about you," she says.

"I don't want to talk about me."

"You love to talk about you."

"Do I? Yeah? I just like to talk. Machu Picchu, do you remember that?"

Machu Picchu they saw on the return trip from Tierra del Fuego, giving themselves a few days in the Peruvian Andes. He had wanted to see the holy mountain.

She nods. Yes, yes, remembering.

"Baloney," he says. "You forget everything."

"I? Me? I remember every inch. It's you who forgets. It was cold on that mountain, when we were there."

361

"But you liked it. It wasn't that cold. The Tower of the Sun, you forgot about that?"

"I remember every time you grabbed for the Maalox. You had such a bum stomach those days."

"Don't remind me."

"Machu Picchu," she says.

"Yeah," he answers, and slides away, onto his back again, head on the pillow, and for a while he's quiet, eyes closed.

Then, as if talking to himself, "Should I have myself frozen?"

It jolts her. She's heard of it, the cryonic preservations, has seen it in the news and in the movies, and it strikes her as grotesque.

"Is that what you want?"

His eyes are open now. "It's a joke, sweetheart. A joke. Frozen Food King Goes into Deep Freeze. Can't you laugh anymore?"

At home that night, it gnaws at her, that idiot question he asked, about how she got into it, doing what she does. Because how, really, do you ever know the reason for the life you have? What she knows is that she likes what she does, she's interested in the men she meets. The lawyers, doctors, the screenwriter, the congressman. The guy who wrote some of the new software for the orbiting telescope. And the Hungarian, the one with a tiger act in the circus. There's a fascination, an excitement. The bad ones too. This clean-cut guy comes home from the war in Iraq, drove a tank there, the four-day desert war, and now he's an enforcer for a drug mob. Blond and Irish, with a fancy upscale haircut and an imported three-piece suit, working for rich Colombians living on Long Island. And he tells her about it, how he whacked three guys. "They deserved it," he says. "They were bums. And the money is smart. How do you think I can afford you?" Crazy. Lunatic. It teases her. A professional killer. He is of interest to her.

And what if she had stayed in Rochester, taking pictures of the falls of the Genesee, and the Kodak

362

smokestacks, would she feel better about herself? With children, a house on an acre of grass. She could do that. With the money she now has, she could buy one of the better homes in Rochester, and could adopt. A girl from Vietnam, or Laos, and she could watch her grow. But she pulls herself away from that, because something inside her knows this isn't right for her. Not now, at any rate. Later. Much later.

The next day she brings oranges and squeezes fresh juice for Harry. He's out of bed, sitting at the kitchen table. He takes a sip, savoring it, then puts the glass down and gives her a dark look.

"Who else have you done it with?" he asks. "The cardinal?"

The idea amuses her, sex with His Eminence. "It could be interesting," she says.

"John Glenn?"

"I wish."

"Rabbi Meir Kahane? Before they killed him?"

She tosses a lazy shrug, lifting her left shoulder.

"But not Clinton," he says, "he likes them fat and young. Have you fucked Al Gore?"

She tells him about Tattafruge, who wants to make her pregnant because his ex-wife took his son to Seattle, and he wants another son to replace him. And Charlie Rohr, who wants to have sex with her in the air, in one of the World War II bombers that he owns. But she's not that crazy.

"Tattafruge? He wants a kid? I thought you went through the change."

"Well, any day. Maybe."

"Who else? Who else you been slumming with? Not that jap Aki Sato, I hope."

"No, not him."

"How come? I thought you made a point of sleeping around with all the riffraff. Sonofabitch was part of the attack on Pearl Harbor. Did you know that? And Rumfarm, him—you do it with him too?"

She shakes her head wearily.

"If you ever do it with that creep, I'll never forgive you. I don't care what he pays. I'll come back from the grave and haunt you till you wet your pants. The bastard wants my penthouse. Can you believe? He can't wait till I'm dead, wants to negotiate a price right now."

He's exhausted. His surge of anger against Rumfarm has robbed him of the little energy he had. With some effort, he pushes himself up from the kitchen table and slowly makes his way back to the bedroom. He climbs into bed, and she pulls the sheet up, tucking him in, and he closes his eyes and sleeps. In a moment there is light snoring. She moves his head slightly, and the snoring stops. Easy breathing, slow and steady. Why can't he live, she wonders. Why can't he slip past this and live forever?

She walks around the apartment, the living room, dining room, the den. In the kitchen she makes coffee. Big windows and views all around. She sees the river, the bay, the Statue of Liberty. Ellis Island. In the living room there's a spiral staircase to the rooftop solarium. She goes up, strolls past the pool and the bar, and steps out onto the open deck, where there are junipers and mimosas. A brisk wind up there, on the roof. The biting March air gives her a shiver. The sun crisp, gleaming off the windows of the financial district, and the two huge towers of the World Trade Center looming so close, only a few blocks away. From here, on the roof, she feels the power of their bigness. When they first went up, she didn't like them. Tall, yes, but not enough imagination, too much like long boxes standing on end. But now she's grown used to them and would miss them if they weren't there, so strong and confident, balancing the skyline, downtown answering the midtown bigness of the Empire State and the Chrysler. All part of the package, New York, the Hudson, the East River and all the bridges, and though she grew up in Rochester, this now, for her, is home.

When she steps back in, downstairs to the bedroom, she finds him awake. He's sitting up, propped up on pillows.

"Don't worry about anything," he says.

"I try not to."

"You're in my will."

This, about his will, comes out of nowhere, and though she should be pleased, she's not. She does well enough on her own and had never thought of him in terms of a bequest.

"Most of it goes to the kids. And something for the ex-wives, I don't want them cursing me in my grave. And a bundle for that damn college in Connecticut, they never stop. But something for you too, you'll have nothing to worry about. You'll be well taken care of."

"I'm not worried about money," she says.

He cocks his head. "Yeah? No kidding."

"It's you I'm worried about."

Something mean wrinkles across his face. "Isn't that sweet," he says. "Real nice of you."

She lets it pass, the self-pity, the sarcasm. He's dying, he has a right to be bitter. If she were dying, she would be bitter too. Or maybe she would just lie there and accept her fate, hope for it to be over fast. Why be angry about things you can't change? What profit was there in that?

He has the round-the-clock sleep-in nurse, Henrietta, and the doctors at Sloan who will give him another session of chemo that won't cure him. And now he also has an Indian medicine man, part Mohawk, part Lenape. Billy Cloud. When María first saw him, she had her suspicions. He wore jeans, a checkered flannel shirt, rawhide vest, and a string of turquoise beads around his neck. And she saw what was happening. Harry was entering a state of denial, looking for a miracle. He was chafing, resisting, refusing to believe he would die. Well, it was understandable. But this? A medicine man shaking a rattle and blowing smoke?

"Don't come back," Harry says to her, late on a Friday afternoon, as she prepares to leave. Darkness already setting in.

"But I want to."

"No," he said.

"I will."

"There's nothing left of me."

He'd always been trim, and now he was gaunt. He's skin and bone, the skin turning yellow.

She touches his forehead, his face. He's cool, not feverish. His left eyelid droops. There is mucus in his chest and he has a hard time bringing it up. He grunts, rasps. Then he's up on an elbow, coughing.

She hands him a tissue, and he spits in it.

"Go," he says.

But she stays, waiting for the cough to subside.

"Don't you understand?" he says. "It's time for you to go."

A few blocks away, on State Street, not far from the ferry, there is a small chapel with a brick front, nestled among high towers of blue glass. Occasionally, when she's downtown, by the Battery, she stops off there and sits a while, in the quiet, away from the trucks and cars and buses outside. The calm, untroubled silence. It's the shrine of Mother Seton, who had worked among the poor, helping widows and children.

Sometimes María sits, and sometimes she kneels. Today, in her scarf and gray coat, she kneels, in a back pew, arms resting on the back of the pew in front of her. The chapel is white, in an oval shape, white walls and white pews, only twelve pews on either side of the main aisle, and a loft upstairs.

It's so different, this chapel, from the pagoda that she liked in Cholon, the Quan Am, with its statue of A-Pho, the Holy Mother. This so plain—and that, in Vietnam, so ornamented with gold and lacquer. Yet somehow, for her, the feeling is the same, a comfort, an ease, a sense of wholeness and completeness.

She likes the smallness, the intimacy. She believes in God. It seems to her that a world with God is better than a world without, so why should she not believe? There is a wooden altar table, and, behind it, a stained glass window. The tabernacle, covered by a red and gold cloth, is off to the left, and to the right, a statue of the Blessed

Mother. Prayers she'd learned in grammar school, from the nuns, filter through in fragments. Queen of Heaven, pray for us. Star of the Sea, pray for us. Tower of Ivory, refuge of sinners. And now Harry Falcon is dying, and he doesn't want to see her anymore. She's known him for twenty years, their lives weaving and intertwining. He might have married her, but instead he chose three women he didn't get along with, and it cost him all that grief. He could linger a few months, maybe more, probably less, and for her it's a sorrow and a loneliness. Virgin most merciful, she prays. Mystical rose, mother most pure. Queen of all saints. She prays for Harry and wants everything to be well for him. Forever in heaven, doing the frozen foods up there, putting them in the microwave, the Alaska crab, the chicken fricassee. It amuses her to think of him that way, in heaven, doing his frozens. It somehow is a comfort. He'd be so popular, all the saints coming for the frozen strawberries. Star of heaven, she prays, star of the sea, wanting everything to be good for him, wanting him to be finally at peace.

Through the doors of the chapel she hears the shrill, piercing siren of a police car, and hates that, the raw turbulence of everything human, and bows her head, trying to shut the noise out.

The Elephant Show

Once a week, in the janitorial room in the basement, Oscar puts down a dollar on Muddy Dinks's shell game, knowing he will lose. Fifty small ones a year, but it's worth it to him, because it makes Muddy feel good, and the others too. All of them looking on as Muddy shuffles the cups, one with an acorn under it. And they really drag this out, Muddy shuffling and Oscar watching, studying, trying to figure which cup the acorn is under, and invariably he guesses wrong. But worth it, the fifty, because for him too it's fun—the feel of it, the expectation, all eyes focused, and in this one moment they are fiercely together, the whole crew, fused. An acorn, or a button, or a dime, and sometimes the cross that Smoke wears in his left ear.

He brings in bagels, donuts, pretzels, peanuts. He's even brought in a TV, putting it in the gray-painted room in the basement, where they have their lockers. They can watch on their lunch hour, and on the coffee breaks. And a VCR too—they can plug in a tape.

As it happens, the only one who brings in any videos is Blue. He has a collection of animal shows that he's recorded, mostly documentaries. Lion tapes, peacock tapes, giraffe tapes, tapes about butterflies, whales, and hummingbirds. His favorites, though, are the ones about the elephants, because elephants are a special thing with him.

If he were in Thailand, he would be a mahout, working in the teak forests. To live with your own elephant and take care of him, to sit on top of him, on his neck, and he responds to your every signal. Press the soft spot behind the left ear, and he turns right. Press behind the right ear, and he turns left. You tap lightly with the prod and he picks up the log with his tusks and moves it from here to there, and you can feel his sense of pride as he does that. An eight-hundred-pound log. Move another? Nothing to it. Blue would like to be the mahout training and caring for that elephant, living with him and feeding him, bringing him the food and the water. So much water they need, over three-hundred quarts a day to swallow down the grass and leaves, the fruit, the cane, the peanuts, the corn.

Blue is stocky, puffy-faced, with a blank look in his eyes, which seem to be always gazing off in the wrong direction. He knows about elephants, but with most things he is slow. It's from the way he was born, a little lazy coming down the birth canal, and something happened to his brain. That, at any rate, was how the doctor explained it. But despite the slowness, he's an adequate worker if you lay it out for him, point for point, exactly what he has to do. He's terrific at dust-mopping the lobby floor, half speed but thorough, not missing an inch, though he sometimes gets in the way of the delivery boys who come and go.

His mother named him Blue because all through the pregnancy she was dejected and sad. After he was born, her blues went away, and she named him Blue so that she would never forget how unhappy he'd made her when he was inside.

His skin is the color of cocoa, like his grandmother's. His mother is the color of pale tea, and his father is as dark as a roasted chestnut. His sister is light, like a cup of coffee with too much cream. His older brother, who is in jail, has skin that gleams like polished mahogany.

Blue's involvement with elephants began when he was six years old, when his cousin Vanada took him to the zoo. She was sixteen, and he was in love with her. In the house, when she visited, he would lie around on the floor, waiting for her to pass by because he liked to look up under her skirt and see her long legs disappearing into her white panties.

"What are you doing down there on the floor, Blue?"

"I'm looking under your skirt."

"What a naughty boy! Auntie, did you hear that? He's looking under my skirt!"

Now he's nineteen and she is twenty-nine, and she has a husband who works on cars, and three kids, ages one, two, and four, and when Blue sees her it's in her Bronx apartment on Webster Avenue, and what they do, when he visits, he sits on the couch with her and they watch cartoons with the kids, old reruns of Bugs Bunny, and a few soaps—*Out of the Shadows* and *Edge of the Dark*—and they eat jelly beans, she taking the red and the cinnamon, and he going for the yellow, and the kids grabbing for anything at all. And when the kids are older, he'll take them up to Van Cortlandt Park and show them how to fly a kite, make it go so far up you can almost not see it anymore. And maybe they too will dream of going off to Thailand, where they will work with the elephants.

When Blue was eleven years old, he fell sick, and for a while he was close to death. His mother sat at his bedside, praying for him, and that always stayed with him, the way she prayed so hard. She attended a storefront church on Lenox, the Live-for-Jesus Church of Christ Resurrected, and she had a beautiful voice for singing the hymns. She was the best voice in the church, and she sang the hymns at home too, while she did the dishes and cleaned the bathroom. When he had the fever and the fever broke, it was a miracle, she said, thankful that God had brought him past the crisis. "Nobody thought you were going to live. Nobody. Jesus did this. Wonderful Jesus!"

But then, three years later, when he was in trouble with the police, she was wishing he had died. He was bad. No good.

"But I *am* good," he said.

"No, you're not," she said. "You're bad, like your

370

brother Seth. If you were good, you wouldn't have done that bad thing you did."

He had walked into a 7-Eleven, late at night, nobody there but the short old man behind the counter, and he pulled out a kitchen knife and told the man to empty the cash register into a paper bag. And then, with the bag full of money, he hung around outside, smoking a Salem, and seemed surprised when the police showed up. The judge had him tested, and when they saw how marginal he was, they sent him home in his mother's custody and arranged for him to work with a court-appointed psychotherapist.

He was fourteen when he robbed the 7-Eleven. Before that, he'd been for a while at a special school where they used pictures on a computer to teach him to read but that wasn't much good at all. Not half as good as the elephants were—or high-flying kites, which he liked almost as much as the elephants, and still does.

He likes elephants not just because they're big but because, despite their largeness, they're so careful and gentle when they move. The way a mother elephant knows exactly where to put her feet, never stepping on her calf, even when the calf is behind her, by her back feet. As if she has some kind of secret radar that tells her where the calf is.

Today, Thursday, he comes in with a video that shows a bunch of females playing in a shallow river. Seven of them lined up side by side in the water, swinging their heads and dipping their trunks, squirting and spraying. Then the one at the left end of the line has a notion to lean on the one next to her, and suddenly they are all leaning and they go down like dominoes. There they are in the water, on their sides, on their backs, seven elephants splashing, swishing their trunks, sucking water and spraying at each other. Fun time at the watering hole, rolling around like a pack of kids, churning the water.

He has another video with him, the one in which a bull elephant comes toward a crowd of females in a field of tall grass, by a stand of trees. One of the cows, in heat, separates off from the others, giving him the eye, and he follows her into the woods, into a clearing. A jaunty swagger in the way he moves, as if to say, Hey guys, she's all mine. The cow spreads her back legs and urinates, which is what the cows do when they're ready. And the bull, coming close, sniffs around her hindquarters. Then, gingerly, he mounts her, his forefeet on her back and his long trunk on her shoulders, steadying her. But something is out of focus for him, so he backs off and nudges her buttocks with his forehead, maneuvering her into position. Then he's on top of her again and she bears his huge weight. Standing behind her, on his two rear legs, he thrusts with his hips, three or four times, and, that fast, it's over. An amazing ease, a lazy gentleness. No haste, no ferocious lunging and pumping.

"That's it?" Muddy says.

"Nine seconds," Smoke says. "That's all the big guy gets?"

"Even Oscar can hold it longer than that," Chase says.

"Speak for yourself," Oscar says.

Verna lights a cigarette. "Want to run that again?" she says.

Blue hits the rewind button and replays that part of the tape, and for the bull it's still only nine seconds.

"Sixty pounds," Blue says.

Verna blows smoke in his face. "Who is sixty pounds?"

"Him. His thing. Stretched out, it's five feet long."

Oscar looks up, surprised, as if, somehow, he's been tricked. "You know that? About an elephant's dick? And you don't know how to polish the damn brass on the damn front door?"

"He's God," Hollis says.

"He's not God," Verna says. "He's just smart. Makes out like he's brain-damaged, and gets away with half the work."

"Tell me about tuco-tucos," Oscar says to Blue, testing him. "How long is the penis of a tuco-tuco?"

Blue gives him a queer look, as if Oscar has just arrived from outer space.

"It's a rodent," Oscar says, "a foot long. They live in burrows. I saw them when I went to Brazil last year. They make a weird sound, like a bell ringing."

"He's been to Brazil," Muddy says in a mocking tone.

"Yeah, Brazil," Verna says, rolling her eyes and lighting up again.

"The Amazon," Chase says.

"The rain forest," says Hollis.

"Lizards," Verna says, sending a long jet of smoke toward the ceiling.

Hollis lights up, and Smoke lights up. Oscar doesn't light up because he quit smoking long ago. Chase lights up.

"Boa constrictors," Muddy says. "Spider monkeys, and sloths."

"How about it?" Verna says to Blue. "You ready for the swamps? You ready for the tuco-tuco?"

Blue is staring at the floor. "Don't got no elephants there," he says. "What good is that?"

On some days, Blue is less confused about things than on others, and this is one of those days. He sees clearly, with crisp intensity. So clearly that his gaze penetrates the walls, and looking out, and up, he sees the street and the traffic, all the way to the World Trade Center, and the Amish Market on Cedar, and the small Greek church where he sometimes goes on his lunch hour because he likes the smell of the incense. Early April rain is falling, but for him it isn't rain, it's purple snow. And the snow isn't snow, it's a field of flowers, and the flowers are neon, brightening the gloomy day. That's what he sees and how he thinks, and how he would like things to be. A tuco-tuco isn't a rodent, it's a bird with big wings, flying far up, high as a kite. And a kite isn't a hippopotamus or a crow, nor is it a bone on the street that a stray dog is gnawing at. A kite, he thinks, is magic, nothing less, blue magic riding the wind. And best of all would be to have an elephant all his own, to care for it and sit on top of it, guiding it gently through the tangled flow of midtown traffic.

* * *

On the same day that Blue showed his elephant videos, the governing board—Rumfarm, Knatchbull, and Neal Noelli—voted unanimously to install the waterfall in the lobby. Rumfarm had persuaded a slim margin of the residents to agree to the waterfall, so Ned Knatchbull and Neal Noelli, both of whom had been strong-armed into signing Rumfarm's petition, felt they were merely ratifying the will of the majority. Farro Fescu was in the room, recording the minutes of the meeting, as he usually did, because that too was part of his job. Later he would feed the minutes into the computer and print copies that would be distributed to each of the residents. But now, this moment, when Knatchbull and Noelli threw in with Rumfarm and voted to move ahead on the waterfall, Farro Fescu stopped writing and let his pen slip from his fingers, onto the table. He was calm, unfluttered. He leaned back, gazing at the ceiling, and all he said was, "I don't think so."

Rumfarm was startled. "What?"

"I really don't think so," Farro Fescu repeated, calm, almost serene.

Neal Noelli peered out from under his gray-black eyebrows. "Is something wrong?" He had timid gray eyes and a pouty mouth that gave his face an expression of enduring sadness.

"I don't think a waterfall," Farro Fescu said.

"Why not?"

"There are other things."

"What things?" Knatchbull asked.

"Broken things. Things that need fixing."

"My God, what's wrong with the man," Rumfarm said, flushed with anger, turning to Knatchbull for support. He knew that Farro Fescu didn't want the waterfall, and that he would probably resign if it were installed. And that, precisely, was what he was after, Farro Fescu's resignation, because he disliked him intensely and wanted to replace him with a uniformed security guard carrying a weapon on his hip. The very notion of a concierge was, he felt, outmoded, an old-world idea that lacked gumption, verve, and a readiness to tangle with the future.

"What needs fixing?" Knatchbull asked.

"Downstairs."

"Where?"

"Come," Farro Fescu said, rising, moving toward the door, with Knatchbull and Noelli following, and Rumfarm trailing behind, irked and exasperated. Out of the conference room they went, across the lobby and down the east elevator to the subbasement. Farro Fescu led them past the boiler room, past the electrical supply and the emergency generator, and the storage room, and, unlocking a wide, steel door, he brought them into the big unused area where the cement walls and floor were painted an unpleasant shade of gray. And there, on one wall and across the floor, as obvious as a shootout in a Western, was the crack that Farro Fescu had been monitoring for almost a year. It was longer and wider than ever.

"When I first saw it, it reached to here," he said, pointing to a chalk mark he had made. "Then it moved to here. Then there. And now—you see."

"The building is settling," Rumfarm said. "It's perfectly normal."

Neal Noelli approached the wall, biting his lower lip. Knatchbull studied the floor.

"Landfill," Farro Fescu said. "It's built on landfill and there is an instability."

Rumfarm laughed. "You think it will fall?"

"Look how it's spread. In only a few months."

"We should have an engineer take a look at this," Noelli suggested.

"Nonsense," Rumfarm said.

"You're right, it's probably nothing," Knatchbull said. "But still, you know, it bears looking into."

"Sheer silliness," Rumfarm insisted. "Have you ever seen a house that didn't have cracks in the basement?"

"This is more than a house," Neal Noelli noted. "And it's a pretty big crack."

"Probably a bad batch of cement," Knatchbull said, squatting down and examining the crack where it was at its widest. "Or bad rivets in the I-beams. We need an engineer."

Farro Fescu watched, enjoying the way they moved away from Rumfarm, who was suddenly isolated, alone, his eyes betraying an awareness that the waterfall in the lobby was being postponed—put off indefinitely, and probably canceled.

"For God's sake," he said, puffing up, swollen, "don't you understand? This crack—it's nothing. Nothing!"

It swayed no one, and as he stood there, arms outstretched in a lingering gesture, something desperate came into his glance, a sudden lack of confidence, as if a trapdoor had opened underneath him and there was no way to save himself from falling.

"Maybe a tremor," said Neal Noelli, who had spent his college years in California. "A mild quake could have done this."

"Yeah?" Knatchbull said, doubtfully. "You think so? New York has earthquakes?" He was still squatting, his fingers deep into the crack, up to his knuckles.

That night, home in his apartment, Farro Fescu was so delighted over Rumfarm's comeuppance that he treated himself, after supper, to a snifter of slivovitz, and later, in bed, he watched an old John Wayne World War II movie and ate a pound of macaroons.

Orchids and Candy Hearts

Harry Falcon knew he was dying, but he was fighting it, holding death off, and each day came as a gift, a surprise, simply to be able to open his eyes and breathe. He was fifty-four, and as he sat on the balcony outside his living room, wrapped in a blanket, he spent a considerable amount of time thinking about his father, who had succumbed at the age of forty-nine. Was death genetic? In the blood? The DNA? This thing, happening now, was his father to blame?

After the Second World War, his father, Wyndham, had fumbled around for a while, doing things that didn't really interest him—and then, surprising even himself, he plunged with great energy into frozen foods and developed a company that he called Arctic Swan. He did well with succotash, broccoli, and green beans but failed in almost everything else. Harry remembers him as warm and generous, a good father, but in business he'd been a dreamer, searching always for things that were hopelessly out of reach. He'd become obsessed with figs, trying again and again to freeze them, with no success. Always, when he thawed them out, they were brownish gray and messy, resembling thick globs of phlegm, and who would ever want to eat anything that looked like that? Again and again he tried, always with the same unhappy result. And Harry came to understand, early on, that his father was doomed to be a disappointed man.

"Someday you will inherit the business," his father would say, "and then it will be your turn. Whoever comes up with a perfect frozen fig is going to be the richest man in America."

Harry Falcon inherited the business sooner than he or anyone else had expected. He was only twenty-one, two months out of college, when his father fell dead while working at home in the lab that he'd built in the basement. And Harry was there, watching. His father was using liquid nitrogen on a fresh batch of figs, thinking the instant freeze might do the trick, but suddenly he leaned sideways, at an odd angle, with a wrenched expression on his face, and fell dead of a massive coronary. Harry bent over him, trying to resuscitate him, pounding his chest and giving him mouth-to-mouth, but his father was gone, and he realized, with a twinge of terror, that all of it, now, was his, the succotash, the broccoli, and the green beans, along with the lab in the basement and the liquid nitrogen, and the uncooperative figs.

Harry was not a dreamer. In high school and at college, he had been an indifferent student, earning mediocre grades, and his lack of distinction in the classroom, in those formative years, helped to shape him as a hard-headed realist, with no illusions about life or about himself. Figs had killed his father, and he was determined not to let that happen to him. When he took over the plant in New Jersey, he did the necessary things to put the business on a solid footing, and he discovered, along the way, that he had a natural instinct for management and an almost mystical sense for what would sell.

At the plant, he tightened procedures, increased the volume, developed new markets in the South and Midwest, and expanded the menu, adding kumquats and kiwis to his father's list of frozens. Within two years, the company was doing so well that he decided to open a plant in Oregon. And soon after that, with demand still rising, he opened a plant in Louisiana. Everything on the move, better and better, and he was percolating with hot new ideas. Instead of buying the peas and carrots and the peaches and blueberries from farmers in Florida and California, he bought the farms and replaced the farmers with college-trained agronomists who supervised platoons of underpaid illegals from Mexico, and the crop more than doubled. And instead of leasing trucks to haul the produce, as his father had done, he bought a whole fleet of refrigerated eighteen-wheelers, and when there was trouble with certain municipalities that objected to the passage of the big trucks on certain roads, he bought the roads. And, on one occasion, he bought the town. That was in Mississippi, where a town, in those days, could be picked up dirt cheap.

In the seventies, when succotash and green beans were not as popular as they had been, he came out with gourmet dinners featuring Alaska crab and slabs of filet mignon garnished with chives and chopped olives. In the eighties, for the health-minded, who were growing in number and shaping the market, he came out with low-calorie, low-fat editions focusing on chicken and fish, and fantasy desserts sweetened with fruit juice rather than sugar. Heart-Smart-and-Body-Wise was the motto. And then, as the nineties came on, noticing that food supplements had become part of the culture, he hooked into the health craze and seasoned his frozens with vitamins and herbs that promised health, quick thinking, stronger bones, and better sexual performance.

When he first met María Gracia, he was already wealthy, and before long he was global, with processing plants in Cape Town, Bombay, Jakarta, and Guadalajara. But what good was money, he would say to María, mocking his own success. Money was just an instrument for making more money, and doesn't it finally become tiresome? He gave a great deal away to the small college in Connecticut that he had attended, and in gratitude they put his name on the library, the chapel, the theater, and a classroom wing, as well as on the soccer field and the waste-disposal facility.

It had been, all in all, a glorious time for him. Early on, after divorcing his first wife, Elsa, he became infatuated with María Gracia but married Roxanne. Then he divorced Roxanne, continued to see María, and married

Hedwig, which was a dreadful mistake, but by then he understood that without mistakes, life, his life, and especially his sex life, would be boring and altogether depressing.

He ate poached salmon at the Arcadia, lasagna at Il Nido, roast duck at the Lafayette, and he danced with María at the Rainbow Room. There were whole days when his mind was filled with songs. "The Beat Goes On," and "Light My Fire," and Sinatra's "Strangers in the Night." And the one he liked best, "Getting Better," the Beatles in an easy, upbeat mode, and that's what he liked to think about his own life, getting better, even though his marriages were catastrophic.

With the profits from his kumquats and kiwis, he bought a bowling alley, a health club, and a motel chain, but the motels ran in the red and he unloaded them, and the health club had to be shut down because polluted city air, pumped in through the ventilation system, was producing upper respiratory problems among the members, and lawsuits were pending. Every summer he donated Eskimo Treats to the Boy Scouts, and that seemed a success—a few sick tummies from too much gorging, but no lawsuits. And on the major holidays he contributed frozen dinners to the shelters housing the homeless. For the homeless who refused to use the shelters, he sent out vans equipped with microwaves. They parked by the bus terminal on Eighth and Forty-second, and at Washington Square and other locations where the homeless congregated, and frozen dinners were served hot at curbside.

But where was it all going? That always bothered him. And what did it mean? All of it sliding by so fast, his father dead in the basement lab, his mother with her mental collapse, his divorce from Elsa, then the mess with Roxanne and the larger mess with Hedwig, and the five children whom he rarely ever saw. And his long time, on and off, with María Gracia. What a treasure she was, María. His whore, his strumpet, his cocotte. His doxy, his wench. His laced mutton. She who had ways of twisting him around and turning his moods upside down, tricking him into laughter. The woman he was always happy with, and the one, he sometimes thought, he should have married. But how do you marry a woman of the night, a demimondaine? And if he had married her, would it too have been a disaster, like the others?

María Gracia had been in Vietnam, and he was jealous of that, thinking now that it had been a mistake for him not to go. He had negotiated an exemption because of his role in a war-sensitive industry that sold huge quantities of frozen meals to the Pentagon, for use on military aircraft and at the officers' clubs in Saigon. But if he'd been to Vietnam, and fought there, he thinks it might have changed everything and given him a different life, a different way of seeing things. The bamboo thickets, thatched villages, the rice paddies and temples. María Gracia told him about all of that. The flares, and the rockets in the night. He could have been part of it, the shooting and the being shot at—it had to change you somehow, make you a different person, and when he was tired of himself, weary of the same old thought processes, he often wished he had been more adventuresome.

But the closest he'd ever come to Vietnam was through the Arctic Swan Ice Cream Eskimo Treats that he shipped to Saigon by the millions. The Treats were a new product line at the plant in Paramus, and they came in five designer flavors—Knuckle Walnut, Strawberry Kiss, Prenuptial Pistachio, Fornication Fuchsia, and Pineapple Tease, each Treat in a plastic cup bearing the Swan logo, with a plastic spoon attached. In 1967, when the troop level was just under half a million, the quartermaster corps was purchasing upwards of three million Treats a week. The plants in Oregon and Louisiana had to suspend their production of frozen broccoli so that they could help meet the demand for Pineapple Tease and Prenuptial Pistachio, which were a greater success than anyone had expected.

In the subtropical heat of Vietnam, most of the Treats melted before anyone had a chance to eat them, yet they were enormously popular because of the redemption value of the lids. Each lid had a peel-off vinyl tab, and underneath, on a winning lid, was a HOT WIN gold star. Five winning lids earned you a smooch from Martha Rae, who was singing for the troops all over Vietnam and willing to pass out smooches for the cause. Ten winners earned you a week in Acapulco when your Vietnam tour was over, if you lived that long. And if you were lucky enough to collect twenty winning lids, you were on your way to a date in New York with Lola Falana, who sang and danced and had appeared as a *Playboy* centerfold.

Empty cups bearing the Swan logo littered the streets of Saigon and Hué. They floated in the rice paddies and blossomed like red-white-and-blue flowers on the trails in the jungle. When the helicopters came and went, the updraft from their rotors sucked the cups up and lifted them into the monsoon winds, which carried them as far as Hanoi, where they were picked up by North Vietnamese intelligence officers who considered them a new and baffling form of psychological warfare.

After the war, when Harry learned from a commercial attaché of the Ho Chi Minh regime about the confusion that his windblown Eskimo cups had caused in Hanoi, he was so delighted with the story that he came up with three new flavors—Ho Chi Minh Chocolate, Rice-Paddy Raspberry, and Jungle Jasmine—which were purchased by Hanoi in huge quantities, with covert loans advanced to them by Israel and underwritten by the State Department, which was only too happy to see the sales go through, on the theory that if you can't beat them on the battlefield, you could win, and win big, by tying them in knots in the marketplace.

But all of that was very long ago, too long, and how terribly fast time had slid by. And now, he knew, time was shutting down on him, and he wanted to scream. He was fifty-four, and the chemo wasn't working. When his last wife, Hedwig, learned of his cancer, she went to her attorney and they were beating the bushes, trying to pump more money out of him while the getting was good. Harry had given her a huge settlement, but she never had enough and was always nagging for more. His first wife too, Elsa, was angling for more before he shuffled off. But from Roxanne, his second wife, he heard nothing. What was wrong with her? Why wasn't she grabbing like the others? That was the problem with her, she used purity and indifference as a weapon and was, therefore, the cruelest of all, above money and greed and crass desire, and in her untainted way, she made him feel dirty and cheap. He would have preferred it if, like the others, she came groveling, drooling for filthy lucre.

The cancer that afflicted him was an aggressive malignancy that had started in his prostate. It had burst through the capsule, migrated into his lymph system, and settled in his pelvis and in his liver. When his oncologist saw the radiology report, how bad it was, five nodes on the liver, he told him surgery was out of the question, and he recommended chemotherapy, but only as a way of buying time. There was no hope for a cure.

"How long?" Harry wanted to know.

"Maybe a year," the oncologist said, making no promises.

"And if we skip the chemo?"

"Two months."

Harry sought a second opinion, and a third, but no one gave him good news. He returned to the first oncologist, at Sloan, and asked for a prostatectomy and a new liver.

"You're too far gone," the oncologist said. "It's in your lymphatic system and in your bone. If we put a new liver in you, it will become as sick as your old one. If you even survive the procedure."

Harry went home and phoned Hector Pouch, who had been with him from the start, in the days when they opened the Oregon plant, and the one in Louisiana. Do-it-all Pouch, Harry called him, because he had a knack for handling the things that nobody else could process. His eyes were slightly crossed, and he had a bony nose that swung off to one side like a broken weathervane.

"I need a new liver and they won't give me one," Harry

said. "Go down to Mexico and see what you can do. Steal one, if you have to."

Pouch returned with a liver, a spleen, and a gall bladder, all belonging to a teenager who'd been killed when his pickup went off the road and into a ravine somewhere between Puebla and Oaxaca. Pouch paid the parents five thousand dollars, which wasn't much, but then nobody else, at the time, was bidding.

When he arrived with the liver, Harry had undergone a change of heart and no longer wanted it. It had finally sunk in, what the doctors had been telling him. A new liver wasn't the answer. He told Pouch to donate the organs to the Albert Einstein College of Medicine, which might or might not have a use for them.

The next few days, he sank into a severe depression, not talking, not eating, not moving off the bed. When Pouch showed up with business papers that required his signature, he turned him away. He didn't answer the phone, didn't use the TV. His hair was long and wild, uncombed, and he needed a shave.

Pouch tried again with the business papers, and this time Harry signed. And Pouch, as he left, mentioned an Indian medicine man that he'd heard about. He lived in Brooklyn and had a reputation.

"This is voodoo?"

"Well, no. It's herbs and broth, and he does a lot of chanting."

"I don't need a damn Indian," Harry said. "All they're good for is to run casinos and get drunk on the reservation."

"He's done some fancy things," Pouch said. "It might be worth looking into."

"'The only good Indian is a dead Indian.' Who said that? Custer? Grant?"

"Sheridan."

"He the one sitting on a horse by the Plaza?"

"That's Sherman, the one who torched Atlanta. Sheridan was at Missionary Ridge. After the war, he was chasing Indians."

Harry was gazing through the window, toward the Twin Towers. "He lives in Brooklyn, you say?"

"Coney Island."

"I thought that was full of Russians and blacks."

"Well, he passes. The Russians are in Brighton Beach."

The Indian's name was Billy Cloud. He was part Mohawk, part Lenape, and part Irish. He used to do steel work on the skyscrapers, walking the I-beams fifty and sixty stories up, and higher, in the wind, but now he was done with that and made his living as a medicine man. Pouch had a cousin who lived upstate, near the Onondaga Reservation where Billy Cloud occasionally visited, and it was from the cousin that he first heard of Billy's powers. The cousin was a pharmacist with a keen interest in alternative medicine. He knew people who healed with tea and people who used scented candles and the laying on of hands. But nobody that he knew had caught his attention as much as Billy Cloud had.

There had been a woman sick with a tumor in her belly, and Billy Cloud sat by her bed for seven days, chanting and blowing smoke into her ears and her nose, and her mouth. He parted her legs and blew smoke there too. He shook a rattlesnake's rattle over her and touched it to her breasts and belly. He had killed the snake himself, a big one with fourteen sets of rattles on the tail, finding it on sacred ground near the Onondaga Reservation. For seven days the woman had no food, only the potions that he prepared for her, brewed from herbs and frogs' eggs and snake venom and rose petals. At the end of the fifth day, the woman was in a high fever. On the sixth, she vomited up a profuse amount of mucus and blood, and the fever broke. On the seventh day, when he touched her, there was no sign of the tumor. "It will come back," he said, "but I'll make it go away again." It never came back. The woman returned to her job with the Welfare Department, in Syracuse, and two years after he had cured her of the tumor, she was struck down by a city bus and was dead on arrival at the hospital.

When Harry Falcon first saw Billy, in frayed jeans and a sweatshirt, he was disappointed. "You?" he said. "You're the best they have?"

The Irish blood in Billy had given him his blue eyes, but what the Lenape blood gave him, he wasn't sure. The Lenapes were the ones from whom the Dutch had bought Manhattan Island, Peter Minuit offering an assortment of things valued at sixty guilders, or about twenty-four dollars. Probably the same kinds of things with which he purchased Staten Island a few months later—axes, hoes, kettles, awls, wampum, a few Jews' harps.

The other part of Billy Cloud, the rough-and-tumble part, was Mohawk, the Mohawks being part of the Iroquois confederation. There was an oral history, centuries old, that his ancestors had been among the ones who tortured the Jesuit missionary Jean de Brébeuf and put him to death. They beat him with sticks, tore out his fingernails, scorched him with burning tar, cut off his nose and lips, gave him a mock baptism with boiling water, and, because he suffered so bravely, they tore out his heart before he was quite dead and ate it, expecting that his courage would become theirs. The story had been passed down from father to son since the seventeenth century, and Billy liked to think that it was the heart of the martyred saint that had given him the courage to walk the steel beams of the skyscrapers in the days when he was doing that.

"Do your chants and your prayers," Harry Falcon told him, "but keep your damn hands away from my heart. I'm going to be cremated. I don't want to be eaten by a cannibal."

Billy Cloud gave him a potion to drink and did some chanting. He smoked his long pipe with the feathers attached to it, and he took out the rattlesnake's tail and touched it to various parts of Harry's body.

"I'll come back next week," he said.

"No," Harry told him. "You stay here. Pouch will fix a room for you."

After a few days, Harry showed some improvement,

but then he sagged and was weak again. He slept, he woke, and he slept again. And then there were times when he couldn't sleep, and those were the times when he and Billy played checkers. Billy won a game, then Harry won. Then Harry won again, and then Billy won. And Harry knew that when he won it was because Billy let him win. He was so soupy from the painkillers, and from the potions that Billy fed him, how could he possibly concentrate on a silly damn thing like a checker game?

He was off the chemo now, and not scheduled to start up again for six weeks. He hardly ate anymore. A grape, a wedge of melon. A thin slice of chicken. And the candy hearts. María Gracia had brought them, and he liked them, tiny wafers of sugar shaped like hearts, the size of a fingernail, in pastel colors, with little messages printed on them: BAD BOY . . . COAX ME . . . LOVE ME . . . DIG ME . . . HUG ME . . . HOT MAMA.

"This is horny stuff," Harry said. "Do you agree, Billy?"

Billy agreed.

And pretty colors—lavender, green, pink.

"You think this stuff is medicine? It's the cure I been looking for?"

He picked up the package and studied the ingredients. The hearts were made of sugar, gelatin, corn syrup, and some other things. K-glycerin, and propylene glycol.

"Sounds like powerful stuff," Billy said.

Harry looked out the window, toward the towers, rising solid and solemn in the afternoon light. "Candy hearts," he said. "Who would have thought?"

They were in the living room, on cushioned high-backed chairs, at a small table from India, inlaid with ivory, the checkerboard on top. The table was in front of a large glass aquarium that contained a school of angelfish, silvery and lithe, their long fins weaving and gliding in the water. Harry tossed a few candy hearts into the aquarium, watching as they drifted down toward the bottom. Some of the fish went for them, picking them up with their mouths but quickly rejecting them. The hearts were not popular. They rested on the bottom, on the gravel, dissolving slowly.

"Billy," he said, "go put some feathers on and do me a war dance. Make war on this damn cancer that's killing me."

"I hate war dances," Billy said, "they wear me out. I don't do them anymore."

Harry's face darkened. "I knew you were no good."

Billy went to the CD player, in an oak cabinet that ran along one wall, and inserted a CD that he had brought along with him. He had brought many CDs with him. This one was drums, nothing but drums and Indians chanting.

"There's your war dance," Billy said. "That's what it sounds like."

They sat a while, listening to the drums, the chanting.

"I'm dying, Billy. You know that, don't you? I am a dying man."

Billy looked at him, stared right at him, but it was as if he hadn't heard. Or didn't want to hear.

Harry threw a candy heart at him. Then another. He threw at the large ficus rising out of a brass pot, and missed. He threw at the orchids, the dahlias, the camellias. Too feeble to throw hard, or far. Tossing. Trying. He loved the orchids. They had always been special for him. And now he was throwing hearts at them and couldn't reach them.

"Hearts are the answer?" he said, wondering.

And still the drums were beating, and Harry threw candy hearts until there were no more to throw. He was thinking of María Gracia, wanting her. He had told her not to come back, because he didn't want her to remember him like this, dying. But she came anyway, and he was glad about that. But sometimes, loaded with painkillers, he didn't know if it was really her in the room with him, or some drug-induced fantasy.

Waking at night, he saw her floating above the bed, naked, hovering close. "Take my breasts," she said. "Take my lips." From her mouth came great clusters of clove blossoms, pinkish green, ripe for taking. So many cloves, how could he handle them all?

"I'm hallucinating," he said.

"No, it's real," she answered. "Don't you feel how real it is?"

"It's better than real."

"You know it is."

Spices poured out of her, from all of her orifices, cloves and cinnamon and peppermint.

And he knew none of it was real, it was a delirium. She wasn't in the room, couldn't be. He had told her not to return. Yet there she was, and now she was drifting away.

"Take me with you," he said.

"No, never," she said.

"Why? Take me."

"You have too much hate and meanness, and too much money. Too much everything."

"I like chocolate. Get me some chocolate."

She dropped chocolate kisses all over him. But still she was drifting away. He tried to unwrap the kisses, peeling away the silver foil, but his fingers were weak and he fumbled. He was helpless.

"Good-bye," she said.

"Bitch," he said.

"Sweetheart," she said.

Then it was Billy there, in the room, the big bedroom with the rosewood wall unit and seven television monitors on the shelves. Billy stood by the bed, his face painted, shaking the rattle, blowing his smoke. Poor Billy, he really believed he was doing something. What a jerk, Harry thought. Couldn't he recognize death when he saw it? Useless. Useless. Because nothing holds death back, not the sun, not the oceans, not the great whales with their deep dives and their epic songs heard by other whales hundreds of miles away. Not even the frozen cuisine of Penguin Mist and Arctic Swan meant anything. So much grandeur and strangeness, and where was the meaning of it all? The Grand Canyon millions of years in the making, and it too would someday be a blip in the past. I love you, Billy. Don't you know how I love you? Blow your smoke, you crazy Indian. Shake your damn rattle. Where's María? Tell her to come back.

He was asleep again, and when he woke, Billy was gone, and a square patch of sunlight was on the wall, and there was a low buzzing sound in his ears.

The Fourth of July

The good news about the crack in the foundation was that it wasn't fatal and the building could be saved. But the repair was going to be long-term and expensive, and rather than face the cost and uncertainty, many of the residents were putting their units up for sale and moving out.

The Smiths were going, as were the Liebermans, the Dimmlers, Judd Winter, and Jenny Vesuvius—most of them newcomers to the condo, rushing off because they were eager to cut their losses. Prices were plunging, and the beneficiary in all of this was Luther Rumfarm, who was snapping up the units as fast as they became available. He repainted, did some updating and refurbishing, and rented out at inflated rates to recent college graduates who were signing on for near-six-figure salaries as Wall Street trainees. In some condo towers, there were regulations regarding the number of units a single owner could acquire, and also about the total number of units that could be put up for rent. But through oversight, or perhaps deliberately, the developers of Echo Terrace had neglected to include any purchase or rental restrictions in the charter, and Rumfarm was in hot pursuit, grabbing everything he could put his hands on.

"He's that loaded?" Oscar wondered when Farro Fescu told him what was happening.

"Rolling in it and getting fatter," Farro Fescu said.

Oscar, who had read some Fourier and Robert Owen

during his college years, and some Karl Marx, still harbored, in his middle age, feelings of hostility toward the big-money capitalists. He'd read Thoreau, who thought life was better when it was simple and cheap, and had built his cabin on Walden Pond for twenty-eight dollars and twelve and a half cents. It was, Oscar thought, a cozy idea, but he knew too that Thoreau had only stayed there for two years, and had visited often for his mother's apple pies.

Later, on a coffee break, when Oscar told Muddy Dinks about Rumfarm, how he was buying up the units, Muddy clucked his tongue. He was taller than Oscar, thinner and far younger, in his twenties, and good-looking, a face like the face of Denzel Washington.

"You mean that son-gun gonna own this whole damn tower? I gotta talk to that man. What I hangin' aroun' here for, climbin' ladders and dustin' cobwebs?"

Oscar leaned against a ladder, steam from his coffee clouding his face. "Knock on his door," he said. "Try your shell game on him."

"Already did," Muddy said woefully.

"He beat you?"

"Son-bitch took me for twenty. Made me pay up too. Who's richer—him or the dude in frozen food?"

"Harry Falcon? He can buy Rumfarm twice over."

"But Mr. Falcon, he's dyin'."

They all knew it now, Harry Falcon was on his way, there was less and less of him as each day passed. Nevertheless, on the Fourth of July, even though his cancer was wasting him away, he threw his annual party for the residents, inviting them to his rooftop deck, with its junipers and red roses, and the solarium, which held a bar and a pool, and baskets of fresh carnations.

Karl Vogel was there, and the Rumfarms and Knatchbulls, and Rabbi Ravijohn, who stayed only briefly. Dr. Matisse, the retired psychoanalyst, came with his son, and Milo Salonika, in his eighties, who had made a fortune in real estate, also came, but he was feeble and had signs of oncoming dementia, and after only a few minutes on the roof, his nurse brought him back to his apartment. Angela, Nora's niece, arrived with Abdul Saad, and Juanita Blaize came with someone wearing a green patch over his left eye. Aki Sato was there, and Louisa Wax, sipping an old-fashioned. Her daughter was with friends, down by the East River, to get a close look when the rockets went up off the barges. And the house staff too, there on the roof—Farro Fescu, and Oscar with his cleaning crew, Blue and Hollis and Smoke, and Verna and Chase, all of them there at Harry Falcon's invitation. It always sent Rumfarm's blood up, seeing the janitors at these rooftop parties. He took it, in a way, as something of an insult, this informal mingling of the residents with the menials. What in the world was Falcon trying to prove?

Even Yesenia came, ripely pregnant, her swollen belly like a gigantic melon under her white maternity smock. She was due to deliver in about a week, though the doctor had told her she might be late. Muddy Dinks had driven all the way to Queens to pick her up. He had grown up in Yesenia's neighborhood, near Jamaica Avenue, but was living now in Harlem and liked it there. The scar on Yesenia's face was gone. Dr. Tattafruge had worked on her, and all that remained was a faint line, an almost invisible reminder of the rapist's knife.

It was Harry Falcon's last party, and a great one. Pouch had hired a Park Avenue catering service, waiters in white shirts and red bow ties, serving champagne, hors d'oeuvres, jumbo shrimp on flaked ice, black caviar from Murmansk on wafers imported from Copenhagen. Mixed drinks at the bar, and for those in need of a sandwich, slices from a saddle of beef, cut thick or thin as desired, by a Sudanese steward with a bald head and a fast hand with the knife. And pastries, no end of cannoli and napoleons, along with espresso and cappuccino.

The gathering began about an hour before sundown. From the roof, they could see up the Hudson as far as the George Washington Bridge, and in the opposite direction, in the bay, the Statue of Liberty and Ellis Island. And directly across, the Colgate clock in Jersey City. To the southeast, a partial view of the Verrazano Bridge as it descended into Staten Island, and, very close, blocking the view to the northeast, the massive upthrust of the two tall towers of the World Trade Center.

Three musicians played tangos and habaneras. They had come over from Cuba with the Marielitos, in 1980. One played a violin, and one was a drummer, working with bongos, a snare, and a tambourine. The third played a bandoneon, a kind of concertina, its odd, husky sound something between a harmonica and an accordion. The violinist was tall, the drummer short and wiry. The bandoneon player had small snaky eyes that roved restlessly, seeking out the women. He never smiled. All three wore white pants and black shirts open at the throat, and they moved about with a lazy shuffle, playing by the bar and the pool, and out on the deck, by the junipers and the roses. The drummer kept his lips parted, showing off a gold tooth.

The Latin music had been at María Gracia's suggestion, because her happiest times with Harry had been, she felt, during their trips to Latin America. They had spent many hours in the bars and cantinas, listening to the habaneras, and the old milongas and zarzuelas. She had even taught him to dance the tango, showing him the steps and the moves, the hook, the sweep, the half-moon, the sandwich. Those were good times, when he took pictures of her in Panama and Buenos Aires, and Rio, and Tierra del Fuego. When he put his hands on her and she put her hands on him, and they were open to each other and warm. And how he had loved the sound of the bandoneon, its friendly zest.

There had been talk, for many months, that the fireworks display would be, this year, less than it usually was, because of the city's budgetary problems. But at the last moment, someone had come forward with an anonymous contribution, and the performance would be everything it was supposed to be. One of the morning papers, using an unnamed source, reported that the contribution had come from Aki Sato. He was less than pleased about the leak, deplored the publicity, and had spent the bulk of the day dealing with the congratulations and thanks that poured in by phone and by e-mail.

Theo Tattafruge drank a Rob Roy, and Muhta Saad, Abdul's father, drank a vodka martini. Juanita Blaize drank a gin fizz, heavy on the gin, shy on the fizz. Maggie Sowle drank a yellow daisy. She leaned over the parapet and looked down, seeing the sidewalk below, where Ira Klempp, falling from the twelfth floor, had hit the ground and his body broke apart. March that was, already more than three months ago. The wreath that Farro Fescu had put there, near the spot where he fell, was long gone.

About a half hour before the fireworks were due to begin, Billy Cloud lifted Harry Falcon off his bed and carried him up the spiral staircase to the rooftop solarium, and sat him in a wheelchair. María Gracia had dressed him in blue pants and a red and white shirt. She was there, making sure he was comfortable in the chair, and she wheeled him out of the solarium, onto the cedar deck. He was gaunt, his skin pasty, his gray eyes sunken in his skull. His hair was gone, from the chemo, and María put a cap on his head to conceal the baldness, but he pushed it off. Aki Sato bowed, greeting him, but Harry gave no sign of recognition. Vogel raised a hand in a casual salute, but from Harry there was no response. His eyes roved across the faces, Louisa Wax, Maggie Sowle, Tattafruge. Then he saw Yesenia, with her huge belly, and something came into his eyes. He held his head at an angle, and with a feeble gesture, motioned for her to come near.

He put his hand on her belly, resting it there a long moment. Then he said something she couldn't hear, and she leaned close. "I felt him move," he said into her ear. "Magic, that's what it is."

"It's a girl," she told him. "When they looked at the sonogram, that's what they said."

He stared emptily. "A girl? That's better. When you go to Tierra del Fuego, say hello to the penguins."

Then something strange happened. There was a sudden need to touch Yesenia's belly, spreading like a contagion. First Maggie, then Karl Vogel. Then Theo, and all the others. The laying on of hands, touching, feeling the movement inside, everyone doing it, lining up, even the musicians. And Yesenia, feeling the touch of all those hands, and the movement of the life inside her, thought that what Harry Falcon had said was right, it was an enchantment. Life, the baby, and the people pressing close, and the roof itself, with the flowers and small trees, illumined now with colored lights. Magical. The sun just down and dark coming slowly on, and Liberty out there in the bay, pistachio green, with her torch, and the sky-scrapers already lit by the fierce brilliance of their flood lamps, purple, yellow, vibrant red. She felt so heavy with her belly, yet she also felt, at that moment, a wild rapture, thinking she could rise up and float away, drift off into the evening sky.

Then it was Angela's turn, coming close and putting both hands on her belly, and they kissed, Angela and Yesenia, and the excitement they shared was not just for the baby but for Angela too, because she had at last made up her mind about Abdul, deciding she would marry him.

"It's too good," Yesenia said, and they held each other a long time, clinging.

Then Angela said something into Yesenia's ear, and suddenly, strangely, they were both weeping, hanging on to each other under the darkening sky.

"How wonderful," Maggie said to Farro Fescu. "Look, they're both crying."

The musicians played again, and the one with the bandoneon sang, his voice high and bittersweet, the tone mournfully joyous, and sad. He sang songs of love and songs of love lost, songs of passion, desire, and desperate yearning, his voice lifting toward the sky, toward the streaks of rose and lavender that lingered even though the sun was down.

Luther Rumfarm, in his forward way, held his glass aloft and proposed a series of toasts. He toasted the building, Echo Terrace, which was cracked in its foundation and a trifle unstable but not, he assured everyone, about to collapse. He toasted Harry Falcon for being such a fine host, and Aki Sato for bailing out the city and paying for the fireworks. And he toasted Maggie Sowle for her UN quilt, which had made her more famous than she already was. And a toast too for Angela and Abdul, who were soon to be married.

"There is still plenty of strength and vitality in this country," he said, rising up on his toes, his pale eyes twinkling in the gloaming. "Don't ever underestimate American initiative—no matter what the doomsday pessimists say about pollution, global warming, poverty, terrorism, the economy, the hole in the ozone. The fact is, things are getting better. Last year only forty thousand dead on the highway. That's three thousand less than the year before. See? Better and better! *Skoal! Salud! Zdorovie!*"

Maggie thought he was pathetic. Yesenia thought he was a pot of overcooked beans. Tattafruge wondered if he was ready for the pump implant that he'd been asking about. Louisa Wax thought he should change his barber. Karl Vogel, knowing how he was buying up the building and converting the units into expensive rentals, thought he was a scoundrel. Harry Falcon, happy that the morphia patch was doing its job, wasn't thinking much of anything at all.

Nevertheless—Angela and Abdul! It was no surprise to any of them, because Abdul had been after her ever since she moved into her aunt Nora's apartment. They knew of the flowers he sent and had seen him waiting again and again to ambush her in the lobby. They saw the dreamy ardor in his eyes. And now they were engaged. He, in deference to her, had suggested a Catholic wedding, and she, in deference to him, wanted an Islamic ceremony, and in the end, rather than wrangle over this, they decided to engage a rabbi to perform the ceremony, and

397

since Rabbi Ravijohn lived right there in the building, so convenient, they chose him.

Abdul's father was in despair. "I don't understand it," he said to Mrs. Wax, who was on her third old-fashioned. "The world changes too fast for me. My son, an Arab, with good Iraqi blood in him, is marrying an actress, a heathen—and a Jew will unite them. How am I to endure it? Why must they put me through this?"

They were by a trellis of roses. His hand, as he spoke, wandered around and came to rest on her hip.

"I'm too old for this," Louisa Wax said with a friendly smile, as she removed the hand.

"You are never too old," he said, placing his rejected hand on her arm.

"I think you're the devil," she said, still with the smile.

"I say my prayers five times a day, as all good Muslims do."

"That doesn't make you a saint," she said.

"A saint I never said I was."

She liked it that he was giving her this attention. She wished Susan Marriocci were here to see it, but she was in New Hampshire, visiting her daughter.

"I think your wife needs you," she said.

Amala was on the other side of the roof, looking across at them.

"Tomorrow," he said. "I'll call."

Loisa Wax tilted her head cheekily, with a coyness that made her all the more desirable, but said nothing.

"Tomorrow," he repeated.

The blimp was up, the Goodyear blimp, circling Manhattan. It was loaded with television equipment, ready to catch the sky's-eye view of the fireworks. On the ground, the sun had already set, but high up, the blimp, still catching the sun, glowed bronze and golden, as did the tallest of the skyscrapers.

"Someday I'm gonna own all this," Muddy Dinks said to Yesenia. He swung his head around, left and right, and she didn't know if he meant the roof, the whole building, or all of lower Manhattan.

"How you gonna do that?" she said. "Pushing your little shell game outside Grand Central?"

"There is ways."

"What kind of ways?"

"Everybody got a shell game one kind or another. Mr. Frozen Foods there, don't you think it's all now-you-see-it, now-you-don't?"

"What you been drinking, Muddy?"

"Don't you wanna be rich?

She touched her belly. "Sure," she says. "But right now there are other things."

At the far end of the roof, away from the solarium, Blue, the youngest on the cleaning crew, was assembling his elephant kite, which Muddy Dinks had told him not to bring, but he had brought it anyway. It was in the shape of an elephant's trunk, long and tubular, and slightly turned at one end, made of lightweight nylon supported by ribs of wire-thin vinyl. When he had all of the parts assembled, the tube was fifteen feet in length and a foot in diameter, with baffles inside to catch the wind. The nylon was pink, and very much to Blue's liking. The only other color option had been chartreuse, and a pink elephant, he thought, was far more interesting than an elephant that was a crazy shade of green.

Muddy, annoyed, gave him a dark frown, black as burnt toast. "Why you doin' this dumb-ass thing at a classy party like this?"

"Ain't dumb-ass," Blue said, making sure the sections were all secure. On the job he was slow, confused, not all there, but now, working on his kite, he seemed to know what he was doing. Muddy had never seen him so focused and determined.

"Ain't even gonna fly," Muddy said. "Everybody gonna laugh."

"It's gonna fly," Blue said. "Ain't no more dumb-ass than your silly shell game."

Karl Vogel, stepping over, asked if Blue had made the kite himself, or if he had bought it.

"Got it second-hand through a magazine," Blue said.

He hooked it to a spool of fish line, then Muddy helped him carry it over to the edge of the roof, one at each end. It was light but awkward, sagging in the middle, and they lifted it over the parapet and let it drop. For several moments it simply hung there, lazy and inert, dangling from the line that Blue held with both hands.

"Didn't I tell you?" Muddy said. "Didn't I?"

But Blue stayed with it, leaning over the parapet, and eventually a breeze caught the kite and filled it, and it started to rise. Soon it was fully up, over the roof and high above them, riding the summer air.

Vogel was amazed. From everything he knew about aerodynamics, the kite, in its tubular configuration, should not have been capable of flight. Yet there it was, long and pink and free-floating, an elephant's trunk, aloft in the thermals and gaining altitude.

Farro Fescu, by a hemlock, watching all of this, knew it was wrong, so wrong. He had talked to Oscar about Blue. The boy was feebleminded, he had to be watched, monitored. He brings this grotesque thing, this kite, to Mr. Falcon's party? And Muddy Dinks, who should know better, he's there, part of it? And Vogel, him too, offering encouragement? Where was common sense anymore? The whole world was conspiring against it, rushing off into petty foolishness. He will talk to Oscar about this, tomorrow, but to what purpose? The boy will do something even more outrageous, and he'll lose his job.

The kite flew. There it was, aloft. Blue had let out all of the line, and now, out of sheer curiosity, wanting to see how high it would go, he released the string, and the kite soared and swung away, out over the Hudson, and hung there a while. Then it drifted back, as if returning, coming home, but a high breeze caught it and took it back over the river, and put it directly in the path of the Goodyear blimp, which was coming downriver, toward Liberty Island.

The blimp moved with enormous slowness, doing, at best, twenty miles an hour, driven by two turboprops, one on each side of the cabin that hung from the blimp's underbelly. The kite was also slow, moving sluggishly toward the blimp, a slowness rising to meet a slowness. The blimp changed direction a few times, to avoid the kite, but the kite shifted direction with it, as if the two were fated to meet. And, soon enough, they did, the kite being drawn into the turboprop on the left side of the cabin, sucked in and chewed to pieces.

And when the kite went in, something went terribly wrong, the blimp dipping its nose and going into a slow, narrow turn over the river, descending, still moving with a ponderous slowness. Everyone on the roof was watching. The waiters watched. The musicians stopped playing, and they watched. Angela and Abdul, holding hands, watched. Farro Fescu and Tattafruge and Maggie. And Yesenia too, she watched, and felt a sudden twinge of pain, holding both hands to her belly.

Blue, expecting he would be arrested and put in jail, was thinking he should run. But, as in a bad dream, he stood rooted, unable to move. And Harry Falcon, lifting his head, observed the slow descent and saw that it would not be long before the blimp hit the water. Feeble though he was, he was conscious of the irony, that the ones aboard the blimp, full of life and far healthier than he, might die before he did, while he sat there, watching.

The blimp was soon below roof level, and now they were looking down at it, not up, and the descent seemed to have accelerated. María Gracia was biting her lower lip. Even if the helium kept it afloat, the cabin was underneath, and how would they ever get out? Why didn't they jump, she wondered, leap into the water and swim away, before that huge thing buried them in the river?

Then, as if the turboprop had finished digesting the kite, the system kicked in again, and the nose of the blimp pulled up, moments before hitting water. The pilot had regained control. The blimp skimmed the surface, the cabin touching water, and then it was rising again, slowly up, across the bay and lifting. And, as if the event had been staged for their entertainment, everyone on the roof burst into applause. On neighboring rooftops too, cheers and clapping.

Farro Fescu, holding his wineglass, did not clap. He was too angry, too annoyed with Blue. See? See what it comes to? He had watched with terror as the blimp nearly went down. A kite, a toy, could do that. A bit of playfulness, but out of place, and it comes to this. Still, as he stood there, wineglass in hand, he felt good to see the blimp was safe. Better that people should live. Yes, better that way, and the good feeling overcame his anger, and he listened as the clapping and the cheers echoed from rooftops all around. And that too was good. Wonderful, yes, that life is so filled with echoes, echoes of all kinds.

The bandoneon player was singing again, and the waiters passed around more champagne. Theo spoke with Yesenia, and Yesenia, turning, spoke with Angela. Abdul spoke with his mother, who still couldn't forgive him for choosing a non-Muslim girl, and his mother spoke with Lyssa Rumfarm, who was redoing the master bathroom, trying to decide whether to go with Mexican tile or Egyptian slate.

In the gathering dusk, Maggie Sowle stood by a dwarf apple tree that grew between a ficus and a pot of euonymus. She was admiring the tiny green apples, touching them, wishing they could be preserved exactly as they were, and never change.

"Junk bonds," Luther Rumfarm said, coming up behind her. "They're a fabulous instrument."

"Really?"

"The smartest move, right now."

"Junk bonds?"

"If you want to invest, I'd be glad to handle it for you." He had a napoleon on a plate, cutting into it with his fork, and offered her a bite.

"I don't think so," she said, declining both the pastry and the invitation to invest. She thought he was pressing too hard, and she had a sense of déjà vu, having just gone through this sort of thing with Muhta Saad. Two months she'd been involved with him, last November and December, and how foolish she'd been, what a silliness.

Rumfarm put his hand on her arm, above the elbow. "Why won't you let me help you?" he said.

She pulled away, taking a step back, and it bothered her that she seemed to appeal, always, to the wrong men.

"Are you trying to seduce me?" she asked, giving him a straight look, and realized, as she said it, that the question was less than gracious, but what other choice did she have?

Her bluntness left him flustered. He grunted, as if something had caught in his throat, then he put his hand to his mouth and coughed.

"Believe me," he said, still clearing his throat, "what you're imagining is—was—the farthest thing from my mind." And then, with a bluntness of his own, he asked if she was planning to give up her apartment.

"Sell?"

"Everyone else is."

"Are they?"

"Well, you know. The structural instability. It makes some people nervous."

"I thought it was being fixed."

"It is, will be. But you understand how people are."

"Tell me."

"Well, people are—people. I ask about your apartment, because if you decide to go, I'll give you a very fair price."

"Junk bonds?" she said. "That's how you do it?"

"They're a gift from the gods. And as I said, anytime you're interested."

"You're very kind," she said, stepping away, heading toward the bar in the solarium, but when she saw that he was trailing after, she threw him off by crossing the deck and approaching his wife, who was still in a quandary, trying to choose between Egyptian slate and Mexican tile.

"Artificial turf," Maggie suggested. "It's the latest thing

in bathrooms. It's mildew-resistant, and waterproof, if the tub overflows."

And she moved right on, into the solarium and down the spiral staircase, into Harry Falcon's apartment, where she was glad to be alone. She browsed, going from room to room. She saw Harry's room, and the nurse's room, and Billy Cloud's room, full of feathers. Three unhappy marriages Harry'd had, three estranged women, and the whore who came and went, María Gracia, with the black hair, and if he liked her so much, why hadn't he ever married her?

She found a bathroom and went in and put down the lid and sat there for a while, feeling disappointed with herself. She thought of the days and nights she'd spent with Muhta Saad, and what had she come away with from all of that? She came away knowing that the best cardamom comes from Guatemala, the finest nutmeg from Grenada, the strongest pepper from Brazil. In the Middle Ages, with a pound of saffron you could buy a horse, and with two pounds of mace you could purchase a cow. Did she have to know any of that? Was she any better for it? Such a waste, she thought. And if she took up with Luther Rumfarm, how was he going to improve the quality of her life? With junk bonds?

She left the bathroom and browsed again through the apartment, looking at pictures, opening closets. Then she went back upstairs, onto the deck, and found Theo, alone, with a half-empty glass, looking across the roof toward Angela, who was at the parapet, gazing at the last glimmers of light in the sky, a few wispy clouds darkening from purple to black.

"Look at her," he said. "She's sad."

"She's watching the sunset."

"But she's sad. She's getting married, she has a part in a movie, and she's unhappy."

"She's worried about her aunt," Maggie said.

"She worries too much. How will she be a famous movie star if she worries so much?"

She was not going to be a famous movie star, not yet. Her role was in a children's film, no people, just talking animals, and she was to be the tiger. It was going to be shot in Long Island City, in a warehouse that had been converted into a studio. The contract offer had just come through a week ago. They were going to glue fur to her her eyes, her teeth, her tongue, and the tip of her nose.

"And that," Theo says, "is better than dying in the third act, before the play is half over?"

"Theo, let her be."

"I said something wrong?"

What he wanted to say was that Angela needed a breast enhancement, it would help her career. But he had tried, months ago, to persuade Maggie to broach the subject with her, and she wouldn't. "Just keep your dirty hands off that poor girl's breasts," she had told him. He remembered that, and she did too, and it was a subject they now stayed away from. Still, it was on the tip of his tongue. If Angela had a better chest, would they be sticking her into a kiddie film?

But all he said was, "She's going to be a beautiful tiger."

"A magnificent tiger," Maggie answered.

"The kids will love her."

"Everyone—everyone will love her."

"But she's so sad. Why is she sad? Does she talk in this movie, or does she just snarl and roar?"

"Of course she talks. But she'll snarl and roar too."

"And move like a cat. Does she know how to do that? To slink around, and purr, and pounce? Not so easy, I would think. And the snarling and the roaring, so much to learn."

"And the fur," Maggie said. "I can't imagine how she's going to wear all that fur glued to her body. All day long, while they shoot. Under those hot lights."

"Life is such a burden," Theo said, in all seriousness. But Maggie, taking it for sarcasm, turned on him and kicked him in the shin.

The last faint light in the sky vanished with a feathery

swiftness, and darkness was fully upon them, arriving with the definiteness of a huge moving van. The first rockets went up, rising from barges on the East River. The barges were hidden from view by the downtown buildings, but the rockets soared high into the night sky, and the roof of Echo Terrace was as fine a place as any to see them. The first shots were wide-bursting pom-poms, red, white, and blue, followed by cherry blossoms, and gold and purple star shells.

If anybody knew about fireworks, it was Abdul Saad, and it had come as a happy surprise to Angela that he knew about more things than just death and cremation. He knew the blue butterfly, the peonies, the palm trees, and the red roses, and the silver spangling chrysanthemums. One summer, when he was an undergraduate, he had worked at a fireworks factory in Rhode Island, in Hope Valley, just above Ashaway. It was Pyro-Pirro, run by the Pirro family. They made strobes and hummingbirds that they sold abroad, in China and Japan, to companies that put their own label on them and then sold them back to America, especially to Grucci, who did most of the big rocket shows. Grucci made their own fireworks on Long Island, but they liked to spice things up with some foreign imports. They knew, of course, that the strobes from China had been made by Pyro-Pirro, but they preferred to buy from China, because Pyro-Pirro was in Hope Valley, in Rhode Island, which didn't have the cachet of Canton or Nanjing. And besides, they paid less to China than they would have paid to Pyro-Pirro, because Pyro-Pirro gave discounts to China that it couldn't give to Grucci, since it was a competitor on American soil—and China, in turn, passed the discounts on to Grucci, because China needed the business, and in the complicated way of things, the international exchange rates helped to make it all possible.

The summer that Abdul worked for Pyro-Pirro was the summer when one of the buildings on their plant-site blew up, killing three employees and a member of the

Pirro family. Abdul had been working in the building, but he had just stepped out for a cigarette break and was strolling across the lawn when the one-story wooden building blew. The explosion shattered the roof and walls, and Abdul, thrown to the ground, lay huddled in a clump of pachysandra while hundreds of rockets whizzed about chaotically, some blazing very close and leaving him with second-degree burns that took a long time to heal. It was this near-death experience that had focused his mind on mortality and led to his decision to devote his life to the dead by becoming a mortician. But now he had Angela, who was full of life, and what he realized was that, undeserving as he was, he'd been given the best of both worlds, death and life too. Standing beside her, on the roof of Echo Terrace, his arm around her waist, he forgot about death for a while and, watching the bright explosions, felt a joy that was, he thought, too much, too wonderful, and more, he was sure, than he really deserved.

He knew the names for them all, the chrysanthemums, the serpents and hummingbirds, the silver strobes and mad lions, the ring shells, the willows. The chrysanthemums were from Japan, a Kyoto specialty. The silver strobes were from Nanjing but made of course in Rhode Island by Pyro-Pirro, and the serpents and the hummingbirds were from a company in Liverpool.

"Which are the strobes," Angela asked.

"There. Those sparkling silver lights—right over there."

She saw the difference between the big, blossoming chrysanthemums and the skitterish hummingbirds. And the weaving serpents. And the golden cross, so astonishing, opening up amid a flowering of blues and reds.

The caterers had rolled a TV onto the deck and had turned up the volume. The sound was up too on rooftops all around—the same sound that went out not just on TV but on loudspeakers all along the East River, echoing through the streets of Manhattan, rising among the glass skyscrapers and rolling down the avenues, the sound of Neil Diamond singing "America," warm and raspy-throated, his song of the immigrants, the ones who came and the ones yet to come.

And when the song was over, there was the enormous pyrotechnical climax, shell upon shell bursting in the sky like some grand celestial orgasm, over five hundred shells, gaudy, glitzy, bombastic, utterly shameless and overdone. And that was the point of it—excess, wildness, extravaganza, burst of national pride, Independence, Freedom, Ellis Island, Statue of Liberty, shells exploding out of other shells, and others out of those, echoes of the long-ago Dutch and the English, slaves and the descendants of slaves, and the Indians, and all the waves of immigrants, old tenements torn down and others going up, Mott Street and Grand and Catherine and Park Row, the concussed air bursting with cascades of flaming color.

And Aki Sato watching, thinking yes, yes, this was better than Pearl Harbor, better than war. Rockets making beauty in the night. This was how it should be. He felt good about it, glad that he had come to America, and happy that he had written the check when the mayor's aide came to him, telling him of the need.

And in the awkward silence after the sound of the last shell, Louisa Wax lifted her voice, singing.

O beautiful for spacious skies,
For amber waves of grain,
For purple mountain majesties
Above the fruited plain!

She wavered through the first few lines, then Angela and Maggie joined in. Karl Vogel didn't know the words, but he hummed along, as did Aki Sato. Farro Fescu knew the words but had a dreadful voice and sang off-key. Blue made up his own words. Hollis and Chase threw in some hip-hop variations as the song moved along. Smoke didn't sing because he never sang. Billy Cloud sang some of the words but not all, because the part of him that was

Mohawk was unhappy with America and traveled on an Onondaga passport.

The Goodyear blimp, all lit up, was still circling, up the East River, and down the Hudson. Planes with blinking lights descended toward LaGuardia, and a helicopter looped toward Staten Island. Maggie Sowle thought of her crazy ancestors fighting on both sides in the Civil War, and Theo thought of Emilio Matoso, dead in that cottage in the Catskills, and wondered when Korn and Bowditch might show up again. Or were they too already dead, victims of the shadowy world they traveled in. Rumfarm, lingering by the bar, was thinking if he could buy three more units in the building, he would have the controlling vote on any issue that might come up. On the other side of the roof, by a pot of tall ferns, his wife, Lyssa, holding an empty champagne glass, decided on Egyptian slate rather than Mexican tile, because she didn't like the way the Cuban drummer had been eyeing her, and between Cuban and Mexican was there that much of a difference? Karl Vogel thought of his wife, Lucille, who had died many years ago, and Farro Fescu remembered the village in which he grew up, where he saw his uncle, at a distance, walking down the road only moments before he was killed by a bomb dropped by an attacking bomber.

"Where's Yesenia?" Angela asked, not seeing her.

"She was having pains," Maggie said. "Muddy drove her home."

"Is she all right?"

"You know how it is," Maggie said. "False labor, it's not uncommon."

"I hope she's all right," Angela said, alarmed that Yesenia had rushed off that way.

The waiters were busy again, bearing trays of hors d'oeuvres and pastries, and, rather suddenly, the sky clouded over, covering the moon and the few pale stars visible above the city. The spring and early summer had seen very little rain and the reservoir was lower than normal. If the clouds brought rain, it would be welcome.

Rumfarm called aloud to Billy Cloud, suggesting that he help things along by performing a rain dance.

"I don't do rain dances," Billy Cloud answered. "I do a harvest dance, a moon dance, a dance to make the fish and the frogs plentiful, and a dance to make the women fertile."

"Improvise," Vogel suggested, and soon they were all clamoring, demanding that he do it, and he did. He gave the drummer a brief instruction on the kind of beat he needed, and, borrowing a lipstick from María Gracia, he stripped to his waist and drew designs on his face and arms. He had muscular shoulders, a thick waist, and no hair on his chest. He used up all of María's lipstick, and he quickly appeared fearsome and strange, a wild man full of dark thoughts and danger.

He danced, and he chanted, his feet stomping on the deck, keeping rhythm with the drums. And as he danced, rocking on one foot, then the other, he seemed larger than he was, taller, light from the lamps gleaming on his sweaty body, the lipstick markings like red fire. He was transformed, moving faster and faster, a force field, a center of energy weaving across the deck, arms bent, shoulders in motion, eyes transfixed, and always that up-and-down motion of his feet. He wore an old pair of sneakers, but even they were transformed, seeming cloudy and ambiguous, like webs of smoke.

And before he was done, the rain came. A crisp snap of lightning illuminated the bay, and drops of rain as big as grapes pounded the deck. And the junipers and the roses took a terrible beating.

They scurried into the solarium, out of the rain, all except Billy Cloud, who remained on the deck, dancing in the rain until he was satisfied that it was really rain and not just a passing shower. He was soaking wet when he came into the solarium, and María Gracia wrapped him in a large white towel.

Karl Vogel, who rarely smoked, accepted a cigar from Rumfarm, who usually smoked a pipe, but on holidays he used cigars. Maggie took a mint from a bowl of mints, and Juanita Blaize stripped off her clothes, down to her bikini underwear, and dove into the pool and swam underwater, surfacing periodically for a breath of air. The musicians stood at the edge of the pool, playing a tango.

Rain pounded noisily on the glass panes of the solarium, and threads of lightning branched down over midtown, striking one lightning rod after another. Across the river, Jersey City was being hit too, peals of thunder rumbling up and down the river like noisy bowling balls. Then the lightning moved closer, hammering the Trade Center, and moments later a single bolt hit the rod on Echo Terrace, striking with a ferocious hiss. The solarium was lit, briefly, with an unearthly glare, and lingering fingers of electrical charge skipped across the glass panels.

María Gracia sat on a chair beside Harry Falcon, holding his hand. His eyes were open, gazing emptily. His thick black hair all gone, the bare head and drawn face making him seem a stranger, not the Harry Falcon that anyone had known. His mouth hung open, arms like sticks dangling from his short-sleeved shirt, and the shirt itself baggy, too large for his emaciated body. There was no sign of life in him, and for all that anyone knew, he might already be dead.

Sitting there, beside Harry, holding his hand while the lightning flickered, María was thinking again of Vietnam, that far time that had become a place in her mind, hills and bamboo, scorched grass, rice paddies, and boiling tropical sunsets, loops and slashes of crimson scribbled across the heavens as the sun went down and darkness moved in. And the helicopters coming and going, rising like clumsy whales, tilting and angling, hovering, overcoming their own awkwardness, and flying. But many of them fell, shot down, breaking apart in the air, and others just went crazy, spinning wildly out of control and plunging to the ground.

And the weather, that too was still with her, the northwest monsoon and the southwest monsoon. One brought rain and the other brought heat, but even when she was there, she couldn't remember which brought what. Never got it straight. And now she was losing him, Arctic Swan Harry, friend, her best guy, mayor of Penguin Mist and maestro of Snow Cuisine, prince of the Eskimo Treats, losing him, and it was more than enough to think about, and too much to bear.

The Bird

Toward the very end of July, on a Friday, Farro Fescu, in the lobby, was on the phone to Oscar, in the subbasement.

"We have a bird loose in the building."

"What kind of a bird?" Oscar asked.

"A big one."

"A pigeon?"

"I don't think so."

"A canary?"

"I think it may belong to Mrs. Sowle."

Some time ago, after completing the United Nations quilt, Maggie had acquired two cuckoo birds, which she kept in a cage that was as large as her stand-up piano. She had thought of bringing home a cat, but it would have clawed her quilts to shreds.

"Did you call her?"

"She doesn't answer," Farro Fescu said in a complaining tone, as if her not answering were somehow an indication of guilt.

"It's probably a bat," Oscar suggested. "Mrs. Wax saw bats circling near her balcony yesterday. They come out when the sun goes down."

"Oscar," Farro Fescu said, in a bad humor, "I want you to come up here with your people and get rid of this thing."

"You want me to catch it?"

"I want you to kill it."

"How?"

"Spray it with a fire extinguisher."

"Kill a bird? A little bird?"

"A big bird. I want you to wring its neck and drop it in the trash."

"I'm not paid for that," Oscar said, putting up the phone.

Nevertheless, a few moments later, he arrived in the lobby with Muddy Dinks and Verna. Muddy, tall and lanky, carried an extension ladder that reached to twenty feet, and Verna carried a fire extinguisher. She was so short, the red cylinder was almost as big as she was. The bird was perched on the ledge above the clock. It was, as Farro Fescu had said, rather large, certainly bigger than a bat or a cuckoo. Its wings and body were richly blue, its chest was white. The eyes were rimmed with red, and the legs too had a reddish cast.

"That's not a bird," Muddy Dinks said. "That's a hawk."

"You know about hawks?" Oscar asked skeptically.

"Seen one in the zoo. Got that funny turned-down beak and sharp talons. Could swoop right down and tear your eyes out."

Oscar too had seen hawks in the zoo, but they were nothing like this. "That nice bird? He wouldn't harm a soul. Look what a fine-looking bird that is."

Farro Fescu was losing patience. "Oscar—"

"Soon as I'm up there, he'll fly," Oscar said. "Open the front door and let him go. That's all he wants, he wants out of here."

"Kill it," Farro Fescu said meanly, and they exchanged fierce glances.

Oscar grabbed the fire extinguisher from Verna and started up the ladder. But when he was a few rungs up, he paused and came back down.

"I'm too old for this," he said, handing the fire extinguisher to Muddy Dinks. "You do it."

"If you're too old," Muddy said, "I'm too young."

"For God's sake," Farro Fescu said, "do it before the damn thing flies again and shits all over the place."

414

It had already left a few big squirts on the leather couch and the easy chairs, and on the desk.

As Muddy started up the ladder, Karl Vogel, carrying a bag of groceries, came through the front door.

"Ah," he said excitedly when he saw the bird perched above the clock. "We have a barn owl in the house."

"It's a hawk," said Muddy Dinks, moving up the ladder.

"A barn owl," Vogel insisted. "Many a barn owl I saw in old Germany, before the war."

The doors on the west elevator slid open, and Luther Rumfarm stepped into the lobby, on his way for the mail.

"A barn owl," Vogel said, pointing at the bird.

Rumfarm glanced up. "That? Looks more like a turkey buzzard to me."

"It's a hawk," Muddy Dinks said with renewed conviction, climbing farther up, slowly, uneasy about the bird's talons.

"A falcon," Verna said. "It's Mr. Harry Falcon come back to haunt us."

"Mr. Falcon isn't dead yet," Vogel said.

"Then it's that other one, the one that fell from the balcony. Mr. Klempp. Swooped down like a bird."

Rumfarm ducked into the mail room and quickly returned, having found in his pigeonhole only two pieces of third-class mail, an ad for hair pieces and a flyer for a new perfume, drenched with aroma.

"Is this all?" he said to Farro Fescu. "Have you sorted it all?"

Muddy Dinks readied the fire extinguisher, and Farro Fescu shouted that he was too far away. "Closer," he called. "Go closer!"

"What are you trying to do?" Vogel asked. "If you are trying to scare the poor thing, I think he is already frightened half to death."

Instead of moving closer, Muddy Dinks took a step down on the ladder. He was having trouble with the extinguisher. He tried to lodge it between his chest and the ladder, but it kept slipping away.

Vogel picked up a pencil from the desk and prepared to throw it. "Somebody hold the door," he said. "That's how to get rid of him."

"No," Farro Fescu shouted, plucking the pencil from Vogel's hand.

"Looks like a turkey buzzard to me," Rumfarm said again, and he went to the door and held it open.

"A bird like that," Oscar said, "it must have escaped from the zoo. We should call them."

"Probably lives on a rooftop," Rumfarm said, still holding the door. "What do you suppose a thing like that would cost? In a pet shop, I mean."

Farro Fescu, dropping the pencil he'd snatched from Vogel, darted across the lobby to close the door, but before he was halfway there he heard a great screeching sound, weird and unearthly, and, turning, he saw the bird still on the ledge above the clock, spreading its blue wings gigantically. "Now!" he shouted to Muddy Dinks. "Spray! Spray!"

Muddy Dinks, shrinking from the bird, lost his footing, and clinging to the ladder with one hand, he went down, onto the floor, pulling the ladder down with him. As he fell, he squeezed the release on the fire extinguisher, and a bath of white foam raged from the nozzle. He rolled about on the floor, in pain, never letting go of the extinguisher. Foam shot out erratically, gushing across the black leather couch, the cushioned chairs, the marble floor, the desk, the palm tree, and the basket of flowers on the lacquered table between the elevators. It covered Vogel's shoes and poured all over Farro Fescu's new green jacket. Rumfarm, completely lathered, head to toe, still held the door—and the bird, with a great whirring of its purple wings, soared from its perch above the clock, arrowed its way through the tall doorway, and vanished into the overcast afternoon.

An hour later, after the foam had been cleaned up, Farro Fescu sat in shirtsleeves at the desk, mad as hell about his ruined jacket. He called a taxi for Mrs. Wax and helped Mrs. Marriocci with her packages. He phoned the window-washing service and berated them for failing to show up last week for the monthly wash. He called the garden shop and complained that the pansies they'd planted last month were wilting, and many had died.

Shortly after three, when Maggie Sowle came in, returning with packages from the mall at the Trade Center, Farro Fescu stepped out from behind the desk and couldn't resist. "Is one of your birds missing?"

She was startled. "I don't think so."

"A large bird. A big purple bird with a creamy chest."

"I only have two small birds," she said, shaking her head. "Two cuckoos."

Farro Fescu thought she was being crafty. Despite her pleasantly calm manner, she was, he concluded, a woman of guile. He liked that, that she should be clever enough to fend for herself. Deceit, he thought, made a woman more interesting.

"Let me know," he said. "Call down and let me know if they're both there."

"Oh, I will."

She went up the elevator, and he waited for her call. Ten minutes passed. He imagined she was groping about from room to room, searching for the missing bird. Behind sofas, under the beds. Calling its name. Twenty minutes went by and he became restless. He clipped his fingernails. When a half hour had passed, he resigned himself to the notion that she had never really intended to call and this was simply her way of putting him in his place. Well, so be it.

He went to the bathroom, not out of any need but simply as a way of changing location, moving his body from here to there. He stood at the urinal but did not pass any urine. He rinsed his hands. He studied his hair in the mirror, noting that it was thinning out. As far as he could recall, baldness had not been a problem in his family. But most of his uncles had died in the fighting in the Balkans, long before baldness had had a chance to develop. Perhaps he would lose his hair after all.

When he returned to the desk, the phone was ringing, and it was Mrs. Sowle.

"Actually," she said, "one of my birds is missing."

"The big purple one?"

"A small silver one."

He knew, now, she was toying with him. Not only was she humiliating him, she was rubbing his face in it. "Mrs. Sowle," he said, "there are no silver birds."

"Oh, yes, yes," she insisted, "one of my cuckoo birds, the missing one. Quite silver. I can't imagine how he could have slipped out. I must have left the cage open. But where in the world is he?"

Farro Fescu remembered the bat that Oscar had mentioned, on the third floor.

"You are sure it was a cuckoo and not a bat?"

"A silver cuckoo. The size of a sparrow."

He had picked up a pen and was doodling on a pad, making Xs of differing sizes. "Gold birds, I know," he said. "Canaries and goldfinches. But I never heard of silver. Such an amusing idea, Mrs. Sowle. You wouldn't be pulling my leg, would you?"

"Why in the world would I want to do that," she said in a flat, matter-of-fact way, making it plain that even if they were the last two people on the planet, pulling his leg would not be something she would care to contemplate.

The day of the bird in the lobby was the day when a Muslim cleric, Sheikh Omar Abdel-Rahman, was indicted by a federal grand jury for conspiracy in terrorist activities—among them, the bombing of the World Trade Center in February. He was cited for instructing and advising the other conspirators. In all, fifteen were named in the indictment.

Rumfarm, in the lobby, was ecstatic. "See? Didn't I tell you we'd catch the bastards?" His pale blue eyes glittered, he was almost gleeful.

On balance, it had been a good month. The economy was improving, unemployment was down, and Congress had passed a bill to reduce the deficit. Pope John Paul spoke at a youth festival in Denver, and the flooding that had afflicted nine states in the Midwest, leaving fifty

dead, was now receding. In Nicaragua, some eighty
political hostages had been released. And the Oslo
Accords brought some hope that the Israeli-Palestinian
crisis might finally be approaching a solution. And now,
with the indictment of the blind sheikh, Abdel-Rahman,
there was a growing sense of closure on the bombing that
had caused six known deaths in the Trade Center.

"Lethal injection," Rumfarm said under the palm tree
in the lobby, "that's what they deserve. Anything less
would be a travesty of justice."

Angela and Abdul passed through, on their way to a
film, and Mrs. Saad rode off in a cab. Juanita Blaize went
walking with her Dalmatians, one with his tail dyed blue,
the other egg-yolk yellow. She varied the colors, changing them every month. Aki Sato went off to the airport.

And a short time later, instead of going home, Farro
Fescu rode the subway uptown, the Lex, to Eighty-sixth,
where he exited and walked. A few blocks south, then
left, to the East River, going to the apartment where María
Gracia Moño lived.

He knew she was a prostitute—and a high-class one—
because it was his business to know such things. A good
concierge had to be alert, wary, knowledgeable. Which
one a prostitute, which into drugs, who a gambler, who
working a scam, who with the police. He had seen her
with Charlie Rohr a few times, and once with Ben Rosen,
a few times with Tattafruge. And so many times now she
was in to see Harry Falcon, helping him in his days of
dying. They had been passing her around, she belonged
to all of them. A few months ago, out of sheer curiosity—
devilishly—he followed her home when she left Harry
Falcon's apartment, wanting to see where she lived. She
took a taxi, and he had to move fast to grab a taxi to
follow. Snazzy part of town she was in, with the river
view, and the park and the mayor's mansion only a handful of blocks to the north. He stood outside, wondering
which windows were hers. Some kind of swanky place,
he imagined, envisioning leather and animal skins and
rugs inches deep. She was doing all right for herself.

And now, at the end of his hard day, the day of the bird in the lobby, he went again, in shirtsleeves, carrying his ruined jacket, by subway this time, and then a short walk. He stood a moment, looking at the place, then went casually in and gave his name to the liveried doorman who sat in a cubicle inside the door. Farro Fescu knew the type—a no-talent flunky, a lump, a mere ornament put there to ward off undesirables. Not a concierge, no, not someone knowing the needs, the desires, aware of the subtleties and innuendos, so closely involved that he feels the pulse, he knows the shadows and the light. They traded looks. The man younger, early forties, haughty, plump, bounced from twenty jobs, no doubt, before he landed this one. He made the call to María Moño, put up the phone, and, unsmiling, pointed Farro Fescu toward the elevator and told him the apartment number. It was a one-elevator building.

Upstairs, when María opened the door, Farro Fescu took two crisp five-hundred-dollar bills from his wallet and offered them to her. All week he'd been carrying them, uncertain about when, or whether, he'd use them.

"I can't," she said. "Don't you understand? It isn't done this way."

"How is it done?"

"I have my client list. Everyone comes recommended." And then, seeing his disappointment, "Look, there are others you can visit. I'll give you someone's name."

"I don't want someone else," he said. "My money's not good enough?"

Again she tried to explain that it wasn't the money, and realized that she wasn't filtering through to him. He simply stood there, at the door, gray slacks, white shirt, the green jacket folded over his arm. And she saw the distress in his gaze, and the way he stood, slumped but rigid, as if stricken, something deep inside him splitting apart and collapsing.

She took the two bills from his hand and stuffed them into his shirt pocket, and then she took the jacket from his arm.

"You're very tired," she said, "come in and rest a moment."

She led him inside, to the living room, and laid his jacket on the couch, and before he sat he was already talking, telling her his story.

"We were Rumanian," he said, "but the family was in Serbia so the men could work at the copper mine. My father, my uncles. Then came the war, and my grandfather was killed, and one of my uncles. The Germans bombed, you know. You can't imagine what a time it was. My other uncles went into the mountains and continued to fight, and they too were killed. My mother is still alive, she lives in Flatbush, but she's old and suffers from heart failure. My father, before he died, was a window cleaner on the Chrysler Building. He was afraid of heights, but that was the job he had."

Then he simply stood there, his deep-set eyes dark with disappointment. He by the couch, she by a cushioned chair, in a strained silence.

"Sit," she said, and she left briefly to fetch some brandy.

On the coffee table, there was a basket of dried flowers, a magazine, her reading glasses, a cup of tea. And a dish with a half-eaten slice of toast on it. A painting hung above the fireplace, a simple scene, sheep in a field of grass, trees in the distance.

Seeing the toast, the tea, her glasses, he had a sudden sense of the ordinariness of her life. She had been relaxing, reading a magazine. She liked dried flowers, and simple country scenes. She was just another person, with ordinary needs and the ordinary aches and pains. It was like long, long ago, when he was young, in New York, without a job, not knowing what his life would be, and one day, on the street, he sees Bobby Thomson, who had hit the famous home run that everybody knew about—he was standing by the curb, trying to flag down a taxi. When he hit that home run, he was one of the gods, but on the street, in a suit of clothes, can't get a cab, he was anybody, just a man in need of a ride. That's what he felt now about María Gracia. No lipstick, no makeup, the hair pulled back, held by a rubber band. She needed glasses to read with. Why had he imagined it was necessary to sleep with her?

She brought in a bottle of Metaxa, and a glass for each of them. She offered him a cigarette, and he took one. He hadn't smoked for years, but now he lit up, and he coughed a few times, inhaling, yet it seemed so simple, as if he had never stopped. And again he was talking, reminiscing, what it had been like, growing up in the Balkans. The trees, the mine at Bor, the shacks they lived in, the creek that flowed down the mountain. All of that. And how he'd been in love with a girl but she was too old for him, and his brother took her, and how he had hated him for that.

And then he was telling her what he thought he would never tell anyone, that he was the one, him, he had done it, he was the one who had killed the young man who lived on the twelfth floor. The clothes designer, Ira Klempp.

"I don't think I truly intended it. I went into his apartment. The door was unlocked, I didn't have to ring. I was angry because he was infesting the building with drugs. I had to confront him. What else could I do? Go to the police? If the building became known as a drug den, the values would drop, and the only ones moving in would be more users."

"Why are you telling me this?"

"I don't know. It's all very strange. I went into the apartment, and he was so high he was helpless. I brought him out on the terrace to give him some air and bring him around. Because I had to tell him to stop, to move out. He was loose, wobbly, he leaned over the railing. Far over. And then it happened. I gave him the slightest nudge, that's all it was. And he went over, as if he wanted to. As if he'd been waiting for it to happen."

"You pushed him?"

"I touched him. What can I say? And he went over."

"And it troubles you."

He shrugged, rocking his head from side to side. "It happened. It's something that happened."

"Is it better now, with him gone?"

"I'm God? I can answer that? Why do you ask such a thing? It's better, of course it's better, but it's also worse. It's always worse."

He was tired, drained, and, swallowing off what was left of his brandy, he felt a momentary stimulus, but then a drop, as if his body was shutting down. When he stood up to leave, taking his jacket, he saw that she too was tired, very tired, and he had simply made a fool of himself.

"I'll send some wine," he said. "Something special."

"Don't do that. Please."

"Just some wine," he said. And then, shyly, "I was a trouble for you. I won't come back," he promised. "I won't bother you again."

Four Adagios and
a Love Letter

1. *Tattafruge*

Theo has given his cat to Mrs. Marriocci, who likes cats and will take good care of it. And, through Farro Fescu, he's arranged that Muddy Dinks and Blue will carry his canoe down to the Hudson River for him. And they do. Monday morning, nine A.M., a warm day in August, no clouds in the sky, they come to his living room, take the boat and bring it down on the freight elevator, then out the rear exit, through the service alley and onto the street, following Theo to a spot he knows where the railing is open and there is access to the water. They set the boat on the ground, positioning it before putting it in.

Muddy Dinks gives the doctor a hard look.

"You for certain about this? One of them big freighters come along, you gonna get swamped."

"It's only a river," Theo says. He's in khaki shorts and a white T-shirt, carrying a paddle and a cooler. A knapsack on his back, and a Greek fisherman's cap on his head. "In Papua New Guinea, they go onto the ocean in these."

He gives them each a big tip, more than they make in a couple of days' work.

"You sure, man?" Muddy Dinks repeats, doubtful about the boat.

"I'm okay," Theo says, appreciating Muddy's concern. "Let's do it."

Into the water the boat goes, and they steady it for him

as he climbs in, situating himself in the stern. He takes off the knapsack and stows it within reach, and the cooler he shoves under the bench he's sitting on. Up front is a duffel containing a sleeping bag and some clothes, a flashlight, a slicker against bad weather, a map.

"Nice boat," Muddy says, his hand on the carved bird on the prow.

"Real nice," Blue says.

"You can swim?" Muddy asks.

"When I was a kid," Theo says, "I swam in the Nile."

They push him off, and he begins paddling, pulling away from shore and heading upriver. He does forty, fifty strokes, then glances back and sees them standing where he left them, on the rocks, looking after him. Several times he glances back, and they grow smaller and smaller as he goes. He sees the top of the condo, Echo Terrace, upper floors and the penthouse, dwarfed by the towers of the World Trade Center. Strange, he thinks, how the things you leave behind seem less important than the things toward which we move. But where is he going, and why? Upriver, but toward what? He only half knows. He dips the oar and pulls, and the boat glides forward, across the surface of the river. And the surface, he thinks, is what matters, it's where we live, where we float and swim and make love and die. The life underneath knows nothing about any of this. The shad and the eels, the perch, the sunfish and the smallmouth bass—what do they know of the good times and the bad, the weddings, the wars, the interaction at the surface, where skin touches skin?

Last night he had called his partner, Lal Chakravorti, telling him he was taking some time off, going to be away for a while. Taking a sabbatical, was the way he put it.

Lal, in his way, was curious, probing, resistant, and, in his overall reaction, less than welcoming.

"Is it medical? Theo, are you sick?"

"No, I'm not sick."

"Then how?" he said. "You have your patients. How can you leave your patients?"

"Lal, I trust you to handle them. That's why we're partners. There's nothing terribly big on the calendar, a nose job and some breast enhancements. A bunch of post-op checkups. If you need help, call Max, he's a glutton for work. He wants to be a billionaire and he's already halfway there."

"Theo?"

"Yes?"

"I think you should talk to someone."

"I'm talking to you."

"What you're doing—you're having, I think, some kind of a breakdown."

"That's what you think?"

"Theo, don't hang up on me."

"Who's hanging up?"

"If you're tired, take a few days off and talk to some-body, get some help. But don't do this. Don't disappear into a midlife crisis."

"I'll keep in touch," Theo said. "I'll send postcards."

"What you need, Theo, is an antidepressant. This will all go away. Take Paxil. Zoloft. You know what to do."

"Lal, I'm not depressed. This isn't a breakdown. This is something I feel good about. If it's a midlife crisis, then I recommend it. You might want to try it yourself someday."

"But Theo . . ." Lal said, intense, not wanting to let go. "Theo . . ."

He dips the paddle and keeps moving, gliding. Up ahead, it's the George Washington Bridge, and beyond that, the bridges at Tarrytown and Peekskill. Then around the bend at Storm King Mountain, and on to Newburgh and Poughkeepsie. How far will he get? How far has he already gone? Nothing is urgent, nothing desperate, he's traveling at his own pace.

In the cooler are two bottles of water and the thermos containing the five embryos that Claudio Nascita has prepared for him. In the knapsack are a few sandwiches from the Amish place, some oranges and pears, and his notebook, into which he's copied his favorite passages

426

from Teddy Roosevelt, who would have cheered this moment of setting forth upon the river, because who in America had been more passionate than he about the great outdoors? *The river gleams like running quicksilver . . . there are no words that can tell the hidden spirit of the wilderness . . . its mystery, its melancholy . . . the awful glory of sunrise and sunset in the wide waste spaces of earth . . .*

After Poughkeepsie, it's Esopus Island, that narrow hump of rock and trees rising from the river, where he'll spend the night, if he gets that far. And beyond that, up to Albany and across to the Great Lakes. And somewhere along the way he will find the woman who will be a nest for one of the embryos in the thermos, some plain-looking, down-to-earth, simple-spoken person with good blood, strong arms, an easy smile, and a sense of humor about the frantic unpredictability of human existence. And he knows this is the best he's ever done, launching out like this, a complete break from everything he knows, into the open weather.

And still he wonders, where will the journey take him? Where will it end? He thinks of the canals that will bring him into the Great Lakes, and all the rivers and their tributaries, and hopes to make it clear across to the Pacific, to the high, rock-strewn shores where the water beats against cliffs and wide stretches of sand, and the setting sun ignites the water with a purple phosphorescence. And the rest of it, one way or another, he will figure out when he's there. But where is there? Who is when? Why is anything the way it is? How marvelous, he thinks, to be adrift. He dips his oar, and up ahead is a big white freighter bearing down on him. It hoots fiercely with its throaty horn, and he paddles strenuously, racing to pull out of the way. And barely makes it, the tall painted hull sliding past like a great building afloat, and what he faces now is the wake, the high swells more troublesome than he'd imagined, up and down, the canoe slanting off, and he knows if he takes a wave broadside, he could lose it altogether and capsize. The

427

waves of the wake come in angles, and despite his work with the paddle, he's spun around, tossing, tipped far over—and, feeling about to go over, he grabs hold of the rim of the boat with one hand, and with the other he hangs on to the paddle, the boat rocking wildly. It's a fierce, riveting moment, and he thinks he's had it, but the rocking slowly eases off, and he's through the worst. He's made it. Done it. He's on his way. Doesn't even look back at the freighter that nearly swamped him, just keeps paddling, pushing on.

2. *Vogel and Farro Fescu*

A few hours after Theo's departure, Farro Fescu leaves the lobby for a short stroll to the river and finds Karl Vogel sitting on a bench, relaxing in the sun. Vogel is in tan chinos and a white shirt, collar open. Farro Fescu takes off his maroon blazer, loosens his tie, and sits down beside him, looking across the water, to Jersey City.

"Look at this," Vogel says, taking a model railroad car from a small, wrinkled shopping bag. "Isn't this interesting?"

It's a car for transporting livestock, with sliding doors that are nicely crafted, with excellent detail. A corrugated roof, markings on the sides, couplings at either end.

"I had one of those when I was a kid," Farro Fescu says. "Something very like that."

"This is German, from before the war. It was made by Bing. Bub and Bing, they were the two big companies. I just brought it to Christie's for an appraisal. What do you think it's worth?"

"A thousand?"

Vogel smiles. "Twenty times that much. They sold one very like this, just last year."

"Impossible," Farro Fescu says.

"Look here, where it says SCHADE. You know what that means? It means pity, as in the phrase, it's a pity. But it should say SCHAFE, which means sheep. This is a car for transporting sheep. Such a wonderful mistake, it makes it more valuable. And there are so few around, most of them destroyed in the bombing. There are only nine others like this that have been documented, with the misprint. If that many."

"What will you do with it?"

"I'm giving it to the girl, Yesenia. For her baby."

They were all contributing something. Some gave money. Mrs. Wax gave a bassinet. Mrs. Marriocci gave a stroller. Aki Sato gave a CD full of lullabies and a Bose unit to play them on. Maggie Sowle gave a mobile for the crib, designed by an artist in SoHo, tiny hummingbirds made of painted aluminum. Mrs. Rumfarm gave a lifetime subscription to *National Geographic*.

Vogel's thought is that Yesenia might hold on to the railroad car until the baby grows up and is ready for college. By then it should be worth even more than now, and Christie's could auction it off for her.

"It's a form of investment," he says to Farro Fescu. And then, gazing at the river, he turns somber and philosophical. "See? A man in a factory makes a mistake like this, a simple misprint, and he loses his job. But other people get rich on it. Which means that mistakes are necessary, essential for progress. Adolf Hitler was a huge mistake, but look how America got rich from fighting him. After the war she emerges as the most powerful nation, and still is. I think of the peasant in Asia, in the rice paddies, working day after day, struggling, imagining that by the sweat of his brow he will get ahead, but he does not. He will barely eke out an existence. Yet here, with something like this, a silly mistake in the production of a toy, a small fortune is made. A postage stamp with a misprint brings riches. Think of a jackass mating by mistake with a horse, and the result is so magnificent—a mule. Farmers forever after persuading their asses to repeat the mistake, because mules are that good. X rays were a mistake, discovered by accident. So too penicillin. Mistakes, sheer craziness, the stuff of life, how we evolve and leap ahead. The very meat of the human tragicomedy."

Farro Fescu seems not to have heard a word that Vogel was saying.

"I'm a dying man," he says.

"What?"

"I have cancer."

"Where?"

"In my penis. They want to cut it off."

"Don't let them touch you."

"That's what I told them. They said I'll die."

It's a carcinoma at the tip, under the foreskin, and it had metastasized to the inguinal nodes. He'd thought it was some sort of pimple, harmless, but no, not so lucky. Haunting him now, obsessing him, are the words the doctors used—penectomy, and inguinal lymphadenectomy. Radiation is of no use for this kind of cancer, and chemotherapy ineffective. Surgery the only option. They want to cut deep, and what would be left?

Vogel puts his hand on Farro Fescu's shoulder. "Don't die," he says.

"I'm trying not to. Is there a choice?"

"Death," Vogel said, "is the biggest mistake of all."

They sit there, silent, a long time. A few gulls gliding above the water, a flight of ducks high up. A tugboat pulling four barges moves slowly downriver into the upper bay. The barges loaded with sand.

"You flew for Germany," Farro Fescu says.

"Yes, yes. You know I did. I wrote about it. I flew in France, Belgium, Holland. I was in North Africa. In the last years, I flew against the bombers that came deep into Germany."

Farro Fescu looks him in the eye.

"You killed my uncle Grigor," he said.

Shocked, Vogel stares sternly. "Me? When? Where?"

"He taught me how to play chess, we had pleasant times together. Memorable. He played the harmonica. He was so happy, making music, doing the old songs."

"This was in Rumania?"

"The family had moved to Serbia, to work in the mines."

"I never fought in Serbia. The Yugoslav campaign was in '41, I was still in school, my last year. I was memorizing Latin poems. I didn't fly until 1942. Why does everyone imagine I killed their loved ones? There was a young woman, some months ago, last November—she sought me out because she thought I had killed her grandfather. He was a bomber pilot, in a raid over Schweinfurt. Why should she imagine such a thing? She was a reporter, she went off to Somalia. She was lovely—but, you know, she was so confused. Anna Harte."

"She had dark hair," Farro Fescu says.

"Yes, dark and full. You saw her?"

"She waited for you in the lobby."

"We went to lunch. I liked her. And yes, it would be pleasant to see her again, but I don't think it will happen."

He takes a piece of paper from his wallet and writes the name of a doctor.

"See him before you let them do anything to you. He's done some remarkable things with cancer."

Farro Fescu accepts the paper with the name on it, but not eagerly. "I don't think you understand," he says.

"I do understand," Vogel answers. "Believe me, in matters like this, it's better to have hope."

The gulls are still out there, wheeling and gliding in the warm air over the river. The tugboat is gone.

"My uncle," Farro Fescu says, "he was a good man, he should have lived. I'm glad you weren't there."

"Yes," Vogel says. "Him and so many others, all of them. That would have been better, if they had all lived."

A helicopter flies over, following the river, heading north, the sound of its rotors like the noise of a stick drawn rapidly across a picket fence. The hard noon sun glares off the water.

3. *Billy Cloud*

Toward midafternoon, Farro Fescu is in the lobby, behind the desk, and Karl Vogel is in his apartment, on the couch, taking a nap. Louisa Wax is on her balcony, sipping a mint julep, and Angela is in her living room, studying the script the studio has sent her. Maggie Sowle, weary of quilting, is searching the newspaper for a good movie.

In the penthouse, Billy Cloud comes into Harry Falcon's room with his rattle and his pipe. The live-in nurse is gone, Harry has given her the afternoon off.

Harry is in bed, propped up on pillows. "No more of this shit," he says to Billy, his voice raspy and thin, as frail as his skin-and-bones body.

Billy Cloud hangs back, and after a few moments Harry lifts a hand, signaling for him to come close.

Billy approaches the bed and leans over, and Harry whispers in his ear.

"Are you sure?" Billy says.

"I'm sure," Harry answers.

"This is what you want?"

"Yes."

Billy goes to the walk-in closet, and after a few moments of searching he finds a set of clothes in a vinyl bag, and brings them to the bed.

"These?"

Harry nods feebly. It's a gaucho outfit, given to him by the governor of Tierra del Fuego. The governor's grandfather had been a gaucho, living in the pampas of central Argentina, and, as a tribute to his grandfather, the governor kept a collection of gaucho clothing, especially the garments worn by the more celebrated gauchos, like Martin Fierro, about whom many poems had been written. The outfit that Billy brings from the closet had belonged not to Martin Fierro but to one of the governor's forebears, who had distinguished himself as a warrior in the time of Julio Roca, using his bolas to great effect against enemy horsemen. The governor gave the clothes to Harry as a way of thanking him for introducing his line of frozen foods into Tierra del Fuego, especially the glazed breast of wild duck, toward which the governor was partial, though he also had a liking for the goose liver and the roast loin of pork.

It's all there on the bed, a linen shirt colorfully embroidered, a vest made of *carpincho* leather, and the jacket, the *chaqueta,* made of blue velveteen and embroidered with silver thread. The large-cut, loose-fitting pants, the *bombachas,* are of a checkered pattern, and there is a wide belt of soft leather, the *tirador,* embroidered with thread of many colors and ornamented with coins and silver medallions.

Billy turns down the sheet and, with some awkwardness, helps him dress. First the shirt, then the pants. Harry wants to button the shirt himself but fumbles, can't, and Billy helps. Then the vest, and the jacket, both of which, like the pants and shirt, are much too large. They had been large when the governor gave them to him, and now, because of the weight loss, they hang like clothes on a stick.

Then the high leather boots, and a pair of embossed silver spurs. With the spurs, Billy is helpless. Harry works at them, feebly, but finally gives up and lets them drop to the floor. The only thing that fits right is the black leather hat, broad-brimmed, the leather made from the belly of a burro.

"Bring me to the mirror," he says.

Billy leans over and, putting one arm under Harry's shoulders and the other under his knees, lifts him. He is surprisingly light. This man who had stood nearly six feet tall is now nothing, yellowish skin stretched across bones that seem as fragile as matchsticks. Billy brings him to the mirror on the back of the door of the walk-in closet, sets him on his feet, and stands behind him, putting his hands under his shoulders and holding him up.

Harry looks at himself, not altogether pleased with what he sees. "Damn jacket don't fit," he says, waving a hand in disgust. Then he leans close to the mirror, studying his face, putting a finger to his cheek, his chin, his lips, as if testing to see if he is still alive.

"Okay," he says. "Now the terrace."

Billy carries him into the living room and through the French doors, onto the balcony, where there is a view of the river. He stands there, by the railing, with Harry in his arms, both of them looking out at the water. Not much happening out there, a few tugs, a few barges. A plane flying in a wide loop over New Jersey, in a holding pattern, waiting to land at LaGuardia.

Harry looks across the river, to Jersey City. "I hate that clock," he says, gazing at the Colgate clock at the river's edge. The big black hands on the white face show ten after three.

"You okay?" Billy asks.

"Right. Sure."

"Yeah?"

"That's enough," Harry says.

Billy carries him back to the bedroom and puts him on the bed, propping him up with pillows, putting him into a sitting position. In the gaucho clothes, he's almost unrecognizable.

"Now mix me that double martini," Harry says.

The gin and vermouth and an ice bucket are on a tray on the bureau. Billy uses the mixer, measuring the gin and vermouth with a shot glass, then shaking the mixer as if in some solemn tribal ritual. He pours the martini into a silver-rimmed glass and adds an olive.

Harry, in bed, on top of the covers, takes the glass and sips.

"Is that okay?"

Harry looks away. "I've had better."

A few slow moments, nothing. Harry sips again, then hovers. Then another sip, and he looks toward the night table. "Okay," he says.

Billy takes a bottle of pills from the drawer and holds it up for Harry to see.

Harry inclines his head.

Billy opens the bottle, sleeping pills, and Harry takes three, swallowing them down with the martini.

"Now the others, the blue bottle," he says.

Billy opens the blue bottle and there are yellow capsules inside. He hands them to Harry one at a time, four in all. When the martini glass is empty, Harry lets it slip from his grasp and it's on the bed, down by his knee.

Then he's just resting there, legs stretched out, his back and his head supported by pillows. His eyes are closed, and he seems asleep.

Billy lingers a moment, watching the shallow breathing. Then, not wanting to see it through to the end, he takes his rattle and pipe and goes to his own room, where he gathers his few belongings and stuffs them into his canvas bag. He washes away the markings on his face and pulls on a shirt. On his way out, he checks in on Harry again and finds him twisted all around on the bed, his eyes open, the breath gone out of him, and a small stream of brown liquid at the corner of his lips. He doesn't touch him, just stands there a moment, gazing, and leaves.

In the vestibule, while he waits for the elevator, he takes a long last look through the window, which faces north, toward the density of glass and stone and steel, the skyscraper jungle, thinking that his people, the Lenape, once owned all of this, the land, the island, and gave it away to a Dutchman for beads and shells, twenty-four dollars' worth—and smart too, smart to unload, because look what it is now, the grit and the noise, even the sky dirty, full of pollution. Who would want it?

On the street, a small crowd has gathered on the corner of South End. There's been a collision, a beer-delivery truck and a VW convertible. Somebody is on the sidewalk, bleeding, being attended to by paramedics.

Billy approaches a police officer, a woman. "Anybody hurt bad?"

"The one in the VW," she says. "They already took him away."

The driver of the truck is in the backseat of a patrol car. The person on the ground is a pedestrian.

"Tough," Billy says. "Real tough."

He walks off, down South End, past the market, the bank, and the restaurant, then across on Rector and into the subway, catching a train that carries him through the tube, into Brooklyn, the long, slow ride to the end of the line, where the low waves of the Atlantic are beating against the beach.

He shuffles across the hot sand, picking his way through the sunbathers on blankets, and drops his bag, peels off his shirt, kicks off his shoes, loosens his pants and steps out of them as they fall, and, moving straight ahead, in his undershorts, he walks into the water, and when it's deep enough he leans forward into a wave, lifting his arms, and swims, the water cooling his thick body, head to feet. On and on, into the low, incoming waves, salt water washing over him, he swims, and swims.

4. *Yesenia at the Window*

In her apartment on Jamaica Avenue, in her bedroom, Yesenia sits by the window, nursing her month-old baby. Marissa Marie, that's the name she's given her. On the other side of the open window is the el, with the tracks and the wooden ties that the tracks are nailed to, and the big steel beams that hold everything up. She likes it, she's grown up with it and would be at a loss without it. The el is a landscape all its own. Some days there are men out there, on the tracks, removing a rail and putting another one in, and she watches, their big sweaty bodies moving and bending as they hammer the new rail into place. And sometimes they change a few of the ties, and you can tell the new ones from the old because they aren't as dark and weathered as the others.

As she sits there, nursing the baby, she remembers when she was up on the roof at Echo Terrace, watching the fireworks, at Harry Falcon's party, and she turned to Muddy and told him she was feeling the pains and it was time to go. And how he asked if she could hold on till after the fireworks, but she couldn't. He took her down the elevator to the garage in the basement and drove her out, heading for the bridge and the BQE, to Jamaica Hospital, but never made it, not even close, because right there on the Brooklyn Bridge it all came apart for her. The pains coming like crazy, and the water broke, and already the baby was coming down.

Muddy pulled over, on the bridge, and came around to her side, and she leaned back, and he helped. Like passing a damn piano, is the way she remembers it—closed her eyes and screamed, a lusty yowl, and when the long scream whimpered down, she opened her eyes and Muddy was there, bending over, with the baby in his hands, not knowing what to do with it. He laid it on her stomach, and she put her hands on it. Then, fast, the police were there, with the hard-bright flashing lights, like some kind of anger in the night, and the ambulance.

And before all of that, before the baby came, same day, up on the roof, at the party, what Yesenia had found out was that Angela's Aunt Nora had died that morning. It was Angela who told her, when they were hanging on to each other, hugging and kissing and crying. So many good things, yes, so many, but not this about Nora, not one of the happy things. Too sad, and they held each other and wept. She had died that morning, and Angela had been there with Abdul, at the hospital. But not telling anyone, not wanting to bring unhappiness to the party. Yet there, on the roof, as they held each other, Angela just broke and it all spilled out, and she said not to tell anyone, not to ruin the day. Better that she's gone, she said, and Yesenia could see she didn't truly believe that, not in her heart.

And now, here, still by the window, the way Yesenia thinks of it is that God took Nora and turned her loose, God set her free. But sad, so sad. And here, at the window, with Marissa at her breast, she knows she will always remember it, Nora dying and Marissa being born on the same day, the two of them linked together like that, joined in some weird sort of dance, coming and going.

And Muddy, what Muddy says—he says, "What's to be sad? Somebody gets on and somebody gets off. That's how it is. How it has to be." As if there are only so many seats on the train, and somebody has to get off before a new passenger can come aboard. Silly Muddy. What's he say a dumb thing like that for? Dumb, she thinks. Dumb.

And alone now with the baby, at the window by the el, Yesenia looks at the tiny fingers, tiny toes, tiny Marissa, wondering who will she be? Will she sing? Dance? Cry? Meet a man who will break her heart? Will she have babies of her own, and will she escape the pain, the suffering, and know how to walk on her own and not be turned inside out by the mean ones waiting to do damage? Her Fourth-of-July baby, her impatient Independence Day angel who couldn't wait and pushed her way into the world. Her firecracker brat who cries for the nipple. What lies ahead for her? What kind of world?

From Muddy, she's heard about the things that are happening. Farro Fescu going into the hospital for an operation, and the Marlins and the Hungerfords, like so many others, moving out. And Mr. Rumfarm buying up those apartments too. And the men to fix the foundation coming in with their big machines tomorrow, going to drill out the bad cement and put in steel beams for reinforcement, and pour tons of new concrete. Going to be a lot of pounding and drilling, and the ones not selling are going off on vacation till the work is done.

And Yesenia, with her baby, by the window, thinking how lucky she is, the only noise to contend with is the noise of the trains on the el, which she's grown up with. And the baby, Marissa Marie, she is more than a comfort, a few wisps of dark hair and skin color like her own, light tan, though her mother says that will probably change. Her mother thinks she looks just like Yesenia did when she was born. But in the lips, the nose, the roundness of the face, Yesenia doesn't see herself at all, or even her mother. She sees her own father, who left long ago, and she can still see him, vivid, like yesterday, a snapshot in her mind. She doesn't see anything at all of the one who assaulted her, who boasted about how many he'd killed, the one she hit on the head with the toilet lid. She is still amazed. So good, and lucky, to get away from him and be alive. So good, and so unreal.

A train comes by, close, right there outside her window. She sees the faces. People standing, people sitting. A woman with blond hair, a girl with braids. A man in a sweatshirt. All the faces going by, and the baby at her breast, Marissa, sucking at the nipple, giving her a warm sensation, a quiet pleasure radiating through her body. The train is gone, and for a while it's just the tracks and the apartments across the street, and the sky with a flimsy veil of clouds and the sun spilling through, and she can see down to the street, patterns of light and shadow, and the cars and buses under the el. Squeal of brakes, toot of horn, somewhere a siren, and then another train coming along, this one slowing down and stopping right there outside her window. Must be men on the tracks ahead, working. The baby has stopped sucking.

All those somber faces right there, on the train, so close. A woman in a red blouse, and a tall boy in a white T-shirt. A gray man reading a book. How wonderful if they could talk! The gray man doesn't see her, goes on reading. The woman in red waves at the baby. Yesenia takes the baby's hand and makes a waving motion in response. The boy in the T-shirt watches. Someone in jeans, with dreadlocks, walks through, going from one car to the next.

Then the train is moving again, and Yesenia holds the baby over her shoulder. Already asleep, she is. The windows of the train flashing by, and the people gone. On the street, would any of them recognize her? Would she recognize them? What if she saw someone—the woman in the red blouse, say, and what if she went up to her and said, "I was the one in the window, with my baby, when you passed by"—if that were to happen, would the woman know who she was? Would she remember passing by on the J train, on that torrid afternoon, and the baby asleep and dreaming?

5. *The Love Letter*

On Esopus Island, on the Hudson, north of Poughkeepsie, Theo Tattafruge has beached his canoe and settled in, opening his sleeping bag on a broad, flat rock by the water, amid pines and hemlocks. So many constellations overhead, stars he doesn't ordinarily see because of the bright lights of the city, and the haze and pollution. Before he sleeps, he sits there, on the rock, in the mild August night, using a flashlight as he peruses his notebook, browsing through the passages from Teddy Roosevelt that he's copied down.

Turning the pages, he pauses over a letter that Teddy wrote to his wife, Edith, in 1909, when he was on safari in Africa. Having just left the presidency, he was restless, on the move, hunting for specimens that were to be mounted and put on display in the Smithsonian. It was an eleven-month trek, and he carried books with him, Shakespeare, Homer, the Bible, *Huckleberry Finn*. With the white hunters and the porters, and a team from the Smithsonian, he moved out from the base camp in the Kapiti Plains, in British East Africa, and pushed on into the interior, into Uganda. The land of sleeping sickness and the fever tick, he called it. He was in a passion to kill a lion, and, very quickly, he did. He bagged an elephant and a giraffe, a bongo, a dik-dik, a kudu, and a klip-springer. But as the weeks turned into months, he grew homesick for Edith, and wrote this to her—

> *Oh, sweetest of all sweet girls, last night I dreamed that I was with you, that our separation was but a dream; and when I waked up it was almost too hard to bear. Well, one must pay for everything; you have made the real happiness of my life; and so it is natural and right that I*

440

should constantly [be] more and more lonely without you.
. . . Darling I love you so. . . . How very happy we have
been these last twenty-three years.

It was Nora Abernooth who had called Theo's attention
to the letter, having found it in a book of letters, and he
in turn showed it to María Gracia, who thought it charm-
ing, lovely, adorable, but something from another age. He
shared it, later, with Maggie Sowle and she fell in love
with it, liking it so much that she copied it in ink onto a
panel in a quilt that she was working on at the time. It
was the quilt that Muhta Saad had purchased from the
Griffin Gallery, and she was glad, now, that he had
returned it to her after their brief and disappointing
affair.

The quilt in question, *Blue Feathers and Memory*, was
a small one, three feet by five, and when Theo last saw
Maggie, only a few days ago, she was working on it again,
incorporating it into a much larger piece that was going
to hang in the Capitol, in Washington.

The new piece was large, with birds in it, and many
pairs of feet. The feet were the feet of George Washington
at Valley Forge, and the feet of the Cherokees on the Trail
of Tears, when they were force-marched from Georgia to
the territory that is now Oklahoma. They were the feet of
Meriwether Lewis and William Clark, who led the over-
land expedition to the Pacific, and the feet of Tom
Thumb dancing at the American Museum. And the feet
of the ones who died at Gettysburg. But mostly, she
explained to Theo, when she showed him what she had
done so far, the feet were the feet of Henry, her poor dead
Henry who had walked the earth for a while and was no
longer around—his feet in the many different moments
of his feet, morning and night, at rest and in motion, and
after a long walk, needing a massage.

"I've already memorialized his hands," she said to
Theo, "so why not his feet?"

"What about me?" he asked. "Can some of those feet be
my feet?"

441

"Yes, why not," she answered. "What size shoe do you wear?"

On Esopus Island, exhausted from his long day of paddling upriver, he puts his notebook and the flashlight back into his knapsack and stretches out on the flat rock he'd been sitting on, lying there now in his sleeping bag, gazing at the stars. So many up there, so far away and wonderful. The constellations. Orion, the Great Bear, Virgo, Gemini. And what he thinks, as he closes his eyes, is that he must remember to write to Maggie and tell her that what her new quilt needs is some stars, bunches of them, amid all those magnificent feet. The feet of Mae West, and the dancing feet of Gene Kelly, and the feet of Abraham Lincoln, whose legs were too long for the bed they put him on when he was dying, and his feet hung out over the end. The stars will make a difference, and maybe, he thinks, as he drowses off, perhaps when he reaches the Pacific, he'll give her a call.

Part Three

And Jonah was in the belly of the fish three days and three nights . . . Then Jonah prayed unto the Lord his God out of the fish's belly, and said, I cried by reason of mine affliction unto the Lord, and he heard me; out of the belly of hell cried I, and thou heardest my voice.

—JONAH 1:17, 2:1,2

The Birthday of
Muhta Saad

Farro Fescu is still there at Echo Terrace, aging but
immutable, anchored, sturdy, a fixture at the desk. His
hair has begun to turn and he colors it black, and, in
his way, he is as solemn as ever, given to gloom, yet he
remains hardworking and diligent, focused on details,
and attentive, alert to everyone's needs.

At the desk, the computer is now a Pentium IV, and
Farro Fescu's files grow like thickets, files inside files
that link to files that are nested in other files. Job assign-
ments for Oscar's work crew, memos to and from the
board, and, most of all, information on the residents. Not
just work numbers and e-mail addresses, but hat size,
belt size, favorite dessert. Religious persuasion and
sexual preference. Lovers. Ailments. Foreign connections. Net worth. Hold Mrs. Snow's mail at the desk,
she hates going to the mail room. A limo for the
Klongdorfs, a city map for Mrs. Sandbar. And the many
presents that come his way at Christmastime, twenty-
year-old Black Label from Vogel, fruit baskets from Mrs.
Marriocci, gift certificates from Tattafruge. But never
the surprises that Renata Negri used to give him, the
cufflinks, the diamond tie clip, the Cossack hat made
from the fur of a Siberian wolf. What a delight she was,
and how he wishes she were still alive.

He's had his operation, the penectomy, and has
survived it physically and emotionally. It had been a
devastating thing for him, having his penis cut away to
remove the cancer, but the operation was successful, and

the fortunate thing is not just that the cancer cells had been reachable but that the surgeon had been able to leave an inch of the penis intact, enabling him to perform his urinary functions without a catheter. And, when he is so inclined, he is even capable of sexual activity, though of an obviously diminished nature. Sex, however, is no longer a major item for him, and he recognizes now that, except for certain desperate moments in his past, it never really was. He has never married, never kept a steady woman, has no children, and has adjusted to the idea that life has its own inescapable rhythms. When one is on in years, as he now is, the tempo slows, and the pulse is no longer the pounding beat of a samba.

Vogel too is still there at Echo Terrace, as are Theo Tattafruge and Maggie Sowle. And Abdul and Angela, with their four-year-old daughter, Emmie. But Abdul's parents have moved on to a house in Glen Cove, on Long Island, and most of the others are gone as well—the Coyles, the Lustlumbers, the Rosens, the Knatchbulls, blown away like leaves in the wind. Rabbi Ravijohn is in his grave, and Aki Sato is at a nursing facility, recovering from an operation on his gall bladder. And Juanita Blaize, whose hip-hop career continues to soar, has departed to an apartment in the Dakota, by Central Park, though she spends most of her time at a ranch in Wyoming.

Luther Rumfarm, buying up the units as they come available, now owns all but a handful of the residences, leasing them to the young trainees coming into the financial district. Over twenty of them are now at Echo Terrace, connected with First Liberty, Fukuoka Bank, Lehman Brothers, Cantor Fitzgerald, Deloitte and Touche. Into stocks and bonds and insurance and banking, learning the trade. It's a compelling view, the river and the bay and the Statue of Liberty, and a leisurely short walk to the Trade Center, where most of them work, and now it's the right weather too, the worst heat of the summer gone and a hint of autumn on the way. No subway, no car, just that easy early-morning river-fresh stroll to the office in the sky. And the sky, here, is everything, it's what you live for—lift, rise, climb, shun the low ground and scramble to the top, because if you're not at the top, where are you and who are you—and when?

Rumfarm is no longer thinking about installing a waterfall in the lobby. His ambition now is to tear the place down and develop a tower three times as tall. He's already talked about it with city planning and has begun to explore financial options. It's a nervous time, the markets sagging and hints of a recession, but real estate is still spiraling up, and he thinks it's time to push on with it. He envisages thirty-three floors, with a Vermont granite sheathing, pinkish brown, and windows with a blue tint, answering the gray-blue of the river.

Having, as he now does, a controlling vote in the run of the building, he could easily dump Farro Fescu, as he's often wanted to do, because there has never been anything between them but ill will and mutual contempt. But he's kept him on because he rather enjoys lording it over the old man, telling him what to do and not do, and where to get off. And besides, the young ones, the trainees, seem, for some strange reason, to be fond of him—and anything, of course, to keep the customers happy.

The crack in the subbasement was repaired years ago, at considerable cost and with plenty of disruption. Noise and dust, big trucks on the street, and the pounding of heavy machinery as bad cement was ripped out and steel supports were tied in as reinforcements. But recently, only a year ago, the crack reasserted itself—nothing so large as it had been, but a teasing reminder, threading its way through the subbasement. Farro Fescu visits it periodically, checking its slow growth as it evolves and develops.

Karl Vogel, on the eighth floor, continues to take his long walk every day, even in inclement weather, attributing his good health to the walks, and to the many oranges that he consumes daily. Whenever he shops, he still leaves an orange at Farro Fescu's desk, and Farro Fescu, suffering always from excessive acid in his digestive tract, drops the orange into the wastebasket as soon as Vogel heads for the elevator.

Vogel is at work on another memoir about his World War II experiences, but the writing moves slowly, and he begins to doubt that he will ever finish. There are images in his memory that float to the surface, and he feels a need to set them down, to preserve them and lock them in place. He wants these images to live beyond him, to survive and have a life of their own. But is it really necessary, he wonders. Is it of any importance that he finish this book? Or is his daily routine of putting words and memories on paper simply a subtle form of compulsive behavior? He would stop, if he could, but nothing else gives as much pleasure, so he writes, and writes, because what else is there to do?

Returning from a long walk along the river, in and out among the tall buildings, he says to Farro Fescu, "2001— that was a movie, wasn't it? or a book? Ten, twenty years ago?"

Farro Fescu remembers the film vaguely, far back, some thirty years, depicting a future world that was, in his recollection, nothing like the world today.

"People should never try to predict the future," he says.

Mrs. Marriocci passes through the lobby, and no, she doesn't remember the film at all. Then Maggie Sowle comes off the elevator, and she does remember, because it had such powerful visual images. But it was science fiction, and sci-fi, she says, is not her thing, it gives her an uneasy over-the-edge feeling, leaving her disoriented and off balance.

She lives yet on the fourth floor, in the Helen Keller, and has recently bought into a loft in SoHo, where she has much more room to work on her quilts. It's what Henry had always been urging her to do, and finally she's done it. Poor Henry, she still misses him, and needs him, though the image has faded slightly, and, although she still visits the grave in Green-Wood, he is no longer the overwhelming presence that he was in the years immediately after his death. Nevertheless, he is still there for her, a barely perceptible summer breeze coming off the river.

Not since her brief fling with Muhta Saad, the spice merchant, has she been with a man, and she feels comfortable about that, spending her days sewing, talking by phone with clients, with galleries across the country, with museum curators, and giving interviews, showing her work and talking about it at the colleges. For companionship she goes to Tattafruge, talking, enjoying his odd-angled view of the world. She likes his fussiness about properly brewed tea, and his passion for Vivaldi. But such a weird profession—the implants, the sex changes. Sometimes she goes walking with Karl Vogel and can barely keep pace with him. So old he is, and still such energy and vigor. And there are men at the gallery who take her to dinner, but it's only friendship, and always in a group, and she finds, on the whole, that it's better that way, simpler and easier.

She has a work arrangement with Yesenia, who sews for her at the SoHo loft three days a week, and sometimes more. The baby, Marissa Marie, is now eight years old, and Maggie foots the bill to put her through a private school in Queens. It had looked, for a while, that something might be brewing for Yesenia and Muddy Dinks, but that has slackened off, and Yesenia still lives with her mother, on Jamaica Avenue, overlooking the el. What Maggie likes about Yesenia is her freshness, her openness, her easy, homespun vitality. And she sews so well. Maggie takes her with her to the galleries, and to the tailors, where they pick up scraps for the quilts.

Muddy Dinks is still on Oscar's cleaning crew, along with Blue and Smoke and Chase, and the woman Zegroba, who does Tattafruge's apartment, but she is always so grim, he misses the time when it was Yesenia who came with the duster and the vacuum cleaner.

Tattafruge too, yes, still there at Echo Terrace. Eight years since he went off in his canoe, up the Hudson, hoping never to stop until he reached the West Coast, but he made it only as far as Pennsylvania, and it was a struggle to paddle that far. The pains in his muscles, the aches in his back, in his shoulders, his arms, nothing but sheer will power driving him on. Past Albany and on to Troy, then west along the main line of the Erie Canal, lifting through the locks, all the way to Buffalo and down into Lake Erie.

And as he went, he had Vivaldi with him, every day, earphones on his head. On the Hudson, an assortment of violin concertos, including *The Four Seasons, Pleasure, The Hunt,* and *Storm at Sea,* the last of which, he reflected, might prove a bad omen. But he was a doctor, a man of science, not given to superstition, and he didn't trouble himself with portents, except to be amused by them. Along the Mohawk, by Rotterdam Junction, an oboe concerto, and in the stretch between Syracuse and Rochester, several concerti for flute and mandolin. Coming through Tonawanda, a bassoon concerto, and as he passed Buffalo, on the way into Lake Erie, a concerto for double winds.

He slept at night in his blanket on grassy slopes by the water, and grabbed coffee and fast food from cafeterias and diners along the way. On Lake Erie, he followed the coast past Lackawanna and Angola, past Farnham and Silver Creek and Dunkirk, Van Buren and Barcelona, and as he came onto Ripley, near the Pennsylvania border, he was hit by a squall and the canoe capsized, and he was fished out of the water by a couple on a small yacht, who were on their honeymoon.

Except for his wallet and the clothes on his back, everything was lost—the canoe, his duffel, his Vivaldi tapes, his maps, the notebook in which he had jotted down his impressions and thoughts, and, hardest to accept, the thermos containing the five embryos, Nora's eggs mated to his sperm, from which he had hoped a son would be born to replace the son taken from him by Estelle. The honeymoon couple brought him on to Pennsylvania, to a berth in Harborcreek, and left him there, and he sat on the pier weeping. Nothing about him, he realized, no aspect of his life, was anything that could be described as normal. The thinness of his body, and the narrow face with the squeezed-together look, the eyes so close, the skull narrow. And the odd way he had of making a living, performing sex changes on people who believed they had been born with the wrong genitalia. Even in having a breakdown he was abnormal—and what else was this, his mad journey in a canoe, with a thermos full of embryos, but a form of nervous collapse? Other people screamed, overdosed, broke windows, hurled themselves in front of subway trains—but him, he slips off in a canoe and sets out for the West, imagining he will find someone in California, a surrogate mother waiting for him to implant an embryo in her womb. What else was this but moon-madness?

It was over. He was past it. He had nearly drowned, and the experience had snapped him out of it, yanking him awake from a foggy dream. He had a son in Seattle that he had to live for, and he knew now that one way or another he must see more of him. Know him better. Must pull himself together and put his life in order. He hitched a ride to Erie, took a hotel, cleaned himself up, shaved his heavy growth of beard, bought himself new clothes, and returned to his practice in New York, on East Sixty-ninth, where his partner, Lal Chakravorti, wasn't entirely happy to see him, because he had run off so unpredictably, and Lal had had to scramble to keep things afloat. Nevertheless, he was back, doing what he knew how to do, the liposuctions and the sex changes, and he felt a quaint contentment as he picked up again with the old routine. But he was unhappy about returning to Echo Terrace, feeling once again, as a few years ago, when Estelle had left, that a new apartment in a fresh location might be a help. He was thinking of something uptown, near the park, and thought he might take up horseback riding.

But now, eight years later, he is still where he was. Habit has gotten the better of him, and though he's made many forays uptown, looking for a place, he is still

451

downtown in Battery Park City. But still he looks, and looking has become a hobby, something to do. Sometimes he brings Maggie Sowle along, and sometimes he goes with María. And he enjoys it, seeing other people's apartments, the way they live, the furniture, the view from the windows, the fixtures. He checks out apartments at the Ansonia and the Eldorado. The Normandy. The Dakota.

Sometimes, when he apartment-hunts with Maggie, he imagines he is married to her and having an affair with María. And when he's with María, it's the other way around, imagining he's married to her and having an affair with Maggie. But with Maggie there is never any sex, because he feels, somehow, it's better that way, and he senses, suspects, that she thinks so too.

In the apartment at Echo Terrace, the place in the living room where he used to keep the canoe is a problem. It's an emptiness, a forlornness, he doesn't know what to put there. A piano won't do, nor would an easel with a painting in a gold frame. He's tried jardinières with dried grasses and flowers, but they didn't seem right. Perhaps an antique harpsichord, or a cello. He misses the canoe, feels its slow, mournful resonance, and misses too that misty morning on the Sepik River, in Papua New Guinea, when he first saw the canoe and knew he had to bring it home. How full of meaning that morning was. It stays with him as a place of wholeness, a place where he felt more right about life than at any other time that he can remember. He would go back, to see the river again, and thinks often of doing it, but fears that a second look might tilt something inside him and spoil the good feeling.

And Angela and Abdul—they too, still here in Manhattan, between the two rivers, the window of their apartment fronting on the Hudson, and, in the opposite direction, an easy walk to South Street, where the Brooklyn Bridge lurches high above the East River and descends into Brooklyn.

After the wedding, Angela sold her aunt's apartment,

and they bought into the two-bedroom apartment vacated by the Swannholds—the Isadora Duncan, on the sixth floor. And a month later, when Abdul had his license in hand, he set up a funeral parlor on Spring Street, in SoHo. His father helped with the financing, though he had done his best to discourage Abdul about Spring Street, considering it not a promising location. But Abdul insisted, thinking it ideal, with Tribeca to the south, Chinatown and Little Italy and the Lower East Side to the east and southeast, and the Village to the north. And all the corporate people in the Trade Center and the Financial Center, with whom he could do advanced planning, with services and burial farmed out to undertakers in any location of their choice. Advanced planning was the coming thing, with all the options, arrangements made worldwide, twenty-four hours, seven days a week, design your own ceremony, ashes scattered anywhere, all major credit cards honored. And besides, Spring Street has the handy parking garage and the restaurants, mourners can visit their beloved without a hassle and dine at their leisure.

Angela makes a joke about the preplanning. "Buy now, die later," she says.

Well, yes, that's what it is. Abdul smiles. She knows how to amuse. How could he live without her? Still, he is serious about this, the need for a comfort level when dealing with death, the consolation that comes of knowing that everything is arranged and you don't have to stick your relatives with the bill. That's important, he thinks. The comfort of knowing. So he goes out to them, to the ones who respond to his flyers, and meets with them in their homes and places of business, where they feel at ease, because who would want to walk into a funeral parlor to plan for the death that you hope—and maybe imagine—will never come? For anyone over sixty, he guarantees today's prices. Younger, he has a scale, and throws in free limo service as an inducement.

Angela has another contract at the studio in Long Island City, doing a film. She never should have taken that role as a tiger in the children's feature. After that came another animal film in which she was a talking zebra, and now they have her as an alligator, and she isn't happy about that at all. She's thinking of going back to work in the theater. Fritz Kovner, who had directed her in *The Jew of Malta*, is back in New York, putting together a sequence of Greek plays, and he wants her as Medea. But it's a hard thing for her, because Medea kills her children, and Angela isn't sure she can do that, put herself into that kind of a mental space.

Today, Tuesday, it's Abdul's father's birthday. Muhta Saad, turning fifty-nine. For Abdul, it's a busy time. He has a wake in the afternoon, starting at four and continuing through the evening. And early, eight in the morning, an appointment at the Trade Center, in the South Tower, with a patent attorney who wants to preplan a funeral for his mother-in-law, who is close to death but not yet there. Then, after the attorney, he'll stop at his father's office, before moving on to Spring Street. His birthday, can't let it pass without seeing him. He occupies a suite in the North Tower, where he keeps a small staff, a traffic manager, an accountant, two secretaries. Most of the work is fax and telephone. Abdul has bought for him a box of cigars, at De La Concha on Sixth Avenue, top-of-the-line stuff that he knows his father will appreciate. Three hundred dollars, a box of San Cristobals.

So first to the patent attorney, then his father, then on to Spring Street to prepare for the wake at four. His assistant, Peter Chen, will already be there, setting out the floral arrangements as they arrive and supervising the maid. The rugs, the dusting, the bathrooms, the smoking room in the back, everything to be neat and clean, impeccable, nothing out of place.

Between Abdul and his father, there is a quiet uneasiness that never goes away, and Abdul has come to understand that this is the way it will be. At certain times the uneasiness is worse than at others. There are tense moments and stabbing remarks. Other times, it's something that is simply there, under the surface, lurking silently. His father has been good to him, and Abdul is grateful for that. He's been generous with money, always helpful and supportive. But he was so angry when Abdul didn't join him in the spice trade, and even angrier when Abdul announced he was going to become a funeral director. "Death is bad enough," his father said, "but to choose it, to embrace it as a profession? Where have I gone wrong? Have I been a bad father? Is that it? I neglected you?" And Abdul saw that his father interpreted his decision as being, somehow, an act of defiance, a rebellion against home, family, everything wholesome, against life itself. Choosing death.

And then, on top of that, he comes home with Angela, a Christian girl, part Italian and part something else, Irish, Norwegian, not an ounce of Arab blood in her. And again Abdul knew what his father was thinking—she is pretty, yes, and talented, but such a woman, an actress, do you marry her? You take her out, you buy her presents, you bring her to dinner in a hotel. He actually said that, something like that. You enjoy her and treat her well, but you don't lose your mind and marry such a person. That's what he said, and Abdul never forgave him.

When his father introduced him to the director of the Bank of Kinki, he said, with casual malice, "This is my son, Abdul. His wife, you know, is an actress. She plays talking animals in the movies." Just like that, making Abdul feel crummy, as if Angela were a joke.

The Bank of Kinki is on the eighty-seventh floor. Abdul's father is on the fifty-first. When he introduced Abdul to the general manager of the Arab Chamber of Commerce, five floors below, he said, "This is my son, the undertaker. He buries people of all persuasions, though he specializes, mainly, in Episcopalians. Isn't that correct, Abdul? He also handles Quakers, Catholics, and Seventh Day Adventists. He lost his prayer rug when he went away to college, but at heart he's still a good Muslim."

Abdul chafes, he suffers. Nevertheless, he does his best, rolling with the punches. Because, after all, your father is your father, your *baba,* and your mother is your mother. They gave you life. If not for them, where would you be? Would you exist? So he swallows his pride and does what he can. He visits them in the house in Glen Cove, on the north shore, bringing the baby, little Emmie, four years old already. The house is a big beast of a thing, old, requiring attention, but his father has no gift for hiring carpenters, so Abdul helps out, hiring repairmen and overseeing the work, and doing the small things himself. He changes the faucet in the kitchen and hangs a new chandelier in the dining room. They should have stayed where they were, at Echo Terrace. He pulls out dead bushes in the garden, and plants pachysandra. Do it, do it. He's handy in ways that his father never was. Keep mellow, he thinks. Fix what you can. Mow the lawn. Plant azaleas. Think of Rumi. The poet Sadi. Think of Walt Whitman. *Urge and urge and urge, Always the procreant urge of the world. . . . And to die is different from what any one supposed, and luckier.*

On the morning of his father's birthday, Tuesday, he's up early, on his way to the eight-o'clock with the patent attorney. It's a clear, warm day, in the seventies, maybe shooting to the eighties, unseasonable, but a lazy breeze blowing, lifting the flag on the pole by the river walk. A man in a green sport shirt sits by the railing, eating a donut, gazing at the river as if he owns it. A woman in white, pushing a baby carriage, and a girl in blue, taking five dogs for their morning walk.

"Eight-thirty," he'd told his father the night before. "Plan on eight-thirty, eight forty-five. As soon as I'm done with the patent attorney." His father is usually at his desk before eight, except when he has jet lag from traveling.

The plaza at the Trade Center is crowded, people still arriving for work, the chefs, the waiters, the attorneys, the janitors, accountants, secretaries, and many, like himself, visiting, doing business—or just on tour. Four nuns by the fountain, snapping pictures of the bronze globe, with disposable cameras. Close by, a bandstand has been set up, and hundreds of chairs, for an afternoon entertainment. Nice, he thinks, music. A baby is crying. A group of Germans hover by Rosati's *Ideogram*, their German-speaking guide using both hands, etching in air the angles and rhythms of the sculpture. And up ahead, stepping into the South Tower, a flock of Mennonites, and he wonders—a Mennonite convention at Dean Witter? Or Charna Chemicals?

At the security check-in, in the lobby, on the line next to his, he spots three girls in halters and hip-hugger jeans, belly buttons pierced by gold ornaments. One is very short, and one is tall, tough-looking, with heavy black eyebrows and bobbed hair, and a long nose that looks as if it had been broken more than once. The third, pretty, noticing his gaze, opens her mouth, displaying a silver button in her pierced tongue. On her left arm, up by her shoulder, she sports a tattoo, a rose with red petals.

He's handled corpses with tattoos, quite a few, both women and men. Truckers, retired sailors, a hair-dresser, a dentist, a woman who had been a vice president at Time-Life. A month ago he had a skinhead who'd been killed on a motorcycle, his scalp tattooed with a skull and crossbones. And a month earlier, a seventy-nine-year-old Chinese woman with a butterfly on her left ankle, and on her right thigh the name DAVE.

The security guard, not satisfied with the X ray, fusses into his briefcase, his big black bag almost as large as a carry-on. Puts her hands into everything, the picture guide for the coffins, the brochure for the urns, the hand-size computer on which he makes his calculations. She points to the gift-wrapped cigars and asks him to unwrap the package. He does, and after eyeing the box and the seal, she sends him on. He pauses at a table, rewraps the box quickly but not well, and catches the express elevator that the three girls are boarding.

Where do they belong, he wonders. Fuji Bank? Empire Health? He doesn't think so. Showtime Pictures? He's about to ask, but it would seem rude, and in any case, here he is already at the seventy-eighth, where he switches to a local for the rest of the trip up. The girls leave the elevator too, but he loses them in the lobby, which is one of the sky lobbies, large, with windows and many banks of elevators, and crowded. Maybe they're the band for the bandstand, he thinks, and the Mennonites are the sing-along chorus.

The patent attorney, Futterman, is on the ninety-first, sharing the floor with Raytheon and an engineering group. The view from his office is to the north, with the North Tower and a slice of the Hudson to the left, and, straight ahead, the long length of Manhattan, skyscrapers crowding and reaching, lifting, and the fifty-mile view into the haze of Westchester and Connecticut.

Futterman, at his desk, has his back to the view. "I find it distracting," he says. The desk is teak, the walls lined with floor-to-ceiling bookcases. One wall holds a walk-in safe, the steel doors open, shelves stacked with folders and papers. Futterman has the avid look of a raptor. Tired, aging, but subtle, still with a hungry eye. Hair thin, a mix of black and gray, combed straight back, flat against his scalp. The three-thousand-dollar suit, five-hundred-dollar shoes, two-hundred-dollar shirt. He's sixty-three, but thin, small-shouldered, the facial skin drawn tight across cheeks and jaw. Abdul wonders if Theo Tattafruge worked on his face. He imagines him eating hundred-dollar meals that arrive in small portions on gold-rimmed plates.

His mother-in-law is ninety-three, in a convalescent home, and not expected to live out the year. She's French, and his wife wants her buried in the village where she'd been born, in the south, near Arles.

"You can arrange this? Everything?"

Abdul can do it—the international papers, the shipping, the care at this end and the arrangements over there. He does it as a specialty, arranging funerals out of state and out of country, almost as easy, in the age of Internet, as sending flowers to Alaska, or Saudi Arabia, but with minor complications one has to know how to negotiate.

Abdul takes down the information on the mother-in-law, her age, name, the convalescent home, the cemetery where the interment will take place. It's a long form. Futterman has everything, names, addresses. The telephone number at the convalescent home. The cemetery in France. But then, close to the end, when he is confronted with the casket catalogue, he is suddenly at a loss, unable to make a decision. He studies every picture, every model, then vacillates between the antique gold, which was made of Vermont oak, and the midnight silver, made of steel.

"It's all right," Abdul assures him. "Take your time. If you want, I can bring you to the showroom, it might be easier."

But Futterman doesn't want that, doesn't have the time. He'll work from the catalogue.

"Fine, fine," Abdul says, "it's important to choose one that you feel good about." And then, excusing himself, he steps into the neighboring room to call his father, to let him know he'll be running late.

The receptionist is a brown-haired woman in a tapioca blouse, busy at her computer. Eyeglasses with dark red rims. Abdul stands by a window, the same view to the north as in Futterman's office, and uses his cell phone, ringing his father, but locks onto a busy signal. Close by, on the roof of the North Tower, the transmissions antenna rises thick and tall, over three hundred feet. It's a pole, a pike, a lance. A gigantic phallus, he thinks, long and shameless in the sky. His eyes graze across the skyscrapers to the north and northeast, slabs of black glass, angled walls, the gleaming art deco chrome of the Chrysler Building. And the Empire State, where his parents had brought him when he was nine, but there was a mist, that day, and the view was a disappointment.

He rings his father again, but another busy signal, and he lingers, gazing idly at the swarm of structures out there, tall and huddled, in all their boastful shapes, the thick and the slender, the squat and the lithe, the lean and the muscular. The steeples, cupolas, domes, flat roofs crowded with machinery, or with gardens. A weird, wild, vertical city, everything up and down, hidden elevators soaring and diving, plunging from the clouds in gut-wrenching seconds. A gluttonous density of steel and glass, defying gravity.

He glances over his shoulder, toward the receptionist, catching her profile, a stubby nose and a sagging chin—and then, looking again through the window, he sees, with heart-stopping astonishment, a passenger jet approaching low, roaring toward the towers with a smart, self-assured swiftness. Big and fast, and he freezes, aghast, eyes riveted on the plane, its largeness, speed—and then, incredibly close, wings tilting, almost upon him, it hooks away, out of his line of vision, and slams into the north face of Tower One.

The blast is immense, a fierce explosion ripping through the North Tower, blowing out windows, pieces of glass the size of taxicabs, a visible shiver running up and down the walls. He can't see the north face, where the plane hit, but sees the sudden loops of flame and smoke shooting out from the east wall and the south, near the top, across from where he stands, and now a great fireball ballooning across the short divide between the two towers, reaching toward him, and he feels the heat, it pushes him back, away from the window, a great bulge of red and orange flame.

He hears the receptionist screaming, and the other women, the paralegals. And Futterman shouting. "Out, out! Everybody down. Documents in the safe and go. Don't dawdle. Go!"

Abdul hangs by the window, mesmerized, vaguely aware of footsteps behind him, a wild scurrying. The fireball exhausts itself and draws back, leaving lines of flame scribbling across several floors, and a gush of black smoke cascading like a waterfall, down across the windows below.

Futterman gives him a heavy tap on the shoulder, almost a shove. "Take your things—in my office. And pull the door shut. We'll talk tomorrow."

Abdul is hardly aware of him. He's focused on the fire, worrying for his father, hoping he was in the office when the plane hit, below the fire, not upstairs somewhere having coffee. He calls again, but for a long time no answer, and when his father does pick up, Abdul is relieved to know the phones over there are still working. His father sounds confused.

"Well," he says, "we have some damage."

"Are you okay?"

"I don't know. A bomb went off."

"It was a plane, Baba. An airliner. It hit the tower. Above you. Looks like the top twenty floors are on fire."

"A plane?"

"Baba, get out of the building."

"I know, yes. Right now, I'm going. I was just on the phone with Brazil, they misplaced a shipment, but we'll work it out. You too, go down. We'll meet in the plaza, by the fountain. A filing cabinet fell on Ramirez, he hurt his leg."

"Can he walk?"

"Yusef will help him. We're getting wet here, the pipes are broken."

"Just go," Abdul says. "I'll see you by the fountain."

"I have to call your mother and let her know I'm all right."

"I'll do that. I'll call. You hear? Just go."

"Don't worry, Abdul. You understand? Don't worry about me. Everything will be all right. You mustn't worry. Be sure you leave the building."

Abdul, looking across, watches the fire and the curling smoke. At first the smoke had been rolling down, like a waterfall in slow motion, but now the movement is upward, black smoke pumping through the broken windows, billowing skyward, and he smells it, the odor coming through the ventilation system, the stink of jet fuel burning, and everything else in there, carpets, furniture, leather chairs, and all of the plastics, the resins. And not just smoke coming out of the windows but paper too, thousands of sheets of paper, fluttering,

461

rising on the hot air, blowing out across downtown, a blizzard of paper.

Something falls, and it's a moment before he realizes that it isn't debris, it's a body. Then another, a man in a blue jacket and khaki pants, arms and legs flailing. Then a woman in red pants and a white blouse, and soon after her, a man in a blue shirt, headfirst, arms wrapped around his head, as if, on impact, his arms might shield him from harm.

He watches, astonished, unable to attach a feeling to it. Horror? Dread? Disbelief? The smoke, the bodies falling, like some crazy hell, unreal as a movie but definite, palpable. People are dying. As he watches. Secretaries, janitors, executives, electricians. They are passing out of existence. He buries the dead, that's his job, his profession. He lays them to rest. But never before has he seen a person die. And here it is, happening as he watches, so grim and simple. Falling, they're alive, but when they hit, they're gone. Lost.

They're lined up by the blown-out windows, crowding. Right there, on the upper floors, so close to him, some two hundred feet away. Through the smoky distance, he makes out something of their faces, their hands, their clothes, the color of their hair. The flames are behind them, and with a fierce, anguished clarity, he knows their dilemma. On the floor where the plane exploded, the stairwells and elevators must have been blown to pieces—and no way to get down. The ones above that point are trapped. It's either the smoke and the fire, or out the windows. Even the roof is involved, giving off smoke, making a helicopter rescue impossible. And as he watches, studying the people crowding at the windows, something inside him tears apart, and he lets out a long, low moan, creased by pain and incomprehension, the sound of a broken animal.

Some fall onto the roof of the hotel, the Marriott, and he sees the bodies there. Many more fall into the plaza, where quick-reaction teams are arriving, firefighters with stretchers and oxygen, with axes, but what can they do?

Windows are popping, bursting from the heat of the flames. Three people leap together, holding hands, two women and a man between them. He watches, gripped. And it's almost as if the watching is making it happen, making them fall. A man diving, as if leaping into a pool, and another stepping out calmly, dropping, feet first. A woman in white, with long black hair trailing upward, above her.

It's unbalancing. He feels a warp, a distortion in his emotional field. The real-but-not-real quality of it tricks him, twists him around, and even though he knows these people are dying, it's as if, magically, they are not. It's simply a bad dream, and in a moment everything will be right again. The plane didn't crash. People aren't jumping to their death. His father isn't in a burning building, working his way down the stairs. And he himself—not standing here, on the ninety-first floor of the South Tower, feeling the blast of heat from the North Tower, feeling it right through the thick glass window. It will pass, vanish. Has to. But it doesn't. And he feels guilty, watching, because he's safe, and the ones at the windows, alive and desperate, are only moments away from death.

He turns away and he rings his mother, to tell her not to worry, but the line is busy, and he suspects it's his father on the line, still in the office, wasting precious time. Doesn't he know he has to get out? Doesn't he know? He rings again, the line still busy, and then he phones through to Angela. She's at the studio in Long Island City, rehearsing. She has Emmie and the nanny with her. That's what she does when she works, brings the nanny and Emmie with her, because she can't bear the thought of separation. She rehearses, she works, she acts, and the nanny, a woman from Colombia, is in another room, close by, with Emmie, keeping her happy.

When Abdul tells her about the crash, he can feel her tensing up. The tightening, the worry in her voice.

"I'm all right," he says. "I'm in the South Tower. It's

okay here. I talked to Baba. You have a television there? Turn it on."

"Abdul, get out of there," she says. "And call me when you're down. Will you? Promise? And let me know about Baba."

"I will, I will," he says, expecting he'll be down in a few minutes, on the elevator. He doesn't mention the people jumping. Doesn't mention that he thinks Baba is still in the office, on the phone, and hasn't started down on the stairs yet. Doesn't mention the stink of the smoke coming through the ventilation, catching in his throat, and the heat of the flames, and that he feels everything is beginning to come apart inside him.

"Call me," she says. "Hurry down and call. Please?"

He wonders about his father. Can he handle the long trek down? At a minute a floor, it will take an hour. But if the people on the stairs move fast, maybe a half hour. Can it be done that quickly? He thinks of the fire, how it will spread and, who knows, involve the whole tower. Just keep moving, he thinks, as if thinking can bring his father down sooner. Come down, damn it. Get out.

And he realizes he's alone up there, in the reception room. Futterman is gone, and the women too. He goes into Futterman's office and gathers his things, the papers and brochures into the oversized briefcase, and notices the doors to the safe are closed. He lingers briefly, gazing across at the long ropes of smoke, and the people at the windows. Then tears himself away and heads for the elevator, feeling now a special urgency, wanting to be down in the plaza, near the fountain, waiting, when his father comes through the doors. That's the moment that he wants and needs, to be by the fountain, and his father out of the burning tower, unharmed.

Black Smoke Rising

He rides the local down to the seventy-eighth floor, but when he exits into the big lobby there, he finds a huge mob waiting for the express elevators down. What the hell, he thinks. Damn. He sees a clot of Mennonites in the crowd and wonders if they're the same ones he saw on the way in. And the nuns, the very ones that were by the fountain, four of them. He moves about, assessing, calculating. Could be a long time, waiting. Maybe he should ride a local to the forty-fourth, the next express stop, and hope for better luck there.

A voice comes over the PA, saying the building is secure, everything is under control. There is no need to evacuate. People restless, out of focus. Secretaries, lawyers, headhunters, accountants. What's to believe? Abdul moving, edging slowly, trying to figure it out, and he comes up short in front of the three girls in hip-huggers, the ones he'd seen at the security check-in. They're scared.

"It's all right," he says, trying to reassure them. "We're okay."

"What's okay?" the tough-looking one says, the one with her left eyebrow pierced with red rhinestones.

"Not to worry," he says, "we'll get there. We'll get down." And is aware, as he says it, that he's really trying to reassure himself.

The pretty one, the one who had put her tongue out at him, showing her silver button, just looks at him, a dumb, empty stare, as if to say what do you know about it. And it hits him—maybe she's right. With the other building burning, the power in the whole complex could go, and who would want to be on an elevator then? He imagines groping through the escape hatch and climbing a ladder in the elevator shaft, searching for a way out. Could he do that? And if he skips the elevator and takes the stairs, from this far up it's too long, too long. His father will already be at the fountain, wondering what happened.

He sees the four nuns and the Mennonites, patient, they seem all part of a group, together. And again the announcement, the softly urgent voice saying the fire in the other building has been contained, it's safe to return to the offices. Secretaries and their bosses grumbling, wondering, the paralegals and computer jockeys, the telephone traders. To stay or go. Several board a local for the ride up, back to work.

And then, while he's waiting there, uncertain, in a crowd by the express elevators, rubbing thumb and fore-finger together, a nervous habit that he has, there is a roar and a resounding thump, a powerful explosion, the building rocking and shuddering. He's thrown to the floor, and someone falls on top of him, across his hips. He hears the splash of shattering glass and sees the ceiling opening, light fixtures yanking loose, flickering and dying. Wires stripped, sparks hissing. The doors have been blown off some of the elevator shafts, one lies angled against the wall, a few feet away. Here and there, on the floor and in the ceiling, small fires are burning. One of the elevators is stuck about two feet above level, the doors a few inches open, hands reaching out and struggling, trying to force the doors apart.

In the light filtering through the broken windows, he sees that the person on top of him is a man, his head turned full around, his neck broken. He pushes up from under him and hears a woman saying she can't see. People groaning, whimpering. Someone wailing. Some attempting to move, others immobile, twisted on the floor. Smoke filtering into the lobby, coming through the elevator shafts. The stink of fuel burning.

A uniformed guard, black, husky, blood on his face, is shouting at them to move, get out. "If you can walk, go to the stairs. Move it. Move it. Don't linger."

Abdul fumbles, puts his hand on the briefcase, grabs the handle, and goes to the woman who can't see, blinded by flying glass. But the guard pushes him away. "Go, go," he says. "I'll handle her." He's pushing everyone to the stairs. "Keep moving," he shouts. "There will be others coming down behind you."

The nuns and the Mennonites are calm, composed. One of the Mennonites has blood on his neck. The tall girl with the crooked nose, and the red rhinestones in her eyebrow, is weeping. Not so tough after all, Abdul thinks.

The stairs are lit, an emergency line has kicked in, and the smoke here is less of a problem than it was by the elevators. The descent is rapid, faster than he'd expected. Everyone with a sense of urgency, get down, get down. There are moments when the ones without injuries are skipping down the stairs, though there are slowdowns too, at some of the landings, as people from the lower floors filter in. But many had started their descent earlier, when the North Tower was hit, and here, at least, on this staircase, there is no clogging and the movement is quick.

Some have radios to their ears, listening to the reports.

"What was it? A bomb?"

"Another plane."

"No shit. A plane?"

"How bad?"

"Bad."

An Asian woman is sobbing, blowing her nose.

"Oh, my God, my God," a black woman moans.

But they're moving steadily, most of them, hurrying down. It's not a stampede, but not a crawl either, it's a swift, steady pace, and Abdul is thinking of Angela and hates himself for having told her to turn on the TV, because now she knows the tower's been hit, and she'll panic.

It's hot on the stairs, the air-conditioning is down and already it feels like ninety. He transfers his wallet into his hip pocket and sheds his jacket, stuffing it into the over-sized briefcase, in with the catalogues and brochures, and the box of cigars that he bought for his father. The briefcase, carried by a handle, is awkward on the stairs, knocking into his leg, into other people's legs.

Radio reports pass up and down the stairs. The president confirming now that the crashes are a terrorist attack.

"That's news?" a paunchy man in a pink suit says, his face ruddy with the exertion of the descent. "Did they think it was a practice drill with sound effects?"

Someone mentions Sheikh Omar Abdel-Rahman, the blind Egyptian cleric who'd been tried for conspiracy in the '93 bombing.

"He's in jail," a wispy, brown-haired woman says, with a pointed chin.

"So? That stops him?"

Somebody mentions Ramzi Yousef, who is also in jail. And Eyad Ismoil.

"Damn fuckin' Arabs," the man in pink says, and Abdul wonders if the remark is for his benefit. What's happening? Is the man trying to pick a fight?

The radio tosses up the name of Osama bin Laden.

"Who?"

"The one Clinton shot a cruise missile at, in Afghanistan. It missed."

Down, down they go, steady and quick. Abdul takes his cell phone off his belt and tries to reach Angela, wanting to tell her he's okay. But he can't get through. He tries his father's office and does get through, but no pickup, and that's good—his father is finally out of the office and on his way down. How many times Abdul has told him to get a cell phone, but he resists, hates the new-fangled things, and wouldn't it be handy now. He tries his mother—but, as with Angela, the circuits are clogged.

Many of the women have taken off their shoes, getting rid of the high heels, the flimsy sandals. Carrying them, or stuffing them into their pocketbooks. The man in the pink suit has taken off his pointed-toe suede Italian imports.

"At least this time we have lights in the stairwells," a heavyset woman says, sweating, mopping her face and neck with a handkerchief. She was there in '93, when the stairs were dark and filled with smoke.

But the light is small comfort. Abdul is hot, his collar open, tie pulled down, shirt soaking. The briefcase is too cumbersome. In a spurt of impatience, he takes out the cigars, holding on to the box, and dumps the briefcase in a hallway off the stairs, abandoning everything, the jacket, the catalogues, the glossy photos of coffins and urns, saving only the application form he filled out for Futterman, folding the pages and stuffing them into his hip pocket, next to his wallet. And the box of cigars, clutching it, not letting go. It's not cigars that he's holding but his father, his father's very self, not wanting to lose him, wanting him safe, wanting him down, out of the burning building.

On the fifty-eighth floor, the descent slows. They have to move aside for firefighters on their way up, lugging stretchers, axes, oxygen. Huffing, breathless from the long climb, faces drawn and grim. Abdul glances about. He's lost some people. The three girls in hip-huggers, and the man in the pink suit. Are they up ahead, or far behind? Still going, descending, feeling it in his knees, turning to the left on the landings and then down again, left and down, wafts of smoke drifting through, not bad, but bad enough. He feels unmoored, mechanical, a vague dizziness. People coughing, wheezing. Grunting. The heavyset woman who was glad for the lights steps aside on one of the landings, giving herself a breather. As Abdul passes her, he sees how limp she is, resigned, as if making up her mind that it isn't worth the rest of the trip down.

He tries Angela again but still can't get through. And still he carries the cigars, the wrapping paper torn and sooty.

On the forty-fourth floor, a man with a bullhorn is telling everyone not to worry, the fire is confined to the upper floors. He urges them to move quickly but carefully, not to trip on the stairs.

On the thirty-ninth, there's a commotion, some shouting, and the descent slows to a halt. Two women are at the door to the landing, one with thick glasses, the other with ash-blue hair. They have an elderly woman in a wheelchair.

The man in the pink jacket is there, telling them in a raised, quavering voice that they have to leave her. The firefighters will bring her down on a stretcher.

"We can't leave her," the one with ash-blue hair says.

"Then stay with her," the man in pink says, pushing past and continuing down.

The line moves again, but slowly, the wheelchair blocking the way. The woman with ash-blue hair is shouting, waving her arms. "We can't just leave her! We can't! Can't!"

The woman in the wheelchair stares emptily. She's gray-haired and hollow-cheeked, eyes sunken, yet in her gaze there is a quiet alertness, a sense of danger. She's aware of what's happening.

Abdul pushes on down to the landing, wanting to get the line moving again. "I'll take her," he says, and awkwardly, still gripping the box of cigars, he reaches down and picks her up, and swings her over his shoulder, like a child. She's light, skin and bone, large dark age spots on her hands and arms.

"Are you okay, Helen?" the woman with thick glasses asks.

"I'm fine, thank you," the old woman says.

Abdul, in trouble with the cigars, asks the old woman if she can hold them.

"If you promise not to drop me," she says, "I'll promise not to lose your package."

There is a spry energy in her voice, but to Abdul, carrying her, she seems frail and vulnerable, and it crosses his mind that by the time they reach bottom, she might not still be alive. He imagines her an unlucky tourist, visiting the towers on the wrong day. But when he asks where she's from, she says she's an accountant. She's with the Aaron Copland Music Fund, thirty-ninth floor. Right next to the Koussevitzky Foundation, and she sometimes works for them too, she says.

And that surprises him. At her age? Still on the job?

"Why not?" she says.

Yes. Why not?

"I need an accountant," he says. "You want to work for me?"

"What sort of business are you in?"

"I'm an undertaker."

"Oh, God," she says, "I'm not dead yet. Is there someone else can take me down?"

She's light, but after he's carried her ten floors, he feels the strain. Still, he keeps moving, descending as fast as he can, despite his burden.

"If you work for me," he says, "I'll give you full benefits. Health insurance, pension, social security. And funeral arrangements at cost."

"I think I'll stay with Aaron Copland," she says.

When they reach the lobby, an emergency worker takes her from Abdul and puts her on a stretcher. She's still holding the cigars and hands them back to Abdul. "Thank you," she says, unsmiling. "You're a very kind man. I do hope you get home safely."

"I hope we both will," he says.

The lobby, crowded with people coming out of the stairwells, is a mess, windows smashed, marble panels shattered. The escalators are immobilized. Doors have been blown from some of the elevators, ripped by the power of the blast as it vented itself and sent jet fuel exploding through the elevator shafts. He sees a charred man with most of his clothes burned off, and a woman holding out her hands, her fingertips melted.

An officer is warning people not to exit onto the plaza, he points to other ways to go out. And when Abdul looks, he sees why. The plaza is littered with torsos and body parts, arms and legs scattered amid the debris, amid chunks of concrete and shattered glass, and the things

471

people dropped as they ran, purses, shoes, briefcases. Especially by the North Tower, many bodies there, the bodies of jumpers. And now others are running, from the North Tower and other buildings, and dropping things, satchels and laptops.

The bandstand by the fountain has been smashed, and many of the chairs have been toppled. He sees plane parts out there, pieces of metal, and pieces of luggage. And there too, among the chairs, he sees broken bodies. The people who fell from the plane, he thinks. Or maybe these were people who were hurled out of their offices when the plane hit. And everywhere there are sheets of paper, blown from the building by the blast, paper on the ground, and paper still in the air. And, in the distance, the wide fountain surmounted by a big bronze globe, Fritz Koenig's *Sphere*, vivid and large, more than twenty feet in diameter, and boldly golden. He scans the five-acre plaza, the buildings at the perimeter, the Marriott to his left, and the North Tower, the Customs House at the northwest corner and Building 5 at the northeast, and closer by, Building 4, with the Cotton Exchange and the Board of Trade, and Gemelli's, where he brought Angela for dinner once. He searches, peering into the smoky air, but doesn't see his father.

He puts the cigar box under his shirt, under his left arm, securing it there, and heedless, with furious intent, he steps through the door and runs, heading for the fountain, halfway across the plaza, sprinting past a de-capitated body, and a pair of shoes with feet in them, pieces of bone showing above the laces. An arm. A leg. A head. Two bodies crushed together, a grotesque merging of trunks and limbs—one, a fireman, hit on the ground by a falling body, someone in a white suit. And before he is quite away from the tower, two more fall, just behind him, the horrible *thrrrmmp*, *thrrrmmp*, like no other sound he knows.

His father isn't at the fountain, and he is nowhere else that Abdul can see. After standing there a moment, watching as others come running, he starts toward a bookstore, close by, at the corner of the plaza, thinking his father may have sheltered there when the second plane hit. But a policeman shouts him away.

"I'm looking for my father," Abdul says.

"If you don't see him here, maybe he's across the street by the Millenium. They set up a triage center there. But you don't wanna be here, it ain't safe. We're clearing the area. You should check on Vesey, the American Express, they're using it for a morgue."

Abdul doesn't go to the morgue. He heads right out to Church Street, along the eastern edge of the plaza, crowded with emergency vehicles. All along the street, knots of people linger, looking up, watching the towers as they burn. The big holes where the planes crashed in. Not just the bankers and traders and secretaries who have just come running out, but people from the shops and eateries in the concourse, the ones who scooped ice cream for Ben and Jerry's, and sold CDs at Sam Goody's. From the coffee shops and pizza takeouts. Lingering, amazed and gaping. Black smoke darkening the sky, the stink of combustion.

On the curb, a young man, twentyish, hair caked with blood, smokes a cigarette, hands trembling. A few feet away, a middle-aged woman who had come barefoot through the glass, her feet bleeding. And a heavyset woman, asthmatic, having a hard time breathing, using an inhalator.

Abdul crosses the street, heading for the hotel, the Millenium, where medical teams have set up a triage out front, along Church Street, between Fulton and Dey. The area is filled with stretchers and gurneys, doctors and nurses moving among the patients. Burn victims and people slashed by flying glass, and some who lost limbs. People bleeding. And only as he crosses the street, making his way through the hoses and a tangle of emergency vehicles, does he notice, for the first time, that the Millenium misspells its name, one *n* instead of two, and why had he never seen that before? And strange, he thinks, completely weird, to be aware of such a thing, so trivial, so empty, in this time of so much suffering and death.

He approaches a paramedic, thickset, thirtyish, with a moustache.

"Is there a list?"

"Well, sort of," the paramedic says, pointing to a woman in a yellow blouse and blue pants, a clipboard under her arm. A pencil in her upswept hair.

Abdul gives the woman his father's name, spelling it out. She scans the list, but the name isn't there.

"It isn't completely accurate," she says apologetically. "We've sent a lot on to St. V's and NYU Beekman. And we have another triage at the Chelsea Piers. If he doesn't turn up, you might try those."

"You have the numbers?"

"Oh, I don't think you'll get through on the phone. I just tried St. V's, and the lines are down. Even if you get a pickup, there's such confusion."

He spends a moment scanning the gurneys and stretchers, looking for his father, hoping. There is a woman with deep burns on her legs, and another with one side of her face melted away. A man whose shirt and pants are rags, wet with blood. A man with his arm severed at the elbow, and many with faces and arms cut by glass. A woman praying the rosary, her lips moving silently. A man groaning. A small, wispy man blinded by glass, saying, quietly, "Where am I, what's happening? Somebody talk to me. Talk to me. Why is it dark?"

"Pray," says the woman on the stretcher next to his.

"Why? Why should I pray?"

"Because terrible things are happening."

"What things? Tell me."

"Prayer makes it easier," she says.

Abdul notices a man with no feet, and another with burns all over his body, waiting for transfer to one of the hospitals. A woman with her lips burned away, teeth and gums showing grotesquely, as in some twisted, feverish nightmare. There was a woman walking about, in a blue dress, carrying a parakeet in a cage, looking for her mother. "She has white hair. Have you seen a woman with white hair and a sweater?" And a man, a tourist from Kansas, looking for his wife. "One minute I saw her, the next she was gone. I can't believe it. Where is she?"

Abdul moves away and hovers at the corner, where Dey Street meets Church, thinking he should double back and look again by the fountain. Maybe his father is just getting down. Maybe. But just then, as he stands there, gazing at the towers in flames, he hears an earsplitting roar and sees the South Tower in a kind of convulsion, the top of it trembling, beginning to fall.

In a great burst and flutter, everyone is running. Abdul leaps down Dey, with a herd of firefighters, away from Church Street and the plaza, toward Broadway, anywhere, east, away from the thundering collapse that roars in his head like an engine, each floor pancaking down onto the floor below, fast, sudden, fierce, windows bursting, steel and concrete wrenching loose and plunging, a blizzard of rubble. He glances back, running, sees it and runs harder, past a man kneeling in the street, arms uplifted in prayer, and a woman clinging to a lamppost, small groups huddled in doorways—the tower imploding, a vast cascade of debris tumbling in a downward rush, and then a huge, boiling cloud, hot with a hellish stink, racing and reaching toward him, and he thinks this is it, he won't beat it, this is how it happens, and already he's choking, sucking smoke and soot into his throat. The cloud, slamming hard, lifts him and tosses him, throws him to the ground, and as he falls, he has a sense of others falling all around him. And then, as the cloud rolls over him, there is only darkness, black density. His eyes burn, as if stung with pepper, and he tastes the soot, it's in his mouth, he's eating it, and he knows that what had seemed many long minutes was merely seconds, and he hasn't run very far at all.

And the other thing he knows is that somehow he's managed, through all of this, to hold on to his father's cigars, the box still there under his shirt, clasped to his body by his left arm, and he takes it as a sign, knowing he must cling to the box and never let go.

In the darkness, a man at a distance is shouting. "It's toxic, don't breathe. If you breathe, you'll die."

And if you don't breathe, what then?

Keep moving, he thinks, forcing himself up, onto his feet, groping in the dark. Get out of it. He stumbles against a parked car, then makes his way around it. He has the top of his shirt up over his mouth and nose, but it's no help, he's gagging. The stuff is in the back of his nose, in his mouth. He's swallowing it. There is no air, nothing to breathe, only the dust, the grit, and small bits of stuff pelting him, hitting his back, his arms, his head. Something heavy punches his left shoulder, and still he presses forward. Then, lacking oxygen, his muscles turn to dough and his legs fold, and again he's on the ground, limp, a rag, eyes burning, all of time and space compressed into this hot volcanic blast that is stealing the breath out of him.

A foot, running past, kicks into him, sending pain through his hip. He lifts an arm and touches nothing. Other feet go by. Then someone with a flashlight is bending over him, pulling, lifting, half carrying and half dragging, advancing through the dark, but he's limp, doesn't want to make the effort, wants to be left there, on the ground, wants not to struggle to breathe anymore. Then he's pulled through a door, out of the darkness and into light. Someone splashes water in his face and wipes the soot away, and someone else hangs an oxygen mask on his face and he's breathing, taking it in, his heart pounding madly against his ribs.

He's on the floor but sitting up, shoulders against a wall. He's in a deli. The fireman leaning over him asks if he's okay, and he nods slowly. His eyes are still burning, but his strength is coming back. Sucking the oxygen, he thinks of the cigars and feels for them. They're still there under his shirt.

The fireman hands him a bottle of water. "Rinse out," he says.

That's what the others are doing, rinsing their mouths and spitting the water onto the floor. Coughing. Grunting, getting the grit out. Washing their eyes.

Abdul pulls away the oxygen and takes the water, squishes it around and spits. All that grit, clearing it out of him. Tilts his head back and runs water up his nose and blows it out, clearing away the pulverized bits of concrete and marble and gypsum and whatever else, getting rid of it, coughing, wheezing, yanking it up from his lungs. Wets a napkin and dabs at his eyes. His clothes are caked with the stuff, white ash, white powder.

It's three firefighters in there, and a blonde in plaid slacks, a guy in jeans and a leather vest, and a cop. All of them covered with gray-white soot, except for the leather vest and the girl in plaid slacks, who had ducked into the store a moment before the tower fell. All of them in a daze, a fuzzy uncertainty. One of the firefighters is stretched out on the floor, by a shelf of pretzels, on his back, gazing emptily toward the embossed tin ceiling. The phone rings, nobody picks it up. It stops ringing. The store clerks have fled. The cop is behind the counter, leaning on his elbows, staring at a bin of bagels. The fireman who dragged Abdul into the store is on the floor, boots off, massaging his feet. He's not old, not young, just over thirty. Abdul looks at him and that's what he thinks, they're the same age. If not for him, he would be dead out there.

And then he sees her, one of the three girls that he had met in the tower, the one with the pierced tongue. She's leaning against the meat counter, white soot covering her hip-huggers and her bare midriff, leaning and sobbing quietly, her face clouded, shadowy. When she sees that he sees her, she nods and continues looking at him, he on the floor and she resting her hip against the glass case with the ham and pastrami in it. Then she's talking to him, through the distance, explaining. "We got separated and I lost them," she says, speaking of the two other girls she was with. "I don't even know if they got out. We stopped to go to the bathroom. When we went back to the stairs, I thought they were right behind me. But a few flights down, when I turned to look, they weren't there."

The phone rings again, and again nobody answers. When it stops, the man in the leather vest picks up the receiver and calls his wife. Then the cop calls home but can't get through. Abdul rings Angela on his cell phone, but the circuits are jammed. He tries calling his mother, but nothing there either.

The firefighter who dragged him in off the street has violet eyes. Two weeks ago Abdul buried someone with the same eyes. He hopes the firefighter will get through the day and have a long life. He hopes that for all of them. For the cop, for the firefighter on his back on the floor, for the woman in plaid slacks and the man in the leather vest. And the girl with the pierced tongue. He thinks of the thousands who may have been in the tower when it fell, and the idea of it, the enormity, is too much to absorb. Outside, the dust cloud is beginning to settle, it seems not as black as before. Men with flashlights are moving about on the street, and he sees them, dim outlines.

"Where's the toilet," he asks.

The cop points to the rear.

He gets up off the floor and explores the back of the store, finding a closet-sized john outfitted with liquid soap and paper towels. He stands long over the toilet bowl, releasing his urine, a long, steady stream. Hadn't realized his bladder was so full. He rolls up his sleeves and washes as well as he can, his arms, his face, his neck, his hair. His eyes still burn from the soot, and he sees in the mirror how bloodshot they are.

When he comes out of the toilet, sunlight is sifting through the dust, and the cloud appears to be dissipating, moving off.

Two of the firefighters pick up their gear and prepare to hit the street. The one who had pulled Abdul into the deli claps him on the arm but says nothing. Abdul says nothing. The one on the floor is still there, on his back, gazing at the ceiling. The cop slams his hand against the counter and, grabbing a bottle of water, shuffles out, onto the street. The girl with the pierced tongue is eating a sandwich, still weeping, tears on her cheeks.

Abdul looks around the store. Loaves of ham and turkey at the meat counter, behind glass, and a row of rotisseried chickens. Bagels and sandwich rolls, and sticks of French bread. Olives, coleslaw. Rock Cornish hens. He has no appetite. There's a slab of baked beef on the butcher block behind the counter, and a large baked turkey, both heavily carved into. He takes a black disposal bag from a box on a shelf, snaps it open, and tosses in a bottle of water and a bagel. And his father's cigars, the wrapping paper long gone, the box scarred and soiled but unbroken. He puts a knot on the bag and slings it over his shoulder. As he approaches the door, he looks back and waves to the girl, who is still eating and weeping. She'll be all right, he thinks. She'll find her friends. The heart-shaped ring in her navel is a glint of gold in the white ash smeared across her body.

Outside, it's all white dust, everywhere, gray-white, an inch or two, and, in places, more. On the street and the sidewalk, covering cars, trucks, fire engines, and clinging to the buildings, heaped up on steps and ledges. White soot, white ash, white cinders, white pulverized concrete and drywall, white chalk, white plaster, white death. Ironic, he thinks, that a cloud so dark, so black, was in fact white. And paper all over, loose sheets, invoices, letters and bills and stock reports.

He walks up Dey Street, climbing across debris, back to Church, needing to return to the plaza, imagining, crazily, that his father will be there, by the fountain. But even before he reaches Church, he sees the terrible devastation, the tower down, nothing left of it but a pile of rubble some seven or eight stories high, burning, sending up a plume of black smoke, and, at the top, a twisted gridwork of steel girders, leaning at a surreal angle. The tower had fallen straight down, spilling hot, smoking debris across the plaza, clumps of crushed metal and fractured concrete, steel columns tumbling into the plaza and onto the smaller buildings in the complex.

On Church Street, along the eastern edge of the plaza, cars are burning, gas tanks exploding. A fire truck flattened by a steel beam, ambulances and police cars crushed. Inches of white soot everywhere, and an eerie quiet. Distant sirens, and occasional shouts from cops and firefighters, but otherwise a disturbing hush, no traffic, no noise of crowds rushing along the street, none of the usual downtown sounds. Just the dust, the black smoke rising, and the silence that comes of doubt, astonishment, anger, and incomprehension.

In front of the Millenium Hilton, no sign of the triage center that had been there, just the debris and a few stretchers and overturned gurneys, patients and doctors gone. The bad cases, he figures, must have been pulled into the lobby, or sent off already in ambulances. He spots the cage with the parakeet, but not the woman in the blue dress who had been carrying it. And all along the street, police and firemen standing around, dazed, some sitting on chunks of debris, using cell phones, calling home. Some just sitting, staring at the ground, weeping. By the subway where Church is met by Cortlandt, two firefighters help a fireman on the ground. The street is crisscrossed by planks, hoses, panels from the collapsed tower, splintered glass. And the dust, the soot, white ash, gray-white. Moondust, someone calls it. Rat poison and lung-killer-gray-shit are other words he hears. The wreckage is unstable and hot, burning, but already, wherever they can, firefighters, alone or in small groups, are venturing in and probing the piles, searching for anyone who might still be alive. One group has found a fireman pinned under a beam, they're working him loose.

Abdul moves up the street, scanning the rubble, and he spots the golden globe, it too covered with dust, but recognizable above the debris. And somewhere below, buried, is the fountain, and he is drawn there, pulled there, wondering if his father ever made it down out of the North Tower.

Cautiously, on the edge of the plaza, on Church Street,

he makes his way onto the pile of debris, stepping from a beam to a steel panel, to a chunk of masonry, aiming to reach the golden globe, and, hidden beneath it, the fountain, feeling a need, an urgency. Crazy, he knows, but he's into it, to the left, to the right, pausing, assessing, and again in motion. The globe is damaged, even from a distance he can see that. A gaping hole in it, and a long crack, but it's there, injured but not destroyed, and he wonders if it's still in place above the fountain or if it has been shoved out of position.

He steps on what looks to be a solid piece of concrete, but it caves in underneath him and his leg sinks down, as far as his knee. He grabs hold of a steel beam, catching his balance, but has a hard time extricating himself. Then he's moving again, slow, cautious, and becomes aware of someone behind him.

"Why don't you clear the hell out of here before you break a leg?" the voice says.

It's the firefighter with the violet eyes, from the deli, his face gray-white with pasty soot.

"I'm okay," he answers.

"What are you trying to do?"

"I don't know," he says fuzzily. "I'm trying to get to the fountain. I was supposed to meet my father there."

"If he's anywhere here," the firefighter says, "he's dead."

"He's not dead," Abdul says defiantly.

"Then he's not here," the firefighter answers. "You got kids?"

"One."

"So go home. Get out of here. You hear? Go home."

Abdul doesn't move.

"I lost three buddies in here," the firefighter says. "You know what that means? Three. Go home before the other fucking tower falls."

They're just standing there, in the wreckage, at the edge of the mound, looking at each other. Abdul sees a fine line wrinkling across the firefighter's face.

"It's okay," Abdul says.

"No, it's not okay," the firefighter says, a thickness in his throat.

Abdul says nothing.

The firefighter looks up at the North Tower, still burning, belching black smoke. "It scares the shit out of me," he says.

"Yeah," Abdul says.

Then, reluctantly, he goes, the firefighter is right. Cautious across the fallen beams, out of the wreckage and back onto Church Street, and when he looks back, the fireman is still where he was, he hasn't moved.

People are coming out of the Millenium now, the ones who hadn't left already, bellhops, tourists, janitorial crews. Coming out of 1 Liberty Plaza too, and the post office, and the East River Savings. Emptying out. Bankers and the gurus of the holding companies. People leaving, and people arriving too, wandering over from Broadway and Nassau and Pearl, and from the Al Smith housing complex on the Lower East Side, needing to see the destruction with their own eyes, shaking their heads, many wanting, in any way possible, to help. But the police are moving them along, telling them to clear the area, because if one tower fell, the other will go too, and soon.

"Go north," they're shouting, pointing the way up Church Street. "Clear the area! Go north!"

And the people move on, some with wet towels against the dust, with satchels, with bottled water. And Abdul is among them, walking briskly, the black vinyl disposal bag slung over his shoulder, up Church, in the middle of the street, past the graveyard behind St. Paul's, headstones cloaked in soot and paper, and past St. Peter's on Barclay, moving along with others who are coming out of doorways, out of delis, a woman saying she hid under a truck when the tower fell, and a man saying he was knocked off the toilet. A college girl, an intern, says she escaped out the lobby only moments before the collapse.

On he goes, crossing Park Place, Murray, Warren, and Chambers, passing a gift shop, a shoe store, the Soup's

On and the Pakistan Tea House, walking with bartenders, waitresses, the girl from the Delta counter in the lobby of the North Tower. Some talking, some not, all hurrying, looking back anxiously. A tall black kid with dreadlocks, and a Hispanic woman with yellow hair. And what he feels, as he steps along, is a weird sense of hope, despite the catastrophe, a mysterious and unexplainable optimism surging inside him. Hope for his father, who may be, at the moment, beyond hope. And hope for Angela, and his mother. And for Emmie, poor Emmie, what kind of a world have they brought her into? Terror, grief, calamity, cancer death, highway death, atomic death, and now skyscraper death. But hope, he thinks, what is there without hope? Wanting to be, now, with Angela and Emmie, close to them, touching them. People weeping all around him. A woman glancing back and putting a hand to her mouth, choking back the tears.

Then, as he crosses Reade, a gift shop ahead of him on his right, he hears what he never wanted to hear again, a thunderous crack, followed by a prolonged, ruffling rumble, the sound coming up through his feet, through his bones, and without looking back he knows the other tower is collapsing. A ferocious, rumbling roar, shaking the ground, and when he does turn, he sees the cloud, black-brown and mean, behind him and racing up the street, and he runs now like never before, pumping, gasping, thinking no, not this time, no way, won't let it catch him—and runs, flying through the corridor of four- and five-story walk-ups and the street-level shops, gift shops and bagel stores and delicatessens, past a parking garage and an Indian restaurant, and the big sign for PARADISE FASHION—WIDE-WIDTH SHOES. Racing, dashing. Darting through the intersections, past Duane and Thomas and Worth and Leonard, and then, near the corner of Franklin, by a small restaurant, he tastes the bitterness in the air, the sour-sick flavor of the cloud. But looking back, he sees that he's outrun it. The cloud is folding, collapsing, dissipating, and all that reaches him is some of the dust, more white powder settling into his hair and clinging to his clothes. But he's out of it, the worst is over.

When he reaches Canal Street, he stops and looks back, both towers gone, an enormous emptiness in the smoky sky. And there is a hole inside him, a darkness, because he thinks, now, his father is gone. The dust in the air is the dust of his father, drifting, dissipating, descending back to the earth, settling on rooftops and on the streets, and something inside him tells him to give in, to stop fighting it, to accept that he will never see his father again.

Maybe, he thinks, and that's as far as he will go. Maybe.

On Canal, traffic is practically at a standstill. A car parked by a sandwich shop has the doors swung open and the radio full blast, a crowd standing around, catching the news. All commercial airports have been closed, the grid is shut down. Incoming planes from abroad are being diverted to Canada. The borders with Mexico and Canada are closed. In New York, everything south of Canal Street is being evacuated. The South Tower collapsed at 9:59 A.M. The North, at 10:28. The Pentagon, hit at 9:40, is still burning. A fourth hijacked plane went down in a field in Shanksville, not far from Pittsburgh. No other hijacked planes are in the air.

What else, Abdul wonders. What's yet to come?

He glances up and down Canal, seeing the signs, the shops, CAR STEREO and SACRED TATTOO, and moves on, heading east, toward the bridge, stepping along at a quick, steady pace, among the thousands of others making the same journey. Past the hardware shops and the bargain dens, AUDIO MAGIC, and PLASTIC CITY, where acrylic is cut to order, into sheets, rods, and tubes. Signs for office furniture, power tools, paint supplies, shoes, fiberglass cloth. Not much is happening here, many of the stores are already closed. None of it seems real. What's real is the towers, and they, as in some upside-down kaleidoscopic nightmare, no longer exist. Nevertheless, there is a comfort in the plainness of the shops, a reassurance that comes from the mundane, the ordinary, the tangible. Buy a clothesline, buy a chair. Buy a bucket of paint, or a hammer, maybe some glue.

Going back to Echo Terrace will be impossible, he knows that. At least for a while. So close to the towers, the whole area shut down. He'll take Angela to his parents' house in Glen Cove, they'll use the spare bedroom. For how long, he wonders. And today, at his place on Spring Street, just above Canal, he has this wake at four o'clock, and how to get back into the city for that? Everything spinning, unbalanced, nothing straight or clean. He'll work on it. The funeral service is scheduled for the morning. What to suggest? What to tell the family? Postpone it? Put the body into cold storage? He'll talk to them, figure it out. Do what he can. After he picks up Angela. Farther along, it's sportswear and novelty stores. Ning Jin's, and Wen Zhou's. And all the others. Shops loaded with candles, kimonos, painted scarfs. Carved chess sets and binoculars. Lacquered jewelry boxes. And, sandwiched among them, above and between the shops, the Chinese dentists doing crowns and fillings and oral surgery. And the practitioners of acupuncture.

People stopping to buy water. And sneakers for the long trek. Someone on his way to Staten Island, and someone to Brighton Beach. Somebody to Bay Ridge. Maybe, in Brooklyn, the trains are still running? Catch a bus. The Manhattan Bridge looms ahead, it will take them over the river and down into Flatbush Avenue. A woman, gray, remembers the days of the Brooklyn Dodgers. "Pee Wee Reese," she says. "Carl Furillo. Duke Snider." Weary, needing a rest, she veers toward a McDonald's, where she will sit on the floor, she says, if she can't find a seat.

Abdul steps into a variety shop and buys a glass buffalo for Emmie. She likes animals. It used to be stuffed bunnies, stuffed parrots, stuffed zebras, now it's crystal, she has a whole menagerie on her shelf and she moves them around so that they can talk to one another, the horse, the rhinoceros, the elephant, the giraffe, and a dozen others. He's spoiling her, he knows. He wants to.

Why shouldn't she have everything? He goes down on all fours for her, a pony, and she rides on his back. He stands her on his shoulders and, four years old, she's on top of the world. Tosses her in the air and catches her, and Angela hates that, can't look. What if he were to drop her? For Angela, he buys jade earrings. Anytime, whenever she wears them—fifty years from now—he'll remember this moment, on his way to the bridge, this terrible day filled with sirens and smoke. But why would he want to remember? And how could he ever forget? The buffalo and the earrings, in protective bubble-wrap, go into the black disposal bag he's been carrying over his shoulder, with his father's cigars.

Again he rings Angela on the cell phone, but nothing, and he thinks he should try a pay phone. There's a phone at a Burger King, but fifty people are waiting to use it. Farther along, near a parking lot, another public phone, but out of order.

A jet fighter passes overhead, patrolling the sky, its sharp, toothy roar radiating muscular vibrations. And the enormity of it all is sinking in, the weight of it, the seriousness. All of downtown closed, and for how long? The financial markets closed, thousands of businesses shut down. And he wonders about Echo Terrace, where they live, what shape is it in, so close to the collapsed towers. The small shops and restaurants will fold. And in the funeral parlor on Spring Street, he has a corpse in an open coffin, and the wake scheduled for four o'clock.

Under the high sun, all along Canal Street, they're heading for the bridge, on the sidewalk and in the street, moving steadily. People near him saying how lucky they are, they made it, they're out. Lucky. Lucky. Escaped just in time. Abdul doesn't think of himself as lucky. How can he be lucky if his father doesn't turn up? He calls his mother and this time he reaches her. But no, she hasn't heard from Baba. She's watching on television and she's frightened, worried.

"Mom, I love you," he says. "Can you hear me? I love you. Everything will be all right."

The line begins to break up and decay. His mother says something, but it's garbled.

"Mom, can you hear me? Mom? Call Angela for me. I can't reach her. Tell her I love her. Will you do that? Tell her I'm on my way and I love her. And I love you. Can you hear?"

Again his mother says something, but he can't make it out, then a long hum and a disconnect. He doesn't think she heard.

His feet are sore, blistering. He should have bought sneakers and fresh socks at that store farther back, where people were stopping. But he didn't. And in any case, here he is, almost at the bridge, passing Mulberry, Mott, and Elizabeth, then on across the Bowery—and there it is in front of him, the high stone arch flanked by curved colonnades, wide and welcoming, the bridge rising, lifting across the river.

It's shut down to traffic, and he sees, far ahead, the long exodus, people moving across, over the river, thousands upon thousands fleeing lower Manhattan, a vast pilgrimage to safety on the other side. Most of them gritty, covered with the soot and dust of the fallen towers. Off to his right, on the Brooklyn Bridge, he sees throngs of people there too, all plodding along, figuring a way to get home. When he looks back, the sky where the towers had stood is black with smoke rising from the ruins. "Oh, God, God," a woman cries, pausing, looking, "there is nothing there. Nothing!"

It's the blister on his left foot that bothers him, more than the one on the right, and he notices he's favoring it with a slight limp. Nevertheless, he still has the cigars with him, the San Cristobals that he bought at De La Concha for his father. Though dirtied with soot, the box is secure, in the black vinyl bag, and he thinks again what he thought before, that if he holds on to the cigars, keeps them with him, everything, somehow, will be all right again. His father will turn up, and, one way or another, things will work out. For all of them. For the crippled old lady he carried down the stairwell, and for the firefighter who lost three of his company in the collapse. For everyone, even for the corpse in his parlor on Spring Street, though he hasn't quite figured out how to handle that yet. If he can make it across the bridge, with the San Cristobals, then everything, he thinks, one way or another, will come together, and before long life will be again as good as it was.

Papers in the Dust

1. *Maggie Sowle and Tattafruge*

Maggie Sowle slept through most of it. She'd been awake through much of the night working at her sketch pad, developing new ideas for her quilts—drawing with a pencil, designing, thinking and rethinking. That's how it is for her. When the ideas hit she has to stay with them, bear with them, even if they rob her of sleep. If she doesn't grab the ideas when they're hot and ready, she can't expect that they'll be waiting around for her the next morning. It was well after three when she went to sleep, and it's almost eleven now when she opens her eyes and pushes herself up out of bed.

There's an odd smell in the room, acrid, bitter, and when she pulls open the drapery and looks through the window, she feels a strangeness, something wrong. And realizes, with a jolt, that the towers are gone, and what she had thought was a cloud is a huge heap of smoke lifting into the sky. That's the odor she smells, the stench of things burning, and in her astonishment she wants to think that she isn't awake yet and is caught in some gauzy, claustrophobic nightmare. But as her senses clear, it sinks in that the scene out there, baffling as it is, is real. A weakness runs through her and her heart races, pounding in her chest.

She moves about the apartment, checking on the windows. Most are closed, but a few are open a crack, and powdery white stuff, gray-white, has sifted in. And the odor, the stench, is deep into the sheets on the bed and the towels in the bathroom. The terrace outside the living room is covered by inches of the grayish powder, like dirty snow.

In the kitchen, she clicks on the TV and gets a lot of fuzz. Then she finds a Spanish-speaking cable station and watches, aghast, as the images rotate through, the same footage again and again—the plane hitting the North Tower, and the plane hitting the South Tower, and the towers burning, collapsing. And the Pentagon, that too, burning, and she's caught, held, can't take her eyes from the screen, the same images over and over again. The massive burst of red flame blossoming from the South Tower when it's hit. Watching, trying to absorb it, as if it were something in a film, yet it's real, as the smell in her apartment is real. And she had slept through it all, the noise, the terror, and still can't believe she did that, slept through and never heard a thing.

She eats quickly, standing, not sitting, toast and jam, a mug of instant coffee heated in the microwave, and still she watches, feeling weird, unbalanced. Every day, she knows, thousands work in the towers, some fifty thousand, and an immense number of visitors pass through, and she's thinking now of the dead, the injured, the thousands waiting to be found and counted. Against such an enormity everything else falls away, meaningless, her own life, everything she's done, her quilts, her work, all of it nothing, a flimsy emptiness. And the mayor on the screen now, Giuliani, not wanting to speculate, saying simply that the casualties will be more than anyone can bear.

She needs to get out of the apartment, needs to do something. To help, somehow. Anything at all. She calls Theo at his office and learns from the receptionist that he left an hour earlier, on his way to a triage center at the Chelsea Piers.

She knows where that is, in the West Twenties, on the river. And that's what she'll do, she thinks. They'll need people to handle the paperwork, sort things out, manage the phones. And at the very least, if they don't want her for anything else, she'll give blood.

She slips into a pair of beige pants and a long-sleeved blouse, and white walking shoes. She takes a large straw handbag and loads it with more things than she thinks she'll need, aspirin, pens, a pad, chewing gum, a packet of tissues, a few crackers that she wraps in a napkin. And some wet handkerchiefs in a plastic bag, if the soot and dust are too terrible.

In the lobby, Farro Fescu is behind the desk, stolid, watching his small Sony.

"I still can't believe it," she says with a shiver. "How could it happen?"

Farro Fescu shrugs, his eyes fixed on the TV. "It happened," he says, "it happened. Look, there it is. Too much freedom in this country, they let the wrong people in and nobody watches."

The ventilation system had been sucking the bad smell into the lobby, and though he's turned it off, the odor lingers, stronger than in her apartment. A thin film of soot coats the marble floor. She sees footprints where people have walked through.

"I'll be at the Chelsea Piers," she says.

"How will you get there?"

"I'll walk if I have to."

The subways are shut down, he tells her, but with luck, she might catch a bus or a cab above Canal Street. From what he's heard, though, he thinks it unlikely. There is talk of everything under Fourteenth being sealed off. He suggests, if she's really bent on walking, that she take the path by the river till she's past the debris, then straight up on West.

"It's ugly out there," he says. "A lot of dust and grit."

Instead of the river route, she decides on Broadway and crosses over on Rector. As she passes Washington, she has a straight-on view of the ruins of the South Tower, and it's heartrending—nothing left but a thick stub of compacted steel and concrete maybe ten stories high and burning, fire glowing from deep inside the pile. Coils of smoke lifting, darkening the sky. At the bottom, steel girders lie strewn like toys, covering the end of Washington, where it runs into Liberty Street. Chunks and clumps of debris, and everywhere that eerie film of grayish powder. The desks, the walls, the phones, the cabinets, all ground down into this dusty stuff. Underfoot, it has the feel of beach sand. And loose sheets of paper that had blown out of the building, scattered everywhere. Up and down Washington, firefighters are sitting around, helpless. One holds his head in his hands, crying. One is slumped in a doorway. One lies on his back on the hood of a police car. A hose on a high boom pumps water onto the burning debris. Smoke pours up into the atmosphere, and there is a stink, the smell of things burning, wood and fabric and plastic and chemicals, flesh and bone.

A policeman leans against the door of his patrol car, hands in his pockets, blue uniform coated with white powder. In his early thirties, she thinks, eyes dark and bleak. He has a long, pointed jaw, in profile it juts out beyond his lips, beyond the tip of his bony nose.

"A girl I know is in there," he says. "She was on the thirty-eighth floor. She had plenty of time, but I don't know. I was on the phone with her, then the line broke up."

They're on the corner, by Moran's, across the street from Giovanni's. Up ahead is a sign for an indoor parking garage, a brick building with fire escapes. Then taller buildings, a hotel, a bank, streetlamps, and down at the end, the wrecked tower, a portion of the windowless facade looming above the smoldering debris. Gothic arches, that's what she sees, a tall row of them, a dozen steel frames emptied of the glass they held, as if from some ruined cathedral, and that moves her, touches her.

"Your girlfriend?" she asks.

"No, just a friend. A good friend. We were in school together. She became a lawyer, I became a cop."

"Well," she says, trying to be reassuring, "she's probably okay, on her way home."

"I don't know," he says. "I think she would have called. Her mother hasn't heard either."

492

She doesn't know what to say. She thinks how words are empty, they slide around, don't say the things you want them to say. When she sews, putting the colors and shapes together, she feels more confident, but even then she is not always sure of herself.

"You're exhausted," she says. "You need a rest."

"Me? I'm fine. Look at those guys," nodding toward the firefighters, slouching in postures of fatigue. "They lost a lot of people in there. We all did."

He asks if she had been in one of the towers, and she shakes her head. She just lives in the neighborhood, she's on her way to the Chelsea Piers.

"You're a nurse?"

"I can help out," she says. "I know a doctor there."

He looks at his watch, then glances toward the wreckage, the ghostly, windowless grid rising above the burning debris.

"Nothing much happening here," he says. "Come on, I'll take you."

They get in and he turns the car around, onto Rector, then maneuvers onto Broadway, slow. There are people on the street, walking, taking pictures. Some heading north, away from the area, others coming south, wanting to see what happened. Reporters and TV cameras everywhere. And a jet fighter patrolling, the bony grind of its engine setting her teeth on edge.

When he's past the site, he hangs a left onto Chambers and crosses to West, and from there it's a fast drive, past Tribeca and the West Village to Chelsea, and he drops her off at Eighteenth, where there's an entrance for the Piers.

"About your friend," she says, "I have a good feeling about her. She's going to be all right."

He looks at her with dead, dark eyes and asks if she's a psychic.

She wishes she were. "Sometimes I just have feelings," she says. "And this time I have a very strong feeling. She's going to be fine."

"I hope you're right."

"Good luck," she says.

"Yeah. We all need it."

The Piers are four old piers converted into a sports village, with a bowling alley, basketball courts, batting cages, and driving ranges. There's a pool and some skating rinks, and a quarter-mile running track. And at the end of one of the piers, a park with benches and picnic tables, and wooden planters filled with sea grasses and flowers. She's been here before, at the park, when they've had musicians. She's never been to the bowling alley, but a few times she's been to the pool, once with a friend from a gallery, and several times with Yesenia. Someone has told her this is where the *Titanic* was to tie up after its first crossing, but instead the *Carpathia* came in with some of the survivors.

She had expected the complex to be crowded with patients, but when she walks through, looking for Theo, nothing much is going on. Doctors and nurses and paramedics milling around, waiting. Cots and gurneys have been set up in the gym, and they're using the skating rink for a morgue.

She finds Theo on the driving range, teeing off and sending one ball after another into a net. His jacket and tie are off, his white shirt open at the collar.

"I never played golf," he tells her. "I could be pretty good at this."

He takes another swing, then drops the club and comes close to her, and they look at each other, seeing the same confusion in each other's eyes.

"It's bad down there? You saw the damage?"

"It's unbelievable," she says.

The officer who drove her had said they expect all of the other buildings in the complex would be lost. And damage to some of the neighboring buildings, 90 West, and Bankers Trust. And Cedar Street, with the little church of St. Nicholas.

"And the condo?"

"Oh, it'll be okay," she says, "but an awful lot of soot and a god-awful smell. Farro Fescu was still there when I left."

494

"We expected thousands of casualties here," he says, "but no one. Earlier, about a hundred. A woman died just as I was about to examine her. Four others I was able to help. But now, more doctors than patients, and I don't know if that's good news or bad."

Downriver, they see the boats ferrying people across to New Jersey. Bringing them to Liberty State Park, and to shelters in Jersey City.

He picks up his jacket and slings it over his shoulder, and they stroll to the pier where the park is.

"How did you find me?"

"Your receptionist told me."

"And you believed her? She usually lies about where I am, to save me from unhappy patients who want to kill me. She thinks all of my patients are unhappy and worries she will suddenly be out of a job."

The pier with the park is Pier 62, with a view to the west and the north. The view to the south is blocked by a building on the neighboring pier, housing a skating rink. But above the roof they see the smoke rising from downtown, an enormous black scarf stretching across the sky.

A yacht goes by, heading downriver toward the ruined towers. Water laps against the pilings of the pier. There are ducks out there, on the water, mallards, rising and falling as the water moves beneath them. And seagulls circling. Except for the smoke in the sky and the distant sirens, there is no hint of the catastrophe that has occurred.

Strange, she thinks, how when danger looms, true danger, everything else falls away. To have someone, that's all that matters, to have someone who means something to you. She doesn't have Henry anymore, except as someone remembered, deeply missed, and wished for. She has Theo, who is not Henry but a friend, and she would not want to be without him. She has Yesenia, with whom she quilts, and Elaine in Riverdale, who will put her up until she can return to Echo Terrace. They take a bench at the end of the pier, between a planter filled with nightshade and another with oleander.

"So what do you think?" she says.

He looks past her, upriver, toward a small brown cloud low in the sky. "I'm trying not to think," he says.

But this, she knows, is not true. He is always thinking, wondering. Exploring. That's why she enjoys being with him.

"I still can't absorb it," she says. "It's unreal. I saw the wreckage, just came from it, but I don't believe what I saw."

"I don't think I want to see it," he says.

"Is it over? Do you think?" But even as she asks, she knows it can't be over, because something this big, this devastating, can only be the start of something larger.

"I imagine, for today, it's probably finished," he says. "But tomorrow, God only knows."

She watches the mallards, drifting on the water as the water lifts and rolls. She's seen the documentary smuggled from Afghanistan, the woman wearing a burqa, brought into a soccer stadium and made to kneel down—and right there, on film, she is shot in the head because she'd been caught in adultery.

"I don't understand any of it," Maggie says. "None of it. None of it makes any sense to me at all."

She's thinking of the way it will be after today, everything changed, heightened security, checkpoints, police wherever there is a crowd. Bomb-sniffing dogs and bomb-sniffing machines. How do you protect against people who want to kill you?

"You know," he says, "long ago, soon after the towers opened, that Frenchman, the high-wire walker—Philippe? Is that the name?"

"Philippe Petit."

"Yes. Him. He hooked a wire between the towers and walked across. It was August, I think. 1974. I saw that. It was wonderful, I stood in the plaza and watched. What courage to walk so high in the open air, a gust of wind could have knocked him down. I was a student, in medical school. It made such an impression."

"You wanted to join a circus?"

496

"Me? No, not one of my temptations. But I understood from that, that life is a high wire, everything far up and risky. Nobody escapes the danger. But that Petit, he was enjoying it. He wasn't defying gravity, he was joining it, playing with it. The woman next to me, she had opera glasses and she passed them over—and you know what he was doing up there? He was laughing, a big smile on his face. Laughing and dancing on the wire, having a hell of a good time."

They're side by side on the bench, looking toward the river, across to New Jersey. He leans forward, elbows on his knees, fingers laced together.

"Doorknobs," he says. "Do you have any idea how many doorknobs there are in those two towers?"

She doesn't rise to it, couldn't care less.

"Forty thousand. Can you believe? Wouldn't you think, in a modern structure like that, they would have figured out how to dispense with doorknobs?"

"And that's what you learned in medical school?"

"That, yes, and much more. Toilets," he says, leaning back now, legs straight out, hands behind his head, eyes roaming the sky. "Seven thousand toilets. Isn't it amazing? Imagine all of them flushing at the same time, a Niagara Falls of human waste plunging from the top floors."

She sees what he's doing, he's deflecting, avoiding, finding solace in irrelevance. Amusing himself. Relieving the pain, holding confusion at bay by thinking of doorknobs and toilets, and God knows what else. Well, at least he has that.

Then, in a change of mood, he turns to her, dead serious, looking at her, long and steady.

"They're evacuating downtown," he says.

"I know."

"You have a place?"

And now too, even more than before, she knows where he's going. She sees how he looks at her and understands what he's asking. That they should go off somewhere and be alone together. He's asking, inviting.

But she draws back, not wanting to follow him down that path. They're friends, good friends, and she likes it that way. Anything more might ruin what they have, and what they have is important to her, she wants to keep it just the way it is. And besides, he has María for every-thing else, and why doesn't he go to her?

"I have a friend in Riverdale," she says. "She'll put me up for a while. And you?"

He lifts a shoulder, tilts his head. "Lal invited me to stay at his place, but I think, you know, I'd rather be alone."

Eight years ago, when a bomb went off in the towers, in the underground garage, he went up into the North Tower, into the smoke, and brought someone out, a child he had thought but it was a midget, a middle-aged accountant. It comes back to him now, and he tells her about it. "It was horrible. I lost my way and could hardly breathe, the smoke was so thick. I thought, for a while, that I was going to die. But all of that, it was nothing com-pared to this, today. Nothing. Those poor people."

"Yes," she says, not knowing what else to say. Pity. And pain, and grief, and anger over the waste of it all, and a terrible wrenching deep in the soul.

When she does her quilting, it's never easy making all of the different patches fit together, especially since she uses so many odd shapes. If a patch doesn't fit, she redoes it, or changes the surrounding patches, but finally all of the pieces have to come together. And so with life, she thinks. There are all these different pieces, and some-how they all have to mix, and match, and blend, all working together. Otherwise it's chaos.

"Good things come out of bad," she says. "One way or another, the pieces fit and it comes out all right."

"Does it?"

"It has to. Doesn't it?"

She had never had children, and that, for her, has been a disappointment. But now, to some extent, she feels reconciled about that. In some ways, she thinks of her quilts as her children. She hopes, through them, that she has reached some people, brought joy and meaning into a few lives. What else was there? To make things better, rather than worse.

"I'm disappointed," she says. "I thought I could lend a hand here. I thought there might be something for me to do."

"Is that why you came? I thought you came to be with me."

She shrugs coyly. "That too," she says.

He tells her about the medical center on East Thirtieth. People are missing, thousands, and the Red Cross is setting up a search facility there. Families will be bringing in photographs, descriptions. Telephone numbers. At the Farkas auditorium.

It sounds like something she can do. She can work the phones, taking names. Meet with the families, help them fill out the forms.

He leans forward again, eyes focused on the river.

"Next week, my son turns fifteen," he says. "It's a hard age for a boy to be without a father around. What I think—I think I should move to Seattle to be near him. So I can see more of him, and help him through his problems. He's had some trouble with the police, you know. Shoplifting, stuff like that."

It doesn't sit well, the thought of losing him, all the way to Seattle. "Yeah?" she says.

"I've been thinking about it," he says. "And today, with all this, it seems like the right thing."

"Seattle is a big leap," she says. She's grown so used to having him around, it's hard to imagine what it will be like without him. "And you have your practice here."

"I'll start over out there," he says. "Even in Seattle they need face-lifts."

"And Estelle? She wants you out there? All these years after the divorce?"

"Of course not. If we meet in the supermarket, she'll go berserk."

"So this is a good idea?"

He's quiet for a moment, then he looks at her. "Maggie, the boy needs me."

And it stops there, she knows she can't get past that. She sees it in his eyes, the boy, how important the boy is to him—and he's right, of course he's right. But she does wonder if he's serious about it, truly bent on making the move, or is he just flirting with it, mentioning it now as a way of punishing her because she let pass his invitation to join him at a hotel.

"Theo," she says, "don't be mean."

"Mean? To you? Never."

Her legs are crossed, and he puts his hand on her knee.

"Why would I be mean to you? You're very important to me. You know that, don't you?"

"Do I?"

"You should."

"Life is good," she says, watching the swirl and glide of the gulls.

"Sometimes," he says. "Not today."

They sit a while, not talking, looking at the water. Another yacht slides by, coming down from the north. From Tarrytown, Peekskill, Poughkeepsie, coming to see the damage. The mallards bobbing in the water, and the sound of the water lapping against the pilings.

She gives him the telephone number of the friend she'll be staying with, and then she's up, off the bench, readying herself to go.

"You're not staying around to have lunch with me?"

"Tomorrow," she says, kissing her forefinger and touching it to the tip of his nose. "Be a good boy. I'm going to see your Red Cross people."

"But I'd rather be bad," he says.

"I know you would."

And she goes, leaving him, and he watches as she walks off in her beige pants and white walking shoes, her aging, thickening body, but still smart, in her way, and lively, with her bright white hair and amber barrettes, and it's a comfort for him to see her, even though she is walking now not toward him but away. And how it saddens him, what she told him about the little church of St. Nicholas, on Cedar Street, where he sometimes stopped to think and collect his thoughts, that it's gone, smashed by the falling towers. And what of the Amish Market by the South Tower? Where will he shop for greens, and for fresh fruit? Where will he buy such wonderful loaves of bread?

Time is a gift, he thinks, and the test, the need, is to be worthy of the gift. But how? What do you do to make yourself worthy? You do your job, and whatever you do, you do it well. Not to do damage. Not to make a mess. Not to ruin what is good. Not to bring pain and loss. And this morning, the ones in the planes, bringing so much confusion, in what way did they add anything? How? And where? Where lies the good? And for whom?

And then, as he sits there, wondering, a strain of music filters through memory, a sequence of notes, poignant, he can't recall from where. *La Fida Ninfa*, he thinks, mournful, piercingly sweet, or perhaps the *Judith,* exquisitely sad. Where lies the gain, he asks. And the sadness rises inside him, the notes repeating themselves, playing over and over, and looking again toward the river, he begins to weep.

2. *Farro Fescu*

It's a few minutes before three. In the lobby, Farro Fescu sits behind the desk, in his leather chair, the small Sony at the desk looping through images that he's seen dozens of times already. He's no longer watching. Early that morning, when the first tower was struck, he heard the impact but thought nothing of it, and heard the sirens too, the wailing and squawking. But that, he thought, was just New York. And then, over the TV, came the message about the crash, and he went to the door and looked, and saw the North Tower burning.

He stood a while, watching, then he returned to the desk and phoned down to Oscar and told him to send the cleaning crew home.

Later, shortly after one, a police officer and two

emergency workers passed by to evacuate anyone still there. Mrs. Sowle had already left, as had the Dillhoppers, and Louisa Wax and her daughter. And Oscar with his crew—Muddy Dinks and Blue and Chase and the others. The only ones remaining were Dr. Matisse, a retired psychoanalyst, and Mrs. Snow, both of them elderly and needing assistance, and a trainee with Cantor Fitzgerald, who had stayed home from work that day, suffering from menstrual cramps. And the retired Greek real estate broker, Milo Salonika, who had dealt in international properties, now eighty-two and bedridden, and suffering from incipient Alzheimer's. He didn't want to be moved. The EMTs took him down on a stretcher, and he was shouting the whole time, making a terrible scene, saying he didn't want to leave, he wanted to stay, wanted to die there. "Leave me, leave me, don't touch me!"

They were all put aboard a boat and ferried to Jersey City, where they were taken to an impromptu shelter set up at a high school.

But Farro Fescu remained behind. Insisted on it, wouldn't hear of leaving. The police officer, a young man with a scar on his chin, tried to reason with him, but Farro Fescu was resolute.

"Somebody has to keep watch," he said.

"That's my job," the officer said. "We'll be patrolling the area." One of his shoelaces was untied, and he stooped to tie it.

"There will be breaking in and looting," Farro Fescu said. "You know that. Always, after something like this, there is looting."

The officer, still working at the shoelace, tried to be understanding. "I know how you feel," he said. "But look, it's the mayor's orders. You know how it is, everybody has to go."

"Give the mayor my regards," Farro Fescu said. "I saw him on the television. Tell him, from me, that he's doing a fine job."

"You have to leave," the officer said, standing now.

"I won't."

"You must."

"I can't. What will you do? Arrest me?"

The officer, hands down at his side, shook his head and through pursed lips let out a long, slow breath. "You have food? A place to sleep?"

"I'll manage," Farro Fescu said.

"I hope so," the officer said, giving him a doubtful look, and stepped toward the door. "I'll check in on you later."

And now, hours later, it's after three, both towers gone and smoke rising from the wreckage. Destruction is so easy, he thinks. It's living that is hard, the going on and the continuing. He's already checked the computer, how many of the residents were working in the North Tower and how many in the South, and others nearby, at the Financial Center and at 1 Liberty Plaza.

Rumfarm, he knows, had gone off to his office in the bank that morning, on the ninety-sixth floor of the North Tower. He dislikes Rumfarm, and though he doesn't hate him enough to wish death upon him, he knows he will not mourn if he is among the lost.

Phone service is spotty. North of the site, as far up as Fourteenth, many phones are down, but here, and eastward to the financial district, and in pockets of Chinatown and Little Italy, the phones are working. Some of the residents who were in the towers, the ones who got out, have called, leaving messages as to where they will be. One, a trainee with Gold Star, is staying with her brother in Brooklyn Heights. Another has ferried across to New Jersey and is already with his parents in Philadelphia. But from four who worked for Cantor Fitzgerald, and two who were with Morgan Stanley, there has been no word.

And Karl Vogel hasn't returned from his morning walk. Farro Fescu suspects he is probably enjoying himself out there, at the site, gaping at the damage, talking, telling the firefighters how to do their job. Or perhaps he's at one of the hospitals, making himself useful. He likes Vogel. If

Vogel doesn't return, he will miss him sorely. But he will return, he's sure of that, and they'll share food in Vogel's kitchen, and Vogel will let him sleep in the spare bedroom. And if he doesn't return soon enough, he'll sleep on the couch in the lobby and figure about the food when the time comes. He's the concierge. That's his job, to figure things.

He fills a pitcher with water and pours it into the wide urn that holds the palm tree, then trims away a few errant twigs sprouting from the trunk. He walks about, touching the marble walls, feeling their cold indifference. He's alone in the building. He kicks his heel against the marble floor. Raps his knuckles against the oak panels in the desk area. After so many years here, who knows it better than he? The nooks and the crannies, the creaks and groans as the building heats or cools. The hum of the elevators, the buzz of the phone. He's killed ants in the lobby and in the mail room. Stepped on them. Sprayed them in the subbasement, in the long crack that widened and finally had to be repaired. He's hated this building and cursed it, but loves it too, because it's his, all his. He knows the comings and goings, the doings and the undoings. Tuned to it, as if sharing the same body, he and the high walls, the same lungs, same sensory system. His domain, his responsibility.

Life is a high-pressure process, he thinks. Raw turbulence that doesn't explain itself. But he's beyond the time when he had a need for meanings and explanations, and he simply wishes now that he were young enough to be with the ones who will be out there, hunting down the people who planned this and making them pay. Like his uncles in the Balkans, in the mountains, fighting the Nazis. That's how he sees it, how he thinks of it, and wishes he could be part of the struggle.

Maybe I should believe in God, he thinks. But not today, not now. He'll save it for later. He had stopped believing in God when a German bomb fell on his village and his uncle Grigor was killed, so long ago. Would God, right now, be a help or, in some eternally complicated way, a hindrance? He pushes the door open and steps out, into the dust and ash, the inch-thick layer, and lying everywhere in the sandy soot are the sheets of paper that flew out of the towers when they went down. Some sailed as far as Brooklyn, descending into playgrounds and parking lots. He's seen it on the Sony, papers in the sky, high up.

He steps out and picks up one, and then another, shaking the soot from them. Some of the papers are singed and torn, but many are intact, undamaged, and that amazes him, that mere paper could survive such violence. Memos, printouts. A page from a manual on skyscraper security. A shopping list written on the back of a page filled with stock quotations. Apples, salmon, vitamin C, chewing gum, kiwis, bread, sherbet. A page from a guide to explosives. And an application form for life insurance. He picks up a spreadsheet from the Chilean Trade Bureau. A letter from one attorney to another. A page from a contract. He moves slowly, bending, taking scraps and whole pages, glancing at them, some recent, many old. A marketing strategy report. The résumé of a young woman applying for a position at Marsh and McClennan, in 1992, the year she completed her degree at NYU. She was magna cum laude and had written for the university newspaper. She had done a semester abroad at the London School of Economics. And she played classical music on the piano. He stands there, in the inches of dust and ash, amid the fallen papers, reading the résumé and wondering if she had gotten the job. And how lucky for her if she had not.

On the street, holding the papers he's picked up, he feels a connection, a human touch. He doesn't want to let them go. They are relics. Mementos. People had handled them, had set down their thoughts on them. Had scribbled messages on them. The spreadsheet with daisies doodled in the margins, and the lunch receipt with telephone numbers written on the back. Heather, Marie, Jen. The cell-phone bill, and the overdue notice from a library. People's fingers had touched them. Their breath had breathed upon them. Their thoughts were expressed in them.

And the one who had submitted her résumé. He'll try to find her. When this terrible time is past, he will call her up and maybe she'll be at the same number. Somehow he'll track her down, and they'll meet in a downtown café for cakes and demitasse, and he'll hand her this résumé that fell from the tower. He sixty-seven, and she so young, perhaps thirty, thirty-one. They'll go to museums together, and he'll help her out if she needs help. He'll give her presents. This is a fantasy, he knows. But, despite his gloomy nature, and perhaps because of it, he is given to fantasy. Imagining is a way of escaping the darkness. So yes, why not? He will look for her. Time, he wants to think, is kinder and stranger than he imagines. And even if they never meet, it will be a joy if he can learn that she is alive and well somewhere. That alone will be enough, to know that she survived this grim day.

He is aware how God comes and goes in his consciousness. Sometimes God is there, but more often not, a kind of vacancy, an absence. The astronomers talk about black holes, and sometimes he thinks of God as an enormous black hole at an infinite distance, something you can't see, yet it draws you toward it, into it, everything vanishing into the darkness of God's density. But this, he knows, is merely something he imagines, a thought that he plays with. He has never been able to make sense out of God—could never reconcile the death of his uncle Grigor with the notion of goodness and mercy and infinite wisdom. And now this, so much worse. All these people. He saw them falling, leaping from the flames. Saw it when he watched from the door and saw it again on television. But how do you complain to God, who, if still there, must be tired of listening. And so old too, he must be in desperate need of a hearing aid.

He goes back inside, into the lobby, glad that he stayed behind. Someone must watch over. Someone must be responsible. When the residents are allowed to come back, he will be here, watching. It's an odd, solemn feeling, being alone in the neighborhood, all of the condos emptied out. Dust clings to the outside of the glass doors, obscuring the view of the street. There will be much to do for Oscar and his people when they return, whenever that might be. And the street itself, such a disaster, the city will have to hire professionals, in masks and moon suits.

He still has in his hand the papers that he picked up and doesn't know what to do with them. He wants to hold on to them, they seem so important, so rich with personal meaning. A prescription for sleeping pills. A faxed airline ticket. A half-written letter to someone's mother. A driver's license. A page from a musical score. A passport. He doesn't want to let them go.

THE END

THE JUKEBOX QUEEN OF MALTA
Nicholas Rinaldi

'RINALDI TREADS A PATH BETWEEN THE TRADITIONAL
WARBUSTER AND THE SUBTLER *CAPTAIN CORELLI* . . . A
RESONANT, THOUGHTFUL NOVEL'
Elizabeth Buchan, *The Times*

It is 1942 and the island of Malta is under siege by a triumphant
German air force. From the smoke and magnesium glare of bomb
blast steps Rocco Raven, native of Brooklyn, New York,
apprentice radioman and expert car mechanic. His only contact is
an American intelligence officer, Jack Fingerley, whose purpose is
known to no-one but himself. Far from finding a role for Rocco,
Fingerley leaves him to face the chaos alone.

On only his third day there his billet, on the top floor of a brothel,
is blown to pieces. Without contacts or belongings, Rocco is left
to wander the devastated streets of Valetta in a bewildered daze
until he sees an apparition, Melita, a beautiful, ethereal woman.

It is the beginning of an extraordinary relationship, at once
passionate and guarded, which flourishes as the island's fortunes
decline. Under the threat of starvation and in a world infused
with the eccentricities of war, Rocco's seems to be the lone voice
of sanity, until he too is infected by the madness around him and
succumbs to the voluntary thrill of danger . . .

'MUCH TO ENJOY . . . RINALDI HAS TREMENDOUS FUN
EVOKING THE RICH CULTURAL PUDDING THAT WAS MALTA
IN 1942, ITS WEIRD COMBINATION OF SUPERSTITION,
FATALISM AND GRAFTED-ON ANGLOPHILIA, OF RICOTTA
AND STIFF UPPER LIP'
Patrick Gale, *Daily Telegraph*

'UNDER THE HEAT AND THE HAMMERING OF BOMBS,
RINALDI PAINTS THE ESSENCE OF THE SECOND WORLD WAR
IN EXCITING MINIATURE'
David Hughes, *Mail on Sunday*

'A BEGUILING, ROMANTIC STORY IN AN ILLUMINATING AND
SURPRISING SETTING'
Joseph Heller

0 552 99810 9

BLACK SWAN

BRICK LANE
Monica Ali

Still in her teenage years, Nazneen finds herself in an arranged
marriage with a man twenty years her elder. Away from the mud
and heat of her Bangladeshi village, home is now a cramped flat
in a high-rise block in London's East End. Not knowing a word of
English, Nazneen must rely on her husband. But unlike him she
is practical and wise, and befriends a fellow Asian girl Razia,
who helps her understand the strange ways of her adopted new
British home.

Confinde to her flat by tradition and family duty, Nazneen fills
her days by sewing for a living – until the radical Karim steps
unexpectedly into her life. Against a background of racial conflict
and tension, they embark on a love affair that finally forces
Nazneen to take control of her fate . . .

0 552 77115 5

BLACK SWAN

THE SOCIETY OF OTHERS
William Nicholson

'HYPNOTIC, FAST-MOVING AND INTELLECTUALLY
CHALLENGING . . . QUITE STAGGERINGLY GOOD'
Daily Mail

He has nowhere to go . . . so he goes there.

An alienated young man can see no meaning in life. He doesn't
even see the point of getting out of bed in the morning. To escape
from his family he decides to set off on a hitchhiking adventure
around Europe, and is picked up by a friendly lorry driver with
an unusual interest in philosophy.

The journey takes him through a violent and Kafkaesque
nightmare to a destination that changes his life.

'A BAFFLING, STAGGERING, GRANDLY AMBITIOUS WORK . . .
QUITE REMARKABLE'
Time Out

'NICHOLSON WRITES WITH SUCH PANACHE THAT
THE SOCIETY OF OTHERS TRANSCENDS GENRES: IT
ENTERTAINS US WHILE IT REFLECTS WITH GREAT
PROFUNDITY ON THE HUMAN CONDITION . . . ONE OF
THE BEST NOVELISTS AROUND'
Piers Paul Read, *Spectator*

'NICHOLSON DESCRIBES IT AS "A THRILLER ABOUT THE
MEANING OF LIFE" AND THAT'S PRETTY ACCURATE . . . A
GENUINELY THOUGHT-PROVOKING READ'
Mail on Sunday

0 552 77202 X

BLACK SWAN

A SELECTED LIST OF FINE WRITING
AVAILABLE FROM BLACK SWAN

77115 5	BRICK LANE	Monica Ali	£7.99
77209 7	BEYOND THE GREAT INDOORS	Ingvar Ambjørnsen	£7.99
99946 6	THE ANATOMIST	Federico Andahazi	£6.99
77105 8	NOT THE END OF THE WORLD	Kate Atkinson	£6.99
99863 X	MARLENE DIETRICH LIVED HERE	Eleanor Bailey	£6.99
77121 X	THE HOTTEST DAY OF THE YEAR	Brinda Charry	£6.99
99986 5	A MOTH AT THE GLASS	Mogue Doyle	£6.99
77078 7	THE VILLAGE OF WIDOWS	Ravi Shankar Etteth	£6.99
99759 5	DOG DAYS, GLENN MILLER NIGHTS	Laurie Graham	£6.99
99204 6	THE CIDER HOUSE RULES	John Irving	£8.99
77190 2	A GIRL COULD STAND UP	Leslie Marshall	£6.99
14240 9	THE NIGHT LISTENER	Armistead Maupin	£6.99
77202 X	THE SOCIETY OF OTHERS	William Nicholson	£6.99
99904 0	WIDE EYED	Ruaridh Nicoll	£6.99
99862 1	A REVOLUTION OF THE SUN	Tim Pears	£6.99
99908 3	STAR DUST FALLING	Jay Rayner	£6.99
77093 0	THE DARK BRIDE	Laura Restrepo	£6.99
99810 9	THE JUKEBOX QUEEN OF MALTA	Nicholas Rinaldi	£6.99
77145 7	GHOST HEART	Cecilia Samartin	£6.99
77166 X	A TIME OF ANGELS	Patricia Schonstein	£6.99
77221 6	LONG GONE ANYBODY	Susannah Waters	£6.99
77102 3	RAINY DAY WOMEN	Jane Yardley	£6.99